PLANTING TREES ON MARS

K STRACHAN

PLANTING TREES ON MARS

ISBN: 9781096987741

For Samantha

Simon, Your exceptional colleagues at Great Ormond Street told me you're a big fan. I wish you all the best at acheiving all I have! I hope all your dreams come true, Kev

"Many a small thing has been made large by the right kind of advertising"

Mark Twain

PROLOGUE

LONDON. ENGLAND JUNE 2014

WANTED!!!

SPACE ADVENTURERS FOR ONE WAY MISSION TO MARS.

NO EXPERIENCE NECESSARY. PLEASE APPLY TO: PO BOX 421, BRISTOL BS1 4GH

The headquarters of project Livingstone were situated within the heart of the city of London in a newly built, high rise glass fronted monstrosity. The interior design was low in content, high in concept and eye-wateringly expensive. However, the view from the executive offices and main conference room was undeniably impressive and never failed to provoke gasps of awe when witnessed for the first time. It was, however, a view that none of the board room's current occupants were enjoying at the moment. Instead the majority of them were staring intently at the highly polished wood of the conference table.

Only one person was unseated and he paced, distractedly around the table shaking his head and mumbling inaudibly to himself. His footsteps echoed around the room as he walked. Each staccato step caused a wave of involuntary flinching to ripple through the room. He continued to circle the table for a few minutes before he finally stopped in front of the giant gallery window that filled the whole of one side of the room, he cleared his throat loudly and forced an unconvincing smile onto his face. Every pair of eyes instinctively snapped towards him.

Kieran McLaughlin was immaculately dressed in a beautifully tailored dark blue, pin-striped suit. He had removed the jacket but retained the waistcoat, which he had kept fully buttoned. A silver watch chain hung from the pocket and his tie was tied in a double Windsor knot. He was five foot eight with a slight but athletic build; the dark Mediterranean skin that he had inherited from his Italian mother was in stark contrast to his Irish father's strawberry blonde hair and piercing blue eyes.

Piercing blue eyes, which he now used to look at each seated figure in turn. He shook his head slowly, sighed and then started to speak,

"There wasn't even a contact number for Christ's sake!" he said, finishing a sentence, out loud, that he had started in his head.

He shook his head again.

"The Globe? Really?" he screwed his eyes closed and shook his head in frustration, "The fucking Globe newspaper. As read by the absolute pinnacle of society. The scientists, the doctors, the engineers," he surveyed the room once more.

"Whose moment of genius was that?" he asked

Every hand in the room stayed resolutely by the side of their owners. Undeterred Kieran continued

"I'm sorry ladies and gentleman," he said," after all, I am told that you are considered to be amongst the finest creative minds within the field of PR."

He looked quizzically at the group as a whole, "and I'm sure that you have a list of credits as long as my arm that would prove that to me," he laughed mirthlessly.

There was more uncomfortable squirming.

"However, in all honesty I've never witnessed such a poorly conceived, half-witted, frankly moronic launch in my entire life."

One of the senior consultants, a young man in his mid-twenties that Kieran seemed to recall was called Henry or Harry, raised a tentative hand. He flinched as he did so, as though expecting it to be blown clean off his wrist at any time,

"With all due respect Mr. McLaughlin," he said timidly,

Kieran waved his hand, "Oh please, call me Kieran," he peered at the young man, "Harry isn't it?"

The executive visibly relaxed, in fact he even returned the smile, "Yes it is, and thank-you… Kieran. We didn't only send the advertisement out to the Globe though," he said nervously.

Again Kieran waved his hand, "Oh really? Please elaborate," he said pleasantly,

"We sent the copy out to every major print outlet." He consulted his folder, "All the Red-Tops. In Scotland too," he looked up at Kieran expectantly, "which represents over seventy percent of the daily newspaper sales in the UK. We also had a broadsheet ad in production but we considered the popular press would represent a bigger bang, as it were," he coughed, "at least initially,"

Kieran nodded, "…And yet the only paper to run the ad was, in fact, the Globe, correct?"

“Ah well,“ the executive bristled, “strictly speaking, that wasn't our fault.”

Kieran raised his brow, “Really?”

“No," Harry continued. "In fact, we sent the copy out to all of the outlets at once,” he looked around for some crumb of support but received none,” we gave very strict instructions for a simultaneous launch, but…” he faltered.

“But what?” Kieran asked, “No, in fact, let me guess! The Editor of the Globe decided to run the advert unilaterally in order to get a scoop over the other outlets?”

The executive nodded, “Exactly. So as you see, it’s not our fault.”

“Except that you trusted a tabloid newspaper to keep their word, when faced with a potentially huge exclusive.”

“Well, we’ve dealt with them before,” he said defensively, "and we've never encountered this issue before."

"You've dealt with them before?" Kieran asked,

Harry nodded,

“Lucky you,” Kieran said dryly,

“And actually," Harry continued, inexplicably emboldened, “the response was extraordinarily high."

He looked down at his open laptop and tapped the screen.

"I don't have the exact figures in front of me," he said reddening slightly

"Pity," Kieran said quietly

Harry looked at him uncertainly before continuing," but I believe we had more than 10,000 respondents from the initial print run alone," he considered his laptop in search of corroboration, but once again found nothing to help his cause.

Kieran watched the flustered young man, allowing his growing discomfort to take hold more fully. He then picked up a glass from the table top and sipped his water.

He looked back at Harry and smiled thinly at him. At least he had said something. At least he had had the courage to defend his work and reputation, he thought to himself, not like the rest of them.

He met Harrys worried eyes, licked his lips, and smiled wickedly,

"Ten thousand, you say?"

"More in fact," Harry continued, utterly misreading the warning signs and grinning widely. He glanced at his computer and finally found what he had been looking for.

He looked back at Kieran and then read confidently, "It was actually ten thousand, six hundred and… twenty-seven," he looked up and smiled.

Kieran stared at him, impassively for a moment and nodded again, he took another sip from his glass, "I must say... that is an impressive response, isn't it? Very impressive numbers there."

A general murmur of agreement resonated around the executives. There was an unexpected flicker of optimism that spread, almost reluctantly, through the room; perhaps things were about to change?

They were, but not for the better.

"Have any of you actually read any of those ten thousand, six hundred and…?"

“Twenty seven Kieran,” Harry added helpfully.

Kieran nodded at him gratefully, “Yes, thank-you. Twenty-seven respondents?”

There was an almost conjoined shake of their heads in reply.

"No," Harry said defiantly.

“You were very clear on that one, if you recall? You asked specifically that all the responses were sent directly to you.”

"That is true," he conceded with a nod of his head, "I was very much looking forward to reading them in fact.”

The room fell into an expectant silence.

“Let me read you a snippet of one,” Kieran paused and an odd smile touched his face, “it is without doubt one of my very favourites. It is fairly representative of the group though.”

Kieran reached into his jacket pocket and produced a single sheet of folded A4 paper. He unfolded it carefully and turned it over to show the room the other side. Beneath the main body of the text there was a neat, but clearly hand drawn picture of some sort of logo. Next to it there was also another drawing of what was, presumably, the authors approximation of an alien. Kieran showed it around the room for a few seconds, ensuring that everyone got a good look.

He then turned it around and started to read;

“Dear Space command," He paused, to let that opening settle over the room, “Dear space command, my name is Darren and I would very much like to join your crew. I have experience in exploration and intrigue and have reached an MMR rating of 2500 on World of Warcraft,” He paused again and glanced around at the bank of the expressionless faces, “is that good?" he asked, "I'm afraid I have no idea.”

There was a vague murmur of approval from towards the back of the room.

"Ah, excellent!" he said, clapping his hands loudly, "Then our problems are solved."

He folded up the paper again and placed it, carefully on the table, an uncomfortable murmur was seeping around the boardroom. Kieran ignored it for moment and then looked up again.

"This gentleman is thirty-seven years old," he paused again to let that sink in, "thirty-fucking-seven! And he included not only a computer game rating but a fucking drawing of an Alien!" He shook his head a walked towards the window, when he turned back he was pleased to notice that every wide-eye in the room was still trained on him.

"He was not alone though," he continued, "let me assure you of that."

He walked over to where Harry sat and leant on the back of his chair. Harry flinched, instinctively but Kieran pretended not to notice.

"So yes," he said, his voice now not much louder than a stage whisper, "I will concede that ten thousand is a lot of respondents, but when it's ten thousand fucking lunatics then there is very little value is there?"

He slammed the table top with the flat of his hand and everyone, gratifyingly, jumped.

An uncomfortable silence once more engulfed the boardroom. The vestiges of hope that had previously been evident had now evaporated.

Kieran sighed and picked up his cellphone, he unlocked it with a press of his thumb and then dialled. As it rang, he lifted it to his ear. He turned his back to the room, closed his eyes and began rubbing his temples with his free hand.

The respondent answered and immediately Kieran's eyes snapped open.

“Hi Gareth, it's me. Yes, I've told them." He listened for a few seconds, before nodding, "Okay," he said, "I'll see you tomorrow. Take care, bye.”

He hung up, sighed again and then turned back to face the room. Everyone in the room looked at him, apparently reluctant to speak.

Kieran looked at Harry expectantly, “Yes?” He asked, "Was there something else?"

“Um,” Harry coughed and licked his lips, nervously, “well I was wondering... that is we were all wondering…what we do now? Do we have a mandate to move forward with this?”

Kieran again nodded his head and sucked at his teeth, “Ah right," he said, "fair enough"

Harry smiled, Kieran didn't.

"Well," Kieran said finally," the way I see it, is that you proceed now by getting the fuck out of the building, before I call security and have you physically removed,” he paused briefly, “and *‘your mandate to move forward’* is to find some other poor bastard to work for.” his voice was calm and quiet and he had an unpleasant, almost painful smile on his face.

There was an agitated shuffling of papers around the table as one by one the executives packed away their belongings and made to leave. When they were all standing, they turned, as one, to face Kieran as if expecting some kind of punchline or release. Instead he stared back at them, his smile replaced by a genuine look of mild bafflement.

“Go on then,” he said, ”off you fuck!” He gestured them out of the room with his hand and without another word, they filed away despondently.

When the last of them had finally left, Kieran returned to his seat and slumped heavily into it. This farce had wasted months of preparation, and cost the business more money that he cared to acknowledge. Gareth was not, by nature, a patient man and was not used to being let down by his employees. What was worse, he had seemingly taken this debacle personally and as a result he had become more closely involved than ever before; to such an extent that he was now taking some of the projects recruitment into his own hands; He was eager to avoid any further delays or mistakes and Kieran was left with an uncomfortable feeling that the idiots he had just dismissed, weren’t going to be the only ones leaving the office with their tails firmly between their legs over the following days and weeks.

PART 1

CHAPTER ONE

NINE YEARS LATER...

MARS COLONY ALPHA. 2023

There was a tangible feeling of excitement throughout the colony in the days and weeks before the anniversary celebration dinner. All the colonists had been assigned extra duties in order make the evening special, but no one was complaining.

It had been an exhausting few months, so the opportunity to relax and have some much needed down time was something that they were all looking forward to. The bio-pods were finally all fully established and operational, in fact they were beginning to produce fruit and vegetables in a sustainable cycle far ahead of schedule. The colony farm was working well and the chickens had proven to be surprisingly adaptable. It was expected that they would lose several of the birds during transit. Yet despite the considerable logistical problems and huge expense of moving poultry through space, the surviving birds had been multiplying as quickly as chickens tend to if left to their own devices. In the two years since their arrival the twenty chickens that had originally left Earth as incubated eggs had now become more than fifty egg-laying hens. The fresh eggs that they produced provided a very welcome dietary supplement for the crew and four of the fatter roosters had been earmarked to become the centre piece of the upcoming banquet.

It had been two years since the Nerine1 landed upon Mars. Two years of blood, sweat and tears. Two years of triumphs, disasters, success and failure. Two years that humanity had lived and survived upon an alien planet.

The Nerine 3 was due to land in only a few weeks and the Nerine 4 was only a few more behind that. The colony would expand from twelve members to over thirty in a little over a month. The close knit band of early settlers were going to be exposed to new ideas, new opinions and new personalities for the first time in almost three years. Some of the colonists were more excited about the prospect of newcomers than others, but one thing was irrefutable; everything would soon change. Whether or not it would change for the better or for the worse was still very much up for debate, but the change itself was as inevitable as it was going to be permanent.

The fully dressed dining table was resplendent. It was laden with more food than any of the colonists had seen in one place for years. There were bottles of rudimentary home brewed wine and a vodka-type spirit evenly placed along the length. The oven roasted chickens were undoubtedly the starts of the show. They looked like film props such was the perfection of their preparation. They were surrounded by at least ten different types of home grown vegetables. Piles of beautifully roasted potatoes were presented in giant serving bowls, along with a mountain of butternut squash and cauliflower and broccoli gratin. Everything was perfect and it looked magnificent.

As the crew filed into the room they each grinned, their expressions bursting with pride. They commented upon how glorious everything looked and congratulated one another on a job well done.

Today was a day for unity and everyone was committed to having a good time.

Jim and Becky picked adjacent chairs at one end of the table. Like proud parents at the head of a Dickensian Christmas feast. They exchanged happy glances with one another and held each others hands in delight as they beamed along the length of the table at the rest of the crew.

As the others colonists settled into their seats the two of them brought their heads together and began whispering and giggling conspiratorially. Apparently, they were suddenly oblivious to the others and the gossip that surrounded them.

Their closeness had initially been the subject of some debate and speculation within the colony, especially as the very lovely Doctor Blank was supposedly still married to the current Vice President of the United States.

From the far end of the table Simon watched them intently. His expression set into an unpleasant sneer. He did not approve of this coupling, not at all. It wasn't a moral objection due to the alleged infidelity. Simon's objection was far more personal than that and it was Becky's apparently terrible taste in men that upset him so thoroughly. During a recent enforced residence in the medical bay, he had got to know Dr Blank quite well. Getting to know women well was not a process that Simon was historically very comfortable with.

Simon was a tall and powerfully built man in his early forties with short, receding, dark brown hair. His face was neither handsome nor unappealing but the perpetual scowl that he wore, made him infinitely less approachable.

Born and raised as a single child in Dusseldorf in Germany, as a boy he had been awkward and shy. With no way of addressing this situation, these traits had perhaps inevitably followed him into adulthood.

Becky had shown him kindness and compassion, and that had been enough to steal his inexperienced heart. He knew that doctors were obliged to act in this way, but that did nothing to halt the fledgling obsession from blossoming. He managed to convince himself that her attention went beyond merely the application of an effective bedside manner. She listened, sometimes for hours at a time, without scorn to his thoughts and concerns and never once tried to talk over him or belittle his opinions.

When he was discharged from the medical facility, she had visited him daily to check on his progress and change his dressings. After a short period of recuperation in his quarters, he had been able to resume his duties which was a great relief to everyone, not least Simon. Unable to work or exercise properly, he had been going slowly out of his mind with boredom sitting for days at a time, literally staring into space. This had given his infatuation time to seed and his imagination had fed it, enabling it to grow into something that it had never been, and was never going to become.

He glared at Jim with hatred in his eyes and nurtured his feelings of betrayal and retribution.

Jim Buchanan was the mission captain and commander of the colony; he had dark ginger, almost brown hair and heavily freckled skin. He was possessed with an indomitable self-confidence and as far as Simon was concerned he represented everything that Europeans found traditionally distasteful about Americans. He had been expensively educated and oozed privilege and natural optimism from his every pore and Simon was in no doubt that he was in no way deserving of Becky's affections.

Simon stared at the two of them and rubbed the scar on his left leg absent mindedly. It had healed well but he still felt the dull ache of the recently broken bones. He closed his eyes and breathed deeply, clearing his mind and remembering her scent. He sighed at the memory of their closeness and smiled. However, the smile faded as quickly as the memory passed

and he turned his attention to one of the bottles of vodka instead. He glared at Jim and took a long swig of the vodka, shuddering as he did so.
The alcohol was as rough as it was crude. It was, nevertheless extremely effective. The wine tasted vaguely of fruit and the vodka didn't. In the current environment though it tasted like the finest vintage champagne and was being warmly embraced by the crew. As a general rule of thumb, alcohol and extra-terrestrial living are not necessarily the most comfortable of bedfellows. The daily challenges and inherent dangers of a fledgling colony and construction site saw to that. Under normal circumstances a clear head was of paramount importance; this evening, however, was not normal circumstances.
Simon gulped another shot, his face twisting along with the burn as he swallowed. With his eyes still fixed upon Jim and Becky he picked through the chicken on his plate, picking up the bones and gnawing on them like a giant rodent.
Anna sat next to him, staring at him as he ate, seemingly transfixed by the spectacle. She watched him with an expression of morbid curiosity and a look of absolute disgust set upon her face.
Anna had joined the project in the early stages along with Captain Benjamin James Sutherland who was second in command for the mission. She had travelled with him to the ISS on his last visit and was a trusted if slightly inexperienced colleague. A member of the Dutch military, she moved into space flight in her twenties and quickly gained a reputation for single-minded determination amongst her colleagues. Anna rose quickly through the ranks and became the youngest captain her unit had ever produced. She had been defying expectations her whole life, so it came as no surprise therefor

to her friends and family when she signed up for Project Livingstone with seemingly no regard for her personal safety. A career soldier and astronaut, she had a natural talent for managing to remain calm in a crisis. Intelligent and versatile she had booked her seat on the Nerine 1 almost before anyone else. She liked working with Ben in particular but found some of the others a little too relaxed in their attitude. However, she had fully embraced the spirit of the evening and was enjoying the rare opportunity to let her hair down a little. In all honesty, she had probably had one or two more vodkas than she had intended, but she wasn't about to let that stop her from having one or two more.

“You eat like a pig Simon,“ she sneered.

Simon glanced at her, shrugged and began licking the chicken grease from his fingers.

Anna shook her head and turned her attention to Ben instead who already had a vodka induced rosy glow. He was leaning back in his chair humming and smiling happily to himself.

"You okay BJ?" Anna asked him,

Ben raised his eyebrows in response but said nothing.

Undeterred, Anna moved her head closer to his.

“This feels wrong doesn't it?” she confided in him with a tiny smile, "Almost...naughty."

Ben turned his head lazily towards her and nodded, “It certainly does captain," he said slowly, "may I suggest that you make the most of it, while you have the chance?”

“Okay sir. If that’s an order?” she said, her smile widening

Ben nodded, ”Absolutely!" he said loudly, "I order you to have another drink. In fact, have a bunch of them!”

Never one to ignore a direct order, Anna refilled her glass.

“Proost BJ!” she said raising her glass.

"Cheers," Ben touched his glass to Anna's and swallowed the contents of his own in one gulp.
He leant closer to Anna," I do wish you wouldn't call me BJ though. Makes me sound..." he struggled for the right word,
"Sexual?" Anna offered.
Ben recoiled at the sound of the word, "What? No!"
Anna winked at him and he felt his face redden.
Determinedly, he looked away from her and gazed around the rest of the room instead. Despite his embarrassment he felt a swell of pride grow in his chest. These were good people sitting around this table. The last two years had been difficult, demanding and exhausting. There had been tears and arguments along the way but the results were beyond anything any of them could have imagined. The Nerine 3 was now only a matter of weeks away from landing and then the next phase of Mars colony Alpha would begin. The new equipment and resources that she had on board were going to prove to be revolutionary. The plan of a fully operational community living, working and thriving on Mars was now no longer a pipe dream. It was a tangible reality and Ben was incredibly proud to be an integral part of it.
As he sat in his quiet reverie he noticed, with a hint of discomfort, that Sophie and Felix were having an animated discussion on the other side of the table. They were too far away for Ben to hear what was being said but neither of them looked very happy with the either topic nor the content of the conversation. The apparently painful discourse continued for a few minutes more. Without any warning, Sophie suddenly stood up and without looking back, walked away from Felix. He watched her go, his face flushed with emotion. He waited for her to look back and when she didn't he also got up from his chair and went over to talk to Andrew.

Ben watched with interest as Sophie slowly meandered over to talk to Jim and Becky. Doctor Sophie Torres was a shade over 5 feet 5 inches tall, she was in her mid-thirties and her time on Mars had made her lean and strong. She had her mothers pale skin and an attractive, heart shaped face, which was framed by a swathe of long, brown, shiny hair.

Without realising it Ben had been staring at her for almost ten minutes. Sophie had noticed though and was heading over to where he was sitting, a coy smile playing across her mouth. She paused briefly to make some small talk with Anna and then placed her hand on Ben's shoulder.

She bent to his ear and whispered, "You okay BJ?"

Ben instantly shot a look at Anna, who laughed instinctively. Any annoyance quickly dissipated though as Sophie's hair gently brushed against his ear, sending a ripple of hyper-sensitivity run through his body. He was unable to prevent a slight shudder or a reactive smile from flashing across his face. Sophie kept her hair pulled into a pony tail, but several strands had made their way loose and hung around her face.

Bens smile broadened, "Never better Doctor," he whispered hoarsely, "never better."

He coughed to clear his throat.

"Can I have a word?" Sophie whispered.

Ben regathered his composure and turned his head and looked into her eyes, "Sure thing, sweetheart," he said, "what's up?"

Her large dark brown eyes were often magnified behind a pair of strong prescription glasses, which gave her a permanently, slightly startled expression. Not tonight though, tonight she wore contact lenses and as she breathed gently into his ear, Ben once again, quivered involuntarily, "I'm worried about Felix" she said.

"I figured as much," he said nodding at Felix's now empty chair, "can I ask what that was all about?"
Sophie shook her head, "It's not really the time or place," she said quietly, “but I think that he's had too much to drink. I'm worried that he might hurt himself."
Ben's face screwed up, "Really?" he said incredulously
Sophie recoiled slightly at the reaction, "Well..." she started but looked away, embarrassed before finishing.
"Sorry," Ben said, instinctively, "go on."
"I don't mean anything horrible," she said, letting the word hang in the air for a moment, "I don't know..."
Ben glanced over to his empty seat. He shook his head.
"Where did he go?" he asked suddenly concerned
"I thought that you might know that," Sophie said, "did you not see him leave?"
"Me?" Ben said, surprised, "why would I know?"
"You know everything that goes on in this colony," Sophie said, putting her hand gently on his arm.
Ben blushed, "I don't know about that," he said.
Sophie shrugged.
"I thought you might have noticed?" she said,
“Nope," Ben replied, "probably just gone to the bathroom. How long's he been gone?"
He looked at his watch and then back at the empty chair.
Sophie shook her head, "I haven't seen him for almost ten minutes," she said.
Ben looked into her eyes, "Is there something I should know about?” he asked.
Sophie shook her head, “No,"
Ben raised his eyebrows, "Really?"
"Not really," she said softly, "just a feeling, like I said, I think that he's had a little too much to drink. Look, he hasn't even

finished his chicken," she nodded her head towards Felix's empty place setting.
Ben looked over at the place setting, Felix still had an untouched drumstick and a pile of coleslaw sitting on his plate and Felix never left food uneaten. His or anyone else's for that matter.
Ben turned back to face Sophie.
"I wouldn't worry about it Doc, he's a big boy. He can look after himself. Ask Andy, after all those two are usually joined at the hip."
Sophie glanced over to where Andrew sat in conversation with Joe. Her worried expression faded slightly and she kissed Ben on his cheek.
"Yeah I'm sure you're right," she said, suddenly serious, "but you shouldn't call him 'Andy' he hates it."
Ben grinned, "Yeah I know," he said and winked at Sophie who wandered off round the table to find another drink.
Ben watched her go with a grin on his face but when he looked back at Felix's empty seat he couldn't help but feel the tiniest spark of concern ignite within him. He resolved to go and check on him if he didn't return soon. In the meantime though, he thought to himself, he might as well have another drink.
The party was in full swing, the vodka and wine were flowing freely and the level of bonhomie had risen to the point that almost everyone had forgotten about the prospect of having to work again in the morning.

Ben continued to enjoy the celebratory atmosphere for another thirty minutes or so, it was only when he went to ask Felix a question that he realised that he was still missing.

He picked up a half-eaten bread roll and threw it across the table at Andrew who looked up at him irritably.
“Hey Andy! You seen Fe?” Ben asked loudly
Andrew physically flinched at the abbreviation of both his name and then Felix's but said nothing. He shook his head, irritably.
“Sure you have,” Ben said.
“Not for a while,” Andrew said with a shrug.
"Well, he hasn't been here for a while," Ben snapped, "and he is your goddamn wife!"
"Neanderthal," Andrew whispered, and rolled his eyes.
"What was that?" Ben asked, pointedly "I didn't quite catch that."
Andrew forced a false smile onto his face, "I said, he’s probably in the bio-pod. You know what he’s like?” he turned back to his conversation with Joe.
Ben shook his head, he considered saying something else but decided against it.
The Bio-pod was way over on the other side of the colony and Ben wasn't sure that he could be bothered with the trip. However, the wine had taken its natural course and he had to visit the bathroom in any case, so he made the reluctant decision to go and look for him.
Swearing beneath his breath, he got to his feet with a slight wobble. He steadied himself against the table top and then set off to the bio-pod. He was fully expecting to have to lecture Felix about the dangers of being an anti-social son of a bitch and also to chastise him about his choice of smugly, annoying British boyfriends.
Ben hummed, happily to himself as he swayed along the corridor. He instinctively patted his breast pocket for a cigar that wasn't there. He hadn't smoked for almost ten years, but

the wine was fuelling an old addiction and he slapped his chest in frustration.
When he eventually reached the bio-pod he carefully checked his reflection in the glass panelled window of the door. He smoothed down his moustache and ran his hand over the stubble of his freshly shaved head. The door slid quietly open and as he entered the pod he immediately noticed the humidity level, he had only taken two or three steps into the dome and already his shirt was sticking uncomfortably to his body. He looked around and noticed Felix tending to one of the larger beds of strawberries.
"Hey Felix!" he called from the doorway, apparently unwilling to venture any further into the sweat box than was absolutely necessary.
Felix turned his head in response to the call and raised his hand in acknowledgment,
"Hey bru," he said happily, "what brings you down here?"
"You do," Ben said simply, "or rather, the lack of you at the party. Where the Hell have you been?"
Felix looked mildly confused as he considered both the question and his current location. He fought down his natural urge to be a smart-arse; instead, he smiled and held up a clear plastic tray that was almost full of fresh, ripe, big red strawberries.
"Dessert!" he said triumphantly.
Ben sighed and looked down at his now saturated t-shirt which had turned from its usual olive green to a much darker mossy colour.
"Dessert?" he said.
Felix nodded, "Yes dessert," he said simply, "I told Andrew where I was going and both Jim and Becky knew that we were having a Pavlova for dessert," he was still beaming at Ben

whose face was now the same colour as the wine that he had been drinking all evening. He turned and headed for the door, leaving a slightly baffled Felix in his wake.
"Are you okay?" he called after him as he opened the door to leave.
"Goddamn limey Bastard," Ben muttered in reply before he trudged back out of the bio-pod and headed off towards his quarters to change his now sweat-soaked t-shirt.
Felix watched him go, shrugged to himself and then returned to his harvest. He was just putting the final few berries into the tray when Andrew walked into the pod, his face flushed with a mixture of wine and the ambient heat, he had a devilish grin on his face and was carrying two glasses of strawberry wine.
"Hello handsome," he said as he entered, he walked up to Felix and kissed him.
Felix pulled away from the attention and shot Andrew a quizzical look.
"What did you do?" he asked his suspiciously
Andrew shrugged, innocently but let his grin linger.
"Have you been torturing Ben again?" Felix asked.
"He called me 'Andy'," he said defensively, "again!"
Felix sighed, "He knows it annoys you that's the only reason he does it."
"Yeah well, I sent him down here for no reason because I knew that it would annoy him, so fair's fair..."
Felix laughed, "You really are a petty bastard, you know that don't you?"
This time it was Andrew's turn to shrug, "Just making a point," he said, "besides it makes me more interesting."
"I'll be the judge of that," Felix said with a smile before turning his attention to the drinks that Andrew carried, "is one of those for me?" he asked hopefully.

"I thought we might grab a moment of private celebration before we head back to the masses," he handed one of the glasses to Felix and they chinked them together.
"Here's to us," Andrew said with an affectionate smile.
Felix blushed slightly and nodded, "Yeah, to us," he repeated.
They kissed again. When they pulled apart, Andrew stared at Felix's face examining every detail, every line. His smile grew.
"I love you," he said softly.
"I love you too," Felix replied staring deep into Andrew's eyes.
Andrew shook his head almost imperceptibly, and looked away.
"What?" Felix asked gently, taking hold of his hand.
"I can't believe that..." he trailed off shyly.
"What?" Felix repeated.
Andrew laughed, "Any of it," he said, "You, me, this place," he shook his head again, "if someone had told me ten years ago that I would be standing on the surface of Mars, picking strawberries with the man of my dreams..."
Felix smiled, "I know," he said softly, "I know."

CHAPTER TWO

The Nerine Three was the flagship of the Livingstone project, its size, scale and cost ensured that. It was indeed magnificent to behold. Its vast presence had hung intimidatingly in low orbit around the Earth throughout its construction but its appearance divided opinion. Some believed it to be an expensive, indulgent eyesore, whilst others regarded it as a constantly evolving work of art. A beautiful monument to the endeavour and aspiration of humanity.

It was, at its core, a fairly utilitarian design and had been conceived to operate as a multi-functional vehicle. Upon its arrival on Mars it would have to absorb as much energy from the distant sun's rays as possible in order to store, convert and then reuse it. The fledgling colonists would then use the stored energy to provide some of the base's huge electrical output as well as help to combat the bitterly cold temperatures that they would encounter upon the planet's surface. The finished craft cast an eerie shadow against the nothingness of space that created the optical illusion of a vast black void that obscured the distant stars. The facets and edges of the craft caught the suns radiance and highlighted the ships outline; this gave it the passing impression of a line drawing made upon black paper with a white pencil.

And now it was only three weeks away from landing on the surface of Mars.

The crew of two was comprised of Major Jon Daniels, Medical Doctor and Captain Cam Harrison, chief designer.

Major Jon Daniels (MD) had been a relatively early recruit for the Livingstone project. The future colonies needed medical professionals that could provide a multi-faceted skill set, therefore a highly regarded and decorated doctor from the Royal Air Force was a combination that proved too tempting to ignore. Privately and expensively educated Jon was blessed with a near photographic memory which meant that he had enjoyed his education immensely. He was studious enough to appear keen, but was also very familiar the various local hostelries of Oxford, safe in the knowledge that he would probably manage to sail through his exams with only minimal effort.

He was from a military family and despite his younger protestations; his progression into the armed forces was as inevitable as it was frictionless. His father had hoped that he would follow him into the Navy but he had instead chosen the Air Force, wary of trying to match the career of the great Commander Daniels. The Air Force provided him with a solid officer's rank and also with the focus that he had been so desperately lacking in his youth.

He was six feet tall and had blonde hair that he kept short and neat. Classically handsome, he had an innate talent to talk to practically anyone about almost anything, he was charming and a natural orator but he was also an attentive listener and understood and empathised with people without any apparent sense of discomfort, awkwardness or insincerity.

He was handsome, intelligent and effortlessly popular.

When Cam had first met him, he had instantly disliked him intensely.

Jon was alone on the bridge of the giant Nerine Three, he sighed heavily and stared at his watch, 3:45 am. He sighed again, he hated the graveyard shift. Absolutely detested it. He knew it was, theoretically at least, no different to any of the other shifts on board and that In the middle of a dark, endless vacuum there was little need to adhere to traditional timekeeping. However, he had been ruled by the order of a twenty-four hour clock ever since he was a child at boarding school and therefore found it impossible to change his mindset now. Everything had its position. Everything had its place. As a doctor, he was used to working through the night, to have to snap awake, and be effectively functional at a moment's notice. He was good at it too, but that changed nothing, he still hated it.

Nothing good ever caused him to be awake and active in the small hours of the morning. It was lonely and stressful in equal measure. Things went wrong. People had heart attacks. People had accidents. People died at 3am. Of course people did those things at every time of the day and night, but there was something unsettling about the darkness that somehow exaggerated the emotion. Lives changed in the blink of an eye whilst the rest of the world slept obliviously. 3am was a terrible time to be awake.

He expected things to go wrong in the window between 3am and 6am. Whilst in the Air Force he had become paranoid about this time of day, so much so that he started to believe that it was somehow cursed.

It was 4am now and Jon looked enviously over at his crew-mate, Cam who was sleeping soundly in his bunk. The ship was calm and his last operations check had shown no alteration with any of the main systems or the cargo bay. He would not relax though, until 6 am arrived and Cam awoke to take over.

Such was Jon's profound dislike of this shift that Cam usually volunteered to take most of them on; he didn't care what the

time was and had no superstitions about the night shift. Jon had insisted on taking on the double shift tonight though because Cam was exhausted. He had been awake for twenty hours trying to fix the main hydroponic system in the main hold and it had taken its inevitable toll.
Space travel presents many unique challenges to horticulture but the colony was reliant on these plants arriving not only in tact but also thriving. Unfortunately the mechanised irrigation system and the artificial daylight system were uneasy bedfellows and would occasionally have disastrous disagreements. Water and electricity are difficult to keep separate in zero-gravity. The inevitable breakdowns and short circuits were often complex and time consuming to repair. Cam had managed it, because Cam, as far as Jon was concerned, was a bonafide genius.
He hadn't always had such a lofty opinion of him though, far from it. When they had first met, Jon had found Cam’s unusual hybrid accent of Glasgow and Yorkshire, more than a little unsettling. He was economic with his speech, and about half of what he did say was expletives, which he used as conversational punctuation.
Cam made little concession to Jons lack of engineering experience and would roll his eyes irritably when Jon didn't fully grasp one of his sophisticated concepts. He would also endlessly shake his head in frustration and mutter inaudibly beneath his breath. He exhibited an effortless, yet entirely unintentional, superiority complex that Jon found extremely irritating, jarring as it did, so completely with his rough syntax. Over time however, he became inured to Cam’s many personality quirks, and slowly began to discover the man beneath the facade. His brilliance shone through the endless swearing though. Jon was wise enough to acknowledge that,

despite his peculiarities, Cam was the reason that that this mission was on time, on budget and going to succeed where other, high profile missions, had failed in the past.
Jon's nighttime pessimism, had often proved to be a self fulfilling prophecy. If you expect the worst, it unfailingly contrives to deliver. Therefore, it came as no surprise, when at 4:13am an unscheduled meteor shower began peppering the hull of the ship with alarming ferocity. He was almost relieved in fact because at least he now knew what was going to go wrong tonight. He briefly toyed with the idea of waking Cam as the tiny fragments of rock hammered against the hull like an interstellar hail storm, but he resisted, deciding instead to wait and see if there was any need. The shower lasted for only a few minutes and Jon immediately checked the ships diagnostics to be certain that there had been no lasting damage. Meteor showers were relatively rare, and whilst the Nerine 3 had been designed to cope with far more severe poundings than the one it had just received. Jon was acutely aware that there was still the potential for significant damage to be caused by even the smallest impact, so he meticulously studied the readouts with paranoia, born out of necessity. Everything was working as it should, he diligently checked the cargo hold for any signs of decompression, but there was nothing detected. He then moved to the main cockpit and checked the hull's condition using the many exterior mounted cameras. The surface was pitted and marked but that was nothing new. Jon was still tense but he exhaled with a long blow. Slowly, he felt his heart rate settle slightly, and his adrenaline levels begin to drop. He relaxed physically and allowed himself a long calming breath.
Crisis averted, he stumbled back into the living quarters of the ship and checked the time, it was 5:15 am and Cam would be

awake and active in less than an hour and then he could sleep.
He needed to sleep.

CHAPTER THREE

MARS COLONY ALPHA

The dining room was dimly lit, relatively quiet, only a few of the chairs were occupied. Any conversation that managed to break the silence was intermittent and unenthusiastic. It was the morning after the night before and as a result those that didn't have to be up and about were still cached away in their quarters nursing fragile heads and unhappy stomachs.

Felix and Andrew were sitting together leaning against one another. Ben, Simon and Anna shared the table next to them. Ben, was being overly and naturally upbeat and had prepared a large pan of restorative scrambled eggs. The eggs were receiving many uncertain glances of mistrust from around the room, but he was sharing them out amongst the crew with a giant grin. In response, he was receiving little in the way of either thanks or enthusiasm.

"Come on guys," he said jovially, "these are my extra special eggs a-la-Sutherland, made with cream, cheddar and just a hint of mustard!"

Andrew blew his cheeks out, "I'm not sure I can face anything at the moment," he said unhappily, "they do smell good though, I'll give you that much."

Ben smiled thinly at Andrew.

"Me either," added Felix supportively, "I think I'll just have a coffee and head off to the bio-pod."

"Come on guys!" Ben said exasperated, "I made these especially for you all."

He looked around at the unenthusiastic faces and visible slumped.

"Look," he said finally, "I promise if you try them you'll like them. They'll make you feel like a million bucks"

Not wanting to continue with this particular battle, Andrew reluctantly handed over his plate, "Go on then," he sighed.
"That's better," Ben said with a huge grin. "Now how about the rest of you?"
Simon held up his hand, "Not for me thank you," he said defensively, "not if there is cream and cheddar in them"
"Worried about the fat?" Anna said patting his stomach playfully.
Simon grunting irritably, "No," he said, "but I am lactose intolerant and I already feel not the greatest this morning."
Ben shrugged, "Ah well, all the more for everyone else then!"
Once the eggs had been divided amongst everyone else they all began to tentatively eat. After a few fork-fulls, Simon stood from his chair and headed over to one of the kitchen worktops.
"Anyone else?" He called back to the group, waving his empty coffee mug at them.
There was a general mumble of ascension so he set about making a fresh pot.
"Could I have tea please?" Andrew replied and the group let out a collective groan.
"What?" he said, "I can't help it if some of us prefer a more civilised start to the day."
He looked around the tables and then stood up as well, pushing his half eaten plate of eggs to one side.
"On second thoughts," he said as he rose, "I think I would rather do it myself. I'm not convinced that anyone else here seems capable of the terribly complex process of adding boiling water to a tea bag!"
He smiled to himself and then took a step towards Simon. As he moved to push his chair back under the table he stumbled, grabbing the back of Felix's chair as he did so, causing him to drop a portion of egg onto his t-shirt.

"Hey!" Felix said, "Careful, I've just washed this."
"Sorry," Andrew croaked and then coughed to clear his throat, "I um... I suddenly don't feel terribly well," he said and coughed again.
Felix turned to face him and his face fell in appalled shock, "Jesus!" he said loudly and everyone else turned their attention to see what was going on, "Sit back down darling," he said, gently.
Carefully, he took hold of his elbow and tried to guide him back onto his chair.
Andrew coughed again, "Yes," he whispered "I think I probably..."
Suddenly, he collapsed onto the floor like a marionette with its strings cut. Felix jumped out of his chair and went straight to his side.
"Andrew!" he shouted, his face twisted with concern.
A few seconds after Felix jumped up, everyone else did as well. Simon hurriedly, replaced the coffee pot and ran over.
"What else was in those eggs Ben?" he asked urgently as he approached.
Ben was looking at Andrew without moving, the colour had drained from his face.
"Ben! What else was in those eggs?"
Ben shook his head blankly, but said nothing.
"Ben!" Simon was shouting now, "What was in the eggs?"
Ben shook himself from his reverie, "Nothing," he said, quietly "just what I said; eggs, cream, cheddar and mustard."
"You're sure?" Simon said calmly, "Nothing else?"
"No," Ben said, his face lined with concern.
"What's happening to him?" Felix asked, his voice frantic.
Andrew was now gasping for breath, clawing at his own throat as if trying to physically open if for the relief it might bring. His

skin around his eyes had swollen to such an extent that they were almost fully closed and his face had taken on an unpleasant bluish tinge. Felix moved Andrew's hands away from his neck and held them tightly in his own, his face now frozen in an expression of pure terror.

"Get help," he shouted, "someone get Sophie!"

"We do not need Sophie on this occasion I think," Simon said calmly and he crouched down to the prone Andrew.

"I don't really give two fucks what you think Simon," Felix shouted, "he needs a doctor, not a fucking labourer!"

Simon flinched slightly at the use of the word labourer but ignored it, "I think not," he said simply and without pausing he rose again and headed back to where he had been sitting. He reached into his jacket and pulled out a yellow plastic cylindrical tube. He removed the lid and returned to where Andrew lay, he bent down and without pause he jabbed the point into Andrew's thigh, pressing the trigger button as he did so.

"What's that?" Felix asked.

Simon said nothing; instead he moved back and watched Andrew carefully. For a few seconds nothing seemingly happened and then, all of a sudden, Andrew emitted a huge guttural gasp which he then converted into a series of hard, fast panting breaths. Simon smiled and stood up again, turning towards Felix as he did so.

"Epinephrine," he said with a shrug, before adding, "Or adrenaline if you prefer."

"Adrenaline?" Anna said.

"Yes," he said, "it counters the effects of anaphylaxis."

"I know what it does," Anna said defensively, "But..."

Simon turned his attention to Felix, "Would I be correct in assuming that Andrew here suffers from some sort of food allergy?" he asked
Felix nodded, "Yes" he said, "Peanuts."
Simon nodded knowingly.
“It was only diagnosed a few weeks ago though," he looked around the room helplessly as though trying to justify himself, “we're not sure what brought it on," he offered meekly
"Ah yes, peanuts," Simon said with a half-smile, "I too suffer from that same problem," he raised the empty EpiPen up to show Felix, "he should have a pen like this as well, no?"
Felix blushed and then glanced down at Andrew who was still recovering," he does yes, but he hasn't got used to carrying it around with him yet," he bowed his head, "I should have reminded him."
"There is no harm this time," Simon said kindly before adding a warning, "but it could have been much worse you know?"
Felix's face continued to redden, and he nodded
"Had I not been in attendance," Simon continued, conversationally, "young Andrew here could have slipped into a coma, perhaps even worse!"
Felix nodded again his face covered with guilt and then he bent his head to give the quickly recovering Andrew a kiss on the cheek. He then stood up and turned to give Simon a grateful hug "Thank you Simon," he said and squeezed him a little harder, "I don't know how I'll ever be able to repay you."
Simon blushed and flinched, almost imperceptibly at this affectionate contact. Felix seemingly didn't notice though, but Anna did and she smiled wickedly to herself. Felix broke off the hug and turned his attention back to the recovering Andrew.

"Are you okay sweetheart?" he asked, his face lined with concern.
Andrew nodded. He looked terrible though, his eyes were still very swollen as were his fingers and neck but his general pallor had certainly improved no end and he managed to produce a weak grunt of affirmation.
"He will be fine now," Simon said with a determined nod, "the swelling will go down over time, but I would still take him to med bay for a checkup."
Felix nodded slackly at Simon, "Sorry about the 'labourer' thing," he said sheepishly.
Simon waved the apology away, "Think nothing of it," he said and then moved to return to the worktop and the unfinished pot of coffee.
Ben meanwhile had moved back into the kitchen and was staring blankly at the remains of the eggs that he had prepared. The cheese, mustard and cream were still sitting out on the counter-top as were the discarded egg shells of the dozen or so eggs he had used. He shook his head and then slowly began the process of clearing away the mess, he put the egg shells into the composting bin and the cheese and cream back into the fridge.
He looked around at the gleaming kitchen and then out of the hatch that led through to the dining room. Felix had departed with Andrew and Anna and Simon were sharing a cup of coffee with each other.
Happy that everything was apparently continuing as normal Ben picked up the small bottle of peanut oil that he had used to coat the frying pan and slipped into his trousers pocket.

CHAPTER FOUR

Cam awoke and as usual it took him a few moments to fully orientate himself. He yawned, flexed his toes and fingers and arched his back, which cracked loudly in response. He massaged his painful right shoulder and scratched at the back of his head. The dull ache that settled in his lower back had become an unwelcomely familiar morning companion over the years and the stiffness that he felt in his shoulder was residual evidence of his preferred sleeping position.

He was forty-three years old and at times he felt every single second of those years. His head ached and his mouth tasted stale and unpleasantly bitter.

Jon carried the demeanour of a man, who if not actually broken, was certainly damaged. He padded inelegantly into the sleeping quarters and stretched extravagantly.

"Morning sunshine" Cam said, brightly.

Jon shot Cam a resentful look and then continued towards his bunk, without saying a word.

"You look like shite, by the way," he added, helpfully.

Jon opened his mouth to respond, but after a seconds pause, he thought better of it and closed it again.

The sleeping quarters on board the Nerine 3 were situated in the mid-section of the habitable portion of the ship. The accommodation's design lay somewhere between functionality and luxury. It was expensively furnished and there were subtle signs of extravagance dotted around. However, everything in the ship had to be reusable or recyclable so aesthetics had been sacrificed for efficiency. The living accommodation on the ship would eventually double as extra living quarters for the colony so were designed as individual module pods. They each had integrated bathrooms as well as separate living, cooking and dining areas. Jon and Cam had been allocated a cabin each but had decided early in the flight that they would share. It was a decision based as much on practicalities and laziness, as it was on camaraderie, but one that they were both glad that they'd made, usually.

Cam yawned and rolled over in his double bed, making himself into a human "X". He stared at the ceiling until the structures and lighting started to swim into focus. He rubbed his eyes and looked over at Jon who, he was slightly disconcerted to notice, was staring at him intently.

"I know I'm gorgeous, but it's rude to stare," Cam said, stifling another yawn.

Jon ignored him and continued to stare.

Cam rolled away from his gaze, pulled the duvet over his head and buried his face into his pillow.

"FFFNKRREW!" He said through a mouthful of feathers.

Jon continued with his impassive vigil, waiting for Cam to crack.

As was usual for Cam his first thoughts inevitably drifted towards his first cup of coffee.

He pulled the duvet back over his head and rolled over again until he was, once more lying flat on his back. He rested his head onto his pillow and let the vibrations of the ship gently massage his body. He smiled as he was serenaded by the familiar percussion of the constantly busy ship.

As the project's chief designer, each electronic whisper gave him a warm feeling of paternal pride. A thousand electronic components, each making its own perfectly unique and beautiful sound, together creating a symphony of endeavour.

It took only a few seconds for him to realise that something was terribly wrong. The ships serenade was out of tune and it jarred against Cam's ear like a misplaced violin in a concerto.

"We had another meteor storm last night Cam," Jon said sleepily.

Cam's head snapped in his direction.

"Good, I have your attention" Jon said, "rise and shine then sleepy head"

Cam scowled at him but did not reply. Instead he once again lay perfectly flat on the bed.

Jonathan rolled his eyes, he had been down this path before and was keen to avoid a repeat visit if at all possible. He walked over to Cam in order to help focus him and he decided to grab the bull by the horns in the hope of moving things along.

He grabbed the engineer by the shoulders and then shook him until Cam swore loudly in protest.

"Fucksake!" he said

“Get up you lazy git!” Jon said flatly.

Cam looked at Jon, his face lined with concern.

"Shhh," he said and held up a hand.

“I beg your pardon?" Jon said, slightly taken aback.

"I said, shhhh," Cam snapped.

“No, I wont 'shush'" Jon said irritably, "I'll tell you what I will do though. I’ll give you thirty-seconds, and then you're getting up regardless of your own personal involvement. Understand?”

Cam was sitting up now and he pressed his ear to the side panel of the sleeping quarters, he held his finger up towards Jon to further encourage his silence. Jon shifted uncomfortably on his feet, the first hint of concern touching his features.

“Meteor shower?” Cam said quietly.

“Hmm?" Jon replied a little distractedly.

Cam moved his ear from the panel and looked at Jon properly for the first time, “You said there was a meteor shower?” he said matter-of-factly

“Sorry? Oh yes about an hour and a half ago, why?”

“And you checked all the systems, right?”

"Did I check the systems?" Jon asked incredulously.

"Aye, did you check the fucking systems?"

"No, I thought I wouldn't bother,"

Cam stared at him horrified.

“Of course I did!”

Cam nodded.

A note of concern entered Jon’s voice, “Why?” he asked

Cam listened again, “you’ve missed something," he said simply, "we've lost the primary power cells."

Without another word, Cam got out of his bed and headed straight for the main computer terminal. He turned it on and a screen sized wall of light appeared in from of him, he flexed his fingers and then started to manipulate the windows on the display, enlarging shifting and discarding sections as he worked through them with a movement of his fingers or a flick of his hand.

Jon eyed him as he worked, but kept his thoughts to himself for the time being. He wanted to ask a hundred questions but he recognised the expression on Cam’s face and was reluctant to interrupt him. He didn't know what was happening, but he knew enough to let Cam work unhindered.

Meanwhile, Cam was busy running quickly through the ships diagnostics. Jon blinked at the display in awe as a steady stream of information began to scroll down it at an eye-watering speed, Cam's eyes flicked around at the different windows and pockets of information, focussing and refocussing on each readout for only a split second before moving on. He regarded the display suspiciously as he did so, as if trying to discover some elaborate electronic ruse.

The ancillary power cells hummed into life as they ramped up their power level to compensate for the shortfall from the main generator. Ordinarily, this was simply a maintenance activity that activated on occasion in order to ensure that the backup cells were working properly. However, it always happened at scheduled intervals and was never supposed to happen spontaneously. It was designed, specifically, to only be instigated by one or other of the crew.

Cam turned his attention to one of the other control panels and then tapped it irritably as if trying to knock out a display glitch. He tapped it again, harder.

He looked back at the display and then turned to Jon who was watching him closely, barely breathing.

An alarm sounded and Jon's head whipped round in surprise, Cam however remained utterly unmoved, still absolutely focussed upon the data in front of him.

"What is that?" Jon asked, as calmly as he was able.

Cam looked at him, "Right!" He said loudly, "Okay, then," he nodded his head.

"What?" Jon asked,

"Well," Cam replied, "I've good news and bad news."

Jon looked at him expectantly, and blinked.

“The good news," Cam continued, "is that I know exactly what's gone wrong and how to fix it!"

"And the bad?" Jon asked, warily.

Cam shifted in his chair, uncomfortably.

"The bad news is that you're going to have to suit up and do a spot of running DIY," he grinned at Jon, apologetically.

Jon blanched, but said nothing.

"Not only that," Cam continued, cautiously, "but I think that we've got about 45 minutes before the secondary power cells are completely drained."

Jon looked at him expectantly.

"Which means if we can't fix it in that time frame, then we are...fucked" his smile widened,

"Fucked?" Jon repeated.

Cam nodded, "Completely and utterly."

He sounded strangely pleased with this situation, Jon fought down his rising concern.

“Just to be crystal clear, 'fucked' in this instance means what exactly?” Jon asked as calmly as could manage.

Cam nodded slowly, “As in ‘*oh fuck I’m dead’"*

“Okay,” Jon said, warily, “what do you need me to do?”

Jon was utterly exhausted, and had been expecting to be asleep by now, or at least well on the way to sleep. However, his adrenaline was kicking in now and whilst he wasn't exactly invigorated he was at least able to stay awake.

Cam looked at his friend, and saw his inner turmoil. He felt a pang of concern but pushed it aside. This was the type of situation that Jon thrived in. He was one of those people that came to life under pressure and Cam was grateful that he was there.

The console beeped and Cam immediately returned his attention to the display panel, where he continued with his calculations as he tried to compose the details of what Jon would have to do when he got outside.

In the background, the tertiary power generator whirred into life meaning that they had about 17 minutes of power left from the secondary cell reservoir. Minutes passed, Jon was still standing behind where Cam was working, he shifted, uncomfortably from side to side.

“What do you need me to do, Cam? ” he eventually repeated, a little impatiently. Cam looked at him, said nothing and then returned his attention to the control panel.

Jon sighed, "Hello?" He said waving his hand in front of Cam's face, "Anyone home?"

Cam looked at him as if for the first time, his face carrying a distracted look of confusion, "Huh?" was all he managed to say.

"If you want me to go out there," he said, pointing to the inky blackness through the window, "then you're going to have to fill me in a little more."

Cam nodded, thoughtfully, "Aye," he said, "you're quite right."

He once again turned away from Jon.

"Cam?" Jon said, exasperated.

"I'm fucking thinking," Cam said, irritably.

Jon huffed loudly, but didn't push the matter any further.

Cam clicked his tongue and tapped his pencil against the console, he remained like this for a few more minutes before finally coming to a decision.

“Just decompress for just now,” he said calmly, “get yourself tooled up. Hopefully I’ll still be able to sort this out remotely.”

Jon grimaced, he could have been doing that for the past ten minutes rather than standing, watching Cam like a spare part. He swallowed his frustration and immediately headed for the airlock and decompression cabin.

The preparation for a spacewalk took careful planning, concentration and most of all plenty of time, but time was limited and shortcuts would have to be taken. This inevitably meant that the inherent risks of things going wrong were increased.

Before he even left the craft Jon risked decompression sickness, seizures or even death if he botched the preparation. They were all risks that Jon was aware of, but he embraced them with a stoic sense of purpose that belied his inner reluctance.

Cam began double-checking the ships external cameras for any obvious signs of damage. Like Jon before him, he could see nothing other than the familiar uniform, if slightly pitted, surface of the hull. The distant sunlight caught on the rims of the many tiny divots, creating irregular pools of light along the ship. The immensity of the hull led his eye, seamlessly from one section onto another. It was silently beautiful, but frustratingly he could see nothing amiss.

Another alarm sounded through the ship, indicating that the secondary power cell was now reaching critical levels and was about to fail. Cam cursed aloud.

“Oh, Fuck off!” he shouted at the flashing light that accompanied it, "I'm trying to think here!"

If the power level dropped below one per cent then the solar recharging process would take considerably longer. The prospect of a prolonged recharge was still purely hypothetical though, unless Cam could somehow get the unit back online. He was running out of options, so he made the executive decision to cut the primary and secondary cells completely. The rationale being that with a few minutes of reserve power left in the tank, there would be enough juice to sustain them during a full cell recharge. It was a decision with its roots firmly planted in unfounded optimism, but it gave him a small psychological boost. They were going to need that power, because they were going to be okay.

The Craft switched completely to its tertiary power cells, the lights flicked to emergency levels and all non-vital systems went into standby. The ship would have become eerily quiet if not for the incessant alarms.

Cam swore again and acknowledged the alarms with the push of a button, silencing them immediately. The console still flashed defiantly but at least the noise had gone. He turned his attention back to the external cameras, one of which was making a pass over the main service hatch. Cam was sure that this was the root of the problem. It slowly panned over the hatch and he felt his heart sink. Everything was fine. He could see nothing out of ordinary. No torn sheet-metal, no picture of desolation or destruction. In fact no visible signs of damage at all. Just a smooth unblemished surface with two small apertures below the access handle to unlock it.

Two. Small. Apertures.

Cam stared at the screen for a few seconds.

"Gotcha, you wee bastard!" he said to himself, a half-smile playing on his features.

He jumped up from his seat and ran back along the cabin, towards the entrance of the decompression cabin. Jon was part-way through the laborious process of inserting himself into his spacesuit. It was uncomfortable and awkward to operate but it also boasted more functions than the world greatest Swiss army knife.

Cam was surprised to see that Jon was already much further along the process that he had any right to imagine he would be.

He pressed the intercom switch and began to talk to the now red-faced Jon.

“Fuck sake,” he spluttered, “you’re no mucking about, are you?”

He shook his head at Cam and shrugged.

“How are your 02 levels?”

He pointed at the monitor above the air hose; it read ninety-nine point four per-cent. He put his thumb up; it was going faster than they could have hoped. Presumably, Jon’s anxiety was helping to oxygenate him faster. He looked at Cam and raised his hands questioningly.

Cam nodded triumphantly, and pointed up to the display screen in the chamber, Jon looked up at the screen and then back at Cam, his flushed face lined with confusion.

“I need you to go to the main access port. It's the big one beneath the main cockpit," Cam spoke slowly and loudly, like an American tourist abroad, "have you got the access key?" he asked.

Jon rolled his eyes but nodded and pointed to the tool-roll that was Velcro attached to the wall by the bike. Cam touched the remote screen that he had carried through with him from the cockpit. The image upon Jon's screen paused and then zoomed into the two holes in the hatch. The high definition image froze in perfect clarity.

“There!” he said, happily, "that's the little fucker there."

Jon looked blankly at the screen and then back towards Cam, he shrugged again.

“There’s only one key!” He shouted, "Because there’s only one key hole, that wee shit there," he said tapping the screen excitedly, "that wee bastard is what’s causing this problem."

Jon shook his head and then continued to stare at the screen. Cam watched his face as the realisation crashed over him like the surf on a rocky beach. Jon's face split into a wide grin, Cam stifled an excited grunt of nervous laughter.

One key for the single keyhole. The second keyhole was not a keyhole at all, it was, in fact, just a hole. A hole that hadn't been there ten hours ago. A hole that was now threatening to kill them both.

CHAPTER FIVE

It was a million to one shot really, so incredibly unlikely as to be virtually impossible; Virtually impossible, but unfortunately not completely.

A tiny ball of an asteroid fragment no bigger in diameter than a five pence piece had punctured and penetrated one of the exterior control hatches. It had managed to pass through the protective Kevlar and ceramic layers and hit a major power coupling, causing it to short and lose communication with the main computer cells. The improbable accuracy of this impact was so unlikely that even a centimetre either side would have caused far less devastation.

The Nerine Three was first and foremost a cargo vessel so Cam and Jon had at their disposal a dizzying supply of spare parts and circuitry. The one resource that was missing from the inventory though was not only the most valuable, but also the one that they needed now more than any other. Time. They desperately needed more time.

Without enough time to replace it, the circuitry became, in real terms, unfixable. If he accepted that, his options became more limited, but equally he became more focussed. Cam was a perfectionist, he was incredibly proud of his work on this project so it irritated him intently that there was no repair possible. However, he was also a pragmatist, and as soon as he had come to his conclusion, he was already considering the alternatives from the limited options available. As he rolled these around in his mind he headed back over to the communication link in order to update Jon with the new information.

"Jon?" the communicator of Jon's spacesuit crackled.

"Are you seeing this?" Jon asked, in response.

Cam looked in horror at the crystal clear, unadulterated view of the charred, electrical mess that was once the main service circuitry. The simple devastation made Cam feel physically nauseous. The circuit board was virtually unrecognisable as a piece of electrical hardware. Its processors had been obliterated and the circuitry itself was nothing more than a blackened mess of melted metal, ceramic and plastic. There is no oxygen in space so a fire will not sustain. However, a conductive element applied at extreme temperature will create the forensic illusion of fire, charred remains and all.

Cam sighed, "Yeah I see it," he said sadly.

"What are our options?" Jon asked, hopefully. "Can you talk me through a repair?"

"Nah," Cam said dismissively, "you can see for yourself, there's nothing to fucking repair." He paused for a moment before continuing, "There is some good news though. We still have choices."

"Choices?"

"Aye, choices," Cam repeated, "there is bad news as well though,"

"You astonish me," Jon said, sarcastically.

"I know,"

"So?" Jon asked as calmly as he could manage, "What's the bad news?"

"The bad news is we haven't the time to do either."

Neither of Cam's possible solutions were guaranteed to work. They were equally time consuming, difficult to perform and hugely labour intensive. This meant he had to pick an option knowing that there would barely be enough time to complete it never mind trying the alternative if it failed. Cam continued to look through the inventory of supplies until he found what he was looking for.

"Okay. Jon?" he said,

"Hello?"

"I've found a replacement board. It's not identical but it'll do." Cam tapped his chin with the edge of his tablets screen, "I think it'll do anyway," he added thoughtfully.

Jon swallowed his anxiety, "What are the compromises?" he asked as calmly as he was able.

"Nothing major. Just wee bits and pieces."

"What will we lose?" Jon pressed.

Cam ignored him and continued to study the image on the screen thoughtfully. He ran through some parallel diagnostics, looking for a third, more realistic option. It was then that he noticed something on the periphery of one of the hull cameras field of view. The primary power cell indicator on the outside of the ship. It was there for when the ship became accommodation on the surface of Mars and it was intended as visual aid. A way of letting the colonists know when the cells were depleting, not unlike the battery icon on a cell phone. Cam halted the cameras movement with the flick go a switch and stared at the screen. His squinted his eyes to be sure what he was seeing was genuine.

The hull indicator wasn't reading empty at all. In fact it was showing quite the opposite. It was showing a full charge.

Somewhere deep inside Cam's chest a spark of hope leapt forward and threatened to ignite his excitement. He steadied himself, and took a slow calming breath. Hope can be a powerful motivator in times of desperation, but, conversely, it can also be a dangerous foe when dealing with tight schedules and fine margins.

Complacency can cause a hazardous situation to become a fatal one in the blink of an eye.

"Jon?" Cam said slowly.

"Still here Cam. What have you got for me?"

"Change of plan," he said carefully, "The power cell is full."

"Excuse me?"Jon said, unable to keep the surprise from his voice,"How is that possible?"

Cam said nothing.

"Cam? Are you there? What's going on?" Jon tapped at his communicator.

Cam remained silent; his eyes darted back and forth across the monitor's readout.

"Hello?" Jon said, becoming increasingly anxious.

Cam cleared his throat, "I'm not sure," he said quietly, "give me a wee second. I need to think."

"That's good though isn't it?" Jon asked, with genuine hope, "We have power and that has to be good?"

"Aye," said Cam, "that is, I think so,"

"What?"

“The problem is not the amount of power, so thats good," he said.

"Go on..."

"The bigger problem now, is getting it reconnected,” Cam scratched at the stubble on his chin thoughtfully.

“I don’t understand, what exactly are we dealing with?”

“The main power cell has lost communication with the mainframe.”

“So?”

“So?” Cam sighed heavily, “So there’s plenty of fucking power okay? But the computer doesn’t know that and it’s switched to back up.”

“Again, so what?"

Cam considered the best way to answer this.

"We are running on the spare battery now," he said, "but it's running out fast."

"Meaning?"

“Meaning, that when the ancillary power cells die. So do we.”

“Really?” Jon sounded appalled,

“Aye, really.”

"But you just said we have full power," Jon protested.

"True," said Cam. "Unfortunately, the ship doesn't know that."

“So, let me get this straight," Jon said thoughtfully. "What you’re basically telling me that there’s a very real chance of dying due to a lack of power whilst the cells are, in fact, actually full?”

Cam considered this for a moment, then nodded to himself, “Aye," he said, "that's it in a nutshell.”

“Oh,” said Jon. He wanted to say more but nothing came to mind.

“Jon?” Cam asked.

“I’m still here Cam," Jon said quietly, "I'm just..."

"I know," cam interrupted, "shite, isn't it?"

"What can we do about it?” Jon asked,

Cam shrugged, “Rejoin the dots.”

Cam stared at the monitor and the charred remains of the circuit board. He was methodically going through his usual problem solving process. He worked his way along a mental flow chart, calculating decisions in an instant before moving on to the next stage. He brought up the main computer display again and once more started moving through the different sections at an impressive speed.

The circuitry that had been destroyed was important but nothing on board had the capacity to act as a terminal on/off switch. The fact that this collision had brought the system to its knees was however a secondary issue to getting the whole thing working again.

“Jon?" He said after a few minutes thought

"Hello?"

"Can you see a serial number on that board anywhere?”

Jon’s camera panned across the blackened remains.

“There’s nothing, just a big melted mess.”

Cam sighed.

"Look at the surrounding hatches and check for any spread of damage would you?" he said,

"Can do," Jon replied and he began methodically moving from one panel to another.

Cam looked deeper into the computer system, digging through layer upon layer of code and diagnostics until he finally found what he was looking for. As he had suspected, the power surge caused by the meteor strike had not only wiped out the circuit board but had also sent an error code into the ships mainframe to report the problem. This error code, however, had corrupted one of the internal servers and triggered a systemic misfire that had somehow managed to cancel the failsafe's from kicking in once the glitch had been detected.

Cam shook his head and marvelled briefly at the level of improbability that had caused this chain of events to unfurl. Had it not been for the severity of the situation he may even of thought of it as poetic. He stared out at the passing stars for moment and just as he was on the verge of reverie he pulled himself back into the situation at hand.

He shook his head to clear his mind and then, with only the briefest pause, he got to work. He began to reboot the many subsystems that would eradicate the issue, and save their life's and all without Jon actually having to do anything to the service panel at all.

"Jon? You still there?" he said casually into the communicator.

"Where on earth else would I be?" Jon asked, a little shortly.

"Fair enough," Cam replied, "you never know though you might have..."

"Might have what?" Jon interrupted.

"I don't know, wandered off, or something," he snorted a short laugh.

"Whatever," Jon said wearily,

Cam laughed again, "Sorry," he said, unconvincingly.

"What's the good word then?" Jon said, desperately trying to ignore Cam's fit of giggles. "Please tell me that you've got some good news for me?"

Jon was currently only a cable's thickness away from floating off into the eternity of space. It was a position that Cam had sent him into, and it was also one that he now realised he didn't need to be in at all. He needed to pitch this correctly so as not to get Jon overly emotional. Laughter at his misfortune, was therefore, perhaps not the best route to head along.

Cam composed himself and cleared his throat, "Don't get too excited just yet," he said as flatly as he was able, "but It looks like our luck's starting to change my friend,"

He rubbed his hand over the side of his face, "I think we can bypass that whole board, at least temporarily."

"Really? That's fantastic! What do you need me to do?" Jon said, unaware of the subterfuge that he was being unwittingly entangled within.

Cam let the silence hang for a few minutes as he continued working through the deeper, more unsavoury levels of code that lingered at the mainframe's core. He managed to isolate the error code and deleted it. He then started to check the systems immediately adjacent and put in blocks to prevent any corruption of any of the other servers. When he was sure that the original error hadn't produced any irritating little babies, he allowed the system to run its own diagnostic check. It reported itself to be clean and fully operational.

His communicator crackled and he flicked his attention briefly back to Jon. He had to tell him something, but he wanted to find something more palatable than the whole truth.

“Well…” Cam said slowly, his mind searching for some words of consolation, “I hesitate to say this Jon, but…” he drifted off again as he spotted a semi-corruption and deleted that as well.

"I've been thinking" Jon said, cutting over Cam's half-hearted confession.

"Have you?"

"Yes, I have," Jon said, defiantly.

"Okay?" Cam replied, "But we've talked about this haven't we? I do the thinking, you do the heavy lifting."

"Shut up, arsehole!" Jon snapped

"Sorry," Cam said, through a barely concealed smile, "please continue..."

"Well, I've been looking at this panel," he began thoughtfully, "and what if we just get rid of it?"

"I beg your pardon?" Cam said, whilst still checking the data-stream.

"If I can run a cable from one side of the board to the other," Jon continued, “then we can bypass that board completely.”

Cam stopped what he was doing, "Yeah?" he said,

"If I can bypass the damaged section of the circuit..."

“It will allow the mainframe to talk to the main cell,” Cameron took over,

“Which will, in turn, switch off the ancillary cells?” Jon finished, excitedly.

“Meaning we can live to fight another day!” Cam finished.

"Think it'll work?" Jon asked, hopefully.

Cam considered it for a moment. It was a simple, elegant solution. In fact, It was far more efficient that the complex solutions that he had initially come up with. Even if he hadn't found a technical bypass, it would have almost certainly saved them.

"Aye," Cam said, "I think it will."

He turned his attention back to the ships diagnostic systems looking for further spikes of impropriety. Happily, the system looked clean again,

“In fact that's fucking genius!” he said, happily.

“Really?” Jon asked.

“Aye," he said, thoughtfully. "Well, the theory’s good, at least.”

"Yes!" Jon shouted, triumphantly, "Not so dumb after all! Eh, professor?"

Cam smiled, "Nope," he said, "crack on with it, then. Time is the enemy."

Jon swallowed, “So help me out here Cam," he said after a few moments pause. "What do I need to get?”

Cam laughed, "Ah, not completely useless then? Am I?"

"Come on," Jon said, "don't be a dick just because I thought of something you didn't."

"No," Cam said with a shake of his head, "quite right, sorry."

He looked at the inventory of Jon's tool pack and his face split into huge grin.

"You're gonna love this" he said, happily.

"Oh no," Jon said. "Now what?"

"No really," Cam said, "you only need a simple length of insulated cable."

Jon opened his tool roll and checked the contents, "Is that all?"

"Absolutely," Cam said, "you'll have to attach a circuit breaker into it to stop it frying either the electrics... or you."

"Nice!"

"I thought so," Cam's voice trailed away as his attention shifted.

He checked carefully as the ship's subsystems entered the final phase of their reboot. Everything was progressing as it should and once again the disparate parts of the ship were communicating happily with one another.

He smiled once more to himself before feeling a fleeting slap of guilt; he had effectively sent Jon out into the unimaginable hostile and dangerous vacuum of space for basically no reason. Not only that, but he was also currently making him engage in a spot of basic engineering "busy work" to save face and possibly prevent a well deserved arse-kicking. He scowled, before consoling himself that perhaps a 'belt and braces' approach wasn't necessarily a terrible plan of action, and that what Jon was doing was in actual fact a very sensible, additional precaution.

He glanced over at the monitor that showed Jon's live feed and was gratified to see that he was already rummaging through his spares and had found the perfect length already attached to a circuit breaker.

Jon laughed to himself, “Jesus Cam, did you make one of these ahead of time?”

Cam blushed, “Aye. Well, it doesn't hurt to be prepared now does it?”

"Apparently not," Jon muttered.

“Thanks.”

Jon clipped the cable into position and connected the circuit breaker allowing the current to flow across the systems again. Cam watched this process anxiously, this was going to require a little bit of theatre. He wanted everything to come together at the same time. With perfect timing the rebooted systems sprung back in to life, the cabin lights came back up to normal levels and the secondary and tertiary cells flicked off automatically in order to begin their recharge. Cam exhaled in relief and smiled broadly to himself.

“How are we doing?” Jon asked nervously.

“It looks promising,” Cam said.

He checked the readouts, when he was certain everything was as it should be, he relaxed. Then he double and triple checked them, and exhaled.

“I hate to be pushy Cam but did it work?" Jon asked, nervously. "Is everything talking to what it should be talking to?"

"Aye," Cam said.

"So, we're going to make it?”

Once again, Cam felt a flush of guilt. Jon was tired and scared and it was, at least partially, his fault.

He nodded to himself, “Aye,” he said quietly, “for another day at least.”

“Oh, thank God!” Jon said, before adding cautiously, ”Any downside?”

Cam took a moment to examine the readouts one more time, “Well the secondary lighting has failed,” he said slowly, “so things will be a little moodier around here for a while”

“Ooh romantic,” said Jon laughing.

"Very," Cam replied.

“Anything else?" Jon asked. "Or can I get my arse back into the warm now?”

“Aye, we’re all good, come on in,” Cam said, then suddenly his heart sank, “Oh fuck!”

He sighed heavily.

“What?!” Jon was suddenly panicked,

"Fuck it," he repeated.

“Cam what’s wrong?" Jon asked, "Did I do something wrong? Has it failed?”

“Naw,” said Cam sadly, “it's okay, come on in.”

“What is it then?” Jon asked, warily.

“It’s nothing; honestly we’ve just lost some of the catering equipment, that's all.”

“Catering equipment? Is that all?”

“Aye” Cam said, but he sounded utterly distraught.

“Cam? What's wrong? Are you all right?”

“We’ve lost the fucking coffee machine,” he said glumly.

"The coffee machine?" Jon repeated and started to laugh.

"Aye, the coffee machine, and it's not fucking funny!"

Jon laughed so hard he almost lost his grip of the panel.

CHAPTER SIX

Only when Jon was safely back on board and unsuited did the two friends allow themselves to share a rare moment of celebration.
“Nicely done,” said Cam with a grin, “that was a wee bit too close though.”
Jon shrugged, “I was just the monkey, and you were the organ grinder.”
"Not at all," Cam said, "it was your plan."
"Good effort all round, I think!” Jon said.
"Aye, okay. I'll take that."
“If we were on Earth I might even consider buying you a beer,” Jon said happily,
“I thought you didn't drink?”
“I don’t, but you do,”
“You’d make me drink alone?” Cam shook his head, appalled.
“No, no I’d happily have a mineral water with you,”
“Body’s a temple eh?”
“Absolutely my friend. Absolutely.”
Cam smiled and pulled Jon into, what he considered to be, a manly hug.
“Careful Cam, people will talk!”
“You can’t fucking help yourself can you?”
"You started it,"
"Really?" Cam said, exasperated.
“Sorry mate, it’s like fuel to a fire,”
“Aye, or shit to a fucking fly!”
The two of them laughed together. Jon had undoubtedly earned some recovery time but not Cam, he had work to do.

“Right!" Cam said with a clap of his hands, "You need some sleep, my friend, and I need to get on.”
Jon sagged visibly, the adrenaline that had fuelled him so effectively through the spacewalk was now visibly ebbing from his body, leaving a drained husk behind it. However, as he trudged off towards the sleeping quarters he did so with heavy legs, but a lightened heart.
Cam’s own adrenaline levels were also levelling out as well. He took a deep cleansing breath, gathered his thoughts and turned his attentions elsewhere.
There was a bigger picture here and now that the crisis had subsided, there was a troubling thought that tugged on Cam's consciousness. The fact that such a potentially major issue had been missed by the ships diagnostic systems, raised the possibility that others systems had been affected by the meteor shower, systems that he was, as yet, unaware of. This translated into a gigantic pain in the neck for Cam who would now have to painstakingly run detailed diagnostics on every system, both major and minor, to discover if any of the ship's capabilities or instruments had been compromised. He also had the usual daily chores to complete.
“No rest for the wicked, mate,” he said to himself with a resigned sigh, “I’d better make sure that this bucket of bolts is going to get us the rest of the way there.”
When he arrived back to the cockpit he gave the main readouts a cursory glance before he began to check over all of the displays and monitors in more detail. Everything was functioning as it should, at least superficially. The main power cells were showing up at full power again. The secondary and tertiary power cells were recharging happily and everything was apparently serene.

Cam checked the display that indicated the condition of the more fragile aspects of their cargo and noticed with some relief that his beloved hydroponic systems had remained unaffected by all the excitement on the bridge.
The biospheres and there contents had been a real labour of love for him. It was one of the more fanciful projects that he had overseen, but was also one of the most undeniably important. Despite the fact that he already had an overflowing work schedule, he had taken extra time and effort to oversee the team that had designed and refined the robotic gardeners, that now so carefully attended to the plants growing in the hold. He had developed a rudimentary artificial intelligence programme that made them able to recognise the early the signs of problems and diseases and deal with them appropriately. This meant that the biospheres functioned entirely remotely, so whilst either Jon or Cam could physically attend to the plants if necessary, the whole process had up until now been self-sufficient. A fact that Cam was rather proud of.

Like a nervous teacher on exam day, Cam monitored these robots via their individual electronic readouts on a daily basis and had taken to giving each of the six of them different names. He would talk to them separately and individually, which provided Jon with further evidence that engineers were a decidedly odd bunch.
He looked at their individual readouts and bid them a good morning.
“Hello, fellas," he said chirpily, "how are we all today?”
He noticed with a tiny swell of pride that they had carried on as normal with no real compromise as a result of the recent power issues.

“We’ve had quite a morning so far, I can tell you,” he continued.
He tweaked one of the service controls and tapped the screen subconsciously
“Looks like you’ve managed to avoid any of the excitement anyway. Excellent!”
This wasn’t the first system that he should have checked in detail, strictly speaking, but he had to start somewhere and it was as good a place as any.
He went on to check if any of the main systems had suffered any power compromises during the outage. It looked very much as though the main systems had all rebooted during the switchover from primary to secondary power cells as a way of protecting themselves from any power spike in the system.
It was a built in safety device and happened in sequence around the major systems; Navigation, oxygen recycling, life support, communication, external surveillance and cargo observation. There were never any two systems rebooting at the same time and none of them shut down completely but merely referred to their default settings unless otherwise commanded.
A red light was blinking on the communication panel meaning that they had missed a message during all the excitement.
Cam remembered that panel from the final draft of the schematics of the ship, he also remembered what it had cost; Half a million dollars, which by Cam’s reckoning must have made it, by some distance, the most expensive telephone answering machine in the world. He pressed the flashing button; which indicated that there was in fact a double communication.
“Two eh?” he said aloud. “Well, aren’t we popular today?”

He assumed that they were both from mission control. He pressed another key so the first message began. The face of his colleague and friend, professor Coupland filled the screen. "Nerine-Three," she said seriously, "this is mission control; our instruments are indicating that you are currently heavily depleting your ancillary power supply, whilst your primary power cell remains at full capacity. Is everything okay?"

Cam rolled his eyes. This was a typical message from mission control, informing them of what they were already experiencing. He wondered, idly, if they had died if they would have had another message to inform them of the fact.

Due to the crafts relative proximity to Mars it had become impossible to hold an actual conversation with Mission control back on Earth due to the time delay. This was frustrating and welcome in equal measure. Mission control was now no longer of any practical use in an emergency. However, they also could no longer offer an opinion on every little aspect of the mission. So overall Cam saw it as a positive because as he was almost certainly the best equipped of the project staff to deal with any technical issue anyway, it meant he no longer had to pretend to care about anyone else's opinion. This had fundamentally altered the way that they communicated with Earth.

There were the inevitable bugs that needed ironing out at the very beginning; consequently the early communications took the form of an almost continuous running commentary. This had inevitably lessened as both the ship and the crew got accustomed to one another and as the time delay started to become more and more significant so the messages dwindled in their regularity and complexity. Until, finally they had reached the point where the crew merely sent in a daily update, as and when they remembered.

Cam realised, a little guiltily, that he hadn't in fact sent an update for at least 48 hours. Jon rarely bothered himself with the “nerds back on Earth” so he quickly composed a brief message that would buy him some time;
“Mission control this is Nerine 3. Captain Cameron Harrison reporting. We had a brief issue with the primary power cell, so decided to use the opportunity to fully test the secondary and tertiary sources. Test was fully successful and the primary cells are once again powering the vessel. Secondary and tertiary cells are recharging within normal parameters. A full system diagnostic is currently under way. The results will be forwarded as they become available”
"That ought to hold them for a while." Cam muttered to the empty room.
He smiled happily to himself and looked out at the passing stars. In truth he enjoyed the 'seat of the pants' stuff far more than when everything was tripping along nicely.
If everything was going well it meant that he and his team had done their job properly. However, there was still the undeniable joy that dwelt within a rush of adrenaline that made him secretly quite pleased when things went, at least a little, awry.
He caught his reflection in the glass of the window and was startled briefly by the severity of the image. Long gone was the slightly chubby Glaswegian that drank too much. He'd been replaced by a lean, muscular, shaven headed man with a long drawn face that showed years of care, drawn across the features.
He barely recognised himself anymore either physically or mentally. He shook his head as he considered the journey that had brought him to where he was currently sitting. It had been a journey laced with joy and sadness, victory and desolation. It

had all started nearly ten years ago on an otherwise terribly normal afternoon in the summer of 2014.

That was the day that Mr. Williams first came to visit

CHAPTER SEVEN

NINE YEARS EARLIER...

SHEFFIELD, ENGLAND. JULY 2014

It was a glorious British summer afternoon, the kind of day that lives long in the memory but was, in truth, depressingly infrequent. The sun was hot and bright, and the trees cast their dappled shadows over the pavements and roads. It was mid-afternoon and Cam had already set off on the walk to his daughters' school for the afternoon pickup.

He he'd set off early so he could go at a leisurely pace, enjoying the heat as he went. He swigged from a chilled bottle of water as he walked and allowed his mind to wander. His route took him past several beer gardens, all of which were full, almost exclusively, with students. Students who had finished their studies for the summer but decided to stay in the city until term time restarted. They were young, uninhibited and filled with the heady combination of optimism, youth and ice cold lager. He smiled to himself as he passed, remembering, fondly his own student days and feeling just the tiniest pang of jealousy.

He arrived at the school with a smile on his face and his mind still bobbing along in a nostalgic haze. Despite his earliness, there were already several other parents assembled in the playground, standing in clusters. He nodded at a few that he recognised but was careful not to join any particular clique. Cam wasn't unfriendly, he just wasn't a big fan of smalltalk. Partly because he wasn't terribly good at it, but mainly because he found it a distraction to his daydreaming. Despite his efforts at dislocation a young woman in her mid-twenties broke away from one of the small groups and sidled over to where he was standing,

"Hiya Cam," she said brightly.

Cam looked at her and smiled.

"Beautiful day isn't it?" she went on,

Cam mentally rolled his eyes, "Aye," he said, looking at the sky, "it's a beauty all right, how are you Lauren?"

Lauren was dressed in a pair of khaki shorts and a purple vest top. Her hair was pinned up into a messy bun and she carried a weary expression on her face.

"Fine thanks, how's Karen?" she asked,

Cam nodded, "Aye, she's really good thanks," cam replied, "busy at work, you know? But really well."

Lauren said nothing for a moment as if waiting for something. Cam took the hint.

"And how's Alan?" he asked,

"Oh, he's fine," She said, "I was just saying to him the other day that we should have you all over for a Barbecue?"

Subconsciously, Cam's eyes widened in fear. Lauren seemed to either not notice or not care and she plowed on regardlessly.

"The girls would love it," she nudged Cam with her elbow, "you boys could have a few beers and Karen and I could have a proper catch up?"

Cam grinned a huge, unnatural grin.

"Aye," he heard himself say, "that would be really nice,"

Lauren placed her hand on Cams arm, "Lovely," she said happily, "I'll get everything sorted. Shall we say 2 o'clock tomorrow?"

"What?" Cam said, shocked.

"Two o'clock tomorrow?" she repeated.

Cam nodded his head, helplessly, "Aye, that sounds perfect. I should probably check with Karen though."

Lauren waved this away, "No need to bring anything," she said as she started to walk back to the group.

Cam watched her leave with a mixture of confusion and awe. He was about to try and argue when he felt a persistent tugging at his arm. He looked down irritably,

"Daddy!" said a small shiny face, looking up at him happily.

Cam's irritation dissolved in a second. He bent down and kissed the top of his daughters head. It smelt of a mixture of Karen's shampoo and factor-fifty sun screen,

"Where's your cap?" he asked

Martha dug into her bag and produced a battered, sun bleached baseball cap. She placed in on her hand and pulled her ponytail through the hole at the back. She grinned up at her father who returned the smile with an air of mild frustration.

"Has that been in your bag all day?" he asked.

Martha shook her head and then started unloading her water bottle, book bag, cardigan and lunch box onto Cam's outstretched arms. He protested weakly but carried them all anyway. He shook the water bottle and confronted Martha accusatorially.

“There’s too much water left in this bottle young lady," he said seriously, "you need to drink more in this heat.”

Martha looked up at him, “I have!" she protested, "That’s the second refill daddy.”

She smiled innocently at her father and Cam narrowed his eyes suspiciously at her,

“Really?” he asked.

She nodded, “Yes really! I promise!”

“Hmm, okay then,” he said and smiled back at her.

He crouched down onto his haunches so that his face was level with hers,

“Hello, sweetheart,” he said, gently and leant close for a hug.

Martha, hesitated, briefly before putting her arms around his neck and kissing him on the cheek.

“Hello Daddy,” she said happily.

She immediately released his neck and ran over to one of her friends. Cam smiled awkwardly at the girl's mother.

Cam stood back up and watched her go. The hesitation for the hug had been a split second but it had been a definite pause. She was only 9 years old, but his little girl was growing up, becoming aware of what her friends might think of her. He shuddered and fought down his instinct to gather her up and run away.

He looked over to where Martha was talking to her friend, Rosie. Lauren walked past with her own daughter and smiled,

"See you tomorrow!" she said as she passed, "I think that Richard and Jessica are coming as well now."

Cam instinctively looked over to the rapidly disbanding group of parents, Richard caught his eye and shrugged helplessly. Cam smiled, at lease he wasn't the only playground wimp. He waved at Richard and then turned his attention back towards his absent daughter.

“Come on sweetheart,” he called after her, “time to go, you’ll see Rosie on Monday.”

“Can Rosie come round for tea daddy?” she called, imploringly at him.

“No darling, not today,”

“Aw! Please daddy?” Martha pulled, what she considered to be, her most adorable expression. Cam wavered for a moment, before shaking his head resolutely.

“Sorry, not today sweetheart, I haven't got the car and it’s a long walk home. Maybe next week if that's okay with her mummy,” he looked at Rosie’s mother who nodded encouragingly.

Martha considered this for a moment, toyed with idea of arguing her point, but then grabbed Cam's hand and they headed out of the school gates. As they left she turned and shouted back to her friend,

“Bye Rosie, see you on Monday, have a nice weekend!”

Rosie responded in kind and they began their journey home hand-in-hand.

“How was your day at school darling?” Cam asked.

It was a question he asked every day after school and it always elicited the same response.

“Fine,” Martha said simply.

Cam nodded, “Fine?" he repeated.

Martha nodded, "mmHmm, Fine."

Cam persevered, "Learn anything today? Maths? English? Tiger wrestling?"

"Daddy!" Martha snorted a laugh.

"What?" Cam asked innocently.

"Don't be silly," she said, "we have English on a Thursday,"

She looked up at her father who couldn't suppress a laugh.

“You must have done something good?” Cam, persevered.

Martha shrugged, “No not really. Ooo we did have pink custard for lunch though, and me and Rosie played “Frozen” at break time. I was Elsa and she was Anna, because I’ve got blonde hair and Rosies is brown…”

“Rosie and I,“ Cam corrected.

Martha’s little face creased in confusion, “Rosie and you what?”

Cam shook his head, “No. It’s Rosie and I, not me and Rosie.”

Martha stopped and stared at her father, her expression one of utter incomprehension. Cam opened his mouth to explain, but he immediately thought better of it and closed it again, “Doesn’t matter darling.” He said, with a shake of his head. Martha considered her farther him for a few moments, then shrugged and continued with her detailed description of what she didn't learn at school.

The retelling of the day's break-times, upcoming social engagements and favoured classmates lasted for about twenty minutes. However, when they reached the group of shops that stood in the heart of their village they stopped to buy an ice cream. They sat on a bench in the play park, opposite the swings, eating them before continuing on the final leg of their journey home . The last part of their walk was all uphill so is was with a weary sigh that they left the comfort of the park and made there way along the sun-bleached pavements.

They lived on a quiet tree-lined avenue in a wealthy, middle class village right on the very westerly edge of Sheffield. The village's history was in fact more closely linked to Derbyshire than Yorkshire. However, it had a Sheffield postcode was populated by the city's professionals.

As Cam and Martha turned onto the road and started up the hill that approached their house they continued chatting. Cam had mentioned the next day's potential barbecue and Martha was excited about picking her most eye caching outfit.

"If I wear my flowery dress with the sparkly shoes then Abbie can wear her Flowery dress as well," she said thoughtfully.

Cam looked at her and nodded, "Hmm," he said, "that's a good plan. Shall I wear my flowery dress as well?"

"Daddy! Don't be silly!" Martha chided, "Your dress isn't flowery, its tartan."

"That's a kilt darling, not a dress," Cameron said, trying not to laugh.

"Well, you can't wear it anyway, it'll clash," Martha said, seriously.

Cam nodded again, "Fair enough," he said, solemnly, "I'll stick to shorts shall I?"

Martha rolled her eyes at him, "No one will be looking at what you're wearing anyway," she said and then launched into a list of possible alternative outfit choices.

Cameron let her babble away excitedly and wiped some of the sweat from his face with his hand.

"Christ, I'm unfit," he huffed to himself.

Martha looked at him, "You don't exercise enough," she said, matter-of-factly "Mrs Laidlaw at school says that 1 in 3 adults don't get enough exercise,"

"Does she?" Cam asked, amused.

Martha nodded and looked at her father's midriff, "You're not fat though," she said thoughtfully.

"Thanks,"

"Just unfit..."

Cam bent down and scooped Martha into the air, before plonking her onto his shoulder.

"Daddy!" she screamed, and started to giggle, uncontrollably.

"I'll show you whose unfit!" Cam said, laughing, "You cheeky wee monkey!"

"Put me down, daddy!" Martha screeched.

"Never!" Cam roared and started to stomp up the hill.

After only a few metres he started to feel the heat intensify. By the time he was a further ten metres up the hill, he was greatly regretting his act of bravado. Martha was still giggling, but she was getting heavier with every step. Cam paused and lifted from her perch on his shoulder. He placed her carefully back on the ground.

"Let that be a lesson to you!" he said, through deep breaths.

Martha grinned and set about straightening her school dress out. Once she was satisfied that it was correctly back in place, she looked up the hill.

"Whose is that car, Daddy?" she asked pointing to a large black Range Rover that was parked midway up the street.

Cam looked up and shrugged, "I've no idea, darling," he said.

"It's parked outside our house," Martha said, and then started to walk towards it.

Cam took a second look and sure enough, Martha was right. It was parked at the end of their drive. Its windows were heavily tinted to blackout levels and the sun reflected brightly from it's highly polished bodywork.

As they got closer Cam could see a dark-suited man standing alongside it, leaning against the passenger door.

The man was tall, a shade over 6 feet and must have weighed about 85-90 kilos. He looked to be in his early forties and sported an expensive haircut that surrounded a handsome, tanned face. He looked fit and trim and his closely fitting midnight-blue suit had clearly been individually tailored for him. He wore a pair of simple, aviator style sunglasses and quite honestly couldn't have looked more conspicuous or out of place if he had tried.

As Cam and Martha approached, he noticed that the man was staring towards their house.

They were almost within touching distance of him, before he apparently noticed them at all. He turned his head in their direction, removed his sunglasses and smiled broadly, revealing a set of immaculate, gleaming white teeth.

"Mr Harrison?" he asked.

“Aye, who wants to know?” Cam's gentle Glaswegian burr noticeably coarsened. He mistakenly thought it made him somehow more intimidating.

The stranger's smiled broadened and he held out his hand, “Hello," he said, "my name's Gareth, Gareth Williams.”

Cam kept his hand by his side, but nodded his head.

"Hullo," he said, "do I know you?"

He thought that he knew that name, but he wasn’t sure from where.

Gareth shrugged, "I can't really answer that," he said, his smile wavered slightly.

Cam instinctively put himself between the stranger and his daughter.

Gareth withdrew his hand, unabashed. He folded his sunglasses and slipped them into his jacket pocket.

Cam looked at this strange man. He didn't appear to be sweating, how was that possible? It was far too hot for a full suit and yet he had the look of someone that hadn't really noticed the heat.

“I know you though," he said, still smiling, "that is, I know of your work,”

“My work?” Cam asked, suspiciously.

“You are Cameron Harrison? The robotics engineer that worked on the Nereus project?” A slight note of uncertainty touched the edge of his voice.

Cam’s eyes narrowed slightly.

“Aye, why?” he replied, cagily.

Cam was sure he knew that name, but how? From where? Gareth Williams… Gareth Williams…

Then it hit him; hit him like a 40 pound sledge hammer. Of course he recognised the name, Gareth Williams. He swallowed hard and physically flinched. Gareth Williams was a name that almost everyone knew; he was famous, rich, powerful and massively influential.

"Oh fuck," he muttered to himself, quietly but audibly.

Mr. Williams tilted his head slightly, "I'm sorry?" he said,"What did you say?"

"Eh? Oh nothing, nothing" Cam said, somewhat feebly, his red face reddening further.

"Are you okay?" Gareth's smile remained, but there was a mischievous twinkle in his eyes.

Cam couldn't detect any obvious sign of malevolence on his face, although his very presence at Cam's home hinted at some indefinable background threat.

Cam began to inwardly panic, his thought processes screamed into overdrive as he searched wildly for a rational explanation.

What was Gareth Williams doing here? He thought to himself.

This was not good; it could not possibly be good. His subconscious mind thankfully kicked in though, and without thinking about it, his arm had raised and he was offering his previously withheld palm to his visitor. He was still instinctively shielding Martha with his body, though. From what, he wasn't entirely sure, but he shielded her nevertheless.

"Mr. Williams, it's a pleasure to meet you," he said, somewhat unconvincingly, "to what do I owe the pleasure? Would you like a drink perhaps? Have you travelled far?" Cam was babbling, but he wasn't keen on letting Gareth talk again now that he'd belatedly, started connecting the dots in his mind as to the reason for his unexpected, presence.

"This is my daughter, Martha," he said, suddenly, "say hello to our guest, Martha!" Abandoning his earlier protective instinct, Cam pushed his only child forward, almost as a sacrifice to the upcoming shit storm. He felt a flush of guilt as she awkwardly shuffled past him, still clinging to his t-shirt and muttered a barely audible "hello" before scampering back to comparative safety, behind her cowardly father's legs.

Gareth smiled, indulgently at the little girl and then crouched down to Martha's level.

"Hello there Martha," he said lightly, "it's very lovely to meet you, my name's Gareth."

Once again he held out his hand, and once again it was completely ignored as Martha tried to get further behind her father.

Undeterred, he continued "Do you like chocolate, Martha?" he asked, in a stage whisper.

Martha glanced up at Cam, apparently uncertain how to correctly answer this question. She had to decide whether or not she should be honest or if it was somehow a trick that she might get into trouble for.

Cam nodded reassuringly at her, "It's okay you can answer, sweetheart," he whispered, trying to untangle her from his legs.

The truth was that Cam was also trying to decide, for himself if this was indeed some kind of trap.

"I'm not supposed to take sweets from strangers, though," she said sadly.

Cam looked at Gareth, "I think you'll be all right," he said, "just this once though!"

Martha looked at Gareth and smiled shyly, "Yes, I do," she muttered.

"Excellent," said Gareth, "but you're quite right, of course. You should never take sweets from strangers, normally. You're clearly a very clever young lady."

Martha's face flushed pink.

"I have a rather large bar of chocolate here in my jacket pocket, that I was going to eat later on."

He reached into his suit and retrieved a large bar of Cadbury's dairy milk. Martha's eye's widened hungrily.

"I'll be honest with you though Martha, I've rather gone off the idea," he whispered, "so if you were to take it off me you would actually be doing me a favour."

He offered it to her, she reached out take it, but then hesitated. She looked, uncertainly at her father again, but he nodded encouragingly at her.

"Sorry it's a little melted, but I'm sure it's probably still okay," Gareth said, gently.

"Are you sure it's okay daddy?" Martha asked.

Cam nodded, "Aye, of course, sweetheart." He said.

"Sorry," Gareth said suddenly, "I really should have checked first, I'm not in the habit of offering chocolate to small children. Honestly!"

Cam's expression flickered with concern, but then he smiled.

“Sorry,” Gareth said blushing, “that was an incredibly odd thing to say wasn't it?”

Martha was looking at her father, still uncertain of how to proceed

Cam looked down at her pleading face and sighed, “I said, it's okay sweetheart," he said, gently, “just don’t eat it all at once okay? You’ll ruin your dinner. Daddy’s made his special pasta sauce for tonight.”

Martha smiled sweetly at him as she reached out and took the bar, tentatively from Gareth.

“What do you say?” Cam prompted.

She held the bar, carefully, like a precious treasure. Without looking up she chanted, “Thank you.”

“You’re welcome young lady,” Gareth said with a smile, “now is it okay if I borrow your daddy for a moment, so I can have a chat with him?”

Martha nodded and without another word, went skipping up the garden with her foil-wrapped prize clutched, proudly to her chest.

Mr. Williams stood up to his full height again and faced Cam. Once more he stared at him, straight in the eyes. Cam looked away, his gaze following his daughter as she went through the back gate and into the rear garden.

“If it’s okay with you Cam," Gareth said, "I’d very much like that drink now please?”

Cam was chewing the inside of his lip, but he managed a nod.

“Aye,” he said, “of course Mr. Williams, what can I get you?”

“Please, call me Gareth," he said with a smile, "you're making me feel as though I’m in the boardroom."

“Aye. Okay, what would you like Mr. Will... sorry Gareth? Water? Orange juice? Gin and Tonic?"

“What kind of tonic is it?” Gareth’s face was suddenly serious again.

“Eh?" Cam said, "Um, I’m not sure. Tesco's, I think.”

Gareth laughed, “I’m only joking, G and T would be lovely, thank you."

He glanced down at his car.

"Actually, perhaps we should make that a 'T' on its own without the 'G'," he reached backwards and patted the wing of the Range Rover

Cam was suddenly very aware that they were still standing on the road side; he turned and began to walk along the drive. He gestured to Gareth as he headed off.

“Please Mr. Will... I mean Gareth, come on in!” he forced a smile onto his face. “We'll go straight round into the back garden shall we?”

Gareth nodded, “Sounds delightful Cameron.”

"Cam" Cam said.

""Hmm?" Gareth replied.

"Well, if I'm to call you Gareth, then you must call me Cam. Only my mother calls me Cameron."

Gareth nodded, "Cam it is," he said.

"And my wife, she sometimes calls me Cameron, but it's never a good thing when she does."

Gareth laughed, "I cant wait to meet her," he said, following behind Cam as he began to make his way along the drive.

The front garden was immaculately lawned with a large gravelled driveway that split and crossed the front of the house. It was a large redbrick detached property that had been extended several times over the years. The most recent addition consisted of a large open-plan kitchen, dining room and conservatory which Cam and Karen had completed themselves only a couple of years previously.

Cam and Gareth walked uneasily along the driveway, without speaking. The only sound was the crunch of their footsteps upon the driveway.

This short journey provided Cam with some much needed thinking time. His calm facade masked his inner panic. After a few further steps he turned towards Gareth and nervously cleared his throat.

“You know what happened to Nereus? It was impossible to predict,” he smiled uneasily, sweat beading on his upper lip.

“Impossible?” Gareth arched a quizzical eyebrow at him, “Really?”

Cam coughed again and swallowed, “Well, maybe not impossible. It was part of the remit of its design though,”

The walk back from school, whilst leisurely had involved a couple of hills. The drive was long and the sun was still warm. Cam was acutely aware of the heavy film of sweat that now had his t-shirt to cling uncomfortably his back.

“The destruction of a twenty-million dollar exploration vehicle was in the remit of its design?” Gareth asked, “Hmmm.”

“Well, it was implied. Surely?” Cam protested.

They rounded the side of the house and Cam opened the gate to the rear of the house,

“Implied?” Gareth’s quizzical eyebrow had returned. Cam stared at it uncomfortably

“Aye, implied. It was an exploration craft," he said defiantly, “and in fact it was charted at a depth deeper than any craft had ever been before, over 6 miles, in fact.”

Gareth nodded, “6.2 I believe," he said, still smiling.

Martha, having inevitably devoured the entire chocolate bar in minutes was now heading, perhaps somewhat ill-advisedly, towards the trampoline. Cam winced inwardly but ignored his instinct and instead ushered Gareth towards the rear patio. It had been recently repointed and still had the distinctive colour and neatness of a newly finished project. Just off centre toward the shade of an overhanging apple tree, laden with ripening fruit, there stood a large glass topped table surrounded by six rattan chairs. Cam gestured towards one of the chairs and then picked one for himself, but instead of sitting down he stood behind it, gripping the back firmly with both hands. His expression was worried but defiant.

“There you go then,” he said, ”it was a pioneering craft. There is no exploration without casualties Mr. Williams, regardless of their dollar value.”

“I absolutely agree and please call me Gareth,” he smiled again.

Gareth’s persistent calm and friendliness was beginning to have an unsettling effect on Cam. His palms were sweating and he was beginning to feel increasingly nauseous. Cam didn't like confrontation particularly, but he was very much of the opinion that if someone was going to say something then they should just go ahead and say it. Even If it meant that he was going to get a lecture or even fired he would rather Gareth just got on with it and then buggered off and left him alone to lick his wounds.

“Yess sorry, Gareth," Cam composed himself a little, "anyway, Nereus had already charted the Marianas Trench in more detail than had ever been seen before. The samples it took have advanced some fields in Marine Biology by years, if not decades.”

“I know,” Gareth looked out over the large lawn and trees, “Lovely garden Cam, by the way, really first rate,”

“I'm sorry?" Cam said, reflexly looking around at the garden, "Oh thank-you, it was more or less like this when we moved in though.”

Gareth nodded, "Still, it really is a lovely space,"

“Thank you," Cam said, "anyway, erm… like I say…”

Gareth interrupted him, “It’s okay Cam. I know the details of what happened. There’s no need for you to go over them again for my benefit.”

“I just wanted you know that what happened was inevitable. We were really pushing the limits.”

“I know.” Gareth’s said calmly, his smile widening. The conversation seemed to be amusing him greatly, a fact that was beginning to irritate Cam.

“With respect then, Gareth. Why single me out for the blame?”

“I’m not. Nothing could be further from my mind,”

“Then why would you mention it?”

Gareth laughed, “Just as an introduction really, nothing more.”

“Oh” Cam’s face fell slightly, “you could have mentioned that earlier?”

Gareth nodded, “True, but then I would have missed an opportunity to see how you reacted under scrutiny.”

All that Cam could manage in response was weak smile.

Gareth shrugged, “You stood your ground though, and you didn't try to blame anyone else,” he smiled “I like that.”

Cam became aware that he had been gripping the back of the chair a little too tightly, his knuckles were white with the strain and the muscles in his arms were taught with effort. He released his grip and instinctively flexed his fingers. His entire body visibly relaxed and the defensive aggression that had been slowly building up within him, drained away. He smiled nervously at Gareth and moved to sit down in the chair in front of him.

Gareth Williams was one of the most influential and wealthy men in Europe, perhaps the world. He had over the years invested hundreds of millions of dollars into oil and gas exploration and development. He was powerful and influential, yet enjoyed a reputation as a great philanthropist. He was intelligent, intuitive and supremely confident in his own abilities. He had an incredible talent for spotting investment opportunities seemingly before they even existed and, more importantly, the skill and financial clout to act on them. He was ruthlessly quick to exploit a situation to its maximum potential and had built up his vast fortune quickly and with brutal efficiency. As a result there existed an almost mythical aura around the man. His private life remained resolutely private and the man himself was something of an enigma. Those that met him spoke of his infectious charisma and enthusiasm but also of a fearsome temper and lack of patience with incompetence. Consequently, he had a reputation as someone that you most certainly did not want to tangle with if you had any alternative.

Cam's initial non-recognition of such an important player within his field of expertise was the engineering equivalent of most people not recognising Tom Cruise. The one mitigating factor being that, in the normal course of things, Tom Cruise was unlikely to visit your home with no warning. Yet here he was, Gareth Williams sitting happily in Cam's back garden, his face turned towards the warm afternoon sun, Smiling. Cam considered the situation and decided that there was only one way of proceeding. He decided to keep quiet and wait until Mr. Williams decided to divulge his reasons for visiting his own tiny little bit of Yorkshire.

"So why are you here?" He blurted out.

He closed his eyes and silently cursed his big mouth, "Sorry that was rude. What I meant to say was…" he searched wildly for a better way to phrase the question, and tried again.

"So..." he said, thoughtfully, "no, sorry. I can't," he shrugged a little helplessly.

"Fair enough," Gareth said, "straight to the point, I like that as well," he laughed as he retrieved his sunglasses from his jacket and put them back on.

"I'm sorry Gareth, but I'm a little confused if I'm honest,"

"I would imagine you are," Gareth said.

"So, are you going to enlighten me then?" Cam asked.

"Tell you what," Gareth said, "why don't you go and make us both that drink you offered and then I'll explain."

He looked at his watch and then back up at the cloudless blue sky

“In fact," he continued, “I rather think that I've had a change of heart. Perhaps, I will have a gin with the tonic after all. I can always get a cab if I need to later on. Would it be okay if I pull onto your drive? I don't want to upset your neighbours.”

Cam blinked, still trying, unsuccessfully, to process what was happening. He shrugged

“Yes of course," he said with a wave of his hand, “please, be my guest. Ice and slice?”

Gareth nodded, “Yes please, I won’t be a minute," he went to move towards the gate.

“No problem, would you like something to eat as well?” Cam offered.

“Not just now, thank you. Perhaps later though? I must confess I’m slightly intrigued about 'Daddy’s pasta sauce' Sounds good!”

“The best you’ll ever taste,” Cam said with a real note of pride in his voice.

Gareth owned a chain of award winning Italian restaurants. Cam immediately remembered this and cringed inwardly. He looked at Gareth but he seemingly hadn't noticed his faux pas and said nothing. Instead, he simply turned and headed back towards his car, whistling as he went. Cam waited until he had passed through the gate and then breathed, like a man that had been holding his breath for too long. He listened to Gareth crunch his way back along the drive but remained seated. As Gareth left the garden, Martha ran over to Cam from the trampoline. She was smiling happily, sweaty, her face still smeared with chocolate.

“Who’s that man daddy?” she asked.

Cam continued to stare at the gate as though expecting it to do something extraordinary,

“Hmm?” he said distractedly.

“That man,” she said, “who is he Daddy?”

He shook his head to clear his thoughts and then refocussed and looked down at his little girl. Her eyes were wide with curiosity and expectation,

“Um…” he said thoughtfully, “he’s my boss I suppose.”

“Are you in trouble Daddy?” Martha’s face crumpled in genuine concern.

Cam smiled reassuringly at her, “No sweetheart. I’m not in trouble. Now go and play and I’ll bring you out a drink out in a minute,” he nodded back towards the trampoline.

This seemed to satisfy her, because she didn't ask any further questions; instead she leaned forwards and kissed him on his cheek, before trotting happily off back towards the trampoline.

Cam heard Gareth’s car pull onto the drive, he opened and closed the car door and then stepped back through the gate, still whistling.

At least I don’t think I’m in trouble Cam thought to himself. Although, If he was absolutely honest, he didn’t really know what he was in.

CHAPTER EIGHT

Cam returned with drinks for himself, Gareth and Martha. The afternoon had worn on but the summer sun retained its warmth. Cam sat down in his chair and slid Gareth's drink across the table towards him. He called Martha and she dutifully ran over, picked up her newly refreshed water bottle and then headed back into the garden, skipping as she went.

The two men sat opposite each other, sipping their drinks in silence. The afternoon shadows continued to lengthen. Cam lifted his drink and held his glass up to the sun; he moved it around, creating a prism of light upon the table top and then looked over at Gareth, who was watching him intently. He blushed, slightly and cleared his throat. Gareth leaned forward expectantly, but Cam had second thoughts and relaxed back into his chair.

Gareth took a bigger sip of his drink and rolled the ice cubes around within the glass, he looked up at Cam.

"Tell me, Cam," he began, "what do you know about the Livingstone Project?"

Cam shrugged, "The Livingston project?" he repeated, "Nothing really. Why?"

"Really? Nothing?" Gareth seemed both surprised and a little hurt by this.

"Do you mean that X-factor thing in the tabloids?" he asked.

"That X-factor thing?" Gareth said, clearly appalled.

"Aye," he said, "you know that stupid competition to find astronauts for some bizarre reason," he laughed, "ridiculous really. I mean what kind of eejit tries to find astronauts in the red-tops?"

Cam looked at Gareth with a smile on his face. Gareth, however, was most certainly not smiling and his face carried a mixture of irritation and embarrassment.

"Indeed," was all that Gareth said.

"Sorry," Cam said suddenly, "I didn't mean any offence."

"No," Gareth said, finally, "it's fine. I'll concede that we have had a few issues around our... public relations,"

Cam stared at Gareth, who continued to look a little crestfallen, it was fleeting though and he quickly reestablished his calm veneer. He had wanted to excite Cam with the dropping of the projects name, and was a little depressed when it hadn't had the desired effect. He grimaced at the thought of the wasted time and money and then regretted, not for the first time, that he had not been there personally to fire that useless bunch of parasitic bastards.

Cam sipped at his drink wearily; he was feeling slightly uncomfortable in the prolonged silence that had suddenly descended. Gareth stared into space though, clearly lost in his thoughts.

Finally Gareth shook himself from his reverie. He smiled at Cam and once again his face was an illustration of relaxation.

"That's a real shame Cam. A real shame."

"Really?"

"Oh yes," he said, "very much so in fact. You see project Livingstone is something that I believe you would, no in fact, you *should* be very interested in."

"Okay," Cam said slowly, his curiosity temporarily piqued.

“So where to begin?” Gareth said dreamily and then looked off into the distance while he considered his next sentence.

“What did you want to be when you were a child Cam?”

Cam stared blankly at Gareth.

“Eh?” he said,

“When you were a little boy what did you want to be when you grew up? A train driver? Pilot? Doctor?”

“Um, sorry Gareth,” he said a little embarrassed “but I’m not entirely sure where you’re going with this.”

“I always wanted to be an astronaut," Gareth said wistfully, “ever since I was a kid and watched the first space shuttle take off. I remember I was at primary school and we were all ushered into the school hall. There was a big old television on a trolley that the whole school huddled around. When the shuttle took off, the noise made the tele and the trolley vibrate. Some of the other kids covered their ears, but not me. I was transfixed.” He sighed happily and shook his head.

He turned back to Cam who was once again watching him a little awkwardly.

“Or an explorer perhaps?” he said.

The cogs in Cam’s brain began to belatedly turn.

“Exploration? Ah, hence project Livingstone I presume?”

“Very good, yes,” Gareth smiled.

“Astronauts though? Is that right? Is this really about going into space?” Cam asked, ” I’m guessing there's a decent budget attached then?”

Gareth nodded. “I don’t have the exact figures with me, of course,” he drifted into thought before continuing, “but I think the final cost will be somewhere in the region of seventy-six, perhaps seventy-seven or seventy-eight," he paused again as he mentally ran over the arithmetic, "definitely, no more than eighty though. Probably," he looked at Cam and laughed then added, "that's in Dollars of course."

"Seventy-six Million?" Cam blew his cheeks out and nodded, "That is a decent amount isn't it is?" Cam laughed, "Not small at all," he shook his head.

"No," Gareth said,

"So where do I come in?" Cam asked

He was genuinely intrigued now, and more than a little excited. The last project of this size that Cam worked on had been the initially successful yet ultimately ill-fated Nereus explorer, and that had gone into development over four years ago.

"Sorry Cam you misunderstand I meant "no" to your question,"

"What question?"

"Your question about funding. You see it's not seventy-six Million,"

"I'm sorry?" This took a couple of seconds to sink in. Cam blinked, confused.

Then the penny dropped.

"Surely not?" he said, leaning forward in his chair, "You can't be serious?" he was now so close that to Gareth that he could smell his cologne.

Gareth smiled, "I can assure you Cam that I am serious. I am always serious about money, always."

"Billion!"

Gareth nodded.

“Seventy-six Billion Dollars?”

“Give or take,” he said calmly. He noticed the shock that registered on Cam’s face, “If you prefer, it’s only fifty-nine Billion in Sterling though?” he said and his smile grew and turned into a laugh.

Cam slumped heavily back into his chair and drank deeply from his glass, his expression curiously blank and disorientated.

“Seventy-six?” he repeated quietly.

“Yes.”

“Billion?”

“Yes.”

“Dollars?”

He nodded again, “Yes. Seventy-six Billion Dollars,” he let the figure hang for a moment in the summer air, “and I’d like you to come on board. If it’s something you’d be interested in that is?” Gareth settled back into his chair, still smiling and sipped at his drink. He maintained direct eye contact with Cam throughout.

“Fuck!” Cam breathed.

Gareth laughed.

Cam was unsettled. He had heard of Project Livingstone but had never paid any attention to it; It was a folly as far as he was concerned, a giant publicity stunt that had no relevance to the real world within which he operated. This kind of backing though was more than a folly; it was a generation defining folly.

"Cam?" Gareth interrupted Cam's train of thought; this mildly irritated him but he already knew better than to let Gareth know that. Cam had been silent for too long apparently and actually now that he looked at Gareth he was looking genuinely concerned.
"Are you okay? You haven't said anything for almost ten minutes, apart from 'Fuck' that is."

Cam blushed, "Sorry. It's a lot to take in, if I'm honest."

"I know, it must be. How can I help?" he said, "Do you have any questions?"

Cam laughed out loud at this and Gareth at least had the decency to look a little abashed.

"Okay, that was a stupid question. What I meant to say was: What would you like to know first?"

Cam was still reeling. He had so many questions that he barely knew how to categorise them in his head, never mind which one to ask first. So he asked the one that was troubling him the most,

"Why have I not heard of this? I mean beyond the realms of fantasy football trivia."

Gareth said nothing.

"I should know about this. Everyone should know about this. This is huge!"

Gareth remained silent, he sipped at his drink.

"Why have you kept this quiet? Why pitch it as a talent contest?"

Cam was prepared for all kinds of explanations involving covert recruitment, secret meetings and clandestine funding streams. He was not prepared for Gareth's actual explanation though. He was also surprised to see Gareth visibly blush.

"We haven't tried to keep this quiet. It was never supposed to be a talent contest," he sighed, "but we, that is rather I, well I made an error, an error that I am now determinedly trying to rectify."

Cam nodded but didn't interrupt.

"In fact I have already made amends in some areas, but I am rather hoping that I can continue to do so today," he sipped his drink again and inclined the glass towards Cam, "with your recruitment to the project in fact."

"Me?"

"Absolutely, I want you as my chief engineer."

Cam laughed again, he looked at Gareth's expression and realised that he wasn't in fact joking.

Cam had assumed that project Livingstone was only a media distraction, a vanity project for some mad American billionaire who had more money than sense.

He looked at Gareth who was still smiling benignly. His presence alone meant that he had not only clearly underestimated the validity of the project's credentials but he had also allowed his professional snobbery to seriously compromise his judgement.

"Fuck," he said again, "I think perhaps I could perhaps do with another drink."

Cam stared blankly at Gareth for a few seconds.

"Why me?" he asked, "I don't understand."

“Are you looking for an ego boost here Cam? You know why you. You have a… reputation.”

“Do I?”

“Yes, and I think that you know that you do,” Cam blushed and tried to brush off the compliment.

“Aye, well, maybe…”

Gareth fixed Cam with his deep brown, almost black eyes and his expression noticeably darkened, suddenly serious,

“I’m not a great fan of false modesty Cam,” he said flatly, “it is often counterproductive and, in my opinion, is worse than arrogance in many ways."

Cam looked suddenly ashamed. He felt a little confused and strangely humiliated, like a school boy caught smoking by a favourite teacher.

"So I would be most grateful if you would please try to avoid it in the future, okay?”

Cam nodded, sheepishly but said nothing.

Gareth immediately relaxed and returned to his previous happy demeanour. The shadow of threat vanished from his face as quickly as it had arrived. Its memory however, played on Cam's mind like an ugly stain.

“My hesitation was personal not professional,” he continued, “you certainly have the necessary expertise and knowledge, but I wasn’t sure about how well you’d operate under pressure,” he took another drink from his glass but maintained eye contact throughout, “however your work on the Nereus project, coupled with what you’ve done within the Arctic exploration fields with Bobby has been very impressive.”

"Bobby?" Cam said, confused

"Yes, Bobby," Gareth repeated, "you do know Bobby Prentice, don't you?"

Sir Robert Prentice was the head of exploration at BP. Cam was reasonably certain though that nobody else had ever called him "Bobby" not even his loveable, white haired, old mother. Cam had briefly met him during the Arctic consultation period and throughout their short time together the urge to call him Bobby had never been a particularly strong one.

Cam had worked for him though, not with him. He had been subordinate in every measurable way. They definitely were not peers, not by any stretch of the imagination.

A rather unpleasant thought suddenly occurred to Cam. It crept up from the depths of his paranoia and started to grumble restlessly at the edges of his conscious mind. After that, It only took a few moments for this paranoid thought to become a fully realised and substantial fear. Cam was abruptly and chillingly aware that Gareth may have got the wrong person. That he had somehow, mistakenly thought that Cam had considerably more influence than he actually had on these projects.

He considered this thought for a moment and then decided to try and dismiss it. After all, it was highly unlikely that the great and powerful Mr. Williams would travel all the way to Sheffield to recruit someone, without first doing his homework. It was possible, but nevertheless, improbable.

Cam was good at his job; he knew that without a trace of conceit. He had, after all, been told so many times in the past and the growing demand for his services as a consultant was evidence of his burgeoning reputation. However, this proposal represented a sizeable step up from his usual projects. The financial level alone was frankly so far beyond his comfort zone that he baulked merely at the thought of it. So much so, that the more he thought about it, the more convinced he became that there had in fact been some sort of terrible, administrative mix-up.

“I’ve got the right man Cam,” Gareth said interrupting his train of thought.

Cam blinked. That was weird, he thought to himself. Gareth had seemingly read his mind almost as he was forming the thoughts. Cam was confused and apparently it was written all over his face, a fact which he felt oddly betrayed by.

“Remind me never to play poker with you,” Cam said, only half-joking.

“I’m good at reading people Cam,” Gareth shrugged, “I have to be.”

“There'd be something wrong with you if you didn’t wonder if I had the right man. I may prefer arrogance to false modesty Cam, but I’m not a fan of either really. After all how arrogant would you have to be not to have any doubts?”

It was a reasonable point, Cam had to admit.

Martha came running over to the table from the bottom of the garden. Cam had almost completely forgotten about her if he was honest; he felt a pang of parental guilt as she bounded up and jumped onto his lap giving him a sweaty kiss on the cheek as she landed.

“I’m hungry daddy” she said. Cam looked at his watch and noticed that it was approaching six o’clock. Karen would be home any minute and he hadn't done anything further about dinner since the earlier promise of pasta.

"Sorry to be a wee bit slow here. But what is this all about Gareth? I mean really?"

Cam scratched his head absent mindedly.

"I mean I've seen some of the hype, of course, but I'm unsure about the truth and I don't know any details. What are you proposing exactly? What is it that you are looking to explore?"

"Life!" Gareth said dramatically.

"I'm sorry?" Cam said, as he struggled to stifle a snigger.

"Life Cam. I want to explore life."

Cam rolled his eyes and shook his head, "Oh right, life. Fair enough then,"

"Don't be like that Cam,"

"Sorry," he said, "but it's all a wee bit vague isn't it?"

"Oh it's not just exploring life," Gareth said, becoming more animated, "it's about the very future of humanity!"

"I'm not sure I'm following you here, if I'm being honest," Cam said, wearily.

This was all becoming increasingly unsettling. For the first time since he had arrived, Cam was worried that Gareth was perhaps not fully attached to reality.

Perhaps sensing Cam's uncertainty, Gareth looked at him, his eyes twinkling again.

"I do hope you will follow me though Cam," he said, wistfully, "that is why I'm here after all!"

“Follow you where?” Cam had an uneasy feeling that he already knew the answer.

“To Mars!” he said with an elaborate sweep of his arms, “To Mars.”

Cam paused for a moment, waiting for the punchline, but it didn't arrive.

“Oh okay then,” he said, eventually, “why not? To Mars eh?”

He nodded his head and looked at Gareth, expecting him to break into laughter at any moment. Only he wasn’t laughing. In fact Cam couldn't recall a time when he'd seen anyone look more deadly serious.

CHAPTER NINE

Cam was still looking at Gareth, waiting for his face to crack into a smile. After a few minutes but when nothing happened he instead considered what he had just heard. He was trying to process it all when Gareth interrupted his train of thought.
"Tell me about the paper that you wrote last year Cam," he asked conversationally.
"Which one?" Cam replied a little suspiciously.
"The one about anti matter propulsion."
Cam laughed, "That wasn't my paper, I only wrote a rebuttal really," he looked at Gareth, carefully gaging his expression, "I'm not a rocket engineer Gareth, I was only offering an opinion really. The fundamental problems of anti-matter propulsion remain the same I'm afraid. I can't offer you a magic wand," he said with a wave of his hand.
"Ah but you did offer a solution," Gareth leaned forward expectantly.
Cam shrugged, "I just took a different perspective."
Gareth sat back in his chair, a satisfied grin spread across his face.
Cam was becoming increasingly confused, and a little irritated by Gareth's increasingly enigmatic behaviour.
"I'm not sure what you're implying," he said, suspiciously, " but the hypothesis of the paper was flawed; They were addressing the wrong problem. It's not so much the creation of anti-matter as it is the ability to trap and store it before annihilation. I suggested that the means of creation should also be the means of trapping, that's all."
"That's not all though is it?" Gareth said, with a grin.
Cam shrugged, "I submitted a theoretical target design, but I have no evidence that it would actually work," he sighed, "the

truth is Gareth, I was only playing devil's advocate really. It kept me amused for an hour or so one afternoon and although I hate to admit it, those aerospace guys can be pretty irritating at times. Sometimes it's fun to poke the bear," he said with a mischievous smile.

Gareth nodded, "It does work though," he said simply.

"What does?" Cam said, "The target trap? It might, but like I said, it's purely hypothetical."

"Not anymore," Gareth said with a shrug, "I built one."

Cameron stared at him, "I'm sorry. What did you say?"

"I built one."

"You built one?" Cam shook his head incredulously, "What do you mean? 'I built one' this isn't a fucking Air-fix model you know."

Gareth arched an eyebrow, but said nothing.

"Sorry," Cam said, "but that's quite some claim."

"I know," Gareth said, still smiling, "but it's the truth."

"How?" Cam said excitedly, "Where? When?"

"Relax," Gareth said and held his hands up to placate him. "It was only in a computer. We modelled it and ran some simulations, then ran them again and then we ran them again and again and again," he paused for effect, "and it works!"

Cam blew his cheeks out and shook his head, "What sort of yield did you get? Was I close with my prediction?"

Gareth nodded, "You were a little optimistic, but close, very close in fact."

"How much did you trap?" Cam asked, "theoretically of course,"

"A thousandth of a gram," Gareth said with a smile

"Over how long?"

"Six months"

Cam whistled, "Wow," he said with a happy sigh.

"Yep."
“Really?" Cam asked, "That's like um...a million times more than the whole of CERN has ever produced in a year. When do you start to build a real one then?"
"I don't," Gareth said, "at least not yet."
Cam face fell in disappointment, "but..." he said quietly
"We will still pursue it Cam, but it's not viable, at least not at the moment. Even at those figures it would still take hundreds of years to produce enough to power a whole spacecraft," he smiled again, "but who knows with you on board..." Gareth let that thought settle for a moment before continuing, "The simple, rather unimpressive, facts are that even with all of the progress in Ion propulsion and with what you've done with the prospect of anti-matter, a good old fashioned chemical explosion is still the best way to get some oomph into your rocket!" he slapped the table so hard that Cam jumped slightly.
Cam considered this for a few seconds and the excitement drained slowly from his face, "Where does that leave me?" he asked.
"I'm sorry?" Gareth replied, "I'm not sure I understand."
"Well, like I said before, I'm not really a rocket scientist. There are many better qualified people for your project than me, and if money is no object?"
"Which it isn't," Gareth said quickly,
"Aye well, if that's the case then I can’t help but think that you could find a better man for the job at NASA, or the European space agency," Cam shrugged, "I don't mean to seem obtuse but I don't get where I fit in to a space voyage."
Gareth nodded, “Okay," he said slowly, "you are not an aerospace engineer that is true and yet you took a premise that had been hypothesised by an aerospace engineer and rewrote it. In what? A couple of hours?"

Cam blushed, “It was an hour actually," he said timidly.
"An hour!" Gareth roared with laughter, "Don't you see Cam it's not your experience that I want on board, particularly,"
"But..." Cam protested weakly.
Gareth ignored him, "It's your potential. I confess that it may have been your wonderfully insightful views on anti-matter that partly brought you to my attention. However, that's not why I'm here...at least not directly. I'm here for you Cam."
He reached over and tapped Cam's forehead with the tip of his forefinger. Cam flinched and pulled his head away, "I want your big, mad, beautiful brain," he said and his eyes widened hungrily.
Cam instinctively pulled further away from Gareth, he put his hands over his temples protectively as though expecting a direct physical assault.
Gareth laughed, "Don't worry, I don't want it in isolation."
Cam let go of his head and smiled nervously.
"I like the way you think Cam. You have an interesting...perspective."
Cam opened his mouth but said nothing and instead merely shrugged.
"You saw a problem and when you couldn't see a viable solution, you looked at it again but this time you changed the parameters. That is a terribly rare, and may I say, valuable asset."
Cam allowed himself a few seconds to begin to process this new information. It was a lot to take in.
"The scale of what we are trying to achieve is beyond anything that mankind has attempted in the past,“ Gareth continued, "and part of that will be to challenge preconceptions of what is, and what is not possible."
Cam nodded slowly, "I don't know what to say."

"You don't have to say anything. I just want you to think about it, that's all."
Cam looked at Gareth, he opened his mouth to reply but was suddenly distracted by a noise from inside the house. He turned his head just in time to see his wife, Karen, walking through the double doors at the rear of the house and out onto the top level of the patio. She looked out over the garden before her gaze settled upon the two seated men.

"Hello my lovely," she said as she walked down the patio steps, her shoes clicking as she went.

She had already abandoned her car keys, briefcase and jacket somewhere in the house, but she had kept hold of her sunglasses which were perched on top of her hair. Her gait was a little laboured, but there was no other evidence of any fatigue. A full day in a hot, busy hospital without any air-conditioning will do terrible things to a body but Karen looked remarkably pristine. Her dark blonde hair was cut into short bob and she wore minimal makeup. She sported a light summer dress and expensive, kitten-heeled shoes.

"Hello!" Cam called, from his chair and moved to stand up.

Karen looked at the table and the drinks that sat upon it.

"Hard day?" she asked.

Cam looked at the glasses and grinned, sheepishly.

He was saved from any attempt to reply by the sudden arrival of his daughter.

"Mummy!" Martha came trotting up the garden and immediately ran over to her mother, wrapping herself around her legs. Karen stooped down and kissed the top of her head.

“Hello my darling. How are you? How was your day at school?”

Martha shrugged, “Fine,” she said, thereby answering both questions in one go, ”Daddy’s friend gave me some chocolate and I ate the whole bar!”

“Really! Gosh, you are a lucky girl? I hope you still ate all of your dinner though?” she said, sternly.

“I haven’t had any dinner yet Mummy,” Martha said.

“Oh really?” Karen glanced at Cam with a little reproach, though her face carried a faint smile.

Cam had been watching this exchange between mother and daughter in a slight trance. The sudden harshness of Karen's tone had bolted him into life though, and he quickly headed up the steps to great her properly.

“Hello sweetheart,” he said putting his arm around her waist and kissing her gently on her salty cheek, “I was just away to sort it out now.”

Gareth stood up and offered his hand, Karen wheeled away from Cam and became the first member of the Harrison family to accept the offer. She shook it briefly and then let it drop again.

“Dr Harrison? Hello lovely to meet you,“ Gareth said and Karen smiled politely at him.

"This is Gareth," Cam said weakly

Karen regarded Cam for a second before returning her attention to Gareth.

“Hello Gareth, it’s a pleasure to meet you."

"Gareth Williams," Cam added.

Karens eyebrows raised, "Oh really?" she said, sounding genuinely surprised, "Not *The Gareth Williams?"*

Gareth bowed his head, "I'm flattered that you've heard of me," he said,

"Oh come now," she said smiling, "only an idiot wouldn't recognised that name."

She looked over at Cam who was now blushing a very deep red,

"Are you all right my darling?" she asked,

Cam nodded and coughed, to clear his throat, "Yes," he said quietly, "yes, I'm fine thanks."

Gareth laughed, "I'm afraid I caught your husband on the hop earlier," he said,

Cam looked from one to the other and decided that it would be best if just kept quiet.

"I'm sorry to have kept your husband somewhat occupied, Doctor Harrison." Gareth said, with a slight bow of his head,

"Please call me Karen," she said

Cam watched with a degree of awe as his wife, once gain, took in a new situation without any apparent discomfort. Nothing ever seemed to throw her off her game, no matter how unexpected.

"Now then," she said, suddenly turning her attention back to Martha, "I think its time that we get you some dinner isn't it young lady?"

Gareth stood, "I'm so sorry," he said, "once again I apologise, it is because I've kept your husband talking that poor Martha here has been deprived of her dinner."

"I'm sorry," Cam said, "I just lost track of the time."

Karen shook her head, "It doesn't matter, it'll take five minutes to cook up some pasta."

Cam went to move off into the house, but as he went Gareth placed a hand onto his arm,

"This is my fault," Gareth said, "and I really don't want to be the cause of any family disharmony,"

"It's no bother," Cam said, "it'll take 5 minutes, like Karen said."

"I know, but how about I take you all out for dinner?" Gareth said.

He looked over to Martha for approval, who was smiling broadly.

"And it seems only fitting that the venue be your choice young lady. If that's okay with mummy and daddy of course?" he looked towards Karen for approval.

"What's a venue daddy?" Martha asked, suddenly serious.

Cam laughed, "Gareth is very kindly asking if we want to go out for dinner with him, and you get to choose where"

"Can we daddy?" Martha said, her smile immediately back in place.

Cam looked over to Karen who shrugged and then nodded in agreement.

"Well, it's not a school night I suppose," Cam said thoughtfully, whilst he looked at his watch, "we might struggle to get in anywhere though on such short notice."

“Leave that to me,” Gareth said, “so where’s it to be then young lady?”

“Cricket!” she shouted

Gareth looked blankly over at Cam for some guidance.

"Cricket?" he repeated.

“The Cricket Inn,” Cam said, “it's a pub in the village. It has a cricket field out the back..." he tailed off.

"That would make sense," Gareth said with a laugh.

"They do excellent beer and burgers though," he said, enthusiastically, "If you like that sort of thing?"

"Sounds perfect!" Gareth clapped his hands together.

"Aye, it's lovely but It will be booked up though,” Cam said with a shrug.

Gareth smiled, “Like I said let me worry about that. Now how far is it? Can we walk?”

“We can…” Cam said, “but it is a fair distance with the wee one. Probably a mile or so?” He looked at Karen who nodded in agreement.

“Not to worry, we’ll take my car.” Gareth eyed his gin suspiciously as If daring it to argue. He had actually only had about half of it, and Cam hadn’t made it particularly strong in the first place.

“On second thoughts..." he said, “please excuse me for a moment?”

"Aye, of course," Cam said.

Gareth pulled his phone from his jacket pocket and disappeared through the gate and back onto the drive.

After a few minutes he reappeared, "Is Seven-thirty too late for Martha?"

Cam shrugged, "No, no she'll be fine," he said.

Gareth held up his finger to stop Cam from continuing, and he fell silent immediately.

"Do you have a car seat I can borrow by any chance?" Gareth asked.

"A car seat? Aye, of course," replied Cam.

Gareth ducked back round the corner for a few more minutes before returning triumphantly.

"All sorted," he said, "the driver will pick us up at 6:50."

He looked at his watch again and then at the half-finished drinks.

"I'd say we probably had time for another gin," he said, "and perhaps we can bring Karen up to speed with a bit of an explanation."

"Explanation of what?" Karen asked, not unreasonably.

Gareth's eyes light up with excitement. Cam looked nervously from one to the other.

"I want your husband to come with me to Mars, Karen," he said, simply, "Or at the very least, I'd like him to help me get there."

"I see," she said picking up Cam's half-drunk gin, and taking a large swallow, "Cam could you make another round of these please?" she smiled.

Cam looked at her, his face lined with concern.

"Aye, no problem," he said, and moved towards the glasses.

“And make it a proper one this time eh? No more of your weedy nonsense!” Karen said.

She handed the glass to Cam and also retrieved Gareth’s from the table top.

“Are you finished with this?” she asked and then handed the half-finished drink to her husband without waiting for a reply.

Gareth opened his mouth to object but Karen cut across him before he had chance to speak.

“As you’re a guest in my house, I shan't have you drinking a barely noticeable gin,” she said matter-of-factly.

Gareth laughed and nodded, "That sounds reasonable," he said.

Cam, once again was blushing, so he took the glasses and scurried away into the house without saying a word.

Karen leaned over closer to Gareth, “You know for a Scotsman, he really doesn't drink enough,” she laughed, “I’ve only just got him drinking gin in the last six months or so,"

"Is he more of a whisky man?" Gareth asked.

Karen laughed, "Oh god no!" she said, a little too loudly, "He cant stand whisky. He never drank any spirits, just beer and an occasional glass of wine with dinner."

"But not anymore?"

"No, I've got him onto Gin. The only downside is that he really is terrible at mixing drinks. He hasn't got a clue!” she continued. “They're either barely alcoholic or so strong you can't stand after half a glass!"

Gareth laughed.

"But he'll learn," she said with a twinkle in her eye, "if it's the last thing he ever does!"

She relaxed back into the chair and slipped her sunglasses back down onto her nose to protect her eyes from the evening glare. She turned her face towards the warm sun and breathed deeply. After a few seconds she opened her eyes again and looked at Gareth, who was watching her intently.

"So Gareth," She said, pleasantly, "may I speak bluntly with you?"

Gareth nodded, "Of course," he said, "please do."

"Okay," she said, "perhaps then you could tell me why you think I'm going to let you rip my husband away from the bosom of his loving family, in order to help you with some damn fool pipe-dream?" She paused and smiled sweetly, "No offence intended by the way."

Gareth returned her smile and waved his hand dismissively, "None taken," he said. "I respect your candour."

"That's a good start," she said smiling, "because I believe that I have something of a reputation for it," she paused before prompting him to continue, "please go on Gareth."

He looked at her, but said nothing. He considered his words carefully before speaking again.

"First of all, It will be a very public project," he began thoughtfully.

"Yes, and?" Karen said, still smiling,

"It will change the field of robotics and engineering forever," he added, "it will explore sources of potential fuel supplies that will keep humanity going for hundreds, perhaps even thousands of years."

“Yes, and?” she asked.

Gareth cleared his throat and swallowed, “There will also be considerable prestige attached to it. There will be a lot of very influential and important people involved in this,”

Cam returned with the drinks and placed the tray onto the table. Karen picked up one of the new glasses, sipped it and smiled approvingly at him,

“You’re getting better,” she said.

She returned her focus to Gareth, inclined her head slightly and although she didn't really have to ask again. She did anyway.

“And?”

Gareth took a large drink from his glass and smiled broadly at them both, “And,” he said confidently, ”I want to pay him ten million dollars to do it.”

CHAPTER TEN

Karen was not someone who was overly impressed by money. She had grown up in a wealthy, middle-class family and had never felt the struggle of poverty. However, the prospect of ten million dollars can certainly add a frisson of excitement to an evening meal. Cam was entirely less blasé than Karen, but he managed to remain resolutely calm and collected during dinner. Internally, though he was buzzing like an over-sugared child.

They were keen for more details but, at the same time, they were also wary of getting involved in such a major discussion with Martha present. Mindful of their reticence Gareth had said nothing about the details of his proposal, or indeed what Cam's potential role would be within it since they had left the house.

Instead he took the opportunity to engage with them all as a family. He and Karen, talked at length about the challenges that an under-funded health service faced against the backdrop of an ageing population and higher public expectancy. Gareth had offered his views on potential new revenue streams and discussed his role in the development of innovative new micro-surgical techniques including Nano technology.

Under normal circumstances Karen and Cam would have enjoyed the opportunity for some adult conversation, but the giant, golden elephant in the room would not allow them to relax and cast its over-large shadow over the whole evening. The beer was helping though and Cam was happily enjoying watching Karen and Gareth discuss the travails of the world, without feeling any compulsion to join in. It was rare that his usually reticent and slightly uptight wife found an intellectual equal to converse with and yet here she was, seemingly trying to impress a man that she had only met a few hours earlier. He smiled inwardly; it was a side of Karen that didn't show itself very often and it was good to see.

Gareth, meanwhile had launched into a major charm offensive so was determined not to ignore Martha. He had listened to her thoughts on music, films and unicorns without a hint of insincerity, and Martha had clearly taken a shine to him as well.

He had not only paid for dinner but had played happily with Martha in the playground while Karen and Cam sat watching contentedly from the sun terrace, enjoying both the last vestiges of the evening sun and the end of a rather fine bottle of Californian Zinfandel.

“You’re flirting with him,” Cam accused Karen, whilst still smiling broadly.

She blushed but didn't try to deny it, “So?” she said defensively.

“Nothing, Just saying that’s all." he sipped at his wine, "You really are terrible at flirting though,”

"Pardon?" Karen asked appalled.

Cam laughed, “I’d forgotten just how bad you are actually.”

“No, I’m not!”

“Yes, you are! You always have been. Even back at Uni. Remember?”

“Well, it worked on you didn't it?” Karen said, a little hurt by the accusation.

“No, it didn’t!” Cam laughed again.

“Well, It must have done we are still together aren't we?”

“Yes, but that had nothing to do with your terrible flirting. That was because you are so insanely gorgeous,”

“So I have a bad personality then?”

Cam laughed again, “Oh no, you're not catching me there. I love your personality. You just happen to be insanely gorgeous as well,” he paused, “as well as a terrible flirt!”

Karen reached over and punched him hard on the top of his arm. Cam continued to laugh

“I mean, who tries to impress someone by reeling off their research articles?”

“He was interested!” Karen said defensively, “He asked me about them anyway.”

“No, he didn’t! All he said was 'you must tell me more sometime',”

“Exactly!” she bristled with irritation, ”He asked me!”

“He was being polite!”

Karen punched him again, but started laughing at the same time.

“Bastard!” she said with a smile and sipped her wine.

Cam rubbed his arm and leant over to kiss his wife.

“Love you too,” he said and stood up to see what Martha and Gareth were up to.

They were sitting together and chatting as Cam approached. When she noticed him coming Martha stood up and ran to her father.

“Hello daddy,” she said happily, ”I’ve been telling Gareth all about the Summer Fair at school.”

Cam looked at Gareth, “Sorry about that,” he said, “she quite likes talking.”

“Don’t apologise, it sounds fascinating,” Gareth said, whilst winking at Martha.

“Well, I think its time to go home perhaps, Madame,” Cam said addressing his daughter.

”Aww,” Martha whined, "is Gareth coming to stay at our house?”

Cam looked at Gareth, “I don't know,” he said, ”perhaps. We have some things to talk about,” he paused, “after you've gone to bed though.”

“Why?” she asked, haughtily,

“Because, I say so," he said simply, “that’s why. Now come on. Let's get you home and into bed young lady.”

They arrived back to the house a little after 9 o’clock. When Martha had, somewhat reluctantly, gone to bed they cheerfully opened another bottle of wine and settled down to listen to Gareth’s proposal in a little more detail.

He suggested an initial four year contract for the development and testing of not only the explorative robotics needed for the planet’s surface, but the systems for the whole mission, including the spacecraft and living environments. This would, theoretically, lead to a further contract of a similar length with a similar dollar value. Cam would potentially be working with some incredible people, some actual geniuses. The timing of the project's launch could hardly have been scripted any better. Space exploration was beginning to inexorably move away from the jurisdiction of Governments and firmly towards private investors. It would seem that the American government's plans to dramatically cut NASA's funding had resulted in a rather disenfranchised workforce. A workforce that was suddenly ripe for the poaching by a wealthy conglomerate with both the desire and the finances to satisfy the collective ambition of brilliant minds. Meaning that Gareth's consortium could approach individuals, that only five years earlier would have been both unapproachable and unobtainable in equal measure.

The consortium, it transpired, was a truly global organisation. It involved many of the wealthiest individuals from across the planet as well as some choice international agencies who had collectively agreed to a level of disclosure and cooperation only previously dreamed of. It had been established over time, largely in secret and Gareth was naturally coy about revealing any of the group's identity, or indeed any intimate details of the project until Cam had officially signed up. He did, however, insinuate that the net worth of those involved dramatically exceeded the one trillion dollar mark, a figure often cited, albeit rather pessimistically and fancifully, in Mars mission budgetary forecasts.

Gareth spoke passionately and at length about not only his involvement but also the grand vision that he had for the whole scheme. This was to represent possibly the first truly globally cooperative project, showcasing humanities indomitable spirit and its insatiable desire to expand its horizons and explore the limitless boundaries of possibility.

By the time he had finished talking it was well after two in the morning and three further bottles of wine had been sacrificed to the cause. Karen and Cam had sat enthralled throughout being unintentionally, yet utterly seduced by Gareth's knowledgeable enthusiasm. By the end, Cam's head was buzzing from the combination of the fervour of Gareth's eloquence, the wine and a general overwhelming feeling of unreality. He went to bed and the alcohol ushered him into a long, deep but dreamless sleep. However when he awoke dry-mouthed and disorientated in the morning, his head was filled with the possibilities of space travel and fantasies of walking on the surface of another planet.

CHAPTER ELEVEN

The next morning, when Cam had finally dragged himself out of bed, Gareth had gone. As he trudged his way, unsteadily downstairs, he passed the lounge where Martha was watching something loud and altogether too perky for his delicate head. He bypassed the worst of it but he found it upsetting even from the relative safety of the other end of the house.

"Morning sweetheart!" he called, as he passed.

Transfixed by whatever she was damaging her mind with, she ignored him which irritated him slightly. It wasn't enough to act upon though and he decided that discretion was the better part of his headache.

He padded into the kitchen and, through clearly eyes, noticed a note and a business card propped up on the kitchen worktop:

Good morning to you both,

I'm sorry to slip away, but I have to be in Rome this afternoon (which means more wine sadly) to discuss the second best pasta sauce in the world!

Thank you for your hospitality and the use of your spare room. I had an excellent night's sleep. I know I've landed a lot on you so I'll give you some time to discuss it all.

I'm back in the UK next Friday so that, perhaps, might be an excellent chance for us to catch up?

Thank you again,

G

Karen was already up and about so Cam presumed that she had already read the note. She was, however, nowhere to be seen. Martha trotted into the kitchen dragging her slightly bedraggled pink rabbit with her. She had been given it for her first birthday and it had rarely ever left her side since. She certainly had never spent a whole night without her increasingly threadbare companion. Martha carefully and meticulously placed her rabbit on one of the stools of the breakfast bar facing the counter top, before turning her attention back to her father,

“I’m hungry daddy and so’s Rabbitty. What can I have to eat?”

“Good morning sweetheart” Cam said, pointedly.

“I said, I’m hungry daddy, not good morning,” she looked at Cam, her face the very epitome of wide-eyed innocence. Cam looked back at her and raised his eyebrows, waiting for her to redeem herself. She waited just long enough then threw her arms around his waist.

“Good morning daddy!” she said with a giggle.

“Good morning, my darling," Cam replied, and squeezed her tightly, "have you had any breakfast?"

“Ages ago!" She looked around her before whispering conspiratorially, “Mummy says you’re a lazy-bones,” before backing away and nodding knowingly at him.

“Does she now? Well, do you know what mummy is?”

“What is mummy?” Martha asked, her eyes wide,

“Yes, what is mummy?” Karen had walked into the kitchen from the office and was looking at Cam expectantly.

She carried a large mug of tea in her right hand, her left hand was resting on her hip and her head was inquisitively cocked to one side.

“Very lovely, mummy is very lovely,” Cam said, hurriedly, ”now off you go sweetheart, go and watch some more of your rubbish.”

He handed Martha a banana from the fruit bowl and tapped her, gently, on the bottom. She paused briefly to retrieve her rabbit then she skipped happily back into the television room.

“It’s not rubbish daddy," she called over her shoulder as she went, "you’re just old.”

Karen snorted a laugh, before quickly lifting her mug to her lips to cover herself. She walked over to where Cam was standing, kissed him on the cheek, and then slipped her hands around his shoulders.

“Good morning sleepy-head,” she said and ruffled his hair.

Cam kissed her back.

“Good morning my love, how are you this morning?”

"Not as bad as I feared. Not as good as I would have liked," she said.

"Lucky you!" Cam said, with a hint of bitterness.

She broke away from his embrace and headed over to the coffee machine that was bubbling gently to itself. She retrieved a mug from the dishwasher, wiped the rim on her jumper and placed it on the counter top next to her own.

“Coffee?” she asked but was already pouring it before he had had the chance to respond.

Cam took the mug, gratefully from her outstretched hand and lifted it up to his face; he inhaled the strong aroma, before blowing gently on it and taking a tentative taste.

“Did you see Gareth’s note?” he asked

“Yes,” Karen said, "he was gone before I got up even."

She blew on her tea before raising her eyes to look at her husband.

“Any thoughts about what you’re going to do?” she asked, casually.

Cam blew his cheeks out and shrugged, “I think…” he began, “I think that I’m going to drink this coffee, and then definitely have another one."

"And then?" she asked, pinning him with her stare.

Cam smiled, "And then, perhaps even a third!” he let his eyes drop from his wife's gaze.

“And then?” Karen pushed, gently.

“And then?" Cam sighed loudly, "Well, then I suppose we need to have a bit of a chat don’t we?”

“Yes, we do,” she said, she shook her head.

"What?" Cam asked.

“Ultimately, it’s your choice, sweetheart. It’s your career after all, and it's your offer.”

Cam rolled his eyes, but wished he hadn't because it hurt.

“Well, it’s not as simple as that now is it?” he said, a little testily.

"There's no need for that tone," Karen warned.

"Aye, sorry." Cam offered weekly.

He felt instantly uncomfortable, like a man wandering ignorantly into an intricately planned ambush. He was already at a disadvantage, his mind was still wrapped in an alcoholic haze. He needed some breathing space before he was going to be ready to get pulled into this discussion. He didn't know what he felt yet, never mind how to justify himself.

Karen was on his side, he knew that, but he wanted to get his own jumbled thoughts in order before facing her, no doubt, eloquent and impenetrable logic. Right now though, he could only operate from instinct, and in Cam's experience, instinct can often be a perilous place to operate from, especially his.

"Anyway, It can be as simple as that," Karen pressed.

She wasn't going to wait any longer, she had been waiting since whatever time she got-up this morning. She was an excellent debater and she employed all of her natural reasonableness, in any given discussion. This was incredibly frustrating to be on the other side of at times and Cam did not have the wit to fight against it this morning.

"No, it can't, and you know it can't," Cam said, with another deep sigh.

He began to pick absent mindedly at a slightly bedraggled bunch of grapes that was sitting in the fruit bowl beneath the bananas. They were perhaps a little past their best but he pulled a few from their stalks and popped them in his mouth anyway. The sweet juice cut through the bitterness of the coffee and he realised that he was in fact actually quite hungry. He decided to try and change the subject, at least temporarily.

"Breakfast?" he asked hopefully.

“It’s almost midday Cam," Karen said, prickly, "breakfast is something that happens in the morning.”

Cam reflexively looked at the kitchen clock and realised that it was in fact already eleven-thirty.

“It’s still morning. At least, technically speaking,” he pointed out, rather weakly.

“Breakfast is a memory now, but feel free to make yourself some toast.” Karen said gesturing to an open loaf of bread.

That seemed fair enough to Cam’s poorly functioning, badly dehydrated brain, so he busied himself with the preparation of said toast. As he did so, he was acutely aware of Karen’s continued stare.

Cam was trying to buy himself a little time but he knew what was coming and could increasingly see no way of avoiding it.

Although they rarely fell out, when they did so, they normally would try to steer clear of anything too contentious until Martha was either in bed or out of earshot. This wouldn’t wait another eight hours, though.

In all honesty, there was little point in arguing with Karen at the best of times. It wasn’t just that she was seemingly always right, but she also had an incredibly effective way of making Cam feel bad about having the temerity to disagree with her in the first place. Frequently, he would end up apologising or consoling her even if she had picked the fight with him initially.

Cam kept this opinion to himself, partly because he knew that it made Karen sound like either a passive aggressive nightmare or an insufferable know-it-all. Neither of which was true. Mainly though, it was because he liked the fact that his wife was a bad-ass that could bury almost anyone in an argument. It was reassuring, unless of course you were the one arguing with her. Then it was just demoralising.

However, Gareth's seemingly golden proposition had already caused friction in the Harrison household.

Initially, they both only saw the positives and were both equally excited about the idea. Cam saw a chance to be involved in a potentially historical project. An opportunity to attach his name to a career defining venture, arguably with the potential to be on a par with the Sputnik or Apollo missions.

Then there was the money, so much money. Cam and Karen weren't poor certainly, they lived very happily without any real financial worries. They had a large, comfortable house with an equally large, but equally comfortable mortgage. They holidayed abroad twice a year as a family and Karen and Cam enjoyed the benefits of living in city with excellent restaurants and theatres.

This wasn't, holidays to Italy and occasional Micheline starred meal money though. This was professional sportsman type of money. This was life changing.

"Martha?" Karen called through to the lounge.

There was no response. She walked towards the patio doors and turned towards Cam just as she reached the threshold. She intimated that he should follow her, which he dutifully did, crunching his toast and steeling himself in anticipation of what was potentially to come as he went. As he entered the sun-lounge Karen was ready to go, but Cam jumped in before she had the chance.

"I'd be away for a year. A whole year!" he said preemptively.

Karen looked a little taken aback.

"That's all that keeps repeating in my head. Round and round like a stuck record,"

“It’s only a year,” Karen said, gently.

"Martha is nine. It's not fair to do that to her,"

"It's only a year," Karen repeated.

Cam knew that Karen would set herself up as the Devil’s advocate but the reality still rankled with him.

"Only a year? Only a year?" Cam was incredulous, "Come on now Karen, a year away from you and Martha? It’s too much, I'd miss too much!"

"Gareth said that you'd be able to come home on weekends."

"Not every weekend though, he said about one in six."

"But it'll go so quickly, I know it would be hard to adjust but just think of all you'd achieve."

Cam shook his head sadly; he knew that a lot of what she was saying was probably true, but he also knew that she would miss him and that she would struggle terribly without him there; especially with the day to day ritual and mundanity, but the real truth of the matter was that Cam was scared. He was the main care giver to Martha, she relied on him so much and the truth was he liked it like that; he wore it as a badge of honour, especially with his friends who barely got to see their children. Cam liked being her constant, her rock. It made him proud to see what a lovely, intelligent and independent young lady she was growing up to be.

He was scared. Not about how much Martha would miss him if he were he to work away for a year, but rather about how little. Children are remarkably adaptable little creatures, and Cam didn’t want her to be fine without him. He wanted her to miss him, he needed her to need him. He knew that this was selfish and irrational but it was how he felt, and so he argued.

“Remember it's initially a year away, yes, but who knows thereafter? I will have a contract that means I could have to go anywhere in the world at a moment’s notice,”

“You already have one of those Cam." Karen said.

Once again, he had to concede that she was right; his current contract said exactly this as well, but he wasn’t going to let little things like facts slow him down, so he brushed it off.

“Yes, but it's theoretical at the moment.”

“But still possible.”

“A year though? It’s too long” Cam shook his head again, “it’s just too long.”

“We’ll cope, we’ll manage,”

“How?”

“Martha will be fine, we can afford a nanny,”

“A nanny! No! Just no!”

Karen threw her hands into the air, her frustration beginning to bubble over now.

“Oh come on, is this some kind of working class outrage bullshit?" Karen asked,

"Can you imagine what my dad would say if we got a nanny?"

"Since when did you give a toss about what your dad thought?"

"I can't..."

"Newsflash, Cam," Karen interrupted, "you’re not working class anymore, look at where you live! Look at your life!”

He looked around at the house and garden. She had a good point, they weren't exactly living in the tenements of Glasgow anymore, but in his cornered state that only added fuel to his argument.

“Exactly!" Cam spat. "We can afford a nanny now, can't we? But we've chosen not to go down that path; we decided that having a constant parental presence was more important, remember?”

“Martha isn't a baby anymore; she doesn't need constant supervision from one of us.”

“What about the school run? The after-school clubs? The holidays?” Cam was, a little unexpectedly, reaching his stride here, he had managed to get a foothold in the argument, and as unaccustomed as he was to this situation he was loathed to let it go without a struggle.

“I could take a sabbatical, do some research from home?” Karen offered.

“Really? You?”

“Sure why not? Other people do it.”

“You're not other people Karen," Cam said with shake of his head, "you'd go mad if you had to stay at home for a year. You know that you would.”

Her previous fervour audibly diminished “I'd be fine,” she offered weakly.

“No, you wouldn't. And you know that you wouldn't,” Cam felt bad, he wasn't cruel and he certainly wasn't enjoying watching his wife flounder.

She deflated slightly, visibly slumping. She knew this was true; a year at home would be torture for Karen, a sentiment she had voiced more than once in the past.

"Don't you want the job?" she asked, suddenly.

Cam froze and looked at her.

"Pardon?" he asked quietly.

"Do you actually want the job?" she repeated.

"I...I," Cam floundered.

Karen stared at him, her arm crossed over her chest.

"Well?" She asked, "It's a simple question. Do you, or do you not want the job?"

"It's more complicated than that," Cam said meekly.

"No, it isn't," Karen said gently, "it's a very simple question. Forget everything else, just for a second and answer this one question, honestly and without considering anything or *anyone* else. Do you want the job?"

Cam stared at his wife, "Yes," he whispered.

Karen smiled, "Pardon,"

"I said yes," he repeated.

“Then you can’t pass this up Cam. Think of the experience, think of the prestige!”

In all Honesty, Cam had thought of little else. The inevitable professional notoriety that would accompany this project meant that he would also be in demand for the rest of his career, and even if Gareth didn’t take up the option to extend his contract beyond the initial four years, the prestige would do him no harm. Apart from anything else his salary expectations would be considerably higher and the offers that would consequently come Cam's way, would be of a calibre and status that was well beyond him at that moment. It would also be a source of continued professional pride. However, Cam was being controlled by his fear and uncertainty and it was these negative emotions that were in the ascendancy, his career vanity was something he could put happily on one side.

Karen was winning, she was being reasonable and sensible and was asking the pertinent questions. Cam was annoyed, he had been out-thought, out manoeuvred and out-argued again.

"Don't pretend you have my career prospects at heart Karen. Please," Cam said, his expression suddenly dark.

She had backed him into a corner and now he knew of only one way out.

"And what's that supposed to mean?" Karen asked, suspiciously.

"We both know very well what your reasons are for me taking this job."

"Oh yes?" she said, a hint of warning in her tone.

She was daring Cam to go to a place that she thought he wouldn't tread, but like a drunken man in a porcelain factory he stumbled onwards, undaunted and undeservedly confident.

"Yes, about ten million of them!" Cam was suddenly angry and shouting

Karen physically reeled, shocked by his sudden crass insensitivity and uncharacteristic ire. She steadied herself and fixed him with her unblinking, beautiful blue eyes. Cam melted inwardly but maintained his outer disdain.

"That's not fair," she said angrily, "that was below the belt!"

She was genuinely upset and Cam knew that he needed to apologise quickly, but he was angry and hung-over, not a wonderful combination. He waited for as long as he dared before apologising. His puffed-up bravado deflating as quickly as it had swollen.

“Sorry,” he said quietly, “I’m sorry, I know you’re right, I shouldn't have said that."

"No," Karen said bitterly, "you shouldn't have."

"But you can't tell me that the money isn’t a factor?”

Karen through her arms into the air in exasperation.

“Of course it’s a factor, you bloody idiot! It’s an awful lot of money."

'I was just..."

"Do you really think so little of me that you imagine I'd sacrifice our daughter’s happiness for money?”

Cam paused, very deliberately. Not a long pause but long enough to inflict the maximum hurt.

“Of course not,” he said quietly, but firmly.

Karen’s face flushed red, her anger hot and dangerous. Tears filled her eyes and something deep inside her snapped. The tenderness that had been a constant on her face throughout, suddenly drained away to be replaced by a cold steel wall.

“Right,” she nodded slightly, as if to a question asked internally, “okay,” the tears continued to well in her eyes but she held Cam’s gaze, unashamed and defiant.

Cam looked at her. He was angry. Karen was right. She had won the argument already. Cam already knew that he would accept the job, just as Karen did. He wasn't sure why he had tried to hurt her so much. Perhaps it was his hangover; perhaps he was sick of always losing arguments.

The truth was much simpler though.

He was scared.

CHAPTER TWELVE

Gareth arranged to meet Cam and Karen at a local restaurant that was as exclusive as it was excellent. It was a place that both Cam and Karen had wanted to try since it had opened some six months previously, and they accepted the invitation gratefully.

Cam wore his favourite, well worn, Hugo Boss suit. He liked the way it fitted, and more importantly, Karen said that she liked him in it.

Karen, on the other hand, had been shopping. Cam conceded that the final effect was worth it though. She looked wonderful, absolutely beautiful, and Cam's heart swelled with pride when he saw her.

They had arranged to meet Gareth at eight o'clock but arrived deliberately early in order to make the most of the babysitter. Cam was also a little anxious and was keen to indulge in a spot of Dutch courage before Gareth arrived.

It was therefore slightly unsettling, when upon their arrival they were ushered straight through to dining room where Gareth was already sitting at the table waiting for them. Despite a bottle of red wine already being open in front of him, Gareth's glass remained empty. Instead he was sipping from what looked to be a large glass of iced water.

He was seemingly lost in concentration and had a serious look on his face. His laptop was open in front of him and he tapped at the keys without so much as a sideways glance. As Cam and Karen reached the table he finally looked up and, noticing them for the first time, his face split into a wide friendly smile. He stood up from the table, closing the laptop as he did so, and then walked around the table extending his arms in welcome. Once again he was dressed casually, yet expensively.

"Cam, Karen! Good evening, lovely to see you again. How are you both?" he said cordially, grabbing Cam's hand and shaking it firmly, before embracing Karen and kissing her on both cheeks; he held her at arm's length, studying her appearance,

"Wow!" he said, "You look beautiful Karen."

Karen's face reddened and she nodded her thanks.

"And Cam," he said turning to examine him, "you scrub up to decent level don't you? Who'd have thought it?"

"I thought I'd make an effort," he said, also blushing, "I'm afraid we don't get out much these days."

Gareth laughed, amiably and patted Cam on the shoulder. A nearby waiter sidled over and pulled a chair out for Karen directly to the right of where Gareth was positioned.

Cam took his own seat before the waiter had the opportunity to address him, Gareth remained standing.

"Aperitif?" he asked them both.

Karen nodded, "Gin and tonic please," she said.

"Make that two," Cam added.

“Three gin and tonics please,” Gareth said to the waiter, who nodded and disappeared off to the bar. When he had left Gareth turned his attention fully back to Cam and his wife.

“How are you?” he asked, “I trust you’re both well?”

They both sighed. “We’re okay,” Said Cam, “we’ve had a tricky few weeks though to be honest,”

“Really?” Gareth asked, his face showing genuine concern.

Cam shook his head and reached out to hold Karen's hand.

“A friend of ours died suddenly,” Karen said solemnly, “we only had his funeral a couple of weeks ago.”

“Oh, I’m sorry,” Gareth said.

Cam shrugged, “Can’t be helped,” he said, “but it was a terrible shock, you know?”

Gareth nodded.

“Are you both okay?”

“Aye,” Cam said and stole a glance at Karen, “kind of. We’ve had a lot to talk about as well, you know?” Cam smiled at Karen who looked slightly uncomfortable.

Gareth nodded his head sympathetically, “Well I suppose that’s only to be expected isn't it?” he picked up his water glass and took a sip before continuing, “So! Do you have an answer for me then?”

Cam physically flinched. He wasn’t expecting to address this quite so quickly. He hadn’t had the chance to partake of any form of courage, Dutch or otherwise and was suddenly uncomfortably aware of both the dryness of his mouth and the dampness of his forehead. Gareth was well practised in this type of meeting and knew how to gain the upper hand from the outset. He felt Cam's discomfort now, he didn't act upon it immediately though and let him sit for a few seconds before taking pity upon him and helping him out slightly.

"Sorry Cam, I didn't mean to make you uncomfortable," he lied, "but there is little point in prevarication is there? We might as well get things out in the open straight away eh? Perhaps then we can all relax a little bit?"

Cam nodded silently, paused again and then took a big fortifying gulp from the recently arrived Gin which went someway to lubricating his suddenly parched throat. He coughed loudly.

"As a matter of fact I do have an answer for you Gareth, yes," he took another drink, "Karen and I have discussed your offer at some length…on and off," he looked over at Karen for some moral support and she smiled encouragingly in return.

"I'm afraid that I've decided…" he paused and stumbled slightly over his words, "that is to say that *we* have decided… um, that I'm going to have to turn down your very kind offer."

Gareth's expression noticeably darkened. Undaunted, Cam soldiered on.

"I do want to thank you so very much for considering me Gareth in the first place and then obviously for offering me this opportunity," he swallowed again, "but it's just not viable I'm afraid, Not at the moment anyway," he paused again, "I'm sorry." He added with a guilty grin.

Cam had practised this little speech over and over again in his head but it still managed to sound trite and disingenuous now that the moment of truth had arrived. Karen squeezed his hand again and he took another mouthful of his drink. Gareth said nothing though. He looked squarely into Cam's eyes, put his hand up to his face and then stroked his chin thoughtfully. He sighed loudly and nodded to himself.

"Very well," he said flatly.

"I really am sorry Gareth," Cam said again, seemingly afraid that Gareth had somehow not heard his earlier apology.

"Is it the money?" Gareth asked, his eyes narrowing, "Because I might be able to find some room in the budget?"

Cam laughed and shook his head emphatically, "No. No of course not, the money is incredible Gareth," he drifted off for a moment then shook his head, "it's…its personal Gareth, complicated."

"Perhaps I can help make it less complicated?" Gareth offered. He looked at Karen and smiled and she shifted uncomfortably in her chair.

"No," Cam said firmly, "thank you but no. It's my family Gareth, It's Karen and Martha, I just can't leave them. I just can't. I thought that I could, but with our friend passing away, we just realised that," he paused and looked at his wife,

"I understand," Gareth interrupted,

"Losing someone close makes you appreciate those that you still have," Cam said.

Gareth said nothing. He looked back at Cam, and studied his flushed yet determined face then raised his glass and sipped his drink. He was considering his next response. Once more he turned to look at Karen.

"And this is a decision that you've both come to, is it?"

Karen inclined her head slightly, "This is Cam's decision," she said lightly, "but if you're asking whether or not I agree with it, then I do, wholeheartedly."

Gareth nodded quietly to himself again, his eyes closed briefly in thought.

"Is there anything I can say to change your mind?" he asked.

Cam shook his head resolutely, but spoke quietly, "Absolutely not, I'm sorry."

Gareth sighed again, "I must confess this has come as something of an unpleasant surprise Cam," he stared at him intently.

Cam shuffled uncomfortably in his chair in response.

"I wanted you for this project. I went out on a limb to convince the team that you were the right man for this position. I still believe that you are."

Cam shrugged. "My mind is set on this I'm afraid, I won't change it."

"Okay," said Gareth quietly, almost to himself, and then again louder, "okay then Cam. I'm not going to lie to you I am disappointed. Bitterly disappointed. I was looking forward very much to working with you, however I admire your conviction and your dedication to your family."

He raised his glass to them both, "No hard feelings though?" he smiled and Cam fought to suppress an instinctive shudder.

Karen and Cam raised their glasses together and shared in the toast.

"Of course not. Cheers!"

They all touched glasses and drank, Cam had already finished his gin so sucked an ice cube instead.

"Are you still happy to stay for dinner? Or would you perhaps like me to leave you on your own? My treat?"

Cam waived this suggestion away with a sweep of his hand, "Of course not! Please understand Gareth it's not personal, if circumstances were different, if it was perhaps five or ten years down the line then I would be biting your hand off, honestly," he shrugged again, "it's just bad timing that's all."

Gareth nodded "It's okay Cam I understand, really I do. Like I said, I'm disappointed but I like you, both of you. I enjoyed our time together in the summer more than I have enjoyed any evening for quite some time. You two are probably the most normal, genuine people that I've met in years," he smiled at them before adding, "and Martha is a credit to you both."

"Thank you." Cam said, he blushed slightly but he knew in that single moment that his decision was the right one.

"I wonder...?" Gareth caught himself and stopped.

"Aye?" Cam asked.

Gareth hesitated before seemingly weighing up the consequences of his next question, “Well I wonder if you might still consider taking some part of the project with less… time commitment?”

“I won't compromise my decision, Gareth.” Cam said firmly.

Gareth instinctively held his hands up in defence, “No, no I don't mean as a resident engineer, I was thinking more as a remote consultant perhaps?”

“Remote consultant?” Cam echoed, “What do you mean?”

“The fact is that I like you Cam, you have been honest and direct with me where most others would have tried to negotiate some way of still getting a pay day from me. I am an instinctive man; I have built my career upon the foundation of being able to back my instincts one hundred percent. It is impossible to operate in the world that I do without that level of confidence.”

Gareth paused, and sipped his drink again allowing his words to resonate with his companions.

Cam nodded his understanding, ”Please go on.”

“And on a personal note I would very much like to stay in contact,” he gestured to Karen, “with both of you,” he lifted his glass to his lips and took another sip, he turned his attention back to Cam, “So what do you think Cam? Would you still be willing to provide some insight as an independent consultant? Strictly non-residential, of course.”

Cam was astonished, having being offered and then turning away a golden goose he had not then expected to be presented with a free supply of golden eggs, he was certainly flattered but also wary, "Yes I'd love to, but..."

"But what?" Gareth was regaining his usual confident air.

"Well, to be honest with you Gareth. I'm not sure that your team will be too impressed with having their ideas discussed with a third party outside of their inner circle," Cam laughed at himself, "we're a funny bunch when it comes to sharing, us engineers. You must have witnessed your fair share of eccentric behaviour from us lot over the years?"

Gareth considered this for a moment, it was true that engineers could be a prickly bunch, but it was also equally true that he paid precious little attention to their complaints. As long as the work was done he didn't really care about the moaning. He didn't want to offend Cam though by insulting his profession so he decided to take a step back.

"Hmm, perhaps you're right. Leave it with me though I'll have the legal boys draw up some kind of non-disclosure contract, and if I pay you a retainer then I can keep you on board without anyone having to get upset."

Cam shrugged again, but nodded his agreement. It was a generous offer and an exciting prospect but he knew deep down that it was fundamentally untenable. The intensity of this project meant that the team would have to know and trust each other implicitly. An outsider, no matter how skilled and knowledgeable he might be, would always be viewed as suspicious. Ultimately, Cam suspected that it meant that he would be included only on the minor decisions, or on the sub-sections of projects that no one else really cared about. Over time, this would become increasingly frustrating and ultimately unsatisfying. He saw little profit from arguing the point now though because he knew that without any support from the main team, the offer, irrespective of intention, would in all likelihood fizzle out before it got really going. Instead he smiled and offered his thanks, which Gareth swatted away.

“Oh no, don't thank me,” he said coyly, “in all honesty it will good to have you on board Cam, even if it is in a reduced capacity,” he picked up his menu and started to examine it, “now then, what’s good here, any idea?” He addressed Karen.

Karen blinked, “The menu changes fairly regularly I think but I’ve heard very good things about the seafood,” she looked at Cam who was examining his own menu, “I must admit though that Cam’s a bit of a carnivore and has a bit of a weakness for steak when we go out, don't you?"

Cam shrugged “Aye well, I know it’s not terribly adventurous. But we never have it at home. The girls aren’t overly keen.”

Karen pulled a face and shook her head “No not really, I get enough blood at work thank-you.”

She smiled again, but now with genuine warmth. Cam returned the smile and took a deep breath. He felt the tension he’d been subconsciously carrying with him for days begin to rapidly drain from his body.

They ordered their meals and settled in to enjoy an excellent evening of fine dining, staggeringly expensive, but delicious wine and good humoured, but quite involved conversation.

The initial tension that had hung over the table after Cam declined Gareth’s offer soon dissipated. Like old friends, they chatted happily and their fledgling friendship continued to blossom. The wine flowed freely and the time passed in an increasingly convivial fashion. As the evening became early morning the three of them became more than slightly merry. The waiting staff had been subtly checking their watches for over an hour, when they finally, and somewhat reluctantly decided to leave the restaurant. As they stepped out in the chill autumn air to wait for their taxi they were laughing and hugging like long lost school friends. They cheerfully began arranging and rearranging future engagements. Meetings that would probably be completely forgotten by the time the next morning's hangover had faded away.

Cam and Karen climbed into their cab for the short ride home, giggling like teenagers. Cam fumbled with the taxi's seatbelt and then slumped heavily into the shiny leather seat. He smiled contentedly and realised that he felt happier now than he had done for weeks. He looked over at his wife who was closing her eyes and nodding her head along with the bumps in the road. He took hold of her hand and instinctively she turned to look at him, albeit somewhat blearily.

"I love you," he said.

"Hmm?" Karen was desperately trying to focus on the passing street without letting her drunkenness overwhelm her.

"I said, I love you,"

Karen nodded and then slumped slightly, "I know," she said, and smiled sleepily, "I love you too," her expression changed and she looked suddenly concerned, "are you all right darling?"

It was Cam's turn to nod, "Aye. I'm fine," he paused to double check, then leaned closer to Karen and whispered conspiratorially, "I'm a wee bit drunk if I'm honest though. How 'bout you?"

The whisper was loud enough for the taxi driver to hear it over the radio station that was playing in the cab; he rolled his eyes to himself and turned the volume.

"I'm fine; I'm not that drunk actually. I think I'm just tired really," Karen's eyes were tightly closed in an expression of concentration.

Cam slid back further into the seat, nodding as he went, "Hmm, yeah, yeah, probably tired that's all," his face twisted into a serious expression although it was one that his facial muscles seemed either unwilling or unable to support.

Karen swayed slightly in her seat and then moved towards Cam, she placed her hand on his chest and looked into his eyes as much as she was able, although he was rather unhelpfully swimming in and out of focus. In an attempt to combat this she closed her eyes again and kissed him hard on his lips. When she pulled away from him, she managed to refocus on his face. Cam was smiling, the same wide, slightly lopsided smile he kept solely for her.

"I love you too," she whispered again and placed her head on his shoulder, closing her eyes.

Gareth, meanwhile, had managed to stumble up the stairs of the hotel, somehow gained access to his room and then collapsed fully clothed onto his bed. He fought with his jacket and managed to shake it off and onto the floor, where it lay in a crumpled heap. He was determinedly still awake and was lying flat on his back staring blindly at his cell phone which had amassed an inordinate number of missed calls and messages during the evening's proceedings. Gareth liked to drink, but rarely got drunk. He knew his limits and although they were pretty high he never normally let himself go beyond them. He had enjoyed this evening though and had enjoyed the company of Karen and Cam more than he was expecting to, especially after the rather inauspicious start to the evening.

The alcohol was fogging his mind. He was desperately tired and he only wanted to fall asleep. The conscious part of his brain though was trying to push a persistent thought to the fore. He reluctantly forced himself to stay awake just a little longer because he knew that there was one call he had to make before he finally went to sleep.

Cam had undoubtedly thrown an engineering spanner into the works this evening and Gareth now had to try and come up with a plan that would resolve things as quickly as possible. He was sure that Cam would still be involved in the project in some capacity or other. He now had the unenviable job of trying to persuade the other engineers and scientists already on board that this was a good thing and not a massive potential pain in their collective backsides. He used the dictaphone application on his phone and left himself a voice message for the morning and then he dialled the number for the call he had to make.

5,000 miles away a cell phone rang and Jacob Mbamwa flipped his cell open to answer it.

“I thought you’d call earlier, it must be kind of late over there now?” he said.

Without pausing for any kind of acknowledgement he launched into his preprepared speech, "I've had an idea," he said, "I think that we should perhaps invite the media to become more actively involved with the project as a whole," he waited for a response, but when none was forthcoming he took it as his cue to continue, "my brother Felix is a journalist over in Cape Town and I think I can persuade him to do a positive piece on us, you know try and remove some of the negativity that rose up after the whole 'Space adventurers' debacle?“ again there was no response, "I know that it might seem a bit unprofessional to try and push my kid brother forward but I know that he'll do a polished job, he's a good kid, you'll like him."

Still there was no reply.

"Gareth?" Jacob licked his lips nervously; "I didn't mean to overstep my role, I just thought that it could work out well for us all" he waited for a reaction,

“Hello?”

As Jacob listened more closely all he could hear was the sound of gentle snoring from the cell phone that now lay on top of Gareth’s sleeping chest.

It was only 7pm in California where Jacob stood on the balcony of his Malibu beach house enjoying the last of the day's sun.

“Gareth, can you hear me?”

The snoring continued so he shrugged to himself and hung up on the call. He would see Gareth soon enough anyway and perhaps face to face was a better way to tackle this subject after all.

Slightly relieved that he hadn't just cost himself either his job or his reputation, Jacob moved back inside his apartment and headed over to his open laptop. He sat down, clicked the mouse pad and studied the e-mail he had been writing to his brother in Cape Town, he read and reread it and after a few minutes of ineffectual tinkering and spell checking he sent it and then closed the screen of his computer.

"Strike while the iron's hot," he said to himself and headed off to his bedroom to finish packing for the journey ahead.

CHAPTER THIRTEEN

CAPE TOWN. SOUTH AFRICA.

Felix couldn't sleep but there was nothing unusual in that. He often struggled immediately after a deadline to shut his brain off. The residual adrenaline of getting an article polished and put to bed meant that his mind was too active to sleep. Unfortunately, at the same time, he was physically exhausted. So he lay in bed, suspended in a pre-dream limbo, staring at the ancient ceiling fan above his head as it rocked noisily from side to side as turned. The almost trance-like *whup, whup whup* of the fan's blades made his eyes grow heavy and he slipped in and out of consciousness. He lay like this, dreaming fitfully, for the best part of five hours before he finally gave the whole process up as a bad idea. He swung his legs over the side of his bed and then, dejectedly shuffled through to his kitchen where he switched on his kettle to make a cup of tea. Despite the age and condition of the bedroom fan, it was still doing its job. The heat throughout the rest of his apartment was thick and stifling, and he went over to open his balcony doors. The Cape breeze that immediately rushed into the room, made his bare skin tingle with relief. He stood in the breeze for a few minutes and smiled to himself. He heard the kettle click off and so he made his way back into the kitchen. However, the five metres or so he had walked had been enough to change his mind entirely about the prospect of tea, instead he made his way over to his fridge where he pulled out an ice cold can of coke, which he held, briefly against his forehead and neck before cracking it open.

He walked back into the lounge area where he headed straight back over to his balcony. He stared out into the night view beyond and smiled. He was close enough to the ocean that if he craned his neck slightly he could see the water lapping against the sand of his local beach. Table mountain stood off to his left and in the moonlight he could make out it's wispy tablecloth covering of mist. He sipped at his coke and looked around at the other balconies in his block. There were no other lights on anywhere, other than the security lights down by old Pauls hut. He took another swig from his can and then turned to head back into his apartment. He reached his dining table cum desk and fired top his faithful old laptop. He was presented with the word document that he had e-mailed to his boss the previous evening. He resisted the temptation to reread it, in case he spotted any mistakes or corrections that he could no longer change and instead closed the document down. He clicked an icon on the desktop and a new article that he had been writing on and off for a few months now, sprung into view.

He wrinkled his nose as he read aloud the headline he had given the piece;

"IS DOCTOR DEATH STALKING THE HOSPITALS OF AFRICA?"

It was a sensationalist banner but despite his misgivings about the title, it was still a genuinely fascinating and chilling story. It concerned a series of more than sixty suspicious deaths that had occurred throughout Sierra Leon, Liberia and Guinea mainly within medical centres and hospitals.

Through some persistent digging, Felix had managed to unearth some fairly compelling circumstantial evidence linking at least twenty or thirty deaths within these regions, but such was the manner of these things that most of the stories had already begun to take on a myth like status.

There was no real link to any one doctor or facility, and frustratingly, no two accounts ever truly corroborated one another. There was a hesitance to implicate any medical staff and when a doctor was described, it was always vague and non-specific. Felix suspected that there was a single linking factor, but he couldn't, as yet, pinpoint it.

He re-read his opening paragraph and sighed, he had been here before and never found the right angle. Undaunted, he opened up the tabs from some of his favourite on-line publications. They were mainly local papers, obscure magazines and independent articles, most of which resided in the less salubrious end of the journalistic universe. They were rich literary seams though, ripe for mining if you had the time or inclination to search. The darker corners of the internet can provide fertile ground for potential sources, provided that you have a strong stomach and a somewhat flexible view of morality.

Paedophile rings, political outrage and sports star infidelities; these were the building blocks of your life when you operated as an independent, investigative journalist. It was either this or travel pieces on "The joys of Franschhoek" or "101 things to do in Stellenbosch". He had spent years scrapping about trying to scratch a living as a freelance reporter, primarily dealing in legitimate and conscientious articles had left him disillusioned, frustrated and with an even bigger overdraft. Conscientious, moral articles are good for the soul, as it turns out, but not for the bank balance.

South Africa had undoubtedly changed hugely in the twenty years post-apartheid, mostly for the better but not completely. The systemic corruption that had been the cornerstone of the government during the apartheid era, maintained its grip on local and national politics. The country-wide appetite for

gossip and celebrity indiscretion had expanded exponentially, its collective desire for scandal and subversion apparently unquenchable. It was into this mire that Felix had plunged, reluctantly but with enough bloody mindedness and determination, that soon his bank account was expanding almost as quickly as his self-respect was diminishing.
Despite this immersion into the more facile aspects of journalism, he maintained his enthusiasm for, what he considered to be, more worthwhile pursuits. These scandal stories gave him a new found financial freedom though, so he balanced his time between what fed his soul and what fed his belly. He was able to take his time and establish a more serious body of work, along side the less salubrious stuff, that he could legitimately be proud of. Always looking for that one elusive story that would establish his reputation and allow him to finally afford an apartment with fully functioning air-conditioning.
Felix stared, unblinking, at the flickering laptop screen, lost in thoughts that had nothing to do with the story in front of him. He was interrupted from his reverie by the electronic chime indicating that he had just received some mail. The sender was his older brother Jacob and the subject line read "Your next story?" intrigued Felix opened the attachment and read the message from his brother in full;

Hey Bru, how are you? Hope things are going well and that you've managed to move out of that shit hole of an apartment by now.

Felix glanced around at his small but neat apartment and bristled. It may have been a shit-hole but only he was allowed to call it one,

"Patronising prick" he said aloud.
He almost stopped reading there and then out of irritation, but his curiosity made him continue. It was unlike Jacob to write at all, never mind with a story suggestion;

I know you're always on the lookout for a new story and I saw this and thought of you.

Felix tapped the attachment icon and the original advert for the Mars space mission opened in his browser. He read it with a mild sense of bewilderment before smiling to himself, closing it down again and finishing his brother's message;

It might seem a bit out there and you would have to leave mum and dad for the first time in your life! However, I am working on a huge project at the moment and we are about to push things up a gear. I think there might just be a role somewhere for you if you're interested? It's not your usual kind of banal bullshit (just kidding) but the money would be good. I've attached some details for you to have a look through which will hopefully whet your appetite. I haven't cleared it completely but I reckon that you would have a pretty free-reign, provided you were (mainly) positive. The angle would be your own choice of course but the final edit would have to be with my boss (obviously) it could really take off though and I wouldn't be surprised if the coverage became international. What do you think? You don't have to let me know straight away but if you are interested I can probably arrange a meeting with Gareth over the next couple of weeks.
Anyway have a think and get back to me. Say hi to Mum and Dad for me, J"

Felix reopened the attachment and reread the advert, before moving on and looking at some of the other material that his brother had sent. Despite the oddly structured newspaper advert, It looked to be a well-structured, viable venture. Jacob was not a superficial kind of a guy, and he certainly wasn't the type to get involved with a folly. Still, the term 'Space adventurers' raised a whole line of red flags in his mind. Felix shook his head.

"Space adventurers?" he said aloud, "Really?"

He smiled, shook his head again and closed the laptop. Neither the caffeine nor the sugar in the coke had made any impact upon his tiredness and all of a sudden he began to feel as though he might actually be able to sleep. He had almost immediately decided that the idea of writing a science fiction piece, based on a flight of fancy from an eccentric foreign national was the very last thing he should get involved with. It was, he feared, almost certain to further cement his undeserved reputation as a superficial, juvenile hack. He yawned and padded back through to his bedroom, still shaking his head and smiling as he went,

"Typical Jacob," he thought to himself, "thinks he knows what's best for me, when in fact he knows sweet F.A"

His bedroom felt cool now, he placed his coke can on his bedside table and then lay down on his bed and closed his eyes. Within minutes, he was fast asleep and dreaming of voyages into space.

CHAPTER FOURTEEN

SHEFFIELD, ENGLAND

Gareth did not keep conventional hours; he worked around the world and would operate in the time zone of whatever country he was working most closely with at any given time. He would often set his watch to Eastern Seaboard time or New Delhi. He would fit his day around the phone calls and meetings he had to participate in, regardless of his actual physical global location. Cam would therefore often get calls from Gareth at odd times of the night or day. Gareth would seem genuinely confused whenever Cam suggested that he called back in a few hours because it was the middle of the night.

Despite the midnight calls, Cam enjoyed the trappings that went along side being friends with a billionaire. The interruptions and strange time keeping were a reasonable trade off against the vicarious thrill of living the life of the super-rich, even if it was only by association.

Cam and Karen were enjoying something of a renaissance in their marriage since their dinner out with Gareth. They had decided that date-night should become a monthly occurrence. Often, it was only a take-away and a Spotify playlist, but they determinedly made an effort to spend some time together as a couple and they had both felt the benefit. This evening they were going out to dinner, though. Martha was spending the evening with Karen's parents so there wasn't even the spectre of early morning childcare to curtail their enjoyment.

They had decided on one of their old favourite haunts, an informal French restaurant within the West end of the city. It was a place they had first visited on Karen's birthday when they were both students and the clientele, although a little different now, was still pleasingly eclectic. Just as they had done when they were younger, they had booked the table for the whole evening and had happily reminisced their way through the starters, entrees and two bottles of wine. The dining room was divided into several small rooms and they had ensconced themselves in one of the dingier corners, oblivious to those around them and effortlessly comfortable in one another's company. When the waiter arrived for the fourth attempt to take their dessert orders they were both mildly surprised to notice that it was almost eleven o'clock and they had already been seated for almost three hours.
Karen ordered the cheese board, as she always did, and Cam ordered the sticky toffee pudding as he always did. They had a glass of port each followed by a brutally bitter French coffee and then paid the bill and reluctantly headed out into the stillness of the night.
It had been a warm day in the city and some of that heat still clung to the stone of the surrounding buildings. It was late September and the air was colder now, hinting at the coming change of seasons. They held hands as they walked towards a taxi rank and when they arrived home they headed straight upstairs to the bedroom leaving a trail of hurriedly discarded clothes throughout the hallway, stairs and landing as they went. They made love like they had when they were younger, with urgency and tenderness and afterwards Karen laid her head onto Cam's chest, her body curled alongside his, her shoulder nestling under the crook of his arm.
"We should do that more often," she said with an impish grin.

“Hmmm,” Cam said, and he kissed the top of her head.
They lay like that, happily entwined until the peace was broken by the beep of Cam’s mobile phone. Instinctively he reached out to his side table with his free arm and started to read the message.
“Another woman?” Karen asked, playfully.
Cam laughed, “Well one of them anyway,”
He read the message and then started tapping out a reply.
"Cam?"
"What?" he asked
“Seriously?” Karen said, "You need me to spell it out?"
“What?” Cam replied.
Karen sighed, “What does he want this time?” she asked, wearily.
“He’s invited me to the test match on Sunday,” he said, “at Lords!”
“To which you presumably said no,” Karen said.
“What? No of course I fucking didn’t!”
“You hate cricket Cam,” she said.
“No, I don’t,” he protested, weakly.
Karen laughed and raised her head from his chest, “What was the phrase that you used with my brother when he invited you last year?”
“I forget,” he muttered quietly
“Ah yes,” she said thoughtfully, “I believe you said that it is, and I quote; ‘an elitist spectacle that only serves to reinforce an outdated stereotype of empirical superiority’”
Cam said nothing.
“I’m sorry,” she said, “I may have misquoted you. I imagine that you swore quite a lot more when you said it!”

Cam shook his head, “Aye, but this is free,” he said, ”and it’s in an executive box!” he grinned hopefully at her, "I've never been in an executive box."
Karen rolled her eyes, untangled herself from his body and then swept out of bed and into the en-suit.
“So can I go?” Cam called through after her.
"I suppose so," she sighed.
"Yes!" Cam said and began typing his reply again.
Karen looked at her reflection in the bathroom mirror and sighed again.
“Doesn’t any of this strike you as a little odd Cam?” she asked, gently.
“What, cricket? Abso-fucking-lutely,“ he replied, “But, like I said, it is free”
“No, not the cricket as such, all of it?”
“I don't understand?” Cam said, whilst still typing.
“All of this attention from Gareth?” Karen said
“No, not really. He’s a generous guy,”
“Hmmm,”
Cameron put down his phone and looked up at the open bathroom door. Karen was drying her hands.
“What does that mean?” he asked, Karen folded the towel and placed it back onto the radiator,
"it's easy when you're rich, though,"
"What is?"
“I just mean, that it’s easy to appear generous when you have everything, isn't it?”
Karen walked back into the bedroom and got back beneath the covers, “You’ve only known him for three months Cam and he’s treating you like you're his long lost brother or something.”
"He has a brother," Cam said, "they get on fine."

"You know what I mean" Karen said.
Cam shrugged, “We just get on, that’s all,” he said, “it’s not fucking complicated!”
Karen laughed, “of course it’s fucking complicated!” she said,
Cam looked at her irritatedly,
“The man is a multibillionaire," she continued, "one of the most powerful men on the planet,"
"I know, what's your point?"
"Despite this, over the past three months he has spent more time with you than anyone else. That doesn't strike you as odd?”
"Not really," Cam said, weakly.
"Well, if it doesn't, it bloody well should!"
Karen had brought a tube of moisturiser from the bathroom and was methodically rubbing it on her arms and legs. Cam watched her for a moment, briefly hypnotised.
“He’s on the phone all the time," he said, finally. "it’s not like he’s not working while he’s with me.”
“And what about you? How much work have you done over the past three months?”
Cam shrugged again, “He is my boss.”
“Exactly,” Karen said, “he’s your boss, not your friend.”
Cam sat up, his face pink with wine and emotion, “He can be both!” he said, loudly.
Karen shrugged.
“Why is it so hard for you to accept that I have a wealthy friend? Is it so hard to believe that someone would want to spend time with me?”
Karen placed a gentle hand on his arm, “No of course not darling, and I’m not trying to be cruel, really I’m not, but..." she hesitated.
"But what?" Cam asked,

"But, you have a family, you have friends," she shook her head, "I'm just worried about you."
"Worried about me?" Cam asked, "I'm a grown man!"
"I know darling," she said gently, "I just think you're spending too much time together and you're losing sight of what's important."
"Fine," he said, sulkily, "I won't go to the fucking cricket then. Happy?"
Cam turned over in the bed so that his back was now facing Karen.
"Oh Cam, it's not about the cricket," she leaned over and kissed his shoulder, "it's about us; You, me and Martha."
Cam rolled onto his back and sighed, "But he's so cool," he said weakly, "I've never had a cool friend before."
"Of course you have."
"Perhaps, engineer cool," he said, "but not private jet and executive box cool."
Karen laughed, "I know sweetheart, but don't you see? He's a man with everything. You're a novelty at the moment, and eventually novelties wear off."
"Ah now, that's a wee bit unfair," Cam said defensively, "I think he deserves a wee bit more credit than that."
"When he gets bored, Cam, and he will get bored. He'll dump you back into your old suburban life, with your boring old middle aged wife and middle class daughter," she sighed, "and then you'll resent us. You'll resent the things that you can no longer do."
Cam shook his head, "No!" he said firmly. "I'll never resent you!"
She smiled and kissed him again, "You won't have a choice my love," she said gently, "and I know you. You'll hate yourself

for feeling that way. But you will and I can't bear the thought of watching you go through that pain."
Cam pushed himself out onto his elbows and sighed, "So what do I do?"
"You don't have to do anything. Just take a step back. Say no sometimes."
Cam nodded, "You're right," he said sadly, "I know you're right. I won't go to the cricket on Sunday," he said determinedly.
Karen laughed, "Don't be daft," she said, "go, have fun, but remember what's important. It's not executive boxes or free champagne."
Cam raised a quizzical eyebrow at her.
"Okay," she conceded, "it's a bit about free champagne, but remember where your heart lies Cam. And it's not with Mr. Billionaire. It's here in this house with the two people that love you more than anything else," she smiled and reached over and kissed him again.
He kissed her back and the two of them fell asleep in each other's arms. Just as they had done when they were younger.

* * *

It was a Thursday night in early October and Cam had a meeting in London about the new budget allocations from one of the educational centres he worked with the next day. His phone lit up and began to vibrate angrily. He picked it up and sighed, loudly;

"Gareth? What the hell?"

"What?"

"It's three o'clock in the fucking morning," Cam stifled a yawn.

"So what?"

"So fuck off, that's what."

"But you're awake now, so what's the difference?"

"The difference?" Cam sighed heavily, "I'm up in three fucking hours. Karen's up in three fucking hours. We need to sleep. That's the difference!" he paused, "Honestly Gareth, you're worse than a fucking child!"

"Why are you up at six?" Gareth asked.

"I've a train to catch," Cam said

Karen rolled over with a pointed sigh and looked at her phone, groaned and then sank her head back into her pillow.

"A train?" Gareth seemed genuinely confused.

Cam sighed, "Aye. A train. Us paupers occasionally have to use public transport to get around I'm afraid."

"I could give you lift if you like? I'm not far away."

"Thanks," said Cam, "but I'm fine."

"We could take the helicopter if you like?"

Cam stifled a laugh, "No. The train's fine Gareth, I'll talk to you tomorrow. Good night."

"But…"

"Good night Gareth!"

The morning arrived far too quickly. Cam had lain awake for what felt like hours before he had managed to get back to sleep. It felt as though only minutes had passed before his alarm started to chime. He reached out a reluctant arm, grabbed his phone and switched it off.

“Bastard,” he muttered a little too loudly.

Karen stirred and rolled over,

“What’s wrong?”

“Nothing sweetheart, sorry, go back to sleep.”

Karen yawned extravagantly, “What time is it?”

“It’s just gone six,”

“What times your train?”

“Half seven,”

“Time for a cuddle?”

“Always!”

Karen shuffled over the bed and rested her head onto Cam’s chest. Cam allowed himself to close his eyes again. He must have dropped off though because the next thing he knew Martha was standing at the side of the bed asking to join the family hug. Cam again picked up his phone and checked the time.

“Oh shit!”

Karen had evidently dropped off again as well and she woke with a start.

“What? What’s wrong?”

"We fell asleep again," Cam said trying to untangle himself, "it's almost 7. I'm going to miss my train."

Cam climbed awkwardly out of bed onto slightly wobbly legs.

"You said a bad word Daddy!" Martha was never likely to let this slip by; she looked accusingly at her father.

"Sorry sweetheart," Cam called as he disappeared into the en-suite.

Karen got out of bed as well and pulled her dressing gown over her shoulders.

"You're not going to make it you know?" She said through a yawn.

"Aye I will," Cam called from the other room.

Karen shook her head, "No, you won't. Even if you left right now, you'd struggle. Get a later train."

"I can't, my meeting starts at 10. I can't be late!"

Karen shrugged. It was impossible and Cam knew it. He ducked back out of the bathroom and picked up his phone again. He checked the time and saw a text message from Gareth that had arrived during the night. He threw the phone back onto the bed and started to undress.

"Bloody Gareth," he muttered to himself.

"I'm sorry?"

"Eh? Oh, nothing, Gareth rang in the night; I couldn't get back to sleep again."

"What did he want?"

"I've no idea. I didn't ask. You know what he's like though."

Cam disappeared back into the en-suite and emerged moment's later, spraying deodorant under his arms. He opened his wardrobe and pulled out the suit and shirt that he was wearing today. He hung the suit on the wardrobe door and started to pull the shirt on. It was then that the thought struck him.

"Bloody Gareth," he repeated quietly to himself, a smile spread across his face. He moved over to the bed, picked up his phone again and dialled. Gareth answered on the third ring.

"Gareth, I need a favour."

"Oh you need a favour now do you? Well, I'm not sure I want to speak to you now."

"Oh, come on, don't be a prick."

"Nice sweet-talk Cam. I wondered how you managed to persuade Karen to marry you, you being such a homely son of a bitch and all. It must have been your beautiful turn of phrase."

"You done?" Cam said impatiently.

"For now,"

"I don't suppose that you were serious about that helicopter offer?"

"Really?"

“Really, I overslept, and as its kind of your fault, I was wondering...”

“Hmmm,” Gareth said, thoughtfully, “How quickly can you get to The Moorlands pub on Baslow Road?”

“Eh? I dunno, about twenty minutes? Maybe half an hour, why?”

“What time do you have to be in London?”

“My meeting's at 10,”

“Where?”

“Docklands.”

“Okay. No worries. See you in twenty minutes. You won’t miss me I’ll be the one in the helicopter.”

Cam said nothing.

“Cam?”

“Sorry,” he said, “I’ll be there.”

“Okay, so I’ll see you in twenty then?”

“Okay. And thanks Gareth, you're a life saver. See you soon,” Cam went to hang up the phone but heard Gareth’s voice still coming through the receiver.

“Cam? Cam? Are you still there?”

Cam lifted the receiver back to his ear and listened, “Hello? Yes?”

“Sorry, is Karen there please?”

Cam shrugged “Aye.”

“Can I have a quick word please?”

“Sure,” Cam covered the phone with his hand, “Karen?”

He called into the bathroom and Karen emerged her hair wrapped in a towel.

“Gareth wants a word.”

“What? Why?”

“He didn’t say,”

Karen rolled her eyes as Cam handed her the phone. Suddenly aware of his time constraints he busied himself with getting dressed, swearing quietly to himself as he went. When he finally left the bedroom to head downstairs she was laughing and chatting happily on the phone.

“What did he want?” Cam asked when Karen arrived downstairs and handed him back his phone.

“Nothing really, just a chat, he had a medical question.”

“Oh right. That all?”

“Yeah. Shouldn’t you be gone?” Karen said pointing at the kitchen clock.

Cam looked at the clock and then checked his phone, “Oh shit! Aye,” he took a swig of tea and grabbed his jacket from the back of one of the kitchen chairs, “Helicopter eh?“ He chuckled,” Talk about lifestyles of the rich and famous, Eh?”

Karen smiled at him, "Yes, Gareth said. Remember what we talked about though? You be careful,"

"I will, sweetheart. Although it's not got much to do with me!"

He pulled his jacket on and took one last swig of tea from his cup.

"Martha. That's me away sweetheart," he called out.

Martha came trotting into the kitchen clutching her new birthday doll.

"Bye-Bye daddy," she said and then stretched up and put her arms around his neck. She kissed him full on the lips, "Urgh tea!" she said, her face contorted into an expression of disgust.

Cam smiled and leaned over to kiss Karen.

He headed for the front door pausing only to pick up his keys, wallet and sunglasses. He opened the door and turned back to the house.

"Bye," he said, "Love you!"

He closed the front door with a bang and climbed into his car. The Moorlands pub was only a short drive away, but there was an established helipad there that was used at the weekends for tourist flights during the summer. As he pulled out of the drive he allowed himself to relax. He looked up and saw Martha and Karen standing in the frame of the door waving. He waved back and pulled into the road.

If he'd known that it was the last time that he'd see either of them alive, he probably would have gone back for another kiss.

PART 2

CHAPTER ONE

THREE YEARS LATER...

LONDON, ENGLAND. AUGUST 2017

It was just after nine o'clock on a Friday evening and Kieran was sitting alone in his office. He stared blankly at the screen of his computer and tried to conjure the enthusiasm for another delve into his inbox. He was tired though, and his apparently endless workload showed no signs of abating any time soon.

He stared at the phone on his desk and picked it up and twirled it through his fingers, thoughtfully. He tapped the screen with his forefinger and then placed it back on the top of the desk. Suddenly, he stood up from his chair and walked to the window of his office, where he looked out over the city and grimaced.

The abandoned phone on his desk lit up as it started to ring, instinctively Kieran moved his head to look at it. He had no enthusiasm for this call and turned his attention back to the view. The phone continued to ring, he sighed a weary sigh and then moved back over to his desk where he hesitantly picked it up. He considered it as though it were made of something deeply unpleasant and then, with reluctance seeping from every pore of his body he answered it.

"Hello?" he said, with a forced enthusiasm.

"Yes,"

"No of course, I understand."

He moved the phone away from his ear and looked at the screen, weariness drawn over his features. He looked at his

watch and then raised the handset back to his ear and listened.
The caller hung up with a click.
He tapped the screen again and tossed the phone over to the leather sofa that was positioned on the far side of the office beneath an original Kandinsky. It landed on one of the cushions and then bounced onto the floor.
"Bollocks!" Kieran sighed and then moved over to retrieve it. He picked up the cellphone and looked at the screen intently for a few seconds before collapsing heavily into the sofa and swinging his legs up onto one of the arms. There he lay, flat on his back, staring up at the ceiling and mentally trying to calculate how much work he now had to do before he would be able to finally go home.
He was interrupted from his reverie by a loud knock at the heavy oak door of his office. There was no one else in the building at this time other than the cleaners.
"Not just now, thank-you!" he called.
There was a pause and then an even louder, more determined knock replied.
"It's okay thanks. I'm going to be here all night. Thank you though," he called again through gritted teeth.
The handle began to turn and the door slowly started to open. Kieran swung his legs back to the floor and stood up. He walked to the door, grasped the handle firmly and pulled it open.
"Sorry, but I don't need the office cleaned thanks. I'm working late tonight."
"Glad to hear it. That's why I pay you the big bucks!" Gareth stood on the other side of the doorway smiling at him.
"Gareth!" Kieran said, startled, "What are you doing here?"

“It is my company," he said with a shrug, "I’m fairly sure that means that I don't need a reason. Doesn't it?”
“What? Yes, of course, It’s just a surprise that’s all,” Kieran's composure had momentarily fractured and he was uncomfortably aware of his increasingly clammy palms.
“Clearly,” Gareth said, with a wry arch of his eyebrow.
Kieran gathered himself quickly, he wiped his hand as subtly as he could on his trousers and then offered it to his employer, who shook it warmly. He walked into the room and sat down on the same sofa that Kieran had so recently vacated. He patted it approvingly.
“Comfy?” he asked.
“Very," Kieran said with a small smile, “it has to be though. I think that I spend more nights on this that I do in my own bed,” he laughed and then realised that this comment could be misconstrued, “not that I’m complaining of course!”
“Of course. You work too hard though Kieran” Gareth said with an admonishing wag of his finger.
Kieran shrugged.
“How are things?”
“Erm... fine thanks,” Kieran answered.
Gareth was picking absent mindedly at a stray thread on the sofa, Kieran flinched, scared that he might begin to somehow unravel the whole thing.
“Good, good, pleased to hear it” He stood up again and smoothed out the crease in his trousers, “Well I won’t keep you. I know you're busy.”
Kieran watched as he walked back towards the door.
“Um…Everything all right?” he asked, tentatively.
“Hmm?” Gareth responded, dreamily.

“Well, I haven’t seen you for almost three weeks. I can’t imagine that you just popped in to ask after my ongoing wellbeing.”
Gareth turned back to look at Kieran.
"No offence, but that's hardly your style is it?"
Gareth looked at him, or rather through him.
“Time for a drink?” he asked.
“Not really,” Kieran said. “You know what with all the work and stuff."
He moved back towards his desk, "Duncan has just dropped another ton of work onto my plate as well."
"I wouldn't worry too much about that," Gareth said with a friendly wink.
"If I don't do it tonight, it still needs doing at some point," Kieran said flatly.
“Hmm yes, of course," Gareth said thoughtfully, "let me rephrase then? Kieran, it *is* time for a drink, and I would like you to join me.” He caught Kieran’s eye and held his stare.
Kieran looked over at his desk, the laptop that stood open on it and then back at his expectant boss, “Okay then…” he said. "If you're going to put it like that."
He walked to the door and grabbed his jacket from the vintage coat stand, slipped his arms into the sleeves and clapped his hands together.
“Where to then boss?”
“I fancy a whisky” Gareth said.
“That doesn't really narrow it down, does it?”
“How about the Whisky Bar in Soho?”
“You need to be member,” Kieran said.
Gareth stared at him with a raised eyebrow, Kieran quickly realised his mistake and smiled “Sorry," he said, "wasn't thinking. Sounds perfect.”

They walked quietly through the office and out through the main entrance to the lobby, as they reached the elevators Gareth reached forward and pressed the call button. They stood in silence for a few seconds as they watched the elevators electronic progress on the wall's display panel.
“How are you getting on with Duncan?” Gareth asked conversationally without turning his head.
Kieran shrugged, “He’s very…efficient” he said.
Gareth smiled, “You hate him, don't you?”
Kieran paused, “Of course not!”
“Sure you do. He got your job,” Gareth said, casually.
Kieran smiled nervously, “I wouldn't say that.”
“No?" Gareth said surprised, "I would. Don't worry though, it’s not for long,”
“Oh? He’s leaving?” Kieran asked hopefully,
“Leaving? Good God no," Gareth laughed, "he’s perfect for the job”
“Um…”
“You are,” Gareth said with a grin.
“I am what?”
“Leaving,"
Gareth let the word hang in the air for a few seconds before continuing, "Come on Kieran it’s not like you to be so slow.”
“You’re what? You’re firing me?” Kieran stopped dead in his tracks. “Sorry, but are you, in fact, firing me?” he repeated.
Gareth looked at him sideways and smiled, “Don’t be absurd!”
“Then what?”
“Let's wait until you’ve got a drink inside you, shall we?”
“What? Why?”
“All in good time my friend”
“Oh, come on!” Kieran said irritably. “Stop pissing me about!”

Gareth regarded Kieran cooly. He smiled, looked him up and down and turned back to the elevator's display panel.
"Project Livingston has finally become too big to deal with remotely. I need a fully dedicated team now," Gareth leaned forward and hit the call button again, "where is this damn lift?" he said to himself.
Kieran looked at him, but said nothing. Gareth glanced back at Kieran and smiled again
"I need someone to take charge," he said, "I need someone that can make the big calls when I'm not available."
"Okay," Kieran said, warily.
"I need someone to come with me," Gareth made eye contact with Kieran and held his gaze, "and that someone, is you my friend."
“Come with you?" Kieran said, "Where to? New premises?”
Gareth shook his head, “No," he said. "Not to new premises," he paused for a moment as a thought wandered through his head. "Well, not exactly anyway."
Kieran shuddered, he knew what was coming, "Don't say it," he whispered under his breath.
"To Mars!” Gareth said triumphantly.
"You said it," Kieran said
Gareth looked at him,"Pardon?"
"I knew you were going to say it, and then you went ahead and said it."
Gareth stared at Kieran, "Did you hear me?"
Kieran blinked and stared back at Gareth silently, his expression oddly vacant. Gareth, however was beaming.
"Yes, I heard you," he said after a few moments silence.
"And?" Gareth asked, expectantly.

Kieran continued to stand in silence for a few more seconds before he finally spoke again, “I’m not going to fucking Mars," he said.
Gareth stared at him, still smiling.
"It’s just not going to happen,” Kieran was adamant.
Gareth considered him for a few more moments, he opened his mouth to speak but as he did so the lift doors finally opened. Gareth stepped forward and pressed the hold button, he turned his head towards Kieran who remained unmoved.
“Come on” he said nodding into the lift.
Kieran shook his head, “No.”
Gareth feigned innocence.
“What?”
“I said No.”
“No what?”
“Fuck you!”
Kieran turned from the lift and walked back through the heavy glass office doors and into the reception area, slipping his jacket off again as he went.
"Kieran!" Gareth called after him.
He looked at the open lift doors and then back at the office. After a moment’s consideration, he reluctantly stepped out of the elevator, allowing the doors to close once again. He followed Kieran who had gone back into his office, slamming the door behind him as he went. Gareth opened the door without pausing and then walked back into the centre of the room where he stood staring at Kieran, who was standing back at the window staring out over the city below.
“You should choose your words more carefully,” Gareth said, the menace in his voice unmistakable.
"So should you!"
"I beg your pardon?"

Kieran didn't turn from his position, “I chose my words perfectly thank-you," he said a little sullenly "You’re not going to bully me Gareth. I’m not one of your little yes men.”

Gareth's eyebrows arched, “Why on earth would I want to bully you?”

Kieran turned around, his face pink with emotion, “Why on earth would I want to go to Mars? It's fucking suicide!” he said, his voice rising slightly.

Gareth’s eyes narrowed dangerously, his smile slipped into a half sneer.

Kieran coughed, “I’m sorry but it is,” he added, the volume of his voice lowered slightly.

“Do try not to be so melodramatic, Kieran,” Gareth said with a roll of his eyes. “It's hardly suicide is it?”

Kieran grunted and took a step closer to where Gareth was standing,

“Okay then tell me this?” he said, “What part of our long and prosperous relationship has led you to the insane conclusion that any part of me would want to be a mother-fucking astronaut?”

Gareth flinched reflexly. Undiminished, Kieran continued.

“Look Gareth. It's a flattering offer, but it’s not my…” he paused searching for the right term. “It’s not my skill set,” he offered.

Gareth sucked at his teeth but didn't interrupt.

“I’m not a pioneer or a bold frontiersman," Kieran pleaded. "I’m a business consultant. And a damn good one at that!”

“One of the best,”

Gareth looked over his shoulder as though expecting a new arrival. Kierans eyes followed him, but there was nothing to be seen.

"Look, can we just go for a drink and then I can explain?" He paused for a moment. "Please?"
Kieran shook his head, "No," he said forcefully, "not if you're going to talk about this all night. I've too much to do without any of this bullshit getting in my way."
“I need you..." Gareth said, suddenly.
Kieran looked at Gareth, "you..."
"Need you, yes!"
"Need me?" Kieran laughed.
"I need you...to trust me,” he said, and held open the office door.
Kieran blinked but said nothing.
“I trust you Kieran,” Gareth repeated, “and I like you. I’m really going to need people around me that I can trust.”
Kieran let out a short mirthless laugh, “You’re not going to flatter me into this Gareth.”
“I’m not trying to. In fact, I’m offended that you think me so shallow.”
“Yeah, right," Kieran said with a hollow laugh. “You forget who you're talking to. I know you, and you're not so easily offended.”
“This isn't about being a pioneer,” Gareth said.
“Bullshit it isn’t," Kieran said with a wave of his hand. "Look, can I speak frankly?”
Gareth raised his eyebrows in surprise, “You mean you’ve been holding back up until now?”
Kieran ignored this, “Well?” he said, "Can I?"
Gareth demurred, “Yes of course you can. You don't have to ask. You know that.”
“This whole Mars thing?”
“Yes,”

"What is it really all about? I kind of understand the "*Because it's there*" thing. I do honestly, but…" he trailed off uncertainly.
"Come on Kieran don't go all coy on me,"
"I don't mean to be indelicate, but is this some sort of…"
"Some sort of what?" Gareth asked.
Kieran swallowed, "I don't know," he said hesitantly, "it just seems like a...folly or something and...well frankly people are worried,"
"Worried? Worried about what? My health? My business?" he paused deliberately, "My sanity?"
Kieran shook his head firmly, "No," he said a little too quickly, "no, of course not!"
"This isn't a joke Kieran. This isn't some vanity project you know. I am deadly serious."
"I know that you are. I just… I just worry is all. I worry that you're losing focus. That this... fantasy is taking over."
"It's not a fantasy!" Gareth's voice was louder now and he narrowed his eyes dangerously, "This is real and I will be successful. It is happening now! Not in the future, not tomorrow, now!" he rubbed his chin, "I would like your help Kieran, but I assure you that I am more than capable of proceeding without it."
Kieran felt the threat settle over him, and calmly accepted its implications without reaction.
"You said I could be honest with you," he said as lightly as he could manage.
Gareth nodded, "I did."
"Well, that's all I'm doing," Kieran shrugged.
"I appreciate your candour, really I do," his voice calmed once again, "this is more important than my personal feelings though, or yours for that matter."

“But why? Come on Gareth enough riddles, no more cryptic teases. If you want me on board then you're going to have to tell me what’s going on. And I mean everything.”

Gareth considered this for a moment and then sighed, “Its...complicated,” he said finally.

“Of course it’s complicated, what else could it possibly be?” Kieran laughed.

Gareth sighed again, heavily and shook his head.

“I don’t know where to be begin,” he said quietly

“How about at the beginning?” Kieran offered.

“Ha!” Gareth snorted.

“What?”

Gareth smiled and shook his head. He closed his eyes for a moment as he composed his next sentence, when he opened his eyes again he seemed genuinely surprised to see Kieran still looking at him.

“Are you okay Gareth?”

Gareth remained silent; a small enigmatic smile flickered across his face

“Gareth?” There was now real concern in Kieran’s voice. “Are you all right?”

“Hmm?" Gareth said dreamily, "Oh, Sorry Kieran, I was just thinking,” he shook his head as if clearing away unwelcome thoughts. “Now, where was I?”

“At the beginning?” Kieran repeated.

Gareth considered this for a moment, “Actually,” he said, “perhaps the end is a better place to start?”

“I don’t follow,”

“Not with a bang, but with a whimper…” Gareth said quietly.

“Huh?” Kieran's brow creased in confusion, he looked at Gareth for a few seconds before the penny belatedly dropped. He opened his mouth to speak again but somehow couldn't

find the right words. Gareth watched him intently, an odd look of tranquility and victory spread across his face.
“Perhaps,” he said finally, “we should get that drink now and then I can tell you a tale of greed, deceit, death and inevitability.” His voice was sedately calm, but his eyes twinkled with mischievous delight.
Kieran nodded blankly and once again slid his jacket on.
"Yeah," he said quietly, "perhaps a drink is good idea."

CHAPTER TWO

The plush decor of the Soho Whisky Bar was as eclectic as it was expensive. Contemporary American and European design sat effortlessly alongside antique, Chesterfield chairs and exquisitely coloured Tiffany lamps. Gareth and Kieran were sitting in two large, French leather chairs, each holding obscenely expensive whisky in Edinburgh crystal glasses. Gareth sipped at his drink whist Kieran swilled his around the glass thoughtfully. He lifted it to his lips, inhaled the vapours deeply, paused, and then lent forward to place it untouched upon a beautifully proportioned arts and crafts side table, which stood directly to the left of his chair. He sighed and then slumped back into the soft leather of his armchair, which creaked satisfyingly. He looked up at Gareth and when he was certain that he had his full attention he spoke.

“So," he said finally with a forced levity, “tell me about the end of the world then?”

Kieran smiled a smile that he didn't really feel and looked into his boss's eyes. They were dark brown, and in the dim light of the club they looked almost black, but they twinkled in the gloom, giving him a slightly unworldly appearance. His face remained placid though and what little light there was highlighted his handsome features. Gareth stared straight back into the face of Kieran. He knew what he had to say and believed it with his whole being, but he was concerned about Kieran’s reaction. He wanted Kieran to get on board, needed him to get on board.

“Will you listen to me Kieran?” he asked earnestly.

Kieran sipped at his drink and nodded.

“No!" Gareth snapped, "I mean it, I need you to listen. To really listen.”
The volume of Gareth’s voice had risen noticeably, his calm facade splintered briefly to reveal a passion and ferocity that he normally kept hidden. Kieran held his hands up.
“Okay Gareth, Jesus!” he took another sip from his glass, "I'll listen *properly."*
Gareth's ire vanished as quickly as it had arrived. He took a deep, cleansing breath and started again.
“Our time is over,” he said simply.
He looked at him and allowed time for this to sink in. Kieran said nothing, he had a mildly confused expression upon his face, but there was no other sign of reaction. Gareth cursed to himself, one sentence into it and he feared that he had already lost him.
“Hear me out Kieran,”
“I am, Gareth,” Kieran protested weekly, “I’m... I'm just tired that's all." He finished his drink and placed it back onto the side table.
“I understand, but this is important. Our time is at an end my friend. Our place in the sun is moving into the shadows.”
“I'm not sure I understand.”
“Look around you. Just in this room alone. Look at the money that’s on display here. Look at the resources that have been utilised just to bring us a decent single malt and a big cigar. We sit here like a Dickensian stereotype, two business men in suits smoking and drinking within spitting distance of some of the poorest people in the country. People that will spend tonight in the same piss addled doorways that we walked past on the way here.”
Kieran had heard this before and his heart sank as he listened to it again.

The businessman that apparently grows a social conscience is a well-established phenomenon. The intentions may well come from a well-meaning place but the reality is that when a businessman grows a heart, he inevitably loses his edge.
Gareth narrowed his eyes, “I know what you're thinking.”
“I'm not thinking anything Gareth,” Kieran said, diplomatically.
Gareth laughed, “Of course not. Don't worry, I haven't found God or anything!”
Kieran laughed as well, “Then what's with all the touchy-feely nonsense?”
“Perhaps if you let me finish you'd find out!”
Kieran shrugged and picked up his empty glass and looked around the room. He had noticed a very attractive waitress when they arrived and was sure that she had noticed him as well. However, he couldn't see her at the moment so instead he gestured to another one of the waiting staff who immediately took his glass.
“Same again sir?" he asked.
“I don't suppose you have a beer do you?” he asked hopefully.
The waiter looked as though he'd been physically assaulted.
“Beer?” he said, as if the words themselves were poisonous.
“Yeah you know? Hops, barely, sugar, water mixed together and fermented? It's quite popular.”
“I'm familiar with the concept sir. You are in a whisky club though.”
“Just a thought,” he sighed. “Yeah, same again then please. Gareth?”
Gareth finished his glass and handed it to the waiter, “Surprise us William, something unexpected. Perhaps Japanese?”
The waiter nodded and walked off, shaking his head as he went.

“May I continue?” Gareth said turning his attention back towards Kieran.
“Please do,” Kieran said.
Although he had only just departed, he looked instinctively around for the waiter and the protection that a stiff drink would afford him. After a surprisingly short wait, the drinks duly arrived and Kieran took a big fortifying sip. This seemed to cause the waiter even more physical pain and he left their table seemingly inwardly lamenting the clubs recent drop in standards.
“It’s not the end of the world as such Kieran, but is the end for us, our society, our way of life.”
“This isn't some kind of socialist utopian dream, is it? Oh God you haven't been reading the Guardian again have you?” Kieran said with a horrified smile.
Gareth shot Kieran another warning glance. Kieran swallowed his grin and took another sip of his whisky.
“Sorry,“ he said, "please go on.”
“Thank you. I’m not talking about socialism, as you well know. I am just telling you the truth. Our way of life is already coming to an end. Our resource consumption and population growth are simply not compatible.”
“Oh it’s not our fault as such," Gareth said with a grand wave of his hand, "it was always inevitable. The very nature and structure of our modern society was doomed from the start.”
Kieran rubbed at his temples, “I’m not sure I’m following you here,” he said honestly.
“Have you heard of the five risk factors for societal collapse?” Gareth asked conversationally.
Kieran raised his eyebrows and shook his head, “I must have missed that memo,” his smile had returned but just barely.

“Okay, let me explain,” Gareth said, ignoring the sarcasm. He was beginning to get into his stride and wasn't going to be derailed by Kieran’s cynicism.

“The five risk factors for collapse are: population, climate, water, agriculture and energy.” Gareth counted them off on his fingers as he spoke.

Unsure of the correct reaction Kieran simply nodded and tried to look as attentive as possible.

“Now, even the most sophisticated and established society will inevitably begin to fall apart when these five factors begin to display two important criteria” Gareth paused and sipped his drink. He shuffled forward in his chair and lent closer to Kieran conspiratorially, his eyes were alive with emotion.

“Firstly, the stretching of resources placed upon the ecological carrying capacity.”

“You mean ‘supply and demand’ then?” Kieran asked.

“Exactly! But more extreme than simple capitalism, I’m talking about when demand drastically outstrips supply.”

Kieran nodded.

“Secondly,” Gareth continued, “the stratification of a society into two distinct factions: Elite and masses.”

“Rich and poor?”

“If you prefer, but to the extent they become completely exclusionary and one no longer has any connection to the other.”

“I’ll drink to that,” Kieran said raising his glass and smiling. Gareth glared at him and he lowered his arm.

“The elite, that is to say you and I," he said gesturing between the two of them, "well we begin to limit the distribution of the resources, in order to create a surplus that will perpetuate our own lifestyle. This in turn eventually cuts off the collection and availability of natural resources to the general public. We will continue with our lavish and comfortable lives while the common man suffers."

"That doesn't paint us in a good light," Kieran's brow furrowed, his smile evaporated.

"No, it doesn't. Worse still, by the time we notice that there's a problem it will already be too late."

"So what are you saying? That we need to redistribute the wealth? Persuade the super-rich to all become philanthropists overnight?" Kieran smiled and shook his head, "That's not going to happen, you know that as much as I do."

Gareth nodded sadly, and waved away the suggestion, "I do," he said, "but it's too late for that anyway I'm afraid. We've already passed the point of no return and the forthcoming collapse is now as inevitable as your hangover tomorrow morning."

Kieran winced slightly at the thought, "How can you be so sure?"

"About your hangover?" Gareth asked with a smile, "Because you're a lightweight, that's how."

Kieran shrugged, "That's not what I meant."

"Sorry," Gareth said, his smile widening, "but you are a lightweight."

Kieran laughed, despite himself.

"It's happened before," he added simply, "check your history. Time and again. Both the Mayans and the Romans ended this way."

"The Romans?" Kieran was incredulous, "Come on Gareth, we're hardly comparable to a civilisation that died out almost two thousand years ago are we?"

Gareth shrugged but said nothing. Undeterred Kieran continued, "We understand these things now. We have a more

sophisticated scientific understanding to prevent this, surely. We have technology that they didn't have."
"Yes, we do," Gareth conceded, "but ironically, it's that very technology that may go on to potentially speed up the process."
"I'm not sure I understand,"
"Put simply, whilst it is true that technological change can raise the efficiency of our resource use," he looked at Kieran who nodded encouragingly, "it is also equally true, that the increase in availability also tends to raise both per capita resource consumption and the scale of resource extraction."
Kieran nodded, "Okay that makes sense I suppose," he said.
"This means," continued Gareth, "that the increase in consumption counteracts against the increased efficiency of resource extraction."
"So back to supply and demand then?"
"Yep," Gareth nodded.
"Increased availability leads to increased demand, which in turn leads to greater consumption, and we're back to square one again."
Kieran had sobered up significantly and his mind was spinning.
"So basically the population has to stop growing so rapidly or in fact decrease dramatically, or people will quite simply continue to starve to death until there's nothing left."
"You want to stop people having kids?" Kieran asked. His voice both louder and shriller than he had anticipated. Several well-groomed heads within the club turned towards them in disapproval.
"Of course not!" Gareth said, leaning closer. "And please, keep your voice down."
Kieran blushed, "Sorry."

Gareth continued, “Like I said though, it’s already too late. We are much further along this path than most people realise. That’s why it is time to go. Time to start again. Take the winnings and run!”

“Run? Run where? And for how long?” Kieran paused for a moment, "Run to Mars? Is that what this is all about?"

Gareth inclined his head slightly and considered this for moment, “It will take about a thousand years for the planet to recover, unless there's some kind of nuclear accident. Then we can come home.”

“A thousand years?”

Gareth shrugged, “Give or take, yes.”

Kieran laughed “I know that you are pretty fit Gareth but I think that a thousand years is beyond the scope of a high fibre diet and a few spin classes.”

“This isn't about us, well not entirely. This is about our ancestors. Our children’s, children’s, children's, children,” he paused, suddenly baffled, “or something like that anyway. I forget exactly how many generations it will take.”

Kieran slumped back into his armchair and took another sip of his whisky. He opened his mouth to speak but instead remained silent and finished off his drink.

“Another?” Gareth offered

Kieran nodded, “Hell yeah!”

Gareth gestured over to the waiter, who immediately arrived with the bottle in his hand,

“Leave it,” Gareth said and gestured to the table.

It was a seven thousand pound bottle of whisky and the waiter placed upon the table without a single comment or raised eyebrow. Gareth leant forward and poured two very large measures into the empty glasses. Kieran retrieved his glass from the table and rolled the contents around the barrel. He looked up at Gareth.

"What's in it for you Gareth?" he asked emboldened by the alcohol, "Sorry to be blunt but...well you know,"

Gareth expression darkened.

"We have the chance to save humanity," he said, "isn't that enough?"

Kieran said nothing; he continued to swill his drink in its glass. Gareth sipped at his drink and stared into Kieran's eyes. Kieran returned the stare unabashed.

"Okay Kieran," Gareth said, "I'll be frank with you then. What happens when we save humanity?" He licked his lips, "What becomes of us?"

Kieran shrugged.

"We become legends Kieran," Gareth said simply, "stories will be written about us. Our deeds will become the bedtime stories for generations to come," Gareth stared directly into Kieran's eyes, "and I, I will be remembered as the father to a new humanity. I will be remembered as a hero!"

"And then what? A God?" Kieran laughed.

Gareth smiled, "I can't see why not?"

CHAPTER THREE

Kieran stared at his reflection in the bathroom mirror and swayed to and fro in an unpleasantly nauseating manner. He rested his forehead against the cool surface of the glass and took what he imagined was going to be a cleansing breath before darting back into the stalls and being violently sick into the toilet. His forehead was clammy and damp with sweat and now the room smelt sourly of depressingly expensive vomit. He groaned and pulled his hand across his mouth before heading back to the sinks where he drank cold water straight from the tap. He withdrew his mouth, splashed some of the water onto his face and shook his head. He screwed his eyes shut and then tried once again to focus upon his alarmingly unfocussed features in the mirror.

"Looking good Kieran," he groaned, with a hollow half laugh. He picked up one of the fluffy hand towels that were stacked by the sink and dabbed at his face with it. The softness felt good against his skin and he longed for the comfort of his bed and a few precious hours sleep.

The evacuation of his stomach had helped clear his nausea and had also sobered him up a little. The payoff for this renewed clarity though was a distant, yet distinct throb in the back of his head that was subtly and unmistakably increasing in intensity with each beat of his heart.

He pulled out his wallet from his trouser pocket and inspected its contents suspiciously, he rarely had any cash on him but he was relieved to see two twenty pound notes nestled together in the lining. He could at least now get a taxi home without the irritation of having to stop at a cashpoint on the way. The door to the bathroom swung open and a large bellied middle aged man with thinning hair and a hypertensive complexion entered the room; he immediately screwed his face up as the acrid smell of Kieran's vomit struck his senses. He gave Kieran the filthiest of looks before entering one of the other cubicles with a disgusted shake of his head. Kieran toyed with saying something to him, but the throb of his head coupled with the dulling of his senses meant that he could think of nothing suitably witty or clever. Instead, he somewhat meekly slid out from the bathroom and headed back to where Gareth was still sitting with his glass in hand, waiting patiently for his return. As he reached the table Kieran held up his hand before Gareth had the opportunity to say anything.

"Before you start," he said slowly, "I'm going to have to go home Gareth, I'm sorry."

Gareth's face fell and he looked at his watch.

"But it's still early," he protested, Kieran laughed, "no," he said, "it isn't. It is in fact not early at all. You might even say that is actually very late indeed," he picked up his jacket from the back of his chair and swung it over his shoulder before grabbing the back of the chair for a moment of assisted support. He licked his lips and pointed a slightly trembling finger at his boss.

"And," he said unhappily, "I'm a little worse for wear. I'm not used to drinking really," he added almost as an afterthought. Gareth raised an eyebrow at this, "I should think not," he said with a smile, "but please, don't make me drink on my own. At least keep me company while I finish off."

Kieran sighed and looked at the table. He wanted to go home but he also did not want to end the evening refusing a direct request from his boss. Reluctantly he slumped back into his chair.

"I got you another drink," Gareth said apologetically gesturing towards the table

Kieran looked at the heavy crystal glass and his stomach did an involuntary flip, he hiccoughed and fought the overwhelming desire to run back into the bathroom for a second evacuation.
"Thank you Gareth," he said uncomfortably, "but I'm afraid that I'm going to have to pass on this one."
"Of course," Gareth said with a smile, "the last thing I want to do is force you to share a drink with me."
Kieran closed his eyes and swallowed a sigh. He reached out a slightly trembling hand and picked up the glass which felt unpleasantly heavy in his fingers, he moved it to his mouth and took a tentative sip. His insides protested and he fought the almost uncontrollable shudder that threatened to course through him. He pushed a smile onto his face and met Gareth's eye.
"I wouldn't dream of making you drink on your own Gareth," he said with as much composure as he could generate.
Gareth watched him carefully, noting his discomfort at each stage. When he had taken his drink Gareth nodded, almost imperceptibly and then took a sip from his own glass.
"Now then, what were we talking about?" he asked innocently.
Kieran knew that this was a test, Gareth never forgot what he was talking about, and he wanted to see if Kieran had been paying close enough attention
"Resource depletion," Kieran said calmly.
Gareth nodded again and Kieran sighed quietly in relief. In all honesty the last twenty minutes or so had become a little shaky and although he had managed to follow the earlier conversation with ease, he had become increasing vague about the intricacies of Gareth's grand vision as the alcohol had gained a greater foothold in his mind.
"Precisely!" Gareth said loudly.

Kieran shifted uncomfortably in his chair and caught the eye of one of the waiting staff, this time he found the young woman that had been smiling flirtatiously with his all evening. Typical he thought to himself, now I look like shit I find the girl again. She immediately moved over to Kieran and he beckoned her down so he could speak to her discretely, as she did so he caught a whiff of her perfume that simultaneously caused a measure of arousal and nausea to leap forward in almost equal measure.

"Could I perhaps have a glass of water?" he whispered into her ear.

She turned her face towards him and smiled pleasantly. Kieran stared at her impossibly white teeth and wondered casually if his own teeth had ever been that straight and perfect. She stood up, and let her fingers brush lightly across the back of his hand.

"If you'd like to come to the bar sir, I can let the you choose from our full range of cigars," she smiled again and Kieran glanced nervously over at Gareth, who was smiling happily at him.

"Excellent idea Kieran," he said. "You see? I knew that you weren't ready to call things to a close just yet. Surprise me," he said with an elaborate rising of his eyebrows.

Kieran stood a little shakily from his chair and then followed the waitress to the bar where she handed him the cigar menu. As Kieran looked at it blindly she produced a glass of ice cold water and two small, white tablets. Kieran looked at her with a look of hopeful confusion.

"Pain killers," she said quietly.

He smiled gratefully at her and swallowed the tablets along with the glass of water in a single gulp. The water was almost painfully cold but it tasted magnificent, she must have added a

twist of lime juice and it cut through the sourness that coated the inside of his mouth with a refreshing tang. Kieran looked into her big brown eyes and felt a further jolt of arousal.
"Thank you...?" he said quietly, and slid a folded twenty pound note onto the bar which she accepted with a wipe of the bar
"Can I recommend one of the Partagas' Cigars," she said, pointedly
Kieran looked around but no one seemed to be taking any notice of their conversation, which almost certainly meant that someone was.
"Excellent," he said, “what would you recommend?"
"Well, if you want something a bit special how about a Gran Reserva Lusitanias Cosecha 2007?"
Kieran shrugged, "Sure why not?" he said.
"Shall I put them on your tab?" she asked looking over at Gareth.
Kieran shook his head, "No, I'll get these separately," he lowered his voice, "and perhaps another one of those?" he said gesturing to the empty water glass.
"Certainly," the waitress said, "that will be three hundred and sixty pounds please."
Kieran slid his debit card across the bar and in the time it took the transaction to complete another glass of iced water arrived upon a folded bar napkin. He lifted the drink and sipped it, once again savouring the coldness as it slid down his tender throat. As he did this the napkin unfolded slightly revealing both the waitress' name and phone number and the return of his twenty pound note. She handed him back his bank card and the two cigars
"I hope you enjoy the rest of your evening sir," she said with a smile.

Kieran returned the smile and slipped the napkin into his trouser pocket along with his wallet. The combination of the water, the tablets and the jolt of self-confidence meant that upon his return to Gareth, he was no longer silently praying for some kind of natural disaster to bring the evening to an early conclusion. He handed the cigars to Gareth and retook his seat.

"You've perked up," Gareth said suspiciously.

Kieran shrugged, "I suppose I've got my second wind." He said as casually as he could manage.

He glanced back at the bar and at Helena who was watching him with a smile on her face, he smiled in return before turning his attention back towards Gareth.

"Anyway," he said with a shake of his head, "please continue with what you were saying," he picked up his glass again and sipped the whisky, the water and drugs had done their job, so he managed to enjoy its warmth this time and felt none of the suppressed gagging that he had only a few minutes earlier.

Gareth rolled his cigar between his thumb and forefinger and studied it closely, "We are going to run out of natural resources sooner rather than later," he said thoughtfully.

Kieran rolled his eyes, "Yes you mentioned that Gareth. Hence your utopian fantasy of a Mars colony"

Gareth raised his eyebrows at this reply and considered his colleague carefully before continuing.

"How is your solar system geography?" he asked, quietly

Kieran shrugged his shoulders, "Beyond the basics, not great," he paused. "To be honest it doesn't come up very often though," he smiled but received no response.

Gareth picked up one of the napkins that was lying on the tabletop and unfolded it; he then produced a pen from his jacket pocket and started to sketch a rudimentary drawing. A

drawing that very quickly Kieran recognised as a simple diagram of the solar system,
"This," Gareth said without looking up, "is the solar system."
Kieran nodded, "okay," he said slowly, "very nice,"
"And this is Mars," Gareth said colouring in the fourth planet from the sun. "The big one next to it is Jupiter."
Kieran bit his lip in an attempt not to laugh, but nevertheless he emitted a tiny grunt of laughter. Gareth's eyes flicked up to him for a second but he ignored him and continued with his drawing.
"Like I said, I'm okay with the basics. Which one is Uranus?" Kieran sniggered.
Gareth looked at him, and then immediately back at his drawing.
"The interesting bit though is what lies between the two," he looked up again but this time a flash of annoyance crossed his face at Kieran's continued amusement.
He sighed, "Do grow up," he said irritably before looking back down at the napkin and drawing some further lines, "now then. This is an asteroid belt that contains millions of orbiting asteroids. Asteroids which contain millions of tons of mineable minerals."
The amusement left Kieran's face as though as switch had been flipped.
"Mineable?" he said, licking his lips.
"Theoretically," Gareth said with a simple nod.
"How theoretically are we talking?"
Gareth shrugged, "Given an appropriate base and the right technology..." he trailed off and pulled his phone out from his pocket, "Here look at this," he said and slid the phone across the table to Kieran. He picked it up and scrolled through the screen.

Kieran studied it for a few seconds before looking back to Gareth, "What am I looking at exactly?" he asked.
"An example," Gareth said, "this asteroid is thirty miles in diameter. It was charted by one of the deep space probes that NASA sent off in the eighties."
Kieran continued to scroll down the screen until he reached a table of minerals at the foot of the page. He read the contents and then looked at Gareth, his face slack with surprise.
"Are these figures accurate?" he asked.
Gareth nodded, “They are a conservative estimate, but close enough for my purposes,“ he said with a renewed cockiness.
"This says that it contains over forty tonnes of platinum," Kieran said in an awed whisper. "That's more platinum than has ever been mined on the planet Earth, ever!"
Gareth nodded again and laughed.
"So if the human race is going to survive this terrible resource depletion, then you will be the man to provide the relief?"
"There is a whole universe of possibilities out there," he said looking out of one of the windows.
"And you plan to be right at the head of the queue?" Kieran said.
Gareth shook his head, "No, not at the head of the queue," he said with a wry smile, "I'm going to be the man behind the counter serving the queue."
Kieran shook his head, "This isn't some altruistic move to save the human race, this is going all the way back to simple supply and demand, is it?"
Gareth arched his eyebrow in an unspoken warning.
"I’m not criticising!" Kieran said defensively, and then laughed loudly, "It's beautiful!"
He slumped into his chair and blew out his cheeks.

"You're going to manoeuvre yourself into a position of maximum profit whilst at the same time looking like the world's greatest ever philanthropist," he shook his head.
Gareth smiled, "You're a cynic Kieran," he said.
"Perhaps so, but I'm not wrong, am I?"
"Mars is the key though," Gareth said suddenly serious again, "if you control Mars then you control it all," he sipped at his drink again, "and I plan to control it all."

CHAPTER FOUR

Kieran was awake, but only barely. He stared blankly at the whiteness of the ceiling above him and swallowed tentatively. His tongue was dry and cracked and it had taken more effort than was strictly comfortable to remove it from the roof of his mouth. His throat was exquisitely tender and his head throbbed painfully along to the beat of his heart. The prophylactic paracetamol that he had taken the previous night along with a pint of flat cola had been, predictably insufficient for the seven hours of whisky consumption that had preceded it. Without looking, he let his arm drop over the side of the bed to where a bottle of water was sitting, warming in the morning sun. He lifted his head tentatively from the pillow and winced, painfully as he did so. He drained the bottle and let it drop back onto the floor beside his bed with a grunt of effort. He picked up his phone from his bedside table to check the time and was dismayed to see a whole list of missed calls and text messages. He scanned through them quickly and pressed the icon that would return one of the calls. The phone rang twice before being answered and Kieran was forced to hold the handset a further three inches from his ear in an attempt at self-preservation.

"Good morning Kieran! How are you this morning? I've been trying to reach you." Gareth's loud, unmistakable voice came booming through the handset.

Kieran swallowed again, but when he spoke his voice was cracked and broken.

"Morning Gareth," was all he could manage, before he had to pause.

The vibration caused by the sound of his own voice had triggered a wave of nausea that threatened to overwhelm him.

“Are you okay?” asked Gareth.

Kieran cleared his throat with a painful cough, “Yes I’m fine,” he rasped.

“Good! Now, have you had chance to think any more about what we talked about last night?” Gareth asked.

Kieran pulled the phone away from his ear and looked again at the screen. It was 9am and he had been in bed for roughly 4 hours.

“Um, no not yet,” he said, “I’ve been asleep.”

“Hmm,” Gareth sounded disappointed, “I’m going to come and get you okay? I want you to meet someone.”

Kieran’s nausea briefly gave way to panic.

“What? Now?” he sat upright in his bed, adrenaline providing him with sudden energy.

“Sure, why not? Give me an hour or so, I’ve got some things to clear up here first and then I’ll come straight over and pick you up.”

“An hour?” sweat instantly prickled on Kieran’s face and neck.

“I suppose I could put these things off and make it sooner if…”

“No!" Kieran said, agitatedly, "No, that will be fine. Finish what you're doing and I’ll see you in an hour.”

“Okay then," Gareth said, "by the way is your passport up to date?”

“Um, yes of course it is. Why do you ask?”

“Hmm? Oh well, you know how it is? You might need it over the next few days. Bye for now.”

With that, Gareth hung up and Kieran dropped the phone down onto the pillow. He desperately wanted to go to sleep again. His mind was fogged, his head was hurting and his mouth tasted sour from the memory of old alcohol. He knew though, that if he lay back down he would stay there for far longer than the 10 minutes or so that the unfolding situation

allowed him. Instead, he reluctantly swung his legs over the side of the bed and forced himself to stand up.
“Oh fuck!” he said to himself with a grimace of discomfort.
"Come on pull yourself together Kieran!" He shook his head and instantly wished that he hadn't.
"First things first," he said out loud, "toilet, shower and coffee.” Without further pause, he headed into the bathroom, deliberately avoiding his reflection as he went.
Sixty-three minutes later he was fully dressed and standing on the balcony terrace of his apartment looking out over the cityscape. His nausea had thankfully abated, albeit slightly, and he had three large, strong coffees coursing confidently through his veins now. He had also partaken of a poppy seed bagel, that he found in the freezer and half a tub of full fat cream cheese. Kill or cure he thought to himself and, perhaps unwisely, burped softly.
He was contemplating a fourth cup of coffee when he saw a big black limousine pull into the courtyard far below. He sighed and headed for the door, grabbing his keys, wallet and jacket as he went. As he reached the door he paused and headed for his office to retrieve his passport from the desk drawer. If Gareth was asking about passports it made sense to be prepared. As he headed back to the door his phone began to vibrate in his jacket pocket; it was Gareth again,
“Where are you?” he sounded irritated.
“I’m on my way down. I’ll be two minutes, Jeez!”
“I said an hour didn't I?”
Kieran hung up, there was no point continuing the conversation. Gareth would make a bigger deal of this the longer he argued with him so he took the easy option and decided to avoid it.

When he got out of the building, Gareth was standing by the door of the car talking on his phone. He waved as Kieran approached, his ire apparently already forgotten.
“No, we’re coming out this evening; I want him to see it with his own eyes. No, no, I have no idea! Talk to Jacob about it. Right, I’ve got to go, bye.”
Gareth hung up the phone and offered Kieran his hand, which Kieran took and shook as firmly as his protesting body would allow.
"You look like Hell," he said, conversationally.
"Thanks," Kieran replied, "I was out last night with my boss."
Gareth nodded, "I wonder if he feels as bad as you look?"
Kieran looked at him, "It would appear not," he said bitterly.
“Okay, let's get started shall we?” Gareth ushered Kieran into the back seat of the limo and got in next to him.
“Here take these” he said, holding out his hand with four capsules on it. He handed him a bottle of water as well.
Kieran reached out and took the tablets; he swallowed all four at once.
“What are they?” he asked almost as an afterthought
“Anti-sickness pills and Tramadol, I figured you might need a little assistance this morning.”
Kieran felt his face redden and his forehead bead with perspiration.
“That obvious eh?”
Gareth shrugged, “Doesn’t make you any less of a man, you know?”
“What, being hungover?”
“No, asking for help when you need it. Not being able to hold your whisky does make you less of a man though," he added with a wicked grin, "in case you were wondering?”

Kieran smiled for the first time that day and relaxed a little. He sipped again from the bottle of water and tried to focus his mind.
“So where are we off to?” he asked.
Gareth beamed back at him.
"California,” he said.
“Okay…” said Kieran cautiously, “any particular reason?”
Gareth regarded him as if he were simple, but said nothing. Kieran was keen not to emphasise this opinion so decided that it was probably wise to keep his counsel for the time being at least. As the car moved slowly through the streets of Chelsea, Gareth began talking on his phone again. Kieran relaxed into the deep leather seats of the car. He considered checking his phone for messages but resisted the urge and closed his eyes instead.
The journey to London City airport managed to take the best part of an hour, although it was less than 20 miles from Kieran’s apartment. Throughout the journey Gareth talked continually on the phone whilst Kieran tried to get some extra minutes of precious sleep.
Kieran had flown on board Gareth’s private jet before and was experienced enough not to look too overwhelmed when they pulled up alongside the aircraft.
There was no denying that the Gulfstream 650 was a magnificent looking plane though. It shimmered majestically in the bright morning sunshine as the ground crew bustled around it making the final exterior checks.
Kieran patted his jacket pocket, instinctively as he got out of the car to check his passport was still with him and headed straight for the staircase that led into the aircraft’s belly. Once on board he went immediately to the simmering coffee pot to pour himself a cup. Gareth followed a few minutes later, still

talking on his phone, but now in fluent Japanese. During a moment of clarity the night before Kieran had apparently cancelled all of his morning meetings when it became apparent that Gareth was intent on drinking well into the night. He picked his phone out of his pocket and considered the blank screen for a moment before reluctantly deciding that he should probably check his messages before they took off. He was not surprised to see that he had a dozen or so missed calls, as well as five or six text messages. He mentally ranked them in order of importance, and spent the next twenty minutes tying up the immediate loose ends. Satisfied, that he had at least covered the bare minimum, he then settled back into one of the supremely comfortable seats and looked out of the window at the grey tarmac beyond. The sky had clouded over and the first spots of rain were beginning to fall. Once again he closed his eyes and breathed deeply. It was a long flight to California, but at least the weather was almost guaranteed to be an improvement upon this. The sunshine was undoubtedly waiting for him at the end of the flight, but he wasn't entirely sure what else was.

CHAPTER FIVE

CALIFORNIA, USA. AUGUST 2017

The flight was uneventful, but each passing mile marked a further emergence from the fog of Kieran's hangover. As the plane began its final descent it quickly became apparent that they were not landing at a commercial air field. His curiosity piqued, Kieran turned to Gareth.

“Where are we?" he asked, "I assumed we’d be going to LAX or San Diego?”

Gareth turned to face Kieran, a huge boyish grin spread over his face.

“This is what I wanted to show you. Welcome to my newest acquisition.”

Kieran whistled and nodded his head.

“Impressive,” he said, “but where are we?”

“We are currently coming in to land at what used to be Vandenberg Military base, which up until nine months ago was one of NASA’s last remaining satellite launch sites.”

Kieran looked at his companion and smiled. He had to admit that Gareth still had the ability to surprise him.

“Used to be? What is it now?”

Gareth grin somehow managed to get even wider.

“It’s mine!” he said.

“Wow,” was the only response that Kieran could think of, but whilst perhaps unoriginal it seemed to him to be appropriate in the circumstances.

“Finally we have an appropriate headquarters for Project Livingstone. Ninety-eight thousand acres, with thirty-five miles of uninterrupted coastline,” Gareth said proudly, “and what’s more, the infrastructure is all in place. Don't get me wrong, it’s

going to need substantial redevelopment but… it's perfect," Gareth said, dreamily.
After a few moments of silence he turned away from the window and focused his smile back onto Kieran," Well? What do you think?"
Kieran breathed slowly and turned to look again out of his window. The immediate view was not overly inspiring. All that he could see was a collection of concrete buildings, tarmac and forest. He shrugged, noncommittally.
"It's kind of hard to tell from up here," he said, "if it's okay with you I'll reserve judgement until we've at least landed?"
Gareth reddened slightly.
"Yes, of course, sorry I was getting a little ahead of myself," he swivelled his chair so that it faced the cockpit again.
Kieran was unsure what to think. Project Livingston was a big deal, and had been so for several years now. However, after the initial teething problems, Kieran had had very little, if anything to do with it. The day to day business of running a business was where his day to day lay. Because of this, he had to admit, he hadn't really taken the time to fully consider the size or momentum that the project had gathered whilst he had had his attention elsewhere. He had taken Gareth's impassioned lecture of the previous evening with a healthy pinch of salt, but the evidence set before him now, made him reconsider his whisky-fuelled scepticism of the night before. This was why he had seen precious little of Gareth for so long. He had wondered if he was in danger of loosing his competitive edge, or getting distracted from the bread and butter of his business by some impossible side fantasy. He now realised that this wasn't a distraction to his main business. This was now Gareths main business and it was everything else that was the distraction.

He looked out of the window at the approaching runway and shook his head again. There was no doubt that seeing this massive facility rapidly expanding beneath him had suddenly made Gareth's side fantasy seem an awful lot more tangible. The logistics of what Gareth had taken on were certainly mind-boggling and Kieran suspected that this aspect of the project was one that he would soon become intimately acquainted with.

Once they had landed they were greeted by a pair of large American security guards with large attack dogs and even larger machine guns.They led them into a small prefabricated cabin at the side of the runway. A large coffee pot simmered, half full, on top of the room's only work surface, appearing a little incongruous next to a hefty bank of security monitors displaying a least a dozen different views of the immediate surroundings. The heat was intense and despite the twelve hours in the air, Kieran's hangover was threatening a third or fourth wind. He moved, instinctively, towards the coffee pot.

"Can I get a cup of that coffee please?" he asked the guard, who nodded and gestured over to a collection of mostly clean white ceramic mugs.

"Help yourself, sir" he said, "It's not the greatest but it's hot and strong."

Kieran poured a large measure, and inhaled deeply of the fumes before taking a tentative sip, his face creased slightly at the bitterness.

"I've had worse," he raised his mug to the smiling guard, "cheers though," he took a bigger gulp this time and then took a cleansing breath.

Gareth checked his phone and then looked impatiently out of the only window. In the distance he could see a dust trail that

indicated that their next mode of transport was on its way to meet them.
A large, black Range Rover pulled up outside the hut and a tall, well dressed, dark-haired man emerged from the driver's seat. He wore large Aviator style sunglasses and a serious expression. Gareth walked over to him, his hand held out in greeting.
“Jonathon!” he said, “Great to see you! How the devil are you my friend?”
The man smiled and inclined his head towards Gareth.
“I'm good thank-you sir. I trust you had a pleasant flight?”
Gareth lifted his eyes in frustration, “How many times? It's Gareth not sir.”
"Force of habit," he laughed, “how was your flight Gareth?”
Gareth smiled, “Excellent thank-you. A little bit of lumpy air mid-Atlantic but nothing too bad.”
Jon gestured towards the car, “Shall we then? We have an awful lot to get through. That is, if you're okay to get straight on with things?”
Gareth nodded, “Of course.”
He began to head towards the car before stopping suddenly, “What am I thinking? Kieran?” he called back into the office.
Kieran was still by the coffee machine, staring blankly at the bank of monitors. He shook his heads and walked towards the door where he stopped suddenly.
“Kieran, this is one of the people that I wanted you to meet,” he turned his head towards Jon whose smile had already faded.
“Kieran Sanderson, may I introduce you to Dr Jonathon Daniels?” Kieran didn't move.
Undeterred Gareth continued, “And Jon, this is Kieran, one of my top…”

"I know who he is," interrupted Kieran, his face set like granite.
Gareth's face wrinkled in confusion, "I beg your pardon?"
"I said, I know who he is. We've met before."
"What?" Gareth said somewhat incredulously.
"We were at university together, weren't we Jon?"
Jon nodded but remained silent.
Gareth clapped his hands together in glee, "That's fantastic! Two of my best men already have a history. Seriously what are the chances?"
Kieran and Jon stood regarding each other, poker faced and still. Finally Jon stepped forward and put his hand out towards Kieran who reluctantly accepted it and shook it, perfunctorily.
"Good to see you Kieran! How are you? Wow, it's been years eh?"
Kieran glared at Jon but said nothing.
Gareth glanced from one to the other, his smile fixed but edged with concern.
Jon turned back towards the car and began to get into the driver's seat.
"Shall we then?"
Gareth opened the rear door for Kieran and then walked around the car to the passenger side. Kieran stood, perfectly still, for a few more seconds before moving towards the car. He slid onto the soft leather seat and pulled his door closed. When he looked up he saw Jon looking at him in the rear view mirror, impassively. A tiny smile just touched the corners of his lips. Kieran returned the look and tried to conceal an old unhappiness that was suddenly reawakening after fifteen years of quiet slumber. He swallowed hard and did his best to remain outwardly calm.
The journey from the landing strip to the main base was only a few miles and took less than five minutes to cover. However,

the awkward atmosphere that had engulfed the car and its occupants meant that everyone was desperate to get out only a few seconds into the trip. Gareth, apparently immune to such mundane problems as social uncomfortableness, chatted happily throughout the journey, seemingly oblivious or uninterested in the tension that surrounded him on every side. When the car pulled into the underground garage Ben was waiting for them by the elevator. Jon got out first and walked round the car with the intention of opening Gareth's door. Gareth, however, was already heading for Ben, his arm raised and a huge smile on his face.

"Ben! How are you?" They shook hands and Ben patted Gareth's shoulder heavily.

"Busy," Ben said, "there's one hell of lot to do here."

Gareth nodded and then turned back to the car, where Kieran was slowly climbing out of the back seat. He looked around the parking garage and was surprised to see so many vehicles filling the spaces.

Jon walked straight past both Gareth and Ben and over towards a bank of three elevators. He offered a small, but friendly nod towards Ben as he went but he didn't break his stride. Kieran followed his walk with his eyes before making his way cautiously over to the other two men. As he approached, Gareth turned and placed his hand upon his shoulder, steering him gently towards Ben.

"Ben," he said brightly, "I would like you to meet Kieran, he's your new boss."

Both Ben and Kieran raised their eyebrows in surprise,

"My new boss?" said Ben.

"Well, not just your new boss," Gareth laughed, "he's here to take over the running of this whole facility. So I guess he's everyones new boss!"

Over in the elevator Jon's head bowed ever so slightly. He removed his sunglasses, folded them into his jacket pocket and swore, almost silently under his breath. Meanwhile Ben grasped Kieran's hand and shook it with more force than was strictly necessary.

"Good to meet you Kieran." he said enthusiastically, but he smiled a smile that didn't extend as far as his eyes.

"And you Ben," Kieran replied.

He turned to Gareth and asked him a question with his eyes. Gareth looked back at him with an innocent grin. He then turned back to Ben and leant in to him conspiratorially.

"I hadn't told him either," he stage-whispered to him, nodding towards Kieran.

Ben looked first at Gareth and then at Kieran. His expression remained unreadable. Then, without warning, he then threw his head had back and laughed loud and long. If a Grizzly bear had either the ability or inclination to laugh, it would sound like Ben, of that Kieran was sure. He took half a step back towards the car before he was intercepted by Ben who once again took hold of his hand and crushed it in a way that Kieran supposed was meant to be friendly.

"Hell, I guess congratulations are in order then," he bellowed, and then more quietly, "although you might want to hold off on the champagne until you've seen what's in store for you," he winked at Kieran and then headed off to join a deflated Jon in the elevator.

Gareth went to move off as well but Kieran caught his arm and pulled him away

"Seriously?" he hissed at him.

Gareth looked slightly bewildered. "What?"

"What the actual fuck Gareth? You can't do this to me...Jesus; you can't do this to anyone. What the fuck were you thinking?"

“It was meant to be a surprise.”
“Well, it’s certainly a fucking surprise!” Kieran shouted.
His words echoed around the concrete garage and every other occupant of the garage, determinedly did not look over. ”We have just spent the best part of twelve hours together on a plane. Did it not occur to you at any time that this might be something that you might want to discuss with me first?”
Gareth shrugged, “But you might have said no,”
“I still might say no,” he said loudly and shook his head, ”you have flown me half way around the fucking planet without letting me pick up so much as my toothbrush. And then you tell me that this is my new home without any warning? Who does that? What is wrong with you?” Kieran shook his head again.
Gareth looked at Kieran, his expression unreadable.
Kieran hadn't finished though, “I know you’re not a fucking idiot Gareth, so what on Earth possessed you to make such demented call?”
Gareth said nothing. Much to Kieran’s annoyance he was now smiling, happily to himself.
"You are fucking unbelievable, you know that, right?" Kieran said.
"I..." Gareth began, but Kieran held up his hand and he immediately fell silent.
"Don't say a fucking word," Kieran fumed, "not a fucking one!" He stormed past Gareth without looking at him again and straight into the open elevator. Both Ben and Jon were uncomfortably looking at the floor. Clearly neither of them were certain how to react. Gareth joined them and pressed a button marked with a “B” The doors closed and the elevator began its descent.

*   *   *

The four men travelled in silence. A small triumphant smile played across Gareth's face, but he tried his best to hide it. This was exactly as he had expected things were going to unfold. Ben and Jon were experts in their fields. Both had a military background and were used to following orders, but Gareth knew that bringing in a civilian as the 'big boss' would be hard for either of them to accept. They had to respect their superior, and that respect had to be earned. Gareth needed the three of them to be able to work together effectively from the outset, he had no time for a long initiation period.

He also knew Kieran was tired, disorientated and vulnerable. He was aware of Kieran and Jon's shared time together at university, and guessed that Jon had probably lorded it over Kieran given all that he knew about their respective backgrounds.

With these ingredients already in place Gareth knew that Kieran would explode at him for his deceit, he had no doubt about that whatsoever. Kieran liked to work with as much information as he could gather. He took risks but they were always calculated ones. Being plunged into an alien environment with no chance to pre-plan represented his nightmare scenario and Gareth knew that he would respond with passion and vigour.

Nobody had ever spoken to Gareth the way that Kieran had just done. Nobody had even been rumoured to have spoken to Gareth that way.

Nobody.

Ever.

Gareth was respected and feared in almost equal measure by all that knew him or worked for him. When he issued an order it was never questioned, it was simply carried out. He was fair, but he was also brutal. The fact that Kieran had just yelled at Gareth with no apparent concern or consequence, immediately communicated everything that the other two men needed to know about the man and his position. There was one more step to bring the others in line. Gareth swallowed his smile and turned his head to Kieran.

"I'm sorry Kieran," he said, the corners of his mouth twitching uncertainly.

Kieran looked at him and sighed.

"Fuck off!" Kieran said but allowed a small smile to touch his lips as well, "This is going to cost you, you know that don't you?"

Gareth shrugged, "Everything costs something," he said.

Ben and Jon looked at each other and then back at the floor, both willing the elevator to hurry up, reach the Basement and let them all out.

CHAPTER SIX

LONDON, ENGLAND. OCTOBER 2017

More than three years had passed since the accident that had robbed Cam of his wife and daughter. Three years of inquests, police investigations and three years of seemingly bottomless grief. The driver of the van had never been found and after what the police deemed to be an appropriate amount of time, the investigation had been quietly closed. Leaving Cam to attempt to reconstruct his life from the tattered, hopeless shreds that remained. Initially he hadn't been able to sleep for more than a few hours a night, the endless nightmares haunting him. As a consequence he had dabbled with drugs, alcohol and all the combinations in-between.

Sleep, was a double edged sword and as time slowly moved to dull the blade of immediacy, so it also brought with it the ghosts of that terrible time. The feelings, the thoughts and the helplessness all replayed in his head while he lay helplessly in his bed, trapped and held hostage to the mercurial appetites of his sleeping mind.

One dream visited him more than any other though, a dream of such perfect clarity and depth that with each replay he awoke with a familiar pain that seared him exquisitely anew like a freshly inflicted wound every night. It was a dream that Cam had endured a hundred times, perhaps even a thousand, but it rarely changed, at least, not in any meaningful way.

It always started in the same place;

He found himself back in the hospital of the evening after the accident, Karen was still in theatre and he had had the unenviable task of going to identify Martha's body. When he had made the journey in real life, he was certain that there had been someone with him, a nurse or doctor perhaps. But in his dream he was always alone as he walked through the endless corridors and down the echoing stairwells. Finally, he reached the mortuary itself. The doorway was black and cold. He stood outside the room, frozen with fear. His sharp, icy breath caught in his throat as he tried to breathe. He stared, unblinking at the painted wooden door for an indeterminate time that could have been seconds or hours. Waiting to move forwards. Occasionally, he wouldn't get any further than this doorway and then he would wake, nauseous and afraid. He preferred those times, but they were rare and tonight's visit was not to be one of them.

Somehow, he managed to summon up the courage to push the door open and timidly he stepped inside. Even now, with the luxury of time passed, he always carried with him the finest vestiges of hope as he made his way into the gloom of the room beyond. Hoping that somehow there had been some sort of ghastly mistake, some tiny chance that it was all simply a terrible case of mistaken identity and that this time, *this time* things would play out differently. This forlorn hope, however fragile had kept him on his feet on his journey through the hospital, and had clutched tightly to his clammy hand as he walked further into the room. It burned in his chest like the glowing embers of a dying fire and kept him breathing.

Hope can be a great comforter in the darkest moments of despair; it can provide a safety rail to guard against the precipice below. However, should that hope fail, then the consequences are magnified, the subsequent fall then becomes infinitely more shocking, more painful and more difficult to accept.

The room had an indelible odour of chemicals and despair, it was dimly lit and Cam's footsteps echoed loudly around the walls as he tentatively approached the mortuary slab. The room swam in and out of focus and he had to clutch a nearby table top in grim determination in order to prevent himself from falling to his knees.

He had looked at the tiny contoured sheet that lay upon the table top and had known instantly, merely by the shape and form of the gentle curves that his hope had been terribly and agonisingly misplaced. It evaporated into the air like an early mist on a hot summer's day.

As the sheet was pulled away from Martha's body, the pain that Cam had been trying to keep subdued, crashed forward and very nearly overwhelmed him completely. He released a low guttural, primeval cry of pain and instinctively turned his face away in disgust. He stood like that, his breathing tight and fast, for a few seconds staring, randomly at an open medical book that had been placed carefully on a table top on the other side of the room. Somehow, he had managed to blink back his tears and he forced himself to look back at the tiny figure lying before him. His beautiful Martha lay in a grim parody of life, broken and covered with dark, blue and purple bruising. The side of her head had been cleaned but there was evidence still of the impact site. Her face however was astoundingly peaceful and unmarked. All of the life that had once made her so very beautiful had gone though, cruelly replaced by a grotesque facsimile of his daughters features.

Perfectly formed but grey and mockingly empty. He reached out, took hold of her tiny hand and lifted it to his face where he breathed in her skin and kissed it gently. He ran her cold fingertips across his cheek and then gently placed it back upon her motionless chest.

The cold touch of her fingers burned his cheek like red-hot pokers.

He turned back to the assistant and she replaced the sheet, before walking silently from the room, leaving Cam alone in the darkness. He closed his eyes and felt a touch on his shoulder, without looking he knew that it was Karen, come to comfort him. Come to take away his pain. He lifted his own hand and placed it gently over his wife's.

"What are we going to do without her?" he sobbed quietly

"You will have to be strong my darling," Karen said gently and kissed his ear.

Cam shuddered at the touch. Karen was stronger than he was. Together they would get through this.

"I love you," she whispered and then she too was gone.

Karen had died on the operating table while he visited the morgue. In the space of less than twenty-four hours he had lost the only two people he had ever really loved, and his subconscious mind tortured him by replaying this moment over and over in his head.

He awoke in his room and stared up at the ceiling. It was three o'clock in the morning. He knew this without having to check. It was always three o'clock in the morning when he had this dream. Time had performed a manner of healing and he no longer awoke in tears, at least not every time. He raised his hand to his cheek where he could still feel the faint burn of Martha's fingers and the phantom kiss of his wife.

He moved his hand to the shoulder where Karen had touched him and sighed. He breathed deeply through his nose as he tried to cherish the lingering memory of his wife's scent, the whisper of her ghostly voice and of the remembered warmth of her gentle touch. He allowed himself this stolen moment of indulgence before he smiled, sadly, to himself and then rolled over in his bed. He looked at the alarm clock. It was eight minutes past six, he smiled at the predictability of this and then shut his eyes again to let sleep take him once more. It took a few seconds for the anomaly to register in his sleep-fogged brain, when it finally did click, his eyes snapped open.

"Six o'clock," he said, alarmed.

He blinked the blurriness from his eyes and looked once more at the display.

"Fuck!"

He swung his legs from the bed and onto the cold tile floor of his hotel bedroom.

Cam had overslept for the first time in over three years, a faint feeling of panic gently bubbled up in his stomach and he rubbed his hand, vigorously over his face. He screwed his eyes tightly shut and shook his head. When he reopened them, nothing had changed, except now he had a headache. The taxi to take him to the airport was due to collect him at six-thirty.

Plenty of time, he thought to himself. If he had a cursory shower then he would have time to grab some toast and coffee on the way out of the hotel. He rose from the bed and headed straight into the en-suite. On the other hand, if he forwent the shower completely he would probably have time for a cheeky bacon sandwich. He considered his options for a moment longer, but a tentative sniff of his underarms helped him make his decision.

"Bollocks!" he said to himself and turned the shower on to full power. He removed his underwear, tested the water's temperature with a tentative hand and then ducked around the shower curtain and into the hot water. He would have to make do with an airport breakfast he thought gloomily to himself, as he lathered his hair with the tiny bottle of complimentary shampoo.

And then he remembered.

Gareth had booked these tickets, he had insisted in fact. He was flying first class and flying first class meant access to a first class lounge, which in turn meant all manner of complimentary goodies would be at his disposal.

In a heartbeat, his mood improved immeasurably. He started to whistle to himself and, as he washed away the suds from the shampoo, he could feel the remnants of the nightmare rinsing away as well.

Gareth had been a constant for him in the last three years. He had given him the time and space that he needed after the accident. He had remained in close contact and, when the time was right, he had also arranged the counselling and therapy that had helped him to get his life back into some semblance of order.

It was almost exactly three years and finally he felt as though he was ready to move on. He would never forget, nor would he want to. The scars that he carried with him would always be visible, to those that chose to look for them. However, despite everything that he had gone through, he had emerged a stronger man on the other side. Diminished, certainly but undeniably tougher. Most importantly though, he knew how to cope with the grief now, how to function again as a human being.

The scalding hot water was beginning to steam his skin lobster-red. He cut the shower off and grabbed a towel from the heated rail. He rubbed at his hair and then walked back into his room where he grabbed his clothes from the bed and checked the time on his phone: 6.27. He quickly dressed and crammed his few possessions into his carry-on case. The rest of his luggage had been sent ahead, so he was travelling light.

As he headed outside, the morning drizzle misted over the carpark, his taxi was waiting and he waved a good morning.

This was his last day in Britain for a while, perhaps ever. This time tomorrow he would be in San Francisco where he was due to spend a month visiting with his brother and his husband. After that, he was going to head over to California to finally take up the role that Gareth had offered him a lifetime ago. As chief designer and senior officer within project Livingstone.

He settled into his seat and grinned.

"You all right mate?" The driver asked.

"Never better," Cam replied, "never better."

CHAPTER SEVEN

NOVEMBER 2017

By the time Cam was due to arrive at the Californian base, he was desperate to get going. Not only was he going to be pushing his mind in ways that it hadn't been for years, he was also due to undergo a bout of physical training that would eventually see him able to take his place alongside the rest of the proposed colony personnel.

The foundations for Project Livingstone were quickly beginning to take shape. And as autumn moved into winter and then into spring the Californian facility finally began to resemble a functional and viable endeavour. With little or no budget constraints, staffing levels on the base had risen as quickly as they were compelled to, and before long the place was a constant hive of activity. Kieran's initial core team of thirty had expanded at a pace and within only six months the number of employees was closer to two thousand. Contractors and specialists arrived almost daily along with physicists, engineers and military personnel. It was at times a logistical nightmare, but there was also a tangible feeling of excitement and expectation throughout the whole staff as the project began to take shape and blossom.

Despite his initial misgivings, Kieran was in his element. Gareth may have had an unorthodox way of introducing him into this environment, but he had been dead right about his suitability for the role. He tried hard to create a working atmosphere that encouraged creativity and unorthodoxy but still maintained high levels of professionalism and personal accountability. At least that was the official line. In truth, he managed the way he always had, by letting people get on with the job that they had been paid to do. The whole project was filled with experts. In his opinion, the last thing any of them needed was some city-boy telling how to calibrate their rocket science. Consequently he didn't interfere unless he had to, which was rarely. This trust was rewarded with diligence, effort and a willingness to work the long hours that were necessary. This ability to avoid micro-micro-management, meant he was able to employ his analytical and structured approach to the considerable logistics of the project.

His reputation made his life easier. His managers all had an easy rapport with him but there was no mistaking who was in charge.

Jon was one of the first recruits and had been on the books for almost two years. He was an officer but he ceded medical lead to doctor Torres. She was to be the chief medical officer on both the Nerine 1 and the fledgling colony.

Jon's primary role was concerned with the staff's mental health, which included, but was not limited to, the application of the crew's psychometric testing. Jon started his career as a physician but over time he had progressed to specialise in psychotherapy and psychiatry as part of his extended roll within the Air Force. He had, primarily worked with personnel that were suffering with clinical depression, some form of post-traumatic stress disorder or often a combination of the two. He had, however, also encountered a long and varied collection of personality disorders: neurosis, psychosis and delusions that ranged from the fairly sedate and run of the mill to the dangerous and violently deranged.

This was the reason for his early recruitment. He compiled the team that assessed the suitability of any and all potential colonists before they even set foot onto the training facility, never mind an actual space craft. As a high ranking officer and core member of the colonies crew, he was also charged with watching for any potential danger signs from within the established colony when they reached Mars.

Jon reported directly to Gareth, but in his constant absence, the chain of command, unfortunately for Jon led to Kieran. The initial surprise at seeing an old university colleague had knocked his equilibrium for a good few weeks after they had met. Kieran didn't like him, he had made that abundantly clear, but Jon couldn't really blame him. Jon was from a wealthy, upper class family and Kieran wasn't. At university these things seemed to matter and Jon had been pretty unpleasant. It made him shudder, uncomfortably when he remembered how he once behaved. He had never been terrible, just obnoxious and supercilious. He could well imagine that anyone that had encountered him at that period in his life would not be in a hurry to do so again. Kieran had not mentioned anything to him, specifically, but he saw how he looked at him when he thought no-one was around. However, he saw no value in trying to pour oil on troubled waters, so he let things be.

Kieran had been away for ten days or so, visiting investors and talking to some potential colony recruits. Jon headed for his office to see how the recruitment had gone and to file his latest progress report.

He spotted him as he was en-route and made a b-line for him.

"Hey Kieran," he called from across the room.

Kieran looked up, he saw Jon and his expression instantly darkened, "Doctor," he said curtly.

"Have you got a moment?" Jon asked. "I've got these reports for you to go through."

Kieran sighed and turned to face Jon, but Jon was now organising the files he was carrying.

"Everyone else on this base, manages to be paperless," Kieran said, snippily.
"Yeah well, I'm a dinosaur I guess," Jon said, still looking down.
"We can agree on that," Kieran muttered.
Kieran tapped his foot, impatiently as Jon continued to sort out his paperwork.
"Was there something specific?"
"Yeah," Jon replied, "give me a second here."
He pulled one of the folders out from the stack and placed it triumphantly on the top.
"Ah, ha!" He said
"Well?" Kieran said
"It's about Captain Harrison…" Jon trailed off. He had looked up at Kieran for the first time. His eyes widened in shock.
"What?" Kieran snapped irritably.
"Jesus Christ Kieran, what happened to you?"
Kieran, instinctively put his hand to his face.
"What?" He said, anxiously. "What is it?"
"You look like shit," Jon said, his eyes still like saucers.
Kieran nodded, "Ah well, thanks for that. That's terribly kind of you to say so."
Kieran turned to leave. Jon grabbed hold of his arm.
"No," Jon said. "You look like actual death. I'm serious, how are you even on your feet?"
"I've been a bit run down I suppose," he conceded.
"It doesn't look like you *are* run down, it looks like you've *been* run down!"
Kieran's face flushed with anger, but only briefly. He was almost grey and his forehead and face were beaded with sweat. Despite being stationary, he was breathing heavily and his body was slumped and painful looking. Jon swung him

around by his elbow until they were face to face. Kieran flinched at the sudden movement, but didn't resist. Jon looked into his eyes which were bloodshot, the whites tinged with yellow. The skin beneath them dark grey and loose.
“I’m getting you to the medical bay now,” Jon said and picked his phone out of his pocket. He pressed two buttons and lifted it to his ear,
“Hi Becky? It’s Jon. Can you send someone down to corridor B, on the way to the main conference room? I need a trolley or a chair. Kieran’s not well,” he paused as he listened.
”Yeah, bring an oxygen cylinder as well,” another pause, "no, I don’t know, but can you see if Sophie’s free as well? She's got more experience with this than me. Yeah, okay, see you soon.”
Jon grabbed a passer by.
"Excuse me Miss? Can you do me a favour will you and grab me a chair out of one of those offices, please?"
The young woman took one look at Kieran and then hurried off to the nearest open door.
Kieran watched her go, opened his mouth to protest, and then he collapsed onto the floor, unconscious.

* * *

When Kieran awoke he was lying on a hospital bed, in the infirmary surrounded by Jon, Becky and Sophie as well as a whole host of other medical staff. He moved his eyes around the room, however he couldn’t see anyone’s face properly as they were all wearing full surgical face masks, gloves and gowns.
He dragged his elbows painfully under his body and tried to push himself up. He was still terribly weak though and his

arms wobbled uncertainly under his weight for a few seconds before he collapsed back onto the bed.
“What’s going on?” he asked, but was surprised at the faintness of his own voice, which struggled out of his mouth in a cracked whisper
Jon’s partially obscured face moved in front of his, his brow furrowed in concern.
“It’s okay Kieran. Don't try to move. You're safe,” Jon’s evident concern was the antithesis of his words though and Kieran felt far from comforted.
“What happened?” he croaked.
“Shhh” Jon whispered as he injected a small syringe of a clear liquid into his arm.
“Ow! What’s that?” Kieran managed to ask, before drifting once again into a dreamless unconsciousness.
Jon checked his vital signs, before moving away from Kieran’s inert body. Sophie went with him, leaving Becky to remain at his side. When they were clear Jon turned to face his colleague.
“Have you got the bloods back yet?” he asked.
Sophie shook her head, her face drawn into a serious frown.
Jon continued, ”I’ve checked with the service log, and he flew back from Cape Town at the weekend, Sunday evening in fact.”
“Did he stay in South Africa for his whole trip?” Sophie asked.
Jon shrugged. “I don’t know” he said, “I don't think so. I have a feeling he was due to visit a few different countries, but I'm not entirely sure.”
Sophie sighed, “We need to keep him in isolation until we get the blood tests back.”
Jon nodded in agreement, “What are you thinking?”
Sophie said nothing.

“Do you think it’s…” he trailed off.
“Ebola?” she asked, and shrugged again, ”It is possible, I suppose, but not very likely. I very much doubt that he will have been exposed to anyone infected. Not in the type of places he would be staying.”
Jon visibly relaxed, “That’s good," he sighed.
Sophie raised her eyebrows at him, “I said it was unlikely, but nothing’s definite,” she paused for a moment. “We don't know where he went or who he interacted with. There are other possibilities as well you know?” she shook her head, “Ebola is only one of a whole myriad of nasties that it could be. Malaria, Typhoid, Marburg, Dengue the list goes on and on,” she shrugged. “There’s no point in idle speculation though until we’ve got some test results. You should know that better than anyone.”
Jon nodded.
“Is there anyone else in the base that travelled with him?” Sophie asked.
Jon nodded again and referred to his computer tablet, “He had a staff of three with him,” he said thoughtfully, “and the aircraft crew are all employees of the project.”
“They need to be isolated as well,” Sophie said seriously, “as does anyone that has come into extended contact with any of them.”
“Already on it,” Jon said and looked again at his tablet, ”the pilot and air crew are all in the old base accommodation and have been off duty since they returned. They are all single and have been confined to quarters at present. There’s no sign of any illness though, but we’ve taken blood of course,” he paused as he checked his tablet’s screen,
“Two of his staff are in some of the new accommodation; they both seem to be okay as well. One of them is married with a

three year old girl; they have all been brought in for surveillance and are in the family facility down the hall."
Sophie nodded approvingly, "And the third?" she asked.
"Kieran's PA, and he hasn't left his quarters since they got back."
Sophie's face softened, "Well that's something," she said, "will you keep me informed of any changes?"
Jon nodded, "Of course."
Sophie smiled, "Now all we can do is wait," she said quietly, "and keep our fingers crossed!"

The lab facilities on the base were small but well appointed, which meant that the test results took less than an hour to get back. When Jon headed back to the med bay he found Sophie examining the lab results on a desktop computer. Her expression carried no clues as to their details though and when she had finished reading she clicked the mouse, looked up at Jon and smiled.
"You can cancel the quarantine Jon," she said, the relief tangible in her voice.
Jon puffed out his cheeks in relief, "It's not Ebola then?"
Sophie shook her head, "I wasn't expecting it to be, to be honest. We had to be sure though."
"Absolutely. What is it then? Malaria? Dengue?"
"It looks like Malaria," Sophie said, "he'll be all right in a week or so. It's not in stage two yet, I think he's been very lucky."
Jon shook his head, "Why wasn't he taking tablets? He should have known better."
Sophie shrugged, "Why don't you ask him?" She gestured over to where a pale, but conscious Kieran lay, "He's been awake for the last half hour or so."
"Does he know yet?"

“No, you saw me; I just got the lab results this second.”
Jon grinned a wicked grin, “Can I tell him?” Sophie did not return his smile. Instead she picked up Kieran’s medical charts are began to flick through them.
“Sophie?”
She looked up at him, her eyes hard and unsmiling, “I’m not getting involved with your petty rivalries, Jon,” she said irritably. Jon blushed but said nothing.
“I know you two don't like each other,” Sophie continued, “everyone on the base has noticed you know? It’s pathetic really watching you try and score points off one another,”
“It’s not just me!” Jon said.
Sophie rolled her eyes at him, ”Just listen to yourself! ‘It’s not just me' really? You sound like a child.”
“I just…”
“Look Jon," Sophie interrupted. "You two are the senior guys on this base. Are you seriously telling me that you can’t get along? In public at least?“
“I didn't realise it was so obvious to be honest,” Jon said, meekly.
She looked up at him, and shook her head again, “Perhaps now would be a good time to bury the hatchet?”
Jon swallowed and glanced over at where Kieran was lying and nodded, “Okay,” he said quietly.
Sophie looked down at the charts again.
She turned to leave, ”This stops now Jon,” she said, "for everyones sake."
She handed Jon the chart and then walked from the room.
Jon watched her go, sighed and turned back to face Kieran again. He walked over to him and looked down at his fevered face.
“You hear any of that?” he said barely audibly.

Kieran's eyes flicked open. The whites were stained yellow from the strain his liver was undergoing and his face was beaded with sweat. He licked his lips which were dry and cracked, but still managed a smile.
"She really let you have it, didn't she?" he laughed a low, painful chuckle and then winced
Jon laughed almost despite himself, "Yeah," he said, "she's right though, isn't she?"
Kieran blinked and then nodded.
"How are you feeling?" Jon asked.
"Oh, brilliant," Kieran whispered.
"Well, you look great, if that's any consolation."
"I'm sorry Kieran," Jon said, he dropped his head.
Kieran licked his lips again. Jon poured a glass of water from a jug that stood on his bedside, he offered it to Kieran who struggled, unsuccessfully to sit up again.
"Hold on," said Jon and headed to one of the cupboards, where he found a drinking straw. He placed it into the glass and again offered it to Kieran who sipped at it gratefully.
"I know that you're never going to particularly like me," Jon said, his eyes focused on the wall behind Kieran's head, "but I really have changed. My time in the Air force gave me a different perspective on life and what with…" he swallowed hard and poured himself a glass of water which he finished in one gulp.
"Do you remember Emily from Uni?" he asked.
Kieran nodded, "Yeah," he said, "pretty girl. Was in the year below me?"
"That's her," Jon laughed hollow laugh. "She was my sister."
Kieran raised his eyebrows in surprise, "I didn't know that."
"No? Well, no one did. Too ashamed," he hung his head.
"Why were you embarrassed of Emily?"

Jon laughed, “I wasn’t,” he said, “she was though. The truth is she was embarrassed of me.”
Kieran said nothing.
“I know, I know,” said Jon, “hardly surprising really, given what a little shit I was,” he smiled wistfully, “she wasn't though. Far from it, she was a good person. Cleverer than I was and better at life than me, even then.”
Jon refilled his water glass, but this time just looked at it. He swilled the contents around and drifted away, briefly, into his own thoughts. Kieran looked at Jon’s face and could see him suffering. He opened his mouth to speak but Jon cut over him before he got a chance to say anything.
“She died the year after she graduated,” his eyes became suddenly glassy with emotion. "stupid really. She was out with her friends on a night out, she had got a bit drunk and got into a taxi for the journey home,” he swallowed and sipped his water, “the taxi driver lost control of the car, went across the traffic and hit a bus head on. She was killed instantly, just like that,” he snapped his fingers, “the driver had a heart attack apparently. He was dead before they even hit the bus.”
"Jesus that's terrible," Kieran croaked.
Jon nodded
“I’m so sorry,” Kieran said.
Jon shrugged, ”Yeah, yeah…” he sighed again, ”anyway, after the funeral, I joined the Air force. I didn't want to stay around London, too many memories. I had to get away, I didn't really care where.”
Jon pulled over a chair and sat down next to Kieran’s bed. Kieran turned his head so he could still look at him.
“Changed my life," Jon said, "and I know that I can’t change what I did or who I was at Oxford. And I really am genuinely

sorry Kieran, truly, but I can't spend the rest of my life apologising for things I did when I was a kid!"
Kieran turned his head back so he was facing the ceiling again. He closed his eyes and took a deep breath, then winced in pain again. Jon offered him more water and he took another sip through the straw
"It's okay," said Kieran
Jon blinked, "Really?" he said
Kieran nodded, "Yeah. I knew that I was being stupid, but seeing you again after all these years made me feel so..." he paused as he searched for the right words, "...so vulnerable, so insecure. I felt like a scared 18 year old again. An 18 year old that was convinced that he was out of his depth, in a place that he didn't belong," he shook his head unhappily, " and I hated you for that Jon," he closed his eyes again, a tear escaped and rolled down his cheek.
"I didn't realise," Jon whispered.
"Yeah well, it doesn't matter now, and I'm really sorry about your sister,"
"Thanks."
Kieran stared off into space, "I had no idea that Emily Daniels was your sister," he said finally.
Jon shot him a sideways glance, "Yeah," he whispered.
"You know that she dated Dan Goodwillie while she was at Oxford?"
Jon nodded, "Erm, yeah I think so, I didn't know that you knew him?"
"Friend of a friend," Kieran said.
"Okay," Jon said, quietly.
"Same friend of a friend that went to their wedding, about 5,6 years ago?"
Jon looked at Kieran.

"You made that whole story up, didn't you?"
Jon nodded, sheepishly.
"What the hell Jon?" Kieran said angrily, "Why would you do that? What kind of person kills off their own sister?"
"I wanted you to like me," Jon said, weakly.
"So you killed your sister?"
"I thought if you felt sorry for me then you'd get over it all."
"You're unbelievable!" Kieran said, "You haven't changed a bit!"
Jon reeled, "I have," he said, defensively, "I just thought you'd like a good old story of misfortune and heroic response."
Jon grinned at Kieran who's expression had soured, significantly, "Besides you're on so many painkillers and drugs, by this time tomorrow, I'll just deny it and blame it on your 'fevered mind!'"
Kieran stared at Jon and shrugged. Then after a few more seconds, he smiled. Jon's grin cracked into a laugh and soon the two of them had dissolved into fits of giggles.
Sophie walked back into the room, carrying more medical records.
“Have you two kissed and made up then?” she asked brightly without looking up.
She stopped in her tracks as she noticed the two of them side by side, giggling like school boys. Silently she rolled her eyes, then without saying another word she awkwardly backed out of the room and closed the door behind her.
Over on the one of the counter-tops, Kieran’s mobile phone began to ring; Jon rose to his feet and went to fetch it, he went to hand it to Kieran, but looked at the screen before he did so “It’s Gareth,” he said.
Kieran took the phone from Jon, "Thanks," he said.

“Do you want me to go?” Jon asked and began to stand up from his chair.
Kieran shook his head, “No it’s okay,” he said and then touched the screen to connect the call.
"Hi! How are you?” he said and then he listened for a few seconds, “No I’m okay, its Malaria apparently?” he looked at Jon who nodded at him, “No, no, I’ll be back on my feet again in a few days, I’m getting excellent care here, Jon and Sophie have been brilliant,” he listened again as Gareth spoke, “yes, you were right,” he said and looked at Jon meaningfully, “no, okay then. Yeah I’ll see you then. Bye,” he hung up and turned back to face Jon.
“What was that about?” he asked before adding, “I’m sorry, none of my business,”
“He’s coming in tomorrow with another band of potential recruits.” Kieran said
“Okay,” Jon said, "I thought that was going to be on Monday?"
"Moved forward, apparently."
"Did he say how many?"
"Don't you have all of their files?"
"Yeah, but it could be one of them or twenty. There's no certainties with Gareth."
“Yeah,” said Kieran, “tell me about it."
"Did he give you any names?" Jon asked
"Not exactly, but he did say that the new chief engineer is amongst them. This Cam bloke, you know anything about him?”
Jon shrugged, ”A bit I suppose; he's been attached for a while now. Confidential stuff though, I can’t really say anything. Wouldn't be very professional of me.”
Kieran nodded, “Anything off the record?”

Jon hesitated, “I’ve read his psych profile and I don't think he’ll be with us for very long.”
“Really?”
“Yeah, really, I'd even go as far as to say that there’s probably not much point in getting too friendly with him. I know I won’t!” Jon lifted his hand to the side of his head and mimed a “crazy” sign.
"That's your professional opinion is it Dr Daniels?" Kieran asked.
Jon blushed, "No, of course not. But he's had a tough life,"
"His sister wasn't killed in a car crash was she?" Kieran laughed.
"No," Jon said, suddenly serious, "but his wife and child were."
Kieran laughed, "Yeah, right!"
Jon blushed again, "No seriously. You didn't hear it from me though, okay?"
Kieran's smile vanished, "Shit," he said,
"Yeah, shit is right."
"No wonder he's a bit fucked up then?"
"I know. Apparently he's over it now though and everything is rosy in his mental garden again,"
"Do you believe that?" Kieran asked.
“No not for a second, you mark my words though,” Jon said, “he’ll be gone within a week.”

CHAPTER EIGHT

PERSONAL JOURNAL OF CAPTAIN CAMERON HARRISON:

Monday:
The way things have started here, I think that I'll be lucky to last a week.
My therapist said that a journal might help me to keep focussed and perhaps keep me away from any dark thoughts.
I am prone to dark thoughts apparently. I can't imagine why?
I have my doubts about this, but she has been right before about this sort of thing I suppose.
I've been asked to watch my language as well; apparently some people find my turn of phrase objectionable. I've no fucking idea why, but if I'm going to commit, I suppose I should try and behave as well.
So here I go!
I suppose if I had to characterise my feelings about this whole thing, I would say that the most generous response I could give would be that of cynical optimism. However I'm going to roll my metaphorical sleeves up and I'm going to give it a go.
See I can be positive!
Basic training begins tomorrow, I've been at the base for 48 hours or so and I have to say that despite my determination to remain cool and impassive, I can't help but be impressed by the military precision that is ingrained into every fibre, every brick, every moment of this place.
The facility has obviously been extensively overhauled for this enterprise. It has a military feel to it, but I've worked for the military in the past and they are not big on comfort or style.
Suffice to say if a passing James Bond villain were to idly drop

by for a visit, he'd be suitably impressed. The whole site used to belong to NASA beforehand; in fact I think I may have visited it about 10 years ago for some meeting or other. If I did then it didn't look like this then though, I'm absolutely certain of that!

I had nothing to do with this part of the project but if this represents the benchmark for what's expected for the rest of the mission then I may have to raise my game significantly. It's very impressive, and so are those that reside within it.

The meet and greet that we all went through this morning was, eye-opening. The recruit list is like a Who's-who of physicists, scientists and engineers. Genuine, bona fide rocket scientists, certifiable geniuses. I recognised several of the names from the journal articles that they have had published. Articles that I have not only read and been influenced by, but have gone on to become industry standards.

It wasn't just physicists and engineers though.

Amongst those out-with the sphere of engineering there were decorated war heroes, internationally recognised doctors, pioneers in the fields of agriculture and biodiversity, philanthropists and entrepreneurs, and by all accounts there are more yet to arrive.

We had a brief introduction and then the plans for the upcoming weeks, months and years were addressed, albeit briefly. Afterwards though I was left in no doubt about the intensity and gravity of what lay ahead. I just hope that I'm ready for it.

The physical aspects of the training are going to be handled by the military personnel within the group, which I suppose is fair enough really. There are, by my count, at least six former astronauts among them and they are being led by the considerable physical presence of Major Benjamin Sutherland.

I met Major Sutherland for the first time, briefly during a visit with Gareth. He was an undeniably impressive man. He was friendly and instantly likeable, but there was an unmistakably serious side to him as well and I got the impression that his joviality masked a man who was not only exceptional, but also almost painfully focussed.
I'm certain that we are in safe hands with him though.

Tuesday:
Today was tough. Tough in a way that I didn't previously believe possible. Tough in a way that I didn't even know existed, I have never physically worked harder and longer before in my life, ever.
I'm not unfit; at least I had never considered myself to be. I used to run quite regularly, I walked whenever possible around the city and I played football occasionally at the 5 a-side centre. I've never been overweight, have never smoked, I generally watch what I eat and I haven't really drunk alcohol for over six months now. I was quietly confident that I would cope with the first few days without too much difficulty. Boy was I wrong! Jesus I am clearly so dangerously unfit. After what Ben described as a "light session" today I pretty much had to crawl back to my room. I forced myself to eat this evening because all I wanted to do was shower and sleep. Actually all I really wanted to do was sleep but I am now a team player, apparently, so a shower was a non-negotiable aspect of my evening.
We split into three groups this morning each of which was placed under the leadership of one of the senior military figures. My group was with Jim, an American guy with an infectious laugh and a torso that looks as though it's been sculpted from granite. Jim pushed us through the exercises

with good humour but a steely determination. We had been divided into ability or at least the other two groups had been divided into ability. My group, group three, got whatever was left. I'm ashamed to say that my group consisted almost entirely of the engineers and physicists. I wasn't the only one suffering by the end of the session and I found myself casually wondering if we were all expected to make it through this section alive.

The dining room was a very quiet place this evening. The excitable babble of the previous two days had been replaced by almost total silence. People focussed upon their plates and treated their meals as merely one more arduous exercise task that had to be completed before the blessed relief of sleep.

Jim asked to speak to me after dinner which I reluctantly agreed to. The dining room emptied with almost alarming speed and barely half an hour after everyone had initially sat down the place was completely empty except for myself, Jim, and Ben.

Jim approached me in his usual friendly way and explained that Ben wanted to add some one-on-one sessions to my training programme. I had laughed because I assumed that he was joking.

He wasn't joking.

The friendly giant that I had previously encountered had vanished. What remained in his place was a big fucking maniac that seemed intent on trying to kill me. He described what he had in store for me and I honestly felt like crying. I'm trying not to dwell on it though, I need to sleep now. Perhaps it won't be as bad as think.

Thursday:

A man died today. It wasn't anyone that I knew personally, he was a PA somewhere high up on the food chain, but I suppose that's not really the point, he's still dead. It's weird but I don't know how to react if I'm completely honest, it's the first time that I've been around death since Karen and Martha and its brought back an awful lot of feelings that I thought I'd managed to work through. I feel less upset than I thought I would, in fact I just feel kind of...empty. As if the normal human response to this has somehow been washed out from me.

I came here to be part of something big, something exciting and something positive. After all this project is all about new life and looking forward, so this has had a big impact on everyone. It's odd though, whereas I thought there would be groups of distraught colleagues crying on one another shoulders there is in fact none of that. Of course people are upset but that's not the overriding emotion. Perhaps everyone is still in shock but it's as if everyone has suddenly forgotten how to interact with one another, it's all a bit disconcerting so I'm trying to keep my head down.

I'm not absolutely sure what happened exactly, but the popular consensus is that this guy had managed to contract malaria and then suffered from some kind of unlucky complication that shut his whole body down. I don't really know (or understand) the details or the medical jargon but from what I can gather it wasn't a particularly pleasant way to go. People are saying that he was poisoned by his own blood and then suffocated by his own lungs. How is that even possible? Is that even possible? Everyone's got an opinion and everyone has a different perspective and at this stage I'm not really sure how much of what I've heard is true and how much of it is bullshit. I just can't really comprehend it all and I'm not really sure that I want to.

Regardless though, whatever the truth, one thing that seems to be unanimous is that it wasn't a very pretty end. If even a tiny percentage of what I've been told is true, then it sounds absolutely bloody terrifying to me. The stuff of horror movies and bad seventies television shows. Five of them went off to Africa last week and three of them came back with malaria, how the fuck does that happen in this day and age? These are meant to be educated men and women and yet they don't even take simple precautions when travelling abroad. The mind boggles, it really does.

One good thing to come out of it all was that today's training sessions were cancelled. I know that sounds really callous and unbelievably selfish but it was genuinely one of my first thoughts. Not pity for the poor guy or whatever family he might be leaving behind. No, my first thoughts were for my own personal welfare. I really am a piece of shit aren't I? But honestly if I had been forced into another session with Major Sutherland I'm not sure that this unlucky PA would have been the only death on the base this week!

Monday:

It's official, karma is in fact a mother fucker.

After my (brief) selfish thoughts about Liam (that was his name apparently, the guy that died) and my barely containable delight at missing a training session, it would seem that Major-bastard-Sutherland has taken it upon himself to ensure that any feelings of smugness were painfully short-lived. The previous break-neck pace that he had adopted through the last week of training has, in fact, merely been acting as warm up to the main event.

There is now no doubt in my mind. He is definitely trying to kill me. There can be no other logical explanation for what he's putting me through. I thought what had gone before was hard but today was absolute fucking torture. Everything aches now, everything. I'm too tired to write even. I have no idea how much more of this I can take, I feel like walking out of door and never coming back. Perhaps I would, if I were still capable of walking. I have reached my absolute limit, both physically and mentally. This man, this giant fucking sociopathic sadist is breaking me down to my constituent pieces. My worry is that when he's finished that I won't have either the inclination or ability to reassemble them again.

CHAPTER NINE

Gareth was in his office when his PA buzzed at the intercom.
"Mr. Williams? There's someone here to see you," she said.
"Who is it Kim?" he asked without looking up.
"It's Major Sutherland."
"Ben? Oh good!" he closed his laptop and smiled, "Well don't leave him standing out there in the hall. Send him in!"
The intercom fell silent and moments later the door to his office opened. Ben loomed into the doorway paused and then moved into the office. Gareth stood from his chair and walked around the desk. His smile had widened.
"Ben! How the Devil are you?" he asked, warmly.
A grin flashed over Ben's broad face. He grabbed Gareth's outstretched hand and shook it.
"Good afternoon sir," he said flatly, "I'm good thank-you. How are you sir?"
"So formal Ben? Please,"
Ben inclined his head to one side, "Twenty years of military service sir. It's kinda hard to put it down again."
Gareth laughed, "Fair enough I suppose," he said, "it's hardly the worst habit I've ever encountered," he gestured to the chair, "please Ben, sit down. What can I do for you?"
Ben looked down at the chair and then somewhat awkwardly folded his large frame into its deep leather upholstery. It took him several moments of readjustment before he seemed to make himself relatively comfortable. Gareth watched him with a mixture of confusion and amused fascination. When he was finally settled Gareth became uncomfortably aware that he was still staring at him, he shook his head and then smiled.
"Would you like a drink? Coffee? Tea?" he checked his watch and then added with a wry smile, "Whisky?"

Ben wasn't much of a drinker, his career choices didn't fit well with alcohol. He did however enjoy a single malt whisky from time to time.
“Whisky?” he said happily, ”Sure! What do you have?”
Gareth went over to an oak console table that was standing in the corner of his office
“Hmmm,” he said as he cast his eyes over the selection. “Not a fantastic choice, if I’m honest. Let’s see...”
He moved a few bottles around and glanced at the labels as he did so.
“Ah, here we go!” he said lifting a green glass bottle from the collection with a smile, “I’ve just picked up this 16 year old Lagavulin.”
Ben shrugged, “I’m in your hands,” he said.
“Well it is lovely,” he said thoughtfully, “if you like a peaty whisky that is,” he shuffled the bottles again and lifted another one, “or there is this 12 year old Glenlivet if you want something a bit lighter or...”
“Like I said, I’m in your hands,” he repeated with a wave of his hand, “as long as its Scottish I don't really care.”
“Okay,” he turned to fix the drinks but continued talking, “but some of the Irish or even Japanese whiskies are really very good you know? Would you like to try one?” he turned back and Ben was staring at him.
Gareth shifted his weight awkwardly between his feet. The environment within the office had just metaphorically dropped several degrees. He suddenly felt unpleasantly like he’d just been caught in a compromising situation with Ben’s mother.
Ben glared at him.
Gareth was not easily intimidated but he had the good sense to recognise when he had inadvertently stumbled onto dangerous ground.

“The Lagavulin it is then!” he added breezily and Ben’s glare visibly softened.
He poured two generous measures, “Ice?” He asked. “Or a nip of water perhaps?”
“No, thank-you,” Ben said reaching for the glass.
Gareth handed him the drink and then returned to his seat behind the desk. He swilled the whisky around the heavy, crystal glass and took a decent sip
“So,” Gareth said, “is there a problem? Or is this just a social visit?”
“No, not a problem sir, not exactly anyway,” Ben teased.
Gareth shrugged, “Okay, what’s up?”
Ben took a sip of his own whisky and physically shuddered. He looked at Gareth and either he hadn’t notice or was wise enough to ignore it, “It’s Captain Harrison Sir,” he said
“Cam?” Gareth asked.
“Yeah, Cam,”
“What’s wrong with him? Is he all right?” Gareth’s eyes narrowed suspiciously, “He’s not struggling with the training is he?”
“No,” Ben said and scratched the side of his face thoughtfully. “Not struggling as such, I’m just kinda worried about…” he hesitated, reluctant to continue.
“Go on. It’s okay Ben” Gareth said encouragingly.
“Well,” he said uncertainly, “I don't want to be unkind sir. I know that the guy has been through the mill,”
Gareth’s expression darkened, “You have no idea, Ben,” he said softly.
“Okay. Sure I understand that. But this mission is not going to be a walk in the park you know? There are gonna be some rough times ahead, real dark days,” he paused and took a fortifying sip of whisky, he coughed to clear his throat before

continuing, "I don't know that Cam will be able to cope. You know when things get tough."
Gareth smiled thinly, "I can assure you Major, Cameron Harrison is an awful lot tougher than he perhaps appears. You could try very hard but I guarantee that you simply won't find a better man," his voice remained quiet, but it was underpinned with steel.
"Oh I know sir," Ben was suddenly a little flustered, "don't get me wrong I think he's a great guy. This has nothing to do with what Cam is like as a man. I just know that things are going to get tough and we are not going to be able to carry anyone."
"Don't worry Major; you won't have to carry Cam."
Ben paused, "With all due respect, I've seen this before, sir."
Gareth nodded, "Listen Major. I appreciate your concerns. Really I do. And I have no doubts as to your experience, but this is different," he met Ben's eyes and held him. "You have no idea how much Cam has gone through to be here. Or what I've been through to get him here for that matter. He is one of the finest mechanical engineers on the planet."
"I understand that sir. But I don't understand why he needs to be a crew member."
"He just does. We are going to need someone like Cam in the colony, and trust me there is none else like Cam. I've looked,"
Ben slammed his glass onto the surface of the desk, "He's weak sir!" he said loudly, "I'm sorry I know you guys are friends but if he breaks down in a tiny space craft or on the surface of Mars," he shook his head. "Well, it aint gonna be pretty that's for damn sure. People are gonna die!"
Gareth looked at the glass and then back at Ben.
"He'll be fine I promise," his voice was soft, calm but loaded with threat. He stared unblinkingly at Ben and took a moment's thought before he continued, "Look if you're that concerned

about him why don't you take him under your wing? Make sure he's up to your standards? He's much stronger than you think. I've seen him on the very edge and still he clawed his way back. You'll see. Give him a chance Ben and I guarantee that you'll change your mind."

"I don't know Sir," he slapped his stomach, "I trust my gut, it doesn't lead me wrong too often."

Gareth smiled, "Well, on this occasion can I ask that you trust me instead?" he said.

Ben picked his glass back up from the desk and offered a toast to Gareth. He looked at Gareth for a moment and then inclined his head at him.

"Okay then," he said, "but if I take him 'under my wing' he's not gonna like it. If he breaks it'll be on your head," he pointed his glass at Gareth and then sipped at it again, "and he's gonna break."

"As I say, he's tougher than he looks," Gareth said quietly.

"He's gonna have to be!" Ben laughed.

They both drained their glasses and Ben stood to leave.

Gareth caught his eye and held it

"Thanks for telling me this though Ben, I know it can't have been easy."

Ben shrugged, "I'm just doing my job, sir."

He nodded to Gareth and then turned and left without saying another word. He paused briefly at the reception desk and offered a friendly goodbye to Kim before heading back to the living quarters where he took some time to consider his new, expanded role as a mentor to Cam. He knew that if Cam was able to survive his tutelage, then he would most probably survive anything.

From that moment on Major Ben Sutherland became Cam's shadow. Wherever and whenever Cam ate, slept or trained.

Ben was there as a constant thorn. Always pushing, always testing and always looking for an opportunity to break him. He didn't have any desire particularly to prove Gareth wrong, but rather to prove that he had been right all along. Ben was a good judge of men, he had to be, and his early impression of someone was rarely wrong.

Cam, however, was an intelligent man and it didn't take long for him to work out what was going on and once he got over the initial shock he took the extra sessions without complaint or comment. He knew any moaning that came from him would merely increase his pain, so he accepted it as the challenge that it was intended to be. In all honesty he had had his own misgivings about the whole process from the very start; it was only Gareth's vociferous encouragement that persuaded him to become a crew member as well as chief engineer.

He had emerged from his prolonged period of mourning, blinking into the bright sunshine of a world that he no longer felt any connection with. The pursuit and enthral of money had become largely irrelevant now. His first cathartic exercise in expressing his newfound freedom saw him sell the family house as quickly as he was able and then pass on the proceeds to his brother, Alasdair. Any financial incentive that had lingered around his involvement in the project had evaporated immediately after Karen and Martha's death. He found himself with clarity of mind and purpose that few seldom discover. He had an opportunity to start with a clean slate and get as far away from his previous life as possible.

He was still an engineer though; his enquiring mind would still need sating. It was therefor after some careful consideration, that he supposed a one way voyage to Mars was probably one of the more conclusive options available to him.

CHAPTER TEN

ONE YEAR LATER...

OCTOBER 2018.

It had taken a long time and had been an arduous, often belittling process but finally, after almost a year of living and breathing life on base, Cam was now as much part of the furniture as anyone else. He was home.

His confidence had grown, along with his physical fitness and mental wellbeing and he now walked the corridors with a relaxed calmness, comfortable within his own skin for perhaps the first time in his life. He had finally fully embraced his role of chief engineer and was proud of the team that he had around him. He was also proud of the work that they were producing together as the weeks and months rolled by. However, he struggled to get used to the endless meetings and progress reports. He had come up with a strategy though. Rather than treat them as the time sapping, inconvenient pain in his backside that they were apparently designed to be, he often used the time to work on some new designs or ideas. His note books represented the physical manifestation of his mental flights of fancy and were as structured and ordered as the average toddlers colouring books. His current one sported a cover that was stained and tattered, and several of the pages had sections missing where he had torn things out. Despite all of its flaws and scruffiness, it was still precious to Cam and he carried it with him wherever he went, crammed into the pocket of his lab coat.

It was currently sitting on top of the highly polished wooden surface of the main conference suite table and was being eyed suspiciously by Cam as if he expected it to jump up and wander off if he took his eyes off it for a second.

Apparently oblivious to his surroundings, Cam scribbled out a doodle irritably and swore to himself; he considered the adjacent equation for a moment and then looked up from his work at the rest of the room's inhabitants. He stared, blankly around the room for a moment, scratched behind his ear with the tip of his mechanical pencil and then started to make another drawing, which he considered for a moment before looking up again.

The conference suite was as busy as Cam had ever seen it; every chair around the large table was occupied as well as some others that had been drafted in from the surrounding rooms. He recognised some of the faces but not all; it was only when all the departmental heads gathered together for an update that Cam really appreciated the full scale of the operation that they were all working on.

Immediately seated to his right was Jason Dickinson, one of his team of engineers. Cam leaned over and whispered to him.

"There's an awful lot of Bertie-big-bollocks in here today, eh?" Cam whispered.

Jason's face crumpled and he leaned closer, "Sorry?" He said and cupped his ear slightly

"I said, there's an awful lot of Bertie-big-bollocks in here..." Cam had raised his voice just as the volume within the room had dropped to a whisper.

"Shite," he said.

Every set of eyes in the room suddenly turned their collective stare towards Cam, who in turn returned his attention back to his note book, his ears blazing red with embarrassment. In response, Jason tried to shuffle his chair away from him, in an

attempt to physically distance himself from the uncomfortable moment that was engulfing the room.
"Did you have something you wanted to add, Professor Harrison?" asked a tall, middle aged woman that stood at the head of the table.
"Hmm?" Cam said without looking up, "No, no. You're fine, Professor McKinnon."
Professor McKinnon stared at him for a moment before turning her attention back to the massed ranks within the room.
"Thank you Cam," she said slightly irritably, "please continue Bilal, with what you were saying."
Bilal was a short, severe looking man with a balding head and an unpleasant sneer permanently attached to his face. He was dressed in an expensive looking suit that somehow didn't seem to quite fit in the right places. His shirt collar was undone and either he had discarded his tie during the meeting or had simply neglected to wear one in the first place. He looked at Cam with utter contempt and then addressed the room again.
"So in conclusion," he said pompously, "it is the opinion of our group that the taking of non-human colony members to Mars represents an unacceptable cost to benefit ratio."
Cam sniggered loudly and then immediately looked up guiltily. Once again the collective attention of the room turned towards him.
"Cam?" Professor McKinnon said with as much restraint as she could muster
"Aye?" Cam said innocently.
"This is an open forum, so please; if you have a point, we would be more than happy to hear it," she said. "However, if not then would you please extent some courtesy to your colleagues?"

"Aye, sorry," Cam said, "I just found the term 'non-human colony members' amusing," he looked around for some show of support but found none.
"Really? No one else thinks that's funny?" He shrugged. "Ah well, must just be me then. Sorry Bilal, please continue."
Bilal's expression dripped with distain and he smiled, thinly at Cam, "the chickens..." he continued
"Chickens?" Cam interrupted, shocked. "You're talking about not taking the chickens? Fuck off!"
"Cam, please!" Professor McKinnon exploded, her patience worn to breaking point. "Please, mind your language, have you even been listening at all?"
"Absolutely!" He replied, unconvincingly. "But the chickens? We've got to take the chickens," he said simply.
Bilal flashed him a serpentine smile, "It is not a reasonable expenditure, *Professor* Harrison."
"I disagree," Cam said, ignoring the attempted slight, "in a confined, finite living space. Non-human interaction is a potentially vital part of this whole concept," he looked around the room again and this time caught someone's eye.
"Doctor Daniels!" He said loudly and Jon shifted uncomfortable in his chair as everyone turned to look at him, "You know what I'm saying is true don't you?"
Jon shrugged, "I did raise this argument with Bilal and his team but they deemed it to be..."
"To be what?" Professor McKinnon asked, pointedly.
"Spurious," Jon said.
Professor McKinnon turned to Bilal who was reddening by the second, "Is this true Bilal?" she asked. Bilal said nothing but nodded, reluctantly.
"Who here has a pet?" Cam said in an attempt to take the focus from his increasingly unhappy colleague.

There was a pause before, slowly, hands started to go up around the room. Professor McKinnon looked around the room and then raised her own hand cautiously.
"Professor!" Bilal exclaimed in surprise.
McKinnon shrugged, "I have a cat," she said, "he's called Eric."
Cam clapped his hands together in delight, "Brilliant!" he said happily.
"And how many of you with your hands in the air have ever talked to your pets?"
Every hand in the room remained raised.
"Exactly!" Cam said triumphantly. "And how many of you feed and house and treat your pets?" He didn't wait for a response. "And presumably, you are all out of pocket as well?"
"Professor Harrison," Bilal interjected, "I fail to see what this has to do with our mission."
"Really?" Cam said surprised, "We all need someone to talk to Bilal, even if they don't answer back, in fact especially if they don't answer back, sometimes," he laughed.
Bilal shrugged, "The chickens that would have been taken to the colony were not to be pets, professor. They were to be used as a resource and as an experiment."
Cam shrugged, "We're talking about a human outpost on another planet, do you genuinely believe that the only other living things within the colony would not be subjected to some form of anthropomorphism?"
"I suppose its possible," Bilal conceded.
"So what we're talking about is the availability of a non-judgmental, perhaps even, affectionate companion."
Bilal shrugged again.
"And your group decided that this was a bad idea?" Cam shook his head, "How did that happen?"

Professor McKinnon looked over at Jon, “Do you concur with Cam doctor Daniels?"
She asked with an arching of her eyebrows.
Jon nodded, "I phrased it in slightly different terminology. But yes, what Cam says is absolutely true. The presence of the chickens would potentially have huge psychological benefits for the colonists," he looked over at Cam and smiled, "plus there will be eggs as well."
Cam threw his arms into the air, "Yes," he said loudly, "I almost forgot about the fucking eggs!"
McKinnon looked at Bilal, "But..." he said weakly
"Chicken shit!” Cam said excitedly
"Okay Cam we take your point," Professor McKinnon said with a roll of her eyes
"No, I mean the chicken shit would be a valuable fertiliser," Cam said and then turned back to face Bilal. "Were you guys high when you came to this decision? Because it's fucking nuts!"
Bilal blushed deeper and looked around for help. There was however none forthcoming.
"I must confess that it does sound like a compelling argument Bilal," professor McKinnon said calmly, "perhaps you and your team could reconsider?"
Bilal was a beaten man, he had visibly deflated and he sank back into his chair without saying another word.
Cam beamed at the room, "So the chickens are going then?" he said happily.
"It would seem so Cam, yes," Professor McKinnon was smiling as well, "now if we could move on from this finally?" she added.

Jason had been staring at Cam's notepad throughout the argument and now it had drawn to a conclusion he leaned over to Cam and whispered in his ear.
"Is this what I think it is?" he asked quietly.
Cam shrugged, "That all depends," he said cryptically.
"On what?" Jason asked.
"On what you think it is," Cam said with a smile.
Jason leaned closer, "Well it looks like a design for a new concept for 3D powder fusion printing," he said.
Cam looked at his colleague and nodded, "Then yes! It is exactly what it looks like then," he said with a chuckle.
Jason shook his head, "This is groundbreaking," he said softly.
"Potentially, " Cam agreed, "I just need to iron out a few of the details but then I think that we're good to go."
"How long have you been working on this?" Jason asked suspiciously.
Cam shrugged again, "A couple of weeks I suppose, it's no big deal,"
"No big deal?" Jason said excitedly. "This will revolutionise the supply of machinery on the colony. You are talking about a fast, safe way of printing in titanium, in hours not days,"
Cam smiled.
"This is the absolute definition of what a big deal is!"
Professor McKinnon shot them both a warning glance.
Jason sighed, "I don't believe you Cam," he sighed
"What?"
Jason laughed quietly, "Well here you are, sitting on a groundbreaking design," he began patiently. "The patent of which alone is probably worth millions, by the way," he picked up a glass of water and sipped it, "not only that but you've been sitting in this room, surrounded by some of the finest brains on the planet arguing about bloody chickens!"

"It was important," Cam protested, "chickens are important!"
"You are a crazy bastard," Jason laughed.
"But you're a fucking genius as well!"

CHAPTER ELEVEN

As Cam left the conference suite, stretching and yawning extravagantly as he went, Jon sidled up to him and touched his shoulder gently. Cam jumped at the unexpected contact and swivelled to face his assaulter, as he rounded on Jon he took a step backwards.

"Whoa," Jon said, "sorry, I didn't mean to startle you!"

Cam looked at Jon and rubbed tentatively at his shoulder, his expression unreadable.

"Professor Harrison?" Jon prompted.

"Hmm?" Cam responded, "Hello?"

"Are you all right?" Jon asked slightly concerned

Cam shook his head as if to clear it, “Aye, I'm fine," he said finally. "Tough session in the gym mixed with a little too much coffee I suspect," he looked at Jon's face as if for the first time. "Doctor Daniels, nice to see you. What can I do for you?"

"Please, call me Jon," he said, "do you have time for a quick coffee?"

Cam shuddered.

"Or something else? A beer perhaps?"

"I don't drink," Cam said simply, "I'll come with you though; I could do with a bite to eat if I'm honest."

The two men turned against the flow of bodies that was still leaving the meeting room and headed off towards the main refectory.

"Thanks by the way," Jon said, as they walked.

"For what?" Cam asked.

"For the show of confidence," Jon shrugged, "for asking my opinion."

They had reached the refectory, although there was no hot food on offer. Cam headed over to one of the vending

machines and ordered a chicken salad sandwich. He had already unwrapped it and started to eat it before they reached a table and sat down. Jon watched Cam eat with a vaguely disgusted look on his face for a moment, before excusing himself to get a coffee. When he returned Cam had finished his sandwich and was tucking into a large banana.
"Why did you let that wee bastard Bilal walk over your recommendation?" Cam asked between mouthfuls.
Jon shrugged his shoulders, "Picking my battles I suppose," he offered meekly.
Cam shook his head, "Naw, I'm not having that doctor," he pointed the stub of his banana at Jon's chest, "you're not a man to be easily cowed in my opinion."
"And what makes you say that professor? You barely know me."
"You have a reputation of sorts," Cam said.
Jon raised his eyebrows questioningly, “Oh, do I?" he said.
"Well, yes frankly," Cam said, "there's no need to be coy about it though, it's not a bad thing!" he laughed and patted Jon amiably on the shoulder.
"Hmmm," Jon said thoughtfully.
"So?" Cam asked.
"What?"
"Why did you let that wee shite treat you like that?"
"It's complicated," Jon said cautiously, "Bilal might seem like a small minded bureaucrat but he..."
"Yes?"
"I barely know you professor," Jon said quietly.
"So?"
Jon inclined his head, slightly and raised his eyebrows.
"Ah," Cam said, "and you don't know if I’m trustworthy or not?"

Jon said nothing, but he looked away from Cam's stare. Cam nodded to himself.
"Fair enough doctor," he said with a smile.
"It's not personal, professor, it's just..."
"Don't worry about it," Cam said with a wave of his hand, "so, what was it you wanted to see me about?"
Jon looked blankly at Cam for a second before he was struck by a flash of remembrance, "Oh yeah!" he said, "I almost forgot, it's about Major Sutherland."
"Ben?" Cam said unable to hide the surprise in his voice, "What about him? Is he all right?"
"Oh yes he's fine, I know that you two spend a fair bit of time together and I wanted to ask your opinion about him, that's all?"
"But why?" Cam said suspiciously.
Jon shrugged, "Can you keep a secret?" he said and leant towards Cam conspiratorially.
Cam said nothing but nodded his head almost imperceptibly.
"Well," Jon said looking surreptitiously over his shoulder, "I've been asked to comprise psych profiles of the main contenders for the first shuttle crew, and Major Sutherland is a strong contender not only for the shuttle but for command as well."
Jon sat back allowing this information to filter through to Cam.
"And you want to know *my* opinion of him?" Cam asked.
Jon nodded, "Not just you of course, but I'm trying to build up a rounded picture of all those that are in contention, and like I said you've spent more time with him than probably anyone else."
Cam nodded in quiet contemplation for a moment as he considered his response, he opened his mouth to speak a few times without saying anything before, finally he managed to phrase his thoughts coherently.

"He's a fucking psycho!" he said with such force and venom that Jon physically reeled from his response.
"I'm...I'm sorry?" he managed to say, as he shifted uncomfortably in his chair.
"I said," Cam said patiently. "That in my considered opinion, Major Ben Sutherland is a fucking psychopath. Further more, he should be in command of nothing other than the tying of his own fucking shoelaces."
"I can't submit that!" Jon said, incredulously.
"You asked my opinion," Cam said with a defensive shrug of his shoulders, "and I have offered one."
Jon stared at Cam, barely blinking, his mind thrashing over the previous thirty-seconds or so, "...but, but I... though you two were friends?" Jon said, stammering a little as he spoke
"Aye, we are," Cam said with a slight smile, "like two peas in a pod."
A look of realisation dawned across Jon's handsome face as he began to understand what was happening, "Ah," he said, the relief tangible in his voice. "You're joking, aren't you?"
He waggled his finger at Cam in a mock scalding, "That's naughty, winding me up like that," a small smile speed across his face.
Cam arched his eyebrows in response, “We are friends, close friends," he repeated, "but my opinion of him is exactly as I said. The man is a monster."
Cam looked at Jon as his expression melted back into one of deep unhappiness.
"I'm sorry professor, but I really am not quite sure I understand what's happening here. Is there any way you could clarify things for me perhaps?"

Cam nodded, "Aye, well fair enough," he said after moments thought. "Do you remember when I first got here doctor? Maybe what? Eleven months ago maybe?"
Jon nodded his reply.
"Well apparently after the first week or so, the great Major Sutherland decided in all of his wisdom that I shouldn't be here," he paused as he tried to recall a moment past, “in fact I believe the exact words he used to describe me were, and I quote: 'A fucking liability'"
He smiled at Jon, who in turn looked uncomfortably at his coffee cup.
"When he approached Gareth about this very fact, Gareth tried to alleviate his concerns-told him that I had been through a lot in the previous few years."
Jon looked back into Cam's face, "The death of your wife and daughter?" he asked quietly
Cam nodded sombrely, "Aye," he said with a sigh, "amongst other things. Things that I'd rather not go in to at this point."
Jon nodded, he knew most, but not all of what Cam had gone through. He knew the battles that he had fought and the demons that he had faced and conquered. He also knew though that this was privileged information so he repressed the impulse to bring it up and instead watched him silently.
Seemingly satisfied that there was to be no further interrogation Cam continued with his reminiscence.
“Anyway, it was decided that Ben should take me under his wing, so to speak. Gareth thought, quite reasonably that if Ben got to know me on a personal level then he might see beyond his initial doubts."
"Which he did, didn't he?" Jon asked hopefully, "I remember that the two of you were inseparable for weeks, months even."

Again Cam nodded, "Aye," he said softly, "Indeed we were," he trailed off from his train of thought for a moment as an apparently particularly painful memory revealed itself to him, "He tortured me," he said at last, his voice barely louder than a whisper.
"Tortured?" Jon asked shaking his head as if clearing his ears, "I'm sorry but did you just say he tortured you?"
Cam looked down at the floor his eyes closed in a moment of contemplation.
"I did," he said at last.
"Surely not!" Jon said with a further shake of his head, "not actual torture, I mean that's ridiculous..."
"The special forces have done it for years," Cam said without looking up. "In order to build you into the person," he paused, before correcting himself, "sorry the soldier, that they want you to become; they must first break you down into your component parts. To remove any trace of fragility or weakness, to make you feel less than human," Cam looked up at Jon again, "they build you back up again of course, reprogrammed and improved. But none of that works without the dehumanisation part first, and Ben is a very effective practitioner of that particular skill set."
"So it was for all the best reasons then, arguably?" Jon asked hesitantly.
Cam's face reddened with anger, "I am not, nor have I ever been a fucking soldier doctor Daniels," he shouted. "I am a fucking engineer! A bloody civilian! I had no frame of reference for what was happening to me, no military background to help me along."
He thumped the table with his fist and looked directly into Jon's eyes.

"He tried to break me doctor, and he came pretty, fucking close to managing it," he raised his fore-finger and thumb in front of his face, and held them millimetres apart, "I was this fucking close!" he said with real bitterness in his voice, if it hadn't been for Gareth..." Once again he trailed off and shook his head, "...I don't know if I'd still be here,"
"And by here you mean?" Jon asked.
"Here," he said thumping his chest with his fist. "Here! Alive!"
The two men sat in silence for a few minutes, both apparently lost in their own thoughts.
"I don't know what to say," Jon said finally.
"Nothing to say," Cam said. "Water under the bridge now I suppose."
"But how can you describe this man as a friend now? This man whom you have every reason to despise?"
"Sometimes," Cam said slowly, "it is infinitely wiser to make friends with the devil than it is to go to war with him. Ben may be a ruthless son-of-a-bitch but I'd much rather have him in my corner that be facing him."
"Making friends with the playground bully?"
"Spare me your psychobabble. You can call it that if it makes you happier," Cam said dismissively, "but I call it survival of the fittest. We can't all be the shark, doctor; and in my experience, if you can't be the shark, you might as well be one of the fish that swim under its belly!"
Jon threw his hands into the air in exasperation, “But that's the point! You are never friends with a shark, ever. Because no matter how close you get, how friendly you think you are with it, it is still a bloody shark and it will still damn well eat you if there's nothing else on the menu."
Cam stared into Jon's eyes, his expression unreadable.

"I'll take my chances," he said simply, "the important thing is that I survived, and now I'm better equipped to deal with any other shit that comes flying at me," he laughed, "I guess when you get right down to the nitty-gritty it worked though didn't it? I am stronger than I ever was before, both mentally and physically."
"Does anyone else know about this?" Jon asked concerned.
Cam shook his head, "Not in any detail, no," he said, "what would be the point?"
"To stop it from happening again to someone else?" Jon said irritably.
"Maybe," Cam conceded thoughtfully, "but arguably the project would be weaker without Ben on board. He's strong and fearless. He has experience of space flight and when he's not being a crazy bastard you can sit down with him, have a civilised chat and perhaps even share a whisky or two,"
"I thought you didn't drink?" Jon said accusatorially
"I don't," Cam replied, "not anymore, but I can still enjoy the aromas of a good single malt, without drinking it."
"Really?"
"If that's all that's available," Cam said with a sigh.
"Will that be all doctor?" he said suddenly pushing his chair back and rising to his feet.
Jon sighed, "Yes I suppose so," he said, "thank you for your time professor."
He stood from his chair and offered his hand. Cam took it and shook it firmly, "And thank-you for your candour as well, you have certainly given me plenty of food for thought."
"You're welcome doctor and please call me Cam, there are so many bloody professors in this place I never know who's who!" he laughed. "So, who's next on your list?"

Jon looked down at his clip board and pretended to read something whilst his face reddened slightly.
"Actually I'm going to talk to Major Sutherland," he said softly, "about you."
Cam laughed, "Oh shite! I'd better start packing now then, hadn't I?"

CHAPTER TWELVE

Ben sat alone, his face like thunder. The other people in the dining hall were giving him a wide birth and consequently he had established an informal exclusion zone around where he was sitting. Cam watched him from across the room, dimly aware that he was perhaps the cause of Ben's unhappiness, at least partially. Ben had been denied the captaincy of the Nerine One and consequently, the mission as a whole. Cam suspected that his blunt character assessment may well have been influential in that decision. Jon had assured him that all of his comments had remained anonymous and strictly confidential. Cam still had an unshakable feeling that Ben was not only aware of what he had said, but was now plotting some sort of terrible Machiavellian revenge against him. It made him uneasy, in the same way that a lamb is uneasy when it's confronted by a bloody great wolf.

He looked down at his Salad Nicoise and pushed the plate away untouched, his appetite suddenly gone. When he looked back over towards where Ben was sitting he was no longer alone, Sophie had apparently taken leave of her senses and was trying to strike up a conversation with him. Cam flinched, involuntarily, as he waited for the inevitable explosion of frustration from Ben, but instead he was surprised to note that not only had Ben remained remarkably calm, but that he seemed to be actually smiling.

Sophie had her hand resting gently upon Ben's shoulder and she was bent over, her face close to his ear and her eyes looking directly over at Cam. Ben's gaze flicked over to him as well and the smile that had previously been touching his features faded back into the earlier scowl. Cam swallowed hard, forced a smile onto his face and lifted his hand in what he considered to be a friendly wave. Ben did not respond in kind and instead pushed his chair back from the table and moved to stand in one sinisterly fluid movement. His eyes unblinking and his stare unfaltering from an increasingly uncomfortable Cam. He moved around the table and began to stride purposefully across the dining hall towards where Cam was sitting. Cam began the process of preparing to defend himself against the inevitable barrage of abuse and accusations that were soon, no doubt, to be heading in his general direction. However as Ben reached his table he merely paused for a fraction of a second, gave Cam a perfunctory nod of the head and then continued past him without speaking. Confused, but mightily relieved, Cam turned in his chair to follow Ben in his path across the room, his heart hammering loudly in his chest, his mouth dry and his palms unpleasantly clammy. Ben continued past another couple of occupied tables without incident until he reached a table right at the back of the room, a table around which was sitting Jacob, Kieran and Jon. When he reached them he stopped and stood silently in front of them his arms folded across his chest. The table top was littered with open folders, piles of paper and portable computer pads and the three men remained deep in conversation even after Ben's arrival at the table. It took them a few seconds to appreciate that, not only was he standing there, but that he was also waiting for them to stop whatever they were doing and acknowledge his presence.

Cam remained twisted uncomfortably in his chair, but he watched this newly formed tableau with bated breath and a touch of morbid curiosity, waiting for the coming events to reveal themselves. Finally, after what felt like a lifetime, the

three men stopped talking and looked at Ben, their faces each composed of expressions of curiosity touched with trepidation
"Ben!" Kieran said loudly yet friendlily. "What can we do for you?"
Ben stared at each of them in turn but remained silent.
Jon looked the most uncomfortable of the three and shifted restlessly in his chair, Jacob sat perfectly still and looked perhaps the calmest of them all.
Kieran sighed, "Is there a problem Ben?" he said a little tersely.
Ben shifted his weight to his other leg and nodded his head, "Yes," he said.
He let the word hang in the air, dripping with hidden meaning.
"I don't really have time for any of your cryptic behaviour at the moment Ben, so if you have something to say please do so," Kieran said, "and do it quickly please, we are in the middle of something here," he gestured to his colleagues.
"I bet you are," Ben said bitterly, "deciding who to screw over next are you?"
"Careful," Jacob said, with a just hint of a dangerous smile, "this isn't the time or place Major."
Ben waved him away, "Actually," he said, "I think that this is, in fact, the perfect time and place for this." He turned his body to survey the rest of the room. "I'm sure everyone here would like to hear your reasons for putting that fuck-witted yank in charge of this whole goddamn thing, rather than an actual fucking astronaut, with twenty years experience and three 'off world' missions already under his belt?"
Jon glanced briefly over at Cam and Cam's face flushed in response. Thankfully though Ben didn't seem to notice.
"I suggest, you return to your quarters to cool off, major," Jacob said.

"I'm perfectly cool," Ben spat back.
"This is not the way a man of your experience behaves," Jacob continued.
Kieran raised a hand, "It's okay Jacob, let the man make his point," he looked at Ben, expectantly. He did not respond.
"Okay, then allow me to remind you major that you are still second in command," Kieran said softly, "currently."
"Currently?" Ben said, "Look here Kieran..."
"Enough!" Kieran said with a raise of his hand, "You have made your point Major and it has been noted. I must say though that frankly this little outburst is making me reconsider your position entirely."
Ben visibly flinched at this thinly veiled threat.
"I can assure you that your experience was considered during this process Major, but I suggest that if you have any further issues that you would do better to raise them in a more professional manner." Kieran looked back to one of the papers that lay on the table top, thereby effectively dismissing Ben.
From his vantage point Cam could see Ben physically shaking with anger and frustration. He prepared himself once again for a verbal explosion, but instead he apparently was able to swallow his irritation and sense of injustice.
"This isn't over gentlemen." Was all that he said, then he turned on his heels and headed straight out of the door.
Every pair of eyes followed him and when he was gone the silence that had engulfed the room throughout the fiery yet brief exchange, began to dissolve into a hum of excitable whisperings and discussion.
When Cam turned himself around to face the table again he was surprised to see Sophie sitting opposite him staring at him intently, he smiled nervously at her and was relieved when she in turn smiled back at him.

"It is a terrible mistake, I think," she said, with a shake of her head.
"What? To piss off Ben? Aye I think your probably right." Cam said with a shudder.
Sophie shook her head, "No," she said softly, "it is a big mistake to pick this other man over Ben. In Spain, a man like Ben is admired. Big, strong!"
Cam considered this for a moment and then shrugged, "Aye, well what can you do, eh?"
Sophie studied him for a moment, "You think that we should do something?" she asked hopefully.
"What? No!" he said hurriedly, "I didn't mean that we should *do* something, I just meant..." he shook his head again,
"What?"
"Doesn't matter, it's an expression that's all," he smiled again, "lost in translation I think."
Sophie nodded thoughtfully, "You could perhaps talk to Gareth though?" she asked her eyes shining with expectation.
"No," Cam said flatly.
"But why?" Sophie's huge eyes, shone glassily.
"If the powers that be have made this decision, then they must have done it for a reason," he shrugged. "Its nothing to do with me really."
Sophie arched her eyebrows, "But you are Ben's friend?" she said, accusatorially.
Cam nodded, "Aye," he said, "of course I am. But I'm afraid that my opinion counts for very little around here."
Sophie shook her head, "That is not true," she said, "I have heard many people talk about how important you are to the mission."
"Have you?" Cam said with a small embarrassed grin.
Sophie nodded.

"Aye, well that's as maybe," he shrugged, "from an engineering point of view, perhaps. But the crew decisions? I'm sorry Sophie, that's not within my remit," he shook his head, "not even almost."
Sophie stared at him, and he could almost feel her huge brown eyes boring deeply into his skull. He shifted uncomfortably in his chair.
"I could have a go, I suppose," he said finally.
Sophie's face split into huge smile, "Thank you," she said happily and leant across the table to kiss him on the cheek.
Cam blushed slightly, "Why do you care though?" He asked. "Why does it matter if Ben is captain or not?"
Sophie shrugged, "He is a good man," she said simply, "and he will be a good leader," she paused for a moment, "and I think that sometimes the Americans think that they run the world, perhaps this will show them that they do not!"
Cam considered this for a moment. Jim was a more than capable officer. He was smart, intuitive and would certainly be a good captain, of that he was certain. However he also knew that his appointment to the position very probably had some external contributing factors. One of those factors was, almost certainly, some degree of carefully applied pressure from the Whitehouse. The president wanted an American to be the poster boy for this mission, so he would talk to Gareth about Ben as he promised, but he was under no illusions as to the effectiveness of that discussion.
There was no doubt in his mind that when the Nerine One touched down on to the surface of Mars, that the man that would be in charge and therefore on every television screen on the planet would be Jim. What he didn't know though was just how much of an effect that decision would continue to have, not only on Ben, but on all those around him.

PART 3

CHAPTER ONE

FIVE YEARS LATER...

MARS COLONY ALPHA.

Simon still walked with a limp and he knew, deep down, that he probably always would. He rubbed at his sore leg, absent mindedly, and groaned as a dull ache spread through his thigh and beyond. He stretched his muscles and then collapsed onto his bunk where he lay flat on his back and stared up at the ceiling. He had practised his relaxation techniques and calmly began breathing his way through the now familiar cramps and protests from his painful bones and muscles. His time in the medical bay had been frustrating and the steady procession of well meaning, but insincere visitors had made him value these moments alone in his quarters, even more than he had done previously.

Because of his physical size, Simon carried with him an innate and effortless sense of presence and intimidation. When coupled with his powder dry sense of humour and his penchant for spending time alone, he had developed something of a reputation of being terribly sombre, serious and unapproachable. This was fine with Simon because he was happier in his own company than anywhere else. Possessed, as he was, with little skill or inclination towards small talk or any of its associates.

Privately, he was the first to acknowledge that this facade did little to disprove the Teutonic stereotype that had followed him throughout his career and beyond; but he played his role as 'the humourless German' with relative good grace and

commitment, even if he did occasionally allow his performance to slip onto the edges of self-parody.
He studied the ceiling above him and sighed. He closed his eyes and allowed his mind to wander back over the events of the past few weeks, until he inevitably settled on the day of his accident. His forehead creased as the pain of the memory replayed across his mind's eye:
He had been working on the construction of one of the new living quarters when it had happened. The giant tubular titanium poles that formed the skeleton of the main construction had fitted together in a satisfyingly, fast and cohesive manner. The section of the works that he had been working on had originally been allocated two days labour. However, because of he and his team's efforts, it was looking as though it would be fully finished and ready for the next layer of construction before the end of day one.
The colonists usually worked together in groups of three, four or five, and would often interchange in order to attempt to prevent any fragmentation of the population into separate cliques.
Simon was as guilty of accepting stereotypical, national generalisations as the next person and was consequently sceptical of working with either the British or American colonists. He thought that they were too easily distracted and would find any excuse to stop for a conversation or to have a break. He also thought that they had a tendency to be too self-congratulatory before a task was completed. This meant that Simon often worked with Anna and Ben because, in his opinion, they were the most "German" in their attitude to work and were apparently as eager as he was to get their hands dirty.

On the day of the accident, his favoured trio was joined by both Andrew and Jim. Despite his natural reservations, both had proven themselves not only to be equally focussed on the task at hand. They had also apparently matched his own limitless enthusiasm for hard work.

As the final pole swung into place, Ben caught it and immediately began clamping it into position. Each pole had been carefully engineered to interconnect with all of the other elements of the construction. This meant that not only did the final framework come together like a giant Meccano set, but also if one element failed for whatever reason it could be replaced or repaired without having to compromise the entire structure.

Each building within the colony had at its extremity a quadruple skin framework, made up of a series of panels of photo-voltaic glass that overlapped to create an intricate, strong, yet simple lattice that could be altered to change the light quality and intensity in the living space below.

Ben carefully climbed down from the apex of the framework and looked proudly up at the newly finished building work; he smiled to himself before turning to Simon and patting him amiably on his shoulder;

"I think that we've earned ourselves an early night and perhaps a tiny Scotch Simon. What do you say?"

Simon turned to face Ben and shook his head defiantly, "No," he said flatly. "What we have is the perfect opportunity to make a start on fitting the outer skin."

Ben said nothing at first and instead merely looked at Simon as though he had requested to drop faecal matter into his spacesuit.

"You're kidding?" he said, "Right?"

Simon shook his head, "Not at all, we still have light enough for another two, perhaps two and a half hours work. Why would we stop now?"
"How about because we've all worked our asses off?" Ben said indicating the others who had now come over to see what was happening. "And I think we've earned a goddamn break!"
Simon clicked his teeth disapprovingly, "We have a task to complete," he said, "I do not see how doing one aspect of it well equates to not having to complete the other aspects,"
"Yeah?" Ben said his voice rising by the second.
Simon shrugged, "Absolutely."
"Well, how about I order you to take a break? How does that sound?" Ben said moving his face closer to Simon's.
"I do not understand why you are getting so irate Ben," Simon continued, "I just would like to make the most of the good conditions while we have them," he waved around at the Martian landscape, "none of us know when the next dust storm will arrive and shut down our construction. The quicker we can protect this section from the elements, the better."
Ben chewed on his Moustache and looked around at the work that they had just completed,
"Very well," he said finally, "but I want everyone to go and get at least a drink and something to eat before we start the next section, Okay?"
Simon nodded, "Of course," he said.
That was the moment that he could have avoided the whole sorry incident if only he had held fast onto his resolve and decided to wait for the others return, instead of blindly following them for a break that he neither wanted nor needed. As he went to leave the construction site he caught his foot on a stray cable that lay, partially buried beneath the powder-fine terracotta dust of the planet's surface. He slipped and

instinctively grabbed out to save himself from falling. The pole that he grabbed, however, was a spare and had not been attached to anything so instead of saving his slip, it swung around with Simon's momentum and crashed into the scaffold-like infrastructure. There was a deafening clang as the metal poles met and then a thud as Simon hit the ground with an undignified splaying of his limbs. His right leg remained caught in the cable and stuck out uncomfortably at right angles from his body, he felt his groin muscle pull and tear in protest at the sudden, unnatural movement, and he gasped in pain. He managed to steady himself and was just beginning to try and work out how to release himself from the troublesome cable, when a hydraulic winch that had been precariously balanced towards the top of the frame came crashing back to the ground, striking Simon squarely across his outstretched knee. He screamed in shock as it ruptured his anterior cruciate ligament and fractured his tibial plateau almost clean away from the shaft of the bone. There was a moment, just a fraction of a second really, when after the initial surprise Simon merely looked at the wreckage of his right leg in an interested, almost dispassionate way. Within that tiny moment, he idly thought to himself that if he were to view this scene from afar then the whole tableau would probably look quite odd, almost comical in fact. A tiny smile brushed the corners of his mouth, and then the pain hit him.

It engulfed him in a tidal wave. It began at his knee but then spread out through his entire body, splintering his concentration and ultimately causing him to pass into blissful unconsciousness.

Lying on his bunk now, he opened his eyes again and his hand reflexly felt for the damage in his knee. His flexed it and winced. It was still excruciatingly painful at times, even more than eight months after the accident.

Despite his discomfort, he could not help but marvel, once more at the incredible job that Becky had done in rebuilding and repairing his leg. He ran his fingertips lightly over the surface of his skin, he could feel the prosthesis moving beneath his touch. He remembered, vividly being shown the replacement knee after it had been printed and being amazed at its simple beauty and functionality. He remembered his surprise at how light the metal felt in his hands and wondering how it would ever manage to support his weight.

He sighed noisily and then allowed himself to relax again. Once again, he closed his eyes, this time with the intention of trying to get some much needed rest and recovery if he could. Despite the persistent throb, over time, his breathing slowed and eventually he drifted into a fitful sleep that was marked with dreams of falling, flying and unrequited love.

CHAPTER TWO

ON BOARD THE NERINE 3

The Nerine Three was on its final approach towards Mars. It was only two weeks away from touchdown and things were moving with a hectic pace and vigour. They were close enough to Mars now to hold regular conversations over the radio. This was great in terms of planning their arrival, but it had resulted in an unexpected shift in the dynamic on board the ship.

Jon and Cam had essentially been alone on the Nerine 3 for months. They had developed an operational and conversational shorthand that was now under threat. Having become accustomed to only each other's company, it had come as something of a culture shock to suddenly be part of a much larger community again.

The time spent in California prior to the first Nerine launching, had been intense, busy and occasionally very difficult. It was inevitable that certain fractions and alliances had developed within the wider group. Kindred spirits naturally sought each other out and alliances coalesced. Friendships had flourished but rivalries had also been seeded. These groups had been somewhat fractured when the first two shuttles had left Earth. However, although dormant, the connections that had been forged during those tumultuous times remained resolute and strong.

After a few days of initial pleasantries between the colonists and the new arrivals, old friendships began to re-establish and past tensions slowly began to simmer once again.

Ben and Cam had picked up where they had left off on Earth. Their natural rapport and easy familiarity had only taken a few minutes to re-establish itself.

Jon, however, began to increasingly isolate himself on board, lying on his bunk for hours at a time, studying and endlessly checking inventories and displays. Cam noticed his withdrawal but put it down to nerves. Jon carried the air of a man supremely comfortable in his own skin, yet despite this outward appearance, Cam had come to appreciate the insecurities and vulnerabilities that defined Jon so much more than his brash, sometimes overconfident exterior.

Cam was busy anyway, and almost giddy with excitement so he didn't have the time to worry about Jon's ego. The landing was fast approaching and he found himself constantly pouring over his calculations, or talking to those on the planet's surface about the mechanics of the colony and technicalities of their day-to-day life.

"How are the pods holding up?" he asked Ben during one of their frequent conversations,

"They're fine Cam. Just like they were yesterday and the day before."

"Yes, but are the compressors dealing with the oxygen levels?"

"The oxygen levels are fine. In fact, better than fine."

"Are the canaries all working properly?"

"I assume so or we'll all start dropping dead!" Ben laughed.

"This is serious Ben!" Cam chided.

"I know, I know. I'm sorry!"

"You can check you know, look at the crystal display, if it ..."

"Cam! They are fine! We have been working with them for almost two years now. I'm pretty sure we can figure out how to check them."

"Aye, but…"
"You asshole!" Ben shouted, "You think I'm too goddamn dumb to work this stuff out don't you?"
"No!" Cam paused, "Of course not."
"Okay 'mister genius'" Ben said irritably, "let's just see how goddamn smart you are when you finally get here, shall we?"
"Fucking smarter than you, anyway" Cam whispered, loud enough to be heard.
"Seriously? Am I going to have to beat that shit out of you?"
Cam laughed.
"Because I'll do it! You know that don't you? Can't you remember the pain?" Ben shook his head sadly, but Cam could see that he was smiling at the same time.
"Aye? Well, you can fucking try old man!" Cam said.
"Old man? Old man?" Ben said incredulously, "Old man or not. Two years down here working my ass off compared to nine months in an artificial gravity field," he sucked his teeth, "boy, you wouldn't have time to lift your hand to object!"
Cam laughed.
"I've missed you, you big fucking psycho! No one else quite reaches your level of sophistication," he said.
"Or your spectacular ability to be the crudest man I've ever met, whilst at the same time being so utterly patronising with only one or two words," Ben replied.
"Aye, well it's not fucking easy. It takes practice." Cam said.
"And yet you make it seem so effortless!" The screen crackled with a resonance pulse and Cam tapped it instinctively, "…11 days my friend. 11 days"
"Aye, I know. I can't believe it," Cam ignored the glitch.
"You guys all set?"
"Aye, More or less,"

“More or less?” Ben’s voice rose in disbelief, “More or less 'aint gonna cut it my little friend. So I’ll ask you again. Are you guys all set?”
“Keep your fucking panties on, Jesus! We’ll be ready, don't you worry your pretty little head about it. I know what I’m doing?”
“Yeah?” Ben laughed, “But what about Doctor Dumb-ass? Does he know what he’s doing?”
Cam sighed, “Aye, He’s fine. And he’s not a fucking dumb-ass. He’s just not an engineer,”
“Or an astronaut,”
“No, nor an astronaut,” Cam conceded. “But he’s saved me on this trip on more than one occasion. He’s a good guy.”
“Hmm,” Ben said uncertainly.
“I don't know why you don't like him. Everyone else does,”
“That’s probably why I don’t," Ben said with a shrug.
"The only reason I like you is because everyone else thinks you're a dick!"
"No, the reason you like me is because I'm the only one that will call you on your Bullshit"
"Not the only one," Ben said coyly.
"Oh really? You finally bumped uglies with the delightful Doctor Torres?"
"No! It's not like that," Ben protested
"Good," Cam said.
"Good? Why good?" Ben asked, confused.
"Because you're massive and she's tiny. You'd fucking crush her!" Cam laughed.
"Careful Cam, there's nothing going on between Sophie and myself."
"Yet,"
Ben shrugged, "Never say never, eh?"

Cam laughed again, "You're filth!"
Ben waggled his eyebrows, "Yeah well we'll see," Ben paused and another voice spoke. Cam couldn't hear what was being said though. "Look, I gotta go Cam. Jim's being an asshole about something or other,"
"Okay," Cam said, "but about Jon,"
"Yeah?"
"Give him a fucking chance, eh?"
"Yeah okay, if its that important to you," Ben had deflated, the excitement drained from his voice.
"You okay?" Cam asked, concerned.
"Sure, nothing I can't handle," Ben replied.
Cam nodded to himself, "Fair enough big man. Remember don't let the fuckers grind you down!"
Ben laughed. "Never have my friend, never will!"
"Okay then Ben, we'll talk later."
"Bye" Ben touched the screen and it went black.
Cam switched off his monitor and sank back into his seat. He looked out of the cockpit window at the steadily approaching planet and smiled to himself. It was beautiful. There was no argument about that, and it would soon become home.
He saw a glimpsed reflection of a figure moving at the back of the pod
"Jon?" he said reflexly.
Cam turned round, Jon was standing in the doorway, he wore a guiltily expression.
"What are you doing back there?" Cam asked.
"Eavesdropping?"
"Sorry," Jon said, "I heard voices. I didn't mean to intrude,"
Cam cringed, "You didn't hear what Ben said did you?"
Jon looked sheepishly down at the floor
"Yeah," he said quietly.

“I’m sorry. You know what he’s fucking like though?”
Jon shrugged.
“You okay?”
“About that?” Jon laughed, “Yeah of course. I don't care what that giant Canadian Neanderthal thinks about me. It’s just...” he paused.
“It’s just what?”
Jon sighed, “Can I ask you something? You know as a friend?”
Cam turned his chair around so he was facing Jon fully.
“Aye," he said. "Of course. What’s up?”
Jon hesitated. “How do you feel about landing?” he asked,
“The landing?” Cam couldn't hide the surprise in his voice.
“Yeah, the landing?” Jon repeated.
“What? You mean the physical part of the actual bumping our arses onto the planet? That landing?”
“No, not that,“ Jon shook his head. "I mean about, you know, seeing everyone again,”
“Oh, right!” Cam considered this for a moment. “Well, it’s a good thing, isn't it? On the whole?”
“Is it?” Jon arched a quizzical eyebrow.
“Aye, of course it fucking is. Why wouldn't it be?”
Jon sighed again, “I don't know,” he looked back at the floor. “It's been a long time though, hasn't it? Things will have changed.”
“Of course things will have changed. In the time since we've been apart, that lot have built a new colony on the surface of an alien planet."
"Not that," Jon said, dismissively.
"Then what? What things are you talking about?" Cam said, “Look Jon, What's bothering you?”

“I don’t know,” he said defensively, “not specifically anyway. But these guys have been on their own for almost two years now,”
“Aye, So?”
“So? So they will have lived things, done things, *endured* things as group,” he shook his head, “things that we don't even know about yet. Things that we can’t possibly imagine. Danger, fear, triumph.”
“So have we,” Cam said irritably, “I’m really sorry, but I just don’t see your point.”
“I think we need to be careful, that's all,” he said quietly,
“Careful? Why would we have to be careful? These people are our friends.”
"Are they?"
"Of course! You're starting to sound like a twelve year old girl, you know that don't you?"
Jon ignored the insult, which irritated Cam a little.
“They were, I agree,” Jon shrugged, “but we’re outsiders now. We’re not part of the group anymore.”
“Oh, don’t be such an old-fucking-woman,” Cam laughed.
"Which am I Cam? A little girl or an old woman?" Jon snipped
"Both!" Cam said with a grin.
"You're impossible," Jon said, "I don't know why I bother," Jon turned to leave.
"No, wait!" Cam called, "I'm sorry. I do think you're overreacting though. I’ve spoken to Ben every day. He’s just the same.”
“Exactly!” Jon raised his voice.
“Pardon?” Cam was confused.
“Doesn’t that strike you as a little unusual?” He asked. “After two years of terraforming, of trying to establish a colony against God knows what kind of danger and hardship. Ben

doesn't seem to have changed at all, he's still exactly the same," he made eye contact with Cam, "don't you think that's even the slightest bit odd?"
Cam considered this for a second and shook his head "No," he said, "not really, he's a pretty fucking even guy,"
"Really? That's not what you said to me all those years ago. You described him as a fucking sociopath."
"True," Cam nodded, "I did say that."
"Do you no longer believe it?"
"No!" Cam said instinctively, and he paused, "okay maybe, but thats not the point"
"Isn't it?" Jon asked.
It was Cam's turn to shrug, "I don't know. Look, what do you want me to say? First of all you're worried that everyone will have changed. Then you're worried that people have stayed the same!"
"I don't know, but you could at least acknowledge the possibility."
Cam shook his head, "Aye okay," he conceded, "its possible...I suppose. Okay? Is that better?"
Jon shrugged, "You don't believe that though do you?"
"Not really," Cam said, "but I honestly don't think you're right. I'm sorry, but I don't."
Jon folded his arms across his chest sulkily.
"Look Jon, Ben and I have been through a lot together. He probably knows me as well as anyone else alive. He helped me find focus when I had none."
"And I don't know you?" Jon sounded genuinely hurt.
"Oh, come on Jon! Don't do that, don't pretend that we were friends from day one. You spent most of your fucking time with the Americans and the other doctors."
"Yeah and you were with the engineers!"

Cam laughed, "What the fuck are you doing?"
"What?"
"You're acting like a fucking child Jon," Cam continued despite Jon's darkening expression, "Ben was with me from the beginning. He saw me at my fucking lowest and he never gave up. Not for a second!"
"Hmm" Jon grumbled. "You described it very differently, not so very long ago."
He was looking blankly at one of the monitors, his face like thunder. Cam put his arm around his shoulders and pulled closer in a hug.
"Come here," Cam said.
"Get off me,"
"I still fucking love you though!" Cam said, kissing him wetly on the cheek, "You know that don't you?"
Jon wrestled himself out of the hug.
"I said, Get off me!" Jon squirmed, but couldn't prevent a snort of laughter from escaping.
Cam took hold of Jon's hand and stared into his eyes, "We will always have this time together though. No-one can take that away from us"
Jon shook his hand free, "Piss off Cam. I'm trying to make a serious point here."
Cam smiled, "I know you are Jon, but I just can't see it. Sorry,"
"There's something not right down there," Jon shook his head again, "either that, or they're really not looking forward to our arrival."
"Of course they are!" Cam threw his hands into the air, "We are carrying enough supplies and equipment on board to ensure that this colony survives until the end of fucking time!"
"You're exaggerating a little I think," Jon said.

Cam shook his head, “No, not really. The sole purpose of this whole fucking mission is to establish a human presence on Mars ... forever...” he whispered the last word and let it drift.
“Yeah, yeah,” Jon waved his hand at Cam, “I read the literature too you know? I am fully aware of the official company line.”
“No, it’s more than that!” Cam was suddenly more animated, “I spent hours, fucking days talking to Gareth about this. This isn’t about us and now, this is about generations to come. We’re fucking pioneers Jon! The work we do now will echo through time!”
Jon rolled his eyes, “Yeah Cam, like I said, I've read the literature.”
“We’re planting the trees here Jon,” Cam said, suddenly deadly serious.
Jon looked at him, “What do you mean? Planting trees?”
“You know," Cam said, "like the Greek proverb?”
Jon shrugged “I don’t follow you, sorry,”
"You're the one that studied ancient Greece at school aren't you?"
"yeah, but..."
"Leave it to a boy from Govanhill to educate an Oxford man, eh?"
Jon sighed, "I don't remember this particular proverb, that's all," he protested.
“Sure you do,” Cam said, “it says that: 'a society grows great when the old men plant trees whose shade they know they shall never sit in'”.
Jon looked at him blankly.
“Don't you see? That’s fucking us, Jon! We’re the old men. We’re the ones who are planting the trees!”
“You’re an idealist Cam,” Jon shook his head.

“And you’re not?” Cam asked incredulously, “How can you be sitting here and not be a fucking idealist?”
“I’m a doctor Cam,”
“So?”
“So, I’m a realist mate. You show me a doctor that’s an idealist and I’ll show you a goddamned fool.”
“Jesus! That's cynical!” Cam laughed, nervously.
Jon shrugged, “Perhaps,”
“Look, when I talk to Ben later, do you want me to say something?”
“Don’t be ridiculous. I’m not a child. I’m just concerned,” Jon said, “and you should be too!”
Cam said nothing. He thought that Jon was just being paranoid, but then again, paranoia doesn't stop the bastards from trying to get you.

CHAPTER THREE

MARS COLONY ALPHA

Jim was sitting a little awkwardly outside the med bay. Apart from a hospital gown, he was only wearing a thin pair of cotton boxer shorts. He jiggled his leg up and down, nervously as he surveyed the corridor for any sign of any of the other colonists. Regular medical checks had become a routine part of life on Mars and although each colonist had become used to them, each visit served as a potent reminder of the extremes that each and every one of them put themselves through on a daily basis.

The living accommodation and vehicles all had an artificial gravity systems that were programmed to replicate conditions back on Earth, in order to make life as familiar and comfortable as possible. The colonists time out on the planet's surface however, brought with it exposure to a much thinner atmosphere. These included, but were not limited to, extremes of temperature and an increased risk of ionising radiation damage from the unfiltered distant light of the Sun. Each of these potential hazards came with a series of possible physical and psychological effects and therefore had to be monitored, not only for the crew's ongoing wellbeing but also for the colony's continued viability as an outpost of humanity. Despite the regularity of these appointments, each and every one of these visits still made Jim feel decidedly uncomfortable. He had never liked the thought of being unwell, and he liked even less the idea of being helpless. As he sat in the featureless corridor impatiently waiting for the med-bay door to slide open. His thoughts began to drift back to when he was only a boy. As a family he, his sisters and parents would go for long vacations to stay with his grandparents out on their old ranch in the heart of Wyoming. He closed his eyes and smiled as he brought forward the image of his grandfather. To a young boy, he was a giant of a man, almost like a superhero in Jim's eyes. He remembered fondly the times that he would sit with him, out in one of the wood barns and watch him chopping wood for what felt like hours at a time, laughing, joking and drinking his grandmother's terrible homemade lemonade. He could see him now, vividly in his mind's eye swinging his old wooden handled axe with apparent ease, its blade glinting in the seemingly endless summer sun and his huge muscles tensing and flexing with each stroke. His thin shirt stretched across his massive chest and a thin rolled up cigarette constantly hanging from his lips.

This image faded from his memory and was replaced by a palely lit and sterile hospital room. He had visited his grandfather just days before he had finally succumbed to the lung cancer that those ever present rollups had gifted to him. He remembered being appalled by the thinness of his skin and how fragile it looked as the dim electric light fell in pools upon his wasted flesh. He remembered the oxygen tubing that ran beneath his nose and poked into his nostrils, but most of all he remembered his eyes. Eyes that had once sparkled with energy and mischief, had become sightless and dull, lined with pain and stained with weariness and defeat.

Jim opened his own eyes again and once more shot a nervous glance along the corridor. There was still no one else around. He sighed a long and drawn out sigh and looked down at his bare feet, he wiggled his toes and then looked once more at the closed door to the med bay.

He had hated hospitals ever since that terrible day, and on every unavoidable subsequent visit that he had made to either a doctor's office, hospital and even dentists, he had always gone accompanied, with the ghost of those memories in close attendance. In his own mind, each one of these visits served as a reminder to the fragility of strength and the temporary nature of health. He knew that one day there would be an issue with one of the tests, perhaps it would be an irregularity in his blood-works or an arrhythmia in his heart beat, but it would be something. From that point on everything would change, perhaps slowly but inexorably. He would slowly begin to deteriorate, he would grow weaker until one day he would be just like his grandfather; old, frail and waiting to die.

The door to the med bay slid open and Sophie poked her head around the corner. She took one look at Jim's careworn expression and her brow furrowed in concern.

"Are you okay James?" she asked as lightly as she could manage.

Jim shook himself from his reverie and looked up into Sophie's wide, expectant face

"I'm fine," he said, "you ready for me now?"

Sophie nodded, "Mmm, hmm," she said.

She ducked back through the doorway, Jim stood up from his chair and followed her. The end of the room had been screened off but other than that it looked exactly the same as it always did. Jim smiled to himself and inwardly berated himself for being so morbid

"Where do you want me doc?" he asked, regaining a little of his usual swagger

Sophie indicated to the screened off portion of the room with a nod of her head and he immediately began to make his way there, his bare feet slapping against the cold hard floor as he went.

"Why on Earth didn't we make these floors heated?" he said as he went.
Sophie shrugged, "I would guess it is because it is only us doctors that spend any amount of time in here," she said dryly, "and we are not very high on the food chain in this particular community."
Jim looked at her, "Really?" he said, surprised, "do you honestly believe that we don't think highly of you guys?"
Sophie shrugged again, "Only when you need us," she replied.
She turned to face Jim and considered him over the rim of her glasses for a moment, "We are all professionals though," she said, "and we have other matters at hand presently," she gestured towards the end of the med bay.
She pulled the curtain to one side revealing a bed and a treadmill, along with a whole host of monitors and equipment.
"If you wouldn't mind removing the robe for me," she said, "and if you could get on to the bed, I will do an EKG and take some blood."
Jim slipped out of his robe and handed it to Sophie, who in turn placed it over the back of a chair. He climbed onto the bed and instinctively stuck his left arm out towards her.
Sophie applied a tourniquet and then turned her attention to attaching the sensors for the EKG.
"How are you feeling?" She said, conversationally.
Jim shrugged his shoulders, "Fine thanks, no worries."
Sophie nodded, “Anything unusual that you would like to report?" she continued.
"Such as?" he asked.
"Any change to bowel habits? Any difficulty sleeping or concentrating?"

Jim shook his head, "Nope," he said and then patted his stomach, "regular as clockwork doc!"
Sophie smiled, "Good."
Just as she turned back to the heart monitor, there was a knock on the wall outside the curtain.
"Sophie?" Becky called through the curtain, "Sorry to interrupt, but can I borrow you for a second please?"
Sophie turned her head and tutted loudly, "I'm doing a medical," she said irritably. "Can't it wait?"
"Would I be interrupting you if it could?" Becky replied with a forced sweetness.
Sophie sighed and turned her attention to Jim, “Would you excuse me a moment?" she said and without waiting for a response headed out of the curtains.
"Yeah, sure! No problem," Jim said to no one in particular, he laid his head back against the pillow and closed his eyes.
The two doctors held a brief, whispered discussion which Jim could neither hear properly or indeed particularly wanted to.
After only a few minutes though Sophie poked her head around the curtain again, her face slightly reddened.
"I'm sorry Jim," she said, "but I'm going to have to go."
"Is everything all right?" Jim asked, concerned.
"Yes," she answered reflexly before adding, "at least I think so..." she trailed off.
Jim looked at her expectantly, “So what do I do?" He said finally. "Wait here in my shorts until you come back?"
"No, of course not," Sophie said, "but I'm afraid that we will have to reschedule."
Jim sighed and closed his eyes, "Really?" he said, exasperated.
"I'm afraid so," Sophie said apologetically, "unless..." she removed herself back to the med bay for a moment where

there were more whispers, she popped her head back around the curtain again.
"Actually, Becky has said she'll finish you off," she said happily, "if that's okay with you that is?"
Jim shrugged, “Sure," he said, "as long as it’s over and done with today I don't really care who actually pokes me with the needle!"
Sophie smiled and then disappeared from view, she paused to thank Becky for the favour and then Jim heard the med bay door slide open and then closed. Then he heard it click as it was locked.
Moments later Becky walked around the closed curtain and smiled at Jim, who was suddenly very aware of his level of nakedness. He returned her smile albeit a little sheepishly.
"You locked the door?" he said quietly.
Becky said nothing but nodded her head in reply.
"Why on Earth would you want to lock the door doctor?" he said, nervously.
Becky stopped walking and considered this question for a moment.
"Because," she said with wicked smile, "the wild goose chase that I just sent Sophie on will probably keep her occupied for a good twenty minutes or so."
As she spoke she pulled her t-shirt over her head and reached around her back to unclip her bra. She walked closer towards Jim and let it fall to floor beside the bed; she locked him with her eyes. Jim swallowed hard.
"And what I've got planned for you may take a few minutes more than that," she said and started to remove her leggings.
"But...but...medical," was all that Jim managed to say.
Becky paused and arched her eyebrows at him, "What about it?" she asked calmly.

"I...I" he stammered.
"Yes?" Becky asked, and slipped off what remained of her clothing.
Jim looked at her now naked body, his face flushed and again, he gulped loudly.
Becky tilted her head to one side and considered him in the way a Labrador might consider a new bone. Her smile remained etched across her features as she reached over and ran her fingers over the waistband of his shorts before tugging gently on them to inch them down slightly.
"Part of your medical is checking your reaction to, and recovery from, prolonged physical activity," she looked over at the treadmill, "it's your choice of course, but I think you'll find my method far more enjoyable."
Jim once again opened his mouth to protest but by now the conversation between the mental and physical sides of his being had become distinctly one sided. Instead, he merely closed his mouth again and invited Becky to join him with a playful pat of the mattress.
In response, she smiled seductively at him and then climbed up onto the bed and straddled him before leaning forward and kissing him lightly on the neck, face and then more firmly on his mouth. Jim's initial reluctance had by now completely thawed and he kissed her back, hungrily.
Half an hour later, when Sophie returned, somewhat irritated by the seemingly pointless diversion, she tried the door to regain entry to the med bay. Upon discovering that it was firmly locked she immediately added two and two together and wisely decided not to investigate the circumstances any further, instead she headed back to her quarters, muttering to herself as she went.

CHAPTER FOUR

Dust storms were not an unusual occurrence on Mars, but this particular one had been raging for almost thirty-six hours and subsequently, the mood within the colony had grown increasingly tense. Thirty-six hours of nothing but artificial light combined with the inability to venture onto the planet's surface was weighing heavily upon the colonists, especially those that had construction work to get on with outside of the main compound.

"They'll be here in a few weeks," Simon said animatedly, "and at the moment there is nowhere for them to sleep."

"I know Simon," Jim said slowly. "But there's absolutely nothing that I can do about the weather."

"You should have had a contingency in place," Simon said simply.

Jim arched an eyebrow in response, but said nothing.

"It is ridiculous that we are unable to make any progress until this storm dies down. If you had looked at things more thoroughly and if the main cover had been erected, like I suggested..."

"Simon!" Jim cut over him, his voice loud but still essentially calm.

Simon stopped suddenly and stared at Jim expectantly, "Ja?" he said.

"I'm sorry that this dust storm has stopped you from completing your work, but I will not be spoken to like that!" Jim said severely, "Not by you, or anybody else. Do you understand?"

Simon blinked, and shook his head, "I do not mean any disrespect," he said flatly, "but I think you have made a judgement error."

Jim rolled his eyes, "Duly noted Simon. If you're bored then there are plenty of chores that you could be getting on with inside."
"Arghh," Simon said with a disgusted wave of his hand. "There are too many people in here. Wherever I go, there are others interfering."
"Then why not take the opportunity to take some R and R?"
"I have rested enough with this," he said patting his damaged leg.
Jim sighed.
"Then why don't you go and see if Andrew and Felix need some help in one of the Bio-pods?"
Simon's brow furrowed
"What?" Jim asked innocently
"I do not think that they would welcome my help," Simon said sternly.
"Of course they would, they're snowed under at the moment," Jim said,
"No," Simon shook his head firmly, "I will go to the gym instead I think, until the weather has cleared."
He turned and left, leaving Jim alone desperately trying to stifle a laugh.
"Homophobic prick," he muttered to himself as he left, and then set off himself to the Bio-pods to check upon their progress.
Felix and Andrew were deep in discussion when Jim arrived into Bio-pod 3, as soon as he entered they looked up in unison and stopped talking immediately. While the storm had been raging outside the two men had been spending most of their time together in here, desperately trying to look after their plants without any natural light whatsoever coming through the panels.

Felix and Andrew's fledgling relationship had taken a long time to establish itself, but now that it had, they were making up for lost time by spending as much time together as humanly possible.
It was only when they had started to work together within the bio-pods, and had consequently become closer as friends, that they had realised that they shared a mutual attraction and finally acted upon it. Since then they had become almost inseparable, they shared everything and Jim suspected that if they could sleep in this damn bio-pod they probably would.
"Good afternoon gentlemen," Jim said, happily as he picked his way over to them through several recently replanted fruit beds.
Felix watched his progress carefully, visibly flinching when his boot skirted too closely to one of the fledgling plants.
"Hi James," Andrew said with a wave, "everything okay?"
Jim nodded, "Yeah, just though I'd check in on you guys. See how you're coping in this shit storm," he gestured to the darkness outside with a nod of his head. "Jesus it's hot in here!" he added, wiping a hand across his face.
"We've had to use the lighting more than we would have liked," Felix said looking up at the ceiling.
Jim's eyes followed his stare and noticed that the banks of ultraviolet lamps were indeed all on at full strength.
"Yeah, that's partly why I'm here guys," Jim said his expression growing more serious, "I'm really sorry, but I can't let you keep these on I'm afraid."
"What!" Andrew and Felix said together. "If we turn them off then we'll lose a full cycle!"
"Not necessarily," Jim said.
"No, but probably," Felix said angrily. "You can't do this Jim; you know how much effort we've put into this?"

"I do guys, but..."
"I don't remember hearing you complain about the strawberries?" Andrew butted in.
Jim raised his hands in mock surrender, "I know guys, but they're absolutely killing the power cells."
"There must be something else?" Felix asked, hopefully.
Jim shook his head, "You are my last port of call. Everyone else has been told."
"Everyone?" Felix asked.
"Yes, everyone!" Jim was getting agitated now, "Christ guys this isn't personal you know? We've got no way of telling how long this goddamn storm is gonna last, though."
"But..." Andrew began, but Jim cut across him.
"Enough! I'm sorry guys, really I am but I haven't got a choice," he shrugged helplessly.
Andrew and Felix looked at each other; each one carried a pained expression on their face.
"Okay," Andrew said, sulkily.
Jim looked at Felix, "And your'e okay?" he asked.
Felix nodded, "Sorry Jim, we shouldn't have overreacted."
Jim sighed, "Look," he said, "I'm not unsympathetic, and you're right I do like the strawberries, so how about if I try to get you some rolling time, enough to try and keep the crop from failing?"
Both Andrew and Felix noticeably perked up.
"Go on..." Andrew said
Jim rubbed at his chin thoughtfully, "Okay," he said slowly, "how about this? If I cut life support in here down to a minimum and limit the gas venting then maybe..." he shook his head.
"Go on," said Felix.
"Well, maybe it will keep things ticking over?"

Felix and Andrew exchanged a look.
"Sounds promising," Andrew said. "theoretically, at least."
"You wouldn't be able to spend any more time in here though; you might have to mix with the rest of the crew again!" Jim said, smiling again.
The two men looked at each other and shrugged, "I guess we don't have much of a choice do we?" Felix said unhappily.
"It's the best I can offer," Jim said, “hopefully, this'll pass quickly anyway and you can get back in no time."
The three of them turned together and started to head towards the exit.
"How long will it take to get back to safe levels?" Andrew asked as they walked. "When the storms over?"
Jim shrugged, "It shouldn't take long," he said, "the Canaries will keep the atmosphere to workable levels and the life support will come back on in a matter of minutes."
They reached the door and Felix turned to take another look at the infant plants, he murmured something under his breath and as they left the bio-pod, it plunged into darkness.
"Did you say something?" Jim asked.
Felix blushed and shook his head. Jim smiled to himself.
"Because I could have sworn that you said something," he pushed, playfully.
Felix once again resolutely shook his head, "No!" he said.
"Oh okay," Jim said, "but it sounded a lot like you just said goodnight to a bunch of strawberries!" his smile had broadened into a grin.
Felix looked at him but said nothing. Andrew however turned back to the door and kissed the glass of the porthole.
"Goodnight my darlings!" he said and then grabbed hold of Felix's hand protectively. Felix looked at him and smiled before reaching over and kissing his cheek gently.

Jim put a hand onto Felix's shoulder, “Just kidding Felix," he said, "no offence, eh?"
Felix smiled and shook his head.
"None taken," he said, "but I'd make sure that you wash your strawberries from now on!"
"Wow! Threats? Really?" Jim shook his head. "You used to be such a nice kid Felix. You just wait till I see your big brother in a couple of weeks!"
Felix blanched. Jim saw his reaction and smiled.
"Yeah," he said, "that got you thinking, didn't it?"
Andrew whispered something into Felix's ear and Felix put his hand to his mouth to suppress a snort of laughter.
"What?" Jim asked.
Felix shook his head, "Nothing," he said sweetly.
Jim narrowed his eyes, "Oh he is *so* going to find out about all this!" he said and the three of them burst into laughter.

CHAPTER FIVE

Ben stood a little awkwardly in Sophie's quarters. He could hear the shower running and he hovered around by the door wondering if he should just leave and come back later. Just as he had made up his mind to go, the sound of running water abruptly stopped and a few seconds later Sophie emerged from the bathroom wearing a snow white towelling robe and a pink towel turban upon her head.

She looked over at Ben and smiled, her face showing no hint of surprise at Ben's presence in her quarters, "Hi Ben," she said with a smile, "please excuse me, I won’t be long."

She walked past him in a cloud of steam and perfumed air and disappeared into her bedroom.

Ben forced a smile onto his face.

"I did knock," he called after her, "I was just checking you were okay, what with this storm and everything."

"You are very kind," she called back.

"Just doing my job," Ben said

"I am fine though, thank-you," she responded happily, ”please, make yourself at home."

Ben looked around Sophie's quarters, in all major aspects they were exactly the same as his own, but she had somehow made them seem more comfortable and inviting. Absent mindedly he started to flick through a pile of papers that lay on the side of the breakfast bar. They were mostly medical journal articles, mixed in with an occasional trashy magazine, that she had clearly read and reread many times over the last two years or so. As he moved to straighten up the papers that he had just messed up he noticed a small, well thumbed, leather bound sketchbook. The cover was intricately stained with all manner of inks and God knew what. Ben gently lifted it up and ran his fingers lightly over the textured surface; he raised it to his face and took a tentative sniff of the leather. It smelled old and familiar and he couldn't help but smile at the comfort that the scent provoked in him. He stood there, holding it a few moments before he went to put it back onto the counter top. The book had several loose pages and one such page was sticking out from the middle of the book. Instinctively he tried to tuck it back into the book, as he did so he noticed an exquisitely rendered portrait drawn in ink on the corner. Intrigued, he opened the book and carefully began to flick through the pages. Most of the sketches that it contained were simple line drawings, mainly of faces and figures. Ben was amazed how beautifully observed they each seemed to be. He marvelled at how so few lines and marks could contain so much information about the subject. Each drawing was dated; named and carried a few personal notes about the sitter. Ben could feel a small smile spread over his face as he examined each drawing. He continued to look through the book until he reached a block of text that was situated towards the back of the book. It was a hand written passage that had been written in Sophie's small and, for a doctor, surprisingly neat handwriting. Without thinking he lifted the book closer to his face and began to read the words that Sophie had so carefully scribed;

I believe in God, I always have.
I was raised to be a good, God fearing Catholic girl. My faith gave me my career and it also brought me Africa, to follow in the footsteps of the missionaries of past times. It has also been my salvation on many occasions. When I have been at my lowest, I have opened my heart to God, I have prayed and I have been lifted.

Six days. That's all it has taken. Six days to shake the very bedrock of my faith. Six days of almost relentless heartbreak and impossible tragedy.
Six days in Hell.
When Ebola hit, we were devastatingly underprepared for what was to unfold, the had no equipment, no facilities, no chance.
People died, good people. People that, like me, were trying to help. Within weeks the front line had been decimated, everywhere was dangerously under-protected, everyone was under informed and in that environment the disease flourished. The people were desperate, desperate and terribly contagious.
Mikosi died today.
So did many others but Mikosi was different. He was one of us. He helped to build this hospital with only his bare hands and his brutal determination. He was a strong man, a handsome man. A son, a brother, a husband and a father. He had become a talisman within the surrounding area. Our good luck charm!
He gave hope to a community that had none. He built an oasis of courage in a dessert of fear and desolation. He seemed superhuman, untouchable, but still he died. He died in the most horrible way imaginable, blood haemorrhaging from his eyes and mouth. In pain and afraid, not afraid to die but afraid of what was to come to those he left behind.
I was with him at the end and I will forever wish that I wasn't. It will haunt me in my sleep, follow me when I wake. To watch this giant of a man, this hero, brought to his knees and crushed, was too much to bare. He was taken by a cruel and indiscriminate disease that swept him aside with no more effort than we would take to swat a fly.

I am a doctor.
A doctor is supposed to help, supposed to heal. Today has brought me nothing but a terrible, disconsolate sadness and a feeling of professional impotence that I can barely bring myself to acknowledge.
I am used to dealing with death and disease, it comes with the territory after all; I have worked in emergency rooms throughout Europe and have witnessed at first hand, man's seemingly endless capacity to inflict pain on their fellow man in graphic and immediate detail. The level of human suffering that I have witnessed here, in this hospital is unlike anything that I have ever seen before. Here there is despair without relief, without hope, without end.
There is nothing I can do to change what is happening here. If the entire hospital was wiped out what difference would it make? We save a life and then send the patient back into the world to die all over again.
Why save a life, only to then watch it ultimately slip away like sand between my fingers?
If it is true then we are all part of Gods plan, then what part of that plan involves children dying alone and scared, unable to kiss their mothers goodbye? What part of God's plan involves burying whole families in mass graves dug with a bulldozer instead of a spade? What kind of God creates a virus so deadly that a hug can kill you?
Two hundred and fifty seven people died here today; men, women and children but Mikosi's death provoked a sadness that was felt by even the hardiest of the hospitals staff;
He was one of us. One of the good guys. He knew the risks and still he tried to help. He was a carer, a counsellor; he was the builder of a hospital in a place where there were no hospitals before.

When all the carers have gone, when the doctors have all left and when all the hospital builders have died. What happens then? Who cares for the sick? And if there are no more new hospitals, then where do the children go to be saved?
So I believe in God, I always have.
I'm just not sure he believes in us anymore.

Ben stared at the words and felt the emotion rise within him. He felt some of the pain that Sophie had clearly felt when she wrote this and it made him ache with sadness to his very core. He noticed that the drawings after this entry were different, the quality of the draughtsmanship remained, but the subject matter became more gruesome. Instead of portraits, the figures that came after this point were clearly of corpses or the very ill. The meticulously beautiful, yet simple lines made by Sophie somehow added a further dimension of grotesquery to the images. He closed the little book, carefully and placed it back onto the breakfast bar next to the papers and magazines. Once it was back in place he patted it gently on the front cover and then turned to leave the room.
"They are not that bad, are they?" Sophie said from the doorway of her bedroom.
Ben looked back, startled and blushed.
"I'm so sorry," he said hurriedly, "I shouldn't have looked...I..."
Sophie waved her hand at him, "It's okay," she said gently and took a step towards him. "It is only a sketchbook. Memories from a different time...a different place,"
"I know but I still shouldn't have..."
"I'm glad you've seen them," she said, a tiny smile touching her lips.

"I have never showed them to anyone before. What did you think?" she walked out of the doorway and headed to where he was standing in the kitchen.
Her face glistened from recently applied moisturiser and it carried upon it a look of expectant dread and hope mixed together. Ben opened his mouth to speak but said nothing, Sophie's smile faded.
"Oh," she said sadly, "you really didn't like them?"
Ben shook his head, "No," he said a little too loudly, "that is, I mean yes! I loved them...they're so beautiful, so perfect."
Sophie's face flushed pink and she moved a little closer to where Ben was standing.
"Do you mean that?" she said quietly, "you are not teasing me are you?"
Ben nodded, "Of course I'm not. You've got a real talent there kid," he said regaining some of his usual swagger.
Sophie stretched up onto her tiptoes, placed her hand lightly on his chest and kissed him gently on his cheek, as she did so her robe caught against his shirt and pulled slightly open revealing a glimpse of her naked breast beneath. Ben noticed immediately but looked away at once; he swallowed and tried desperately not to look again at her exposed flesh.
Sophie smiled wickedly, "You are so sweet," she said to him but made no effort to cover herself back up.
Ben took half a step backwards, "I'll let you get dressed," he said awkwardly and forced a smile onto his face, "I’ll come back later."
Sophie smiled and nodded, "Okay then." She said with a tiny smile and then turned to head back over to her bedroom, refastening her robe as she went.
Ben watched her go and remained staring at the closed door for a few seconds before he finally shook himself from his

trance and left her quarters. As he walked along the corridor he tried to process what had just happened, before ultimately deciding that he was reading far too much into what he was sure was just a minor wardrobe malfunction.

CHAPTER SIX

Felix was staring, entranced at the flickering screen of this laptop. His fingers hovered above the keys, poised to move into action at the precise moment that inspiration struck. They remained poised for almost ten minutes before he reluctantly let them drop onto the table top with a gentle thud. Inspiration was a fickle mistress and she was steadfastly refusing to turn her favour towards Felix today. He swore quietly under his breath and decided to check his emails instead.

He opened the page, then without looking, almost immediately stood up from his desk and headed over to the fridge, where he pulled out a bottle of strawberry wine that he and Andrew had made for the party. He unscrewed the top and poured a large measure into one of the clean mugs that stood drying by the side of the sink.

He was off his game, and had been for more than a week. The incident with Andrew's allergic reaction in the dining hall had affected him more than he had initially realised. As a consequence, his ability to concentrate had apparently all but evaporated and he found that he couldn't work on anything for more than a few minutes at a time. Now that this dust storm had pushed him out of the bio-pod, he had the perfect opportunity to catch up with some work. The truth was, it was the wrong kind of work, and he really wasn't feeling any enthusiasm for it at the moment.

Andrew had recovered well from his brush with anaphylaxis and he had been shocked into carrying an epipen with him wherever he went. That didn't help Felix though; he was new at the whole relationship thing and as a consequence was reluctant to leave his side for any extended period of time. Mindful of both his concern for his safety and his ongoing literary struggles, Andrew had gently insisted upon giving Felix some time on his own in an attempt to refocus his mind and to give him a chance to catch up on his column. Felix had argued of course, fearful of letting Andrew out of his sight, but common sense along with a series of rapidly approaching deadlines had finally persuaded him otherwise. He had started well in his newly imposed isolation but now, as he sat there devoid of all distractions, all he could think about was how much he missed Andrew and how much he longed to be with him. He sighed, took a long draught from his mug and then refilled it before heading back over to his laptop.

'Postcards from Major Tom' was the name of the regular column that Felix wrote for the information hungry inhabitants of the planet that he and his colleagues had left behind. It had begun life as a short travelogue that he wrote, as a jokey, semi-autobiographical diary entry. However, such had been the impact of it that it had quickly blossomed into a much anticipated, widely read column. It ran in some of the largest publications on the planet and was carried by over thirty 'homepage' websites including the BBC, CBS and MSN. Within weeks he was receiving hundreds of daily e-mails about the column, most of which were friendly and complimentary with only an occasional alarming message from some religious or fanatical zealot.

He normally enjoyed writing the column but as with all such things, the monotony of the familiar occasionally becomes hard to ignore and his enthusiasm would inevitably waver from time to time. He kept himself focussed by diversifying and he continued to write other articles unrelated to either Mars or space travel. Due to his somewhat isolated location, his ability to personally investigate any breaking stories had become severely limited. He had, reluctantly, had to accept that he could no longer operate as a frontline journalist and had adapted his working methods accordingly. He was still able to get information from Earth but while any internet capability on Mars was impressive. It wasn't exactly fibre-optic in its speed, nor was it overly reliable. This meant he found that he had to delegate and rely on friends, colleagues and Jacob to provide him with the raw materials that he fed upon to launch a new story. One benefit from his new acquired minor celebrity status was that that for the first time in his journalistic career, he was able to write about issues that he had a genuine interest in and still be virtually guaranteed some column inches, somewhere. In the main, he wrote about recently occurring, perhaps overlooked and occasionally controversial historical events. Cold cases that still had plenty of evidence available if you knew where to look. Stories that could capture an imagination, that had the potential to grab the public's attention if given the right set of circumstances.

He looked once again at the open window on his screen and scrolled, listlessly, through the most recent batch of fan based e-mails and, without raising any enthusiasm, he deleted the whole batch without even opening a single one. He parked his e-mail account and instead opened his desktop folder of half-finished articles and stories in search of inspiration. He spent a few minutes here, picking over the literary carcasses of his still-born projects, with as much enthusiasm as he could muster.

He opened a story that he had begun way back in Cape Town, half a life time ago. He had abandoned it when the excitement of Project Livingstone had come calling. It was the one story that he found himself returning to, constantly re-examining the evidence, always looking for a new angle, a different perspective. He scanned through the half written body of the

text and considered the paragraphs of half formed ideas and without finding anything new. Then he started to look through some of the resources articles and journals that he had brought, electronically, with him.
His eyes flicked over the old yet familiar lines of text searching for a way in. As he read further he noticed, almost subconsciously, an anomalous snag in the text. A word that didn't fall into the familiar pattern, something he had somehow failed to notice before. He checked some more documents until he found it again and then scanned more and more until finally he had six references all to the same point.
His heart rate quickened as he tried to process what this new information might mean. It might be nothing after all, coincidence and nothing more. But then again it might be the way in he had been looking for.
The article was about a series of suspicious deaths that had occurred throughout West Africa and Europe in the mid-noughties. Deaths that no one seemed to either notice or particularly care about. The clinician that many suspected of being behind the deaths had never been caught or even questioned and he had continued to move, unrestricted, from hospital to hospital with devastating impunity. Felix had tried to find a way to make it into some form of cohesive story, but had always struggled for a narrative hook. The victims were invariably considered to be of low status, and in countries where hundreds die every day, the evidence was hard to compile and almost impossible to collate. There was plenty of rumour and conjecture, but without any empirical evidence, there remained no case to answer, and no one to answer it.
Felix checked the texts again to be certain that his excitement wasn't clouding his analytical judgement, but with each check and with each article he found more and more references.

Each article had quotes from interviews from other health care workers as well as porters and cleaners that had all worked alongside the suspected doctor. Medicine can be a closed shop to outsiders, especially when the efficiency or competence of the profession is being called into question. Therefore, perhaps unsurprisingly, there had been a distinct shortage of medical staff that had been either willing to speak about what had happened or waive their right to anonymity. This was the rule, but there were exceptions. Some had stepped forward and spoken up for those that could no longer speak for themselves, and of those that did, one of the names that kept reoccurring was a young, newly qualified doctor called Dominguez.
Sophie Torres-Dominguez.

*   *   *

Ben had just come off duty and was heading slowly towards his quarters, where he planned to have a shower and perhaps a cheeky nap before heading along for his evening meal. The dust storm was finally slowing down and between the clouds, the pale Martian light flooded through the photovoltaic glass panels of the corridor. He allowed himself a moment's pause to enjoy the magnified warmth. He stared out over the alien landscape and smiled to himself. The view could hardly be described as beautiful, at least in a traditional sense, but the shadows cast by the rock formations and surface craters were certainly dramatic.
As he stood, lost in his thought, he suddenly became aware of the sound of approaching footsteps. He turned his head to greet the owner of them, but as he did so he heard of an angry, whispered exchange. Without thinking he ducked

around the corner of the corridor and hid himself from view. The voices came closer and he was uncomfortably aware of the vulnerability of his hiding spot, as soon as the arguers came around the corner they would see him poorly secreted and apparently eavesdropping on their conversation. He cursed inwardly at his instinct to hide; after all if he had just stayed where he was then he would have nothing to explain. He looked around in an effort to plan his next move and ultimately decided that he would try and slink off to the end of the corridor and into the main pod before he could be seen. As he went to move off he heard the footsteps come to a halt and, for the first time he could make out some of what was being said;

"I don't know what you want from me," came the first voice which Ben released, almost instantly belonged to Sophie. Instinctively he stopped, his muscles tensed and then he edged a little closer to the conversation so that he could better hear what was being said. The acoustics within the corridor were surprisingly effective and despite the fact that he was a least twenty metres away from them, he could hear the two of them clearly despite their hushed tones.

The second voice was even quieter than Sophie's but Ben still recognised it, "Why are you being so defensive?" Felix said in a whispered growl.

"I'm not being defensive!" Sophie said angrily, "I have answered your questions."

"Have you?" Felix said, "You were there, not just once but three maybe four times."

"I don't remember," she shot back, "it was twenty years ago. I was fresh out of med school."

"You must remember something?" Felix was almost pleading with her now.

Ben realised that he could see the two of them in a reflection in part of the corridor, which logically meant that they would be able to see him too if either of them looked in the right place. As a result he tried, unsuccessfully, to push himself further into the wall. Fortunately for him they both seemed sufficiently distracted by one another to notice anyone else. He looked at the two of them and Ben could see the expression on Sophie's face, she looked upset and Felix was clearly angry.
"I’ve told you what I remember," Sophie said defiantly, "now, if you don't mind I have work to do!"
She turned to leave but Felix grabbed her by the arm forcing her to stop dead in her tracks she gasped in surprise and pain.
"Let me go!" she said a little desperately. "You’re hurting me!"
Ben tensed further, he wasn't going to stand idly by whilst Sophie was clearly being harassed. He pulled himself up to his full height and then started to walk along the corridor, whistling loudly as he went.
Felix looked up in alarm at the sound of the intrusion and hurriedly let go of Sophie's arm.
Ben plastered a wide smile onto his face and walked up to then pair of them, staring intently at Felix the whole time.
"Evening guys," he said, jovially.
Felix reddened and grunted sullenly. He looked directly at Sophie his eyes narrowing dangerously as he did so.
Ben followed his gaze, “Everything okay here?" he asked as lightly as he could manage, "I haven't interrupted something have I?"
Felix didn't take his eyes from Sophie who moved closer to Ben and put her hand on his arm gently. Ben arched his eyebrows and considered Felix a little more closely.
"Felix?" he said.

Felix tore his stare away from Sophie's face and forced himself to look at Ben
"No," he said, through a clenched smile, "you're not interrupting. Everything's fine thanks," he looked back at Sophie. "Isn't it Soph?"
Sophie looked at Felix and swallowed awkwardly, "Yes" she said quietly.
Ben stroked his moustache and turned back to Sophie.
"Well, if your all finished here, perhaps young Miss Torres would like to accompany me to dinner this evening?" he said.
Sophie looked up at Ben, her eyes wide with gratitude and smiled.
"I think," she said, "that that would be lovely."
She wrapped her arm through the crook of Ben's elbow and the two of them turned to leave. They had only moved a few paces before Felix called after them.
"I'll see you later Sophie," he said loudly, barely trying to hide the warning in his voice. "We can finish off then."
"Not if she sees you first." Ben called behind them without turning his head.
The two of them then they continued on their way, leaving Felix to cut a forlorn and frustrated figure in their wake, his expression like thunder.
After what Ben considered to be an adequate distance he looked down at Sophie and was surprised to see her smiling, serenely.
"You okay?" he said.
Sophie nodded; "Mmm hmm" she said and pulled herself closer to Ben's arm.
"What was that all about?" Ben pressed.
Sophie shook her head, "Nothing really," she said, simply.

"It didn't look like nothing to me," he said gruffly, "did he hurt your arm?"
Sophie glanced down at the spot where Felix had grabbed her and considered the red mark that still showed there with an expression of vague surprise.
"What that?" she asked, "Oh that was nothing, he just got a little overexcited, that's all."
Ben looked at her arm, "Looks painful," he said seriously.
Sophie shrugged, and they continued their journey towards the dining hall.
"It is fine," she said.
"You know if he's hurting you or..." Ben hesitated.
"He's worried about Andrew that's all, after what happened in the dining room last week."
Ben blushed reflexly at the reference but Sophie didn't seem to notice.
"He's okay isn't he?" Ben said as casually as he could manage.
Once more Sophie shrugged, "Yes, he's fine," she said, "if anything it taught him a valuable lesson. To always carry an epipen with him."
Ben swallowed, "You're sure that's all?" he asked again.
Sophie nodded, "Of course. What else could it be?"
Ben shook his head, "I don't know."
"Exactly," she said and kissed his arm, "now come on, you promised that you'd buy me dinner."

CHAPTER SEVEN

Ben and Sophie walked into the dining hall arm in arm, there was no one else around and they headed straight for the smallest of the tables that were set up around the room. Ben pulled out the chair facing the wall and gestured for Sophie to sit down; he then moved around the table and sat opposite her with his back against the same wall so he could see not only her but also the rest of the room.

"Do you want a drink?" he said and moved to stand again.

Sophie nodded and Ben walked over to one of the vending machines where he ordered two bottles of water. He retrieved them and then turned back to face the table.

"You hungry?" he called across the room.

Sophie looked over at him but said nothing, merely shaking her head by way of a reply.

Ben made his way over to one of the refrigerators and helped himself to a large bowl of pre-wrapped noodles, which he placed directly into the microwave and started to heat.

Sophie had turned back to face the wall, where she sat motionless until Ben returned with his steaming bowl of food a few minutes later. He placed the bowl onto the table and put a set of chopsticks by the side of it, he handed Sophie one of the bottles of water and opened the other himself, taking a long draught from it before sitting himself back down again. He picked up the chopsticks and pulled them through his fingertips before diving into his dinner.

"You sure you don't want some?" he asked through a mouthful of half chewed chicken chowmein.

The barest flicker of distaste touched Sophie's face and she once again shook her head. Ben shrugged and then continued with his meal hardly pausing to swallow as he did so. Within

five minutes the bowl was completely empty and even as Ben wiped the remains of the sauce from his moustache he was looking back over at the fridge as he contemplated going back for a second helping.
Sophie reached across the table and placed her hand on his arm just as he made the decision to go back. Instead of standing, Ben remained seated, seemingly glued suddenly to his seat. He looked over at Sophie and noticed for the first time that her eyes had reddened a little and were glistening with newly formed tears. Tears that her glasses magnified to alarming proportions.
He swallowed, "What's wrong?" he asked and then continued without waiting for a reply, "Is this about what just happened with Felix?"
Sophie looked up at him, she was biting her top lip nervously, she nodded, but just barely
"Do you want to talk about it?" Ben asked tentatively.
Sophie looked at him and as the bulging tears began to roll down her face she spoke.
"It wasn't about Andrew," she said quietly,
Ben shrugged, “I guessed as much," he said, "look if you'd rather talk to one of the other girls about this rather than..."
"No," she said cutting over him, “I want to talk to you."
Ben shuffled, a little uncomfortably in his chair. This wasn't exactly within his wheelhouse of expertise. He didn't like it when people cried, especially women and he never really knew how to react when someone tried to confide in him. It wasn't that he was devoid of empathy or emotion, he just simply wasn't built that way. As a career soldier he also didn't exactly have a wealth of experience to call upon when it came to matters of the heart. He knew enough to wait for Sophie to begin to speak though.

Sophie picked up her bottle of water and opened it before taking a slow gulp; she removed her glasses and wiped the sleeve of her cardigan across her face, drying the tears that had streaked down her cheeks. She fixed Ben with an unblinking stare and then let her eyes drop to the table top.

"It was when I first graduated from medical school," she began slowly.

Ben nodded encouragingly.

"I thought I could change the world," she sighed wistfully, "after only six months, I went straight from my first job in Valencia to join Medicine sans Frontiers in Western Africa."

"Wow," Ben said, "thats pretty impressive, you must have only been a kid?"

Sophie shrugged, "I was 24 years old," she said, "I met some remarkable people and saw some terrible things. When you share terrible times with other people it makes you close, you know?" She raised her eyes to look at Ben, his face was serious but smiled, encouragingly at her.

She continued, “Mark was already well established within the group. He was an American and I had never met an American before," the hint of a smile touched her face but disappeared as soon as it had arrived, "what's more, he was friendly, kind and handsome," she said blushing, "very handsome, in fact. We became friends straight away. I think he felt sorry for me at the beginning so he took me under his wing. We soon became inseparable and I followed him from field hospital to field hospital, country to country, crisis to crisis. We quickly became closer as friends and colleagues and then we became..."

Sophie hesitated.

Ben held his hand up, “It’s okay I get the idea."

Sophie nodded her thanks and carried on with her story, "We had been together for six months and were working in The

Ivory Coast when I first noticed something...unusual," She took a sip of water, "the hospital that we were stationed at was well established, well stocked and well run but..." Sophie stumbled.
"It's okay," Ben said, "take your time."
Her eyes fell back to the table top and she started to spin the bottle of water in her fingers,
"I came onto shift one morning and one of my patients, a young girl called Sabella; a really beautiful girl had died suddenly during the night. She was seventeen years old and there was no warning, just dead." She clicked her fingers to punctuate the word. "Mark was working that night and said that her temperature suddenly spiked through the night and by the time they had tried to take control it had taken her over and she had gone within an hour."
"Can that happen?" Ben asked shocked, "I mean that quickly?"
Sophie nodded, "I'm afraid so, when the body is weak it is quick to surrender to a virus. It is not uncommon, not in these places. However this time... something felt wrong this time...I couldn't be sure what exactly but I felt it in my heart," she tapped her chest.
Ben watched, whilst simultaneously trying not to stare at her breasts.
"What did you do?" Ben asked, shaking his gaze back to her face.
Sophie's head remained bowed and she shook her head unhappily, "Nothing," she said simply. "As I said, these things do happen sometimes and the place was busy. There was no time to indulge a gut feeling. My shift had started and there was a lot to be done," she looked up at Ben again, "there was always so much to be done. We never finished. So I put it out

of my head and carried on with my work as best I could," she tapped her head this time, "but it kept coming back to me throughout the day. It is hard to describe but it was as though my insides were..." she paused as she searched for the right word, "...crawling, itchy almost," she said, finally.

Ben screwed his face up at the unpleasant thought and Sophie smiled fully for the first time since they sat down.

"A week or so later we moved again," she said.

"Is that normal?" Ben asked, "To move around so much?"

"It was not unusual," she said with a small shrug of her shoulders. "There is always another crisis to attend and we were young and idealistic. We thought we were going to save the world...at least I thought we were."

She paused for a moment, as if ordering her thoughts.

"We moved on from place to place as before, but now my discomfort followed me like a shadow, wherever we went. I couldn't stop thinking about Sabella and how quickly she had gone from getting stronger and better to simply nothing at all within a few short hours. I asked Mark if he could recall anything from that night but he denied even remembering her name and when I pushed him he suddenly became evasive and angry. He told me to forget about it and I felt something new. There was an edge to his voice, a half hidden threat that caught at me, frightened me. That was when I became more than simply suspicious, but still I could not bring myself to believe it. He was good man and a good doctor. He was my friend and I loved him."

"Were there others then?" Ben asked, warily.

Sophie continued to look at the table top for what felt like an age before slowly, but determinedly nodding. Ben slumped in his chair as though punched in the gut.

"Oh shit," was all that he could manage, "I'm so sorry Sophie. What did you do?"
"We were working in some awful conditions," Sophie replied, "people died more often than they lived. An extra death here or there, who would notice that?"
"But why?"
"Power, control, who knows?" she said, "The point is I could prove nothing. I was twenty-four years old and alone in a foreign land with a man that I was becoming increasing scared of...I...I did nothing," she said quietly, "I was weak when I needed to be strong and people died because of it."
"Couldn't you tell someone?"
"Mark had been involved with Medicine sans frontier for more than five years when I joined. Who would believe a tiny little Spanish girl, fresh out of med-school?"
"What happened?"
"He died," she said with a humourless laugh, "he contracted Ebola and died in one of the hospitals that he had killed so many others in. I left Africa and moved to America to try and put it all behind me,"
"I'm sorry," Ben said sadly, "I really am."
"And now Felix wants to drag it all up again," she said and her voice began to crack, "oh Ben! I don't want to remember it anymore...it's too...hard." She stopped talking and once again the tears came, but this time they were more persistent.
Ben rose from where he was sitting and walked around the table. He grabbed another chair and dragged across the floor until it was next to Sophie. He sat down, then reached out for her and carefully pulled her towards him until her head lay against his chest. He held her closely and then gently kissed the top of her head. He felt her shoulders quivering beneath his arms as she wept freely, so he stroked her hair and tried to

comfort her in the only way he knew how. He had no words for these moments, so instead he held her tightly in his big arms. After a few minutes she pulled gently away from his hug and looked up into his face, her face was wet and her eyes glistened with tears. She smiled weakly and then stretched her neck so that her face was level with his. She held it there for a moment, their noses only a few millimetres apart and then she leant forward and kissed him on his mouth.

Her lips were salty from her tears and although seemingly reticent at first, Ben finally relaxed into the moment and kissed her back. When they broke off from the kiss she looked into his eyes, her face full of sadness, her anxiety heavy and tangible.

"Don't worry," Ben said soothingly, "I'll take care of it."

Sophie smiled hopefully and opened her mouth to talk.

"Shh," Ben said. "It's okay."

He kissed her again and then held her tightly, "It's okay," he repeated, "nothing's going to hurt you while I'm around."

They sat like that for a few minutes, silently embracing, then Sophie lifted her head and looked into his eyes.

"There's something else," she said quietly, "and I don't know how to tell you,"

Ben smiled at her soothingly, "It's okay," he said, "you don't have to if you don't want to."

Sophie withdrew from him a little; Ben looked at her, his brow furrowed in concern. Her face may have been tear-stained and puffy, but her eyes burned with a fierce determination.

"Do you remember the party?" she asked.

Ben nodded, "Of course," he said, "why?"

"I spoke to Felix that night as well," she said and shook her head, "about his brother."

"Jacob?" Ben said, and then nodded again. “Actually I do remember. The two of you were quite cozy at one point if I remember rightly?"
Sophie looked confused, "What is 'cozy'?" She asked.
Ben looked at her, "Erm, I dunno...close I guess. You guys looked kinda close for a while."
Sophie nodded apparently satisfied, "He was drunk," she said, "and his tongue was loose,"
Ben shrugged, "He wasn't alone," he said.
"Hmmm," Sophie agreed, "but he told me something that night. Something that I do not think he was supposed to tell anyone," she hesitated for a moment and bit her lip.
"It's okay," Ben said. "you're safe with me,"
He smiled at her and she returned it with gratitude.
"I know," she said. She took another deep breath and settled herself.
"He told me that his brother, Jacob, had done many terrible things in the past. Things that he would not want others to know about."
Ben arched an eyebrow at her, "I can’t say that I'm surprised," he said.
Sophie recoiled from him, "You know?" she said accusatorially.
Ben shrugged, "I don't know any specifics, but he had a certain...reputation."
"But how could someone do such a terrible thing?" she said with a shiver.
"What do you mean? Did Felix give you details?"
She nodded sadly.
"Such as?" he asked, casually.
"Violence, corruption," she swallowed hard, ”even murder." Her eyes once again became heavy with tears.

"Murder?" Ben said, "Jeeze, I always knew that that he had some skeletons in his closet," he shook his head, "but murder? Are you sure that you didn't misunderstand him?"
Sophie smiled at him, "You are a kind man," she said, "always forgiving."
Ben blushed.
"I am sure of what he told me, but it is worse than it sounds," Sophie said solemnly, her expression once again serious.
"Worse than murder?" Ben said. “How does it get worse than murder?"
Sophie hesitated and swallowed hard, she looked away from Ben, "Children, women," she whispered, "Felix told me that he had killed people that stood in the way of the Project going forward. Innocent people, people like..."
Ben's eyes bulged with shock, "No!" he said loudly.
Sophie flinched and then looked at him, her face the very picture of unhappiness.
The colour drained from Ben's face, he shook his head, "Not Cam's family?" he said, "Tell me you don't mean, Cam's family?"
Sophie looked down at the table top and nodded.
"Shit!" Ben said.
He wiped his hand over his face “I can't believe it!"
"I know," Sophie sniffed unhappily, "I think that Felix had carried it with him for so long that he had to tell someone else."
"And that someone was you?"
Sophie shrugged, "As I said, he was drunk. I do not think that he knew what he was saying."
Ben sighed, "Fuck," he said quietly.
"But now, with everything that has happened today...I'm scared Ben," Sophie said, her voice trembling, "this man will

be here soon, this monster...and if Felix decides that he wants to make life difficult for me or brings up my past," she paused for a moment, "then, who knows what he might do to me?"
Ben gently took hold of her chin and tilted it up until he was looking at her directly into her eyes.
"He won't hurt you," he said gently, "I promise."
"But this man, he has no limits, no conscience," Sophie said desperately.
"Yeah," said Ben. "Well, I aint exactly a pussy cat, either. If he wants a fight then he'll have to go through me first."
Sophie smiled.
"I'll talk to Felix as well if you like? He's a good guy I'm sure he'll back off."
Sophie's eyes flicked open again, "No," she said, "please, I would rather just try and forget it," she looked at Ben pleadingly.
Ben shrugged, "If that's what you want?" he said, and Sophie nodded.
Once more she allowed herself to relax, she settled her head back against Ben's chest and sighed happily, her eyes were closed and her mouth was stretched into a contented smile.

CHAPTER EIGHT

Jim was alone in the printing room, with the storm finally showing signs of abating, he had decided that he would make sure that the newly formed components were fully functional and ready to be utilised immediately, once they were able to get back onto the surface. He picked up a section of a deep surface drilling mount and studied it admiringly. The precision and level of the finish was truly astonishing and even though he had used this facility hundreds of times over the previous months and years, he still couldn't help but be impressed by the intricacy of what they were able to produce, so very far from home with little more than a vat of titanium powder and set of schematics. Simon knocked on the door frame and when Jim turned to face him he wasn't quite quick enough to hide the disappointment completely from his expression, if Simon noticed this, he decided not to mention it.
"James," he said with a thin smile touching his lips, "can I assume that I am clear to leave the compound now that this storm has passed?"
Jim raised his eyebrows in surprise, "Is it over then?" he asked.
Simon nodded, "Ja," he said, "or at least it has diminished sufficiently to enable our work to continue."
Jim shook his head, "No Simon," he said, his voice heavy with exasperation, "I have told you that we will not resume normal activities until the storm has fully cleared,"
"But..." Simon began.
Jim sighed, "Look Simon, do we have to keep having the same conversation?"

Simon shook his head, “I just assumed that because Felix had been given the go-ahead to re-enter the bio-pod, that you felt that the storm had reached a safe level."
"You are talking about going back onto the surface of an alien planet, not checking on a few strawberries!" Jim put the drill mount back onto the workbench.
Simon shrugged, "The principle is the same," he said simply, "if Felix can go back into the pod then clearly the shutdown has passed and I can resume my duties?"
"Wait," Jim said his face creasing in thought, "I haven't given permission for anyone to resume normal duties. As far as I am aware the bio-pods are still in shut down."
Simon shrugged, "I saw Ben only five minutes ago and he said that Felix and Andrew had been given the go-ahead to re-enter."
Jim went over to one of the wall mounted communication panels and tapped in a code, as he waited for a response he turned back to Simon.
"I hope your wrong about this Simon," he said, his face suddenly lined with concern, "because if one of them has..."
"Hello?" Ben's loud gruff voice issued from the communicator.
"Oh Hi Ben, its Jim,"
"Hey Jim, what’s up?"
"You any idea where Felix is? Coz I've got Simon here and he thinks that you saw him heading to the bio-pod?"
"He's right," Ben said simply, "I saw him not half an hour ago, why? What's this about Jim?"
Jim said nothing for a moment; instead he looked at the communication panel as he considered his next move.
"Get down to bio-pod three as quick as you can. I think Felix might be in trouble," he paused again for a few seconds, "I'll be there as soon as I can."

"Gotcha," Ben said and with no further questioning or comment, the communication panel clicked into silence.
Jim turned back to Simon.
"Go and find Sophie and ask her to head to the med bay, we might need her."
"What shall I tell her," Simon asked
"Just tell her to hurry," Jim said.
Simon hurried out of the room and Jim followed close behind. His mind suddenly in turmoil.
Ben arrived at the bio-pod quickly but there was no sign of Jim, undeterred, he unlocked the door and braced himself for what he might find inside.
The door slid quietly open but as he entered the pod he immediately noticed the humidity level was way beyond even the uncomfortable levels that Felix and Andrew liked to keep the place in. Ben's skin became instantly slick with sweat and his clothes clung unpleasantly to his body. He cursed the conditions but still ventured further into the dome. The lighting was still at emergency levels and even though he had bypassed the controls it would still take a few minutes for the main lights to illuminate. Because of this he had to peer through the gloom in an unsuccessful attempt to recognise any distinguishable figures.
"Felix?" he called, "You in here?"
His voice echoed, eerily around the pod. He listened intently for any kind of response but there was no answer. He ventured further in, carefully picking his way through the plants. He was headed straight for the closest canary, which was beeping sedately at him. As he went he walked directly past where Felix lying face down amongst the plants. Upon inspection, the canary seemed to be working perfectly. After a cursory check he headed towards the second one which was

situated towards the rear of the dome. As he got closer the power override kicked in and the lights started to blink on in succession. Ben instinctively shielded his eyes. It was several seconds after the dome had been fully illuminated until Ben was able to take a second, more thorough look around the dome.

As his eyes swept over the foliage he finally noticed Felix or rather he noticed Felix's boot, which was poking out from between two rows of strawberries.

"Oh shit!" he said loudly.

He instinctively rushed over.

"Come on, don't you dare be dead," he said worriedly and looked up at the security camera that was pointing almost directly at them. He waved at it to get whoever was watching's attention. Sweat ran freely from Ben's face and onto the hard floor, and he considered his limited options as he looked at his companions face.

Felix was ashen grey and lying on his side in what looked unpleasantly like a pool of vomit and urine. Without hesitation, Ben turned him over onto his back and put his ear to his chest. He was breathing, just, and soaking wet with what Ben hoped was sweat. Next Ben checked Felix's airway was clear and then his pulse. It was fast, thin but regular; he didn't know how much time he had so he acted instinctively. He needed to get him to the med-bay as quickly as possible and from Ben's perspective there was only one way that was going to happen. Felix was tall, fit and strong but Ben, fired with adrenaline, picked him up as if he were a child's toy. He strode quickly out of the bio-dome and began the short journey through the colony towards the medical wing. Both Jim and Rebecca intercepted him on his way out of the bio-pod and without saying a word they fell in behind him and followed him.

"Let me take some of the weight," Jim demanded.
"I've got him," Ben said shortly, his breathing heavy.
"It'll be quicker if I help," Jim persisted.
Ben shook his head, "I've got him balanced," he gasped, "I don't want to waste any time."
Jim opened his mouth to argue but fought the urge and instead remained quiet.
As they entered the med bay Sophie was already in position.
"What the hell happened?" she asked as they entered the treatment area
Ben's breathing was increasingly laboured and he merely shook his head and headed straight for the closest of the beds where he placed Felix carefully, but heavily onto the covering sheet. Sophie and Rebecca clicked immediately into full medical mode and began checking his vital signs thoroughly whilst Ben picked up a towel from one of the counter tops and wiped some of the sweat from his face.
"I have no idea," he said finally through gaps in his breathing, "he was already out cold when I got there."
"His heartbeat is very weak," Sophie said as she wiped a swab across his mouth which was stained with what looked like fresh blood.
"Was this blood there when you found him?" she asked
Ben shook his head, "I didn't notice, but it could have been," he paused, tried to focus and then nodded, "yes, I think it was actually."
Jim moved over to Ben's side and passed him a fresh towel to replace the original one which was now soaking wet.
"What's wrong with him doc?" he asked, "is he gonna be okay?"
"I don't know," Becky was cannulating his left arm and Sophie prepared a saline drip to attach to it,

“He’s very dehydrated; we’ll know more when we’ve got some fluids into him. It looks like he may have had a seizure though.”
“A seizure? Christ! He's not epileptic is he?” Ben asked.
“Not that we know of, or he wouldn't be here. But…” Sophie hesitated
“Yeah? But what?”
“Well, things change. Look guys we’ve got a lot to do here and without being rude it’s going to be a whole hell of a lot easier to do it without you two hovering over us.”
“We could go back to the bio-pod see if we can see anything?” Jim offered as he tried to slide Ben towards the door.
Ben looked at him and opened his mouth, but closed it again without speaking and started to head towards the exit. As he reached the doorway he stopped again.
“If you’re sure there's nothing we can do to help?”
The two doctors were moving quickly and confidently around Felix, methodically taking baseline observations and discussing possible procedures. Jim once again took hold of Ben’s arm.
“Come on Ben, I think the ladies are just fine in here by themselves.”
Ben shook his arm free and turned angrily towards him.
“Get the Hell off me!” he shouted.
Jim flinched, his eyes widened in surprise but Ben quickly calmed and his face relaxed into a thin smile.
“Yeah. Okay. Come on lets go,” he conceded.
They headed out of the room and then Ben turned back to Jim, “I just want to swing by communications first, maybe Cam can help?”
“Cam?” Jim asked, “Why do you need Cam? I’m quite capable you know?”

Ben rolled his eyes and sighed heavily, "Oh, for fuck's sake Jim! Do you have to turn every little goddamn thing into a pissing contest?"
"I'm not!"
"Sure you are,"
"No, I'm just pointing out that I have been looking after things for the last two years without Cam's help,"
"Yeah? Do you want to go back in there and ask Felix what he thinks about that?"
"Are you suggesting that this is somehow my fault?"
"I aint suggesting nothing Jim!"
"Yes, you damn well are!"
"No I'm not, it's just…"
"It's just what Ben? What is it just?"
"It's just that if there is something wrong with the canaries I'd rather talk to the guy that designed the damn things!" he paused. "That is if that's okay with you?"
Jim fell silent. Ben was right. Cam was the best qualified person to deal with this, but he didn't like it. He'd worked too hard on this colony to hand over the running to some pasty faced Brit, At least not without a fight.

CHAPTER NINE

ON BOARD THE NERINE 3

All was quiet on board the Nerine 3. Cam had given up trying to contact the colony for the time being at least. They were clearly busy and he had more than enough to do to keep himself occupied. Muttering and swearing, he had disappeared back onto the main flight deck to go over some of his calculations for the umpteenth time. Jon let him go without trying any interaction. Cam had been talking to himself more and more as the weeks went by and was now ignoring even direct questions from Jon. He was hardly sleeping and when he did, he would toss and turn and mumble mostly incoherent gibberish. Jon was worried about him at first, but had soon become inured to the background noise of Cam's mutterings and tapping pencils. He had already established the fact that any attempts to contribute or help Cam in any way were going to end in an argument, so instead he'd taken what he considered to be the wisest option and given up on him. He decided to attempt to use the time productively and began studiously going over some of the hundreds of schematics and manuals that he would need to be familiar with when they finally landed. As the chief project engineer, most of these had been at least partly designed by Cam and Jon felt an odd feeling of associated pride whenever he saw Cam's name on a document.

There was however a growing palpable tension on board. Whilst Cam was intensely focussed upon the upcoming landing sequence, Jon was increasingly full of nervous energy about what was waiting for them when they finally reached Mars.

He had tried again to talk to Cam about it but found it impossible to maintain any kind of dialogue with him, he could see his eyes glaze over, or his mind dart away after only a few seconds.
Jon felt increasingly isolated and lonely and as a result he found himself calling down to the colony more and more in his down time. Without Cam to talk to he had rekindled some old friendships. He had been friendly with the other medical doctors throughout the training period and had been particularly close with both Rebecca and Sophie. Sophie had seen war-zones and worked in an Ebola ravaged Africa and had still somehow managed to emerge from the experience altered but still apparently sane. She said that she "had lost her faith but found her humanity" which Jon found beguiling if somewhat enigmatic. She was an idealist, which amused Jon, but also one of the most capable and adaptable doctors he had ever met. He maintained that he had learned more from her during their training than he had during his entire time in military or civilian medicine.
Jon was waiting for a call from Sophie when the communication panel lit up. He picked up the handset and pressed the button that opened the channels up. The screen however remained blank.
"Hello?"
"Hi Cam, it's Ben. Look I haven't got time to chat I'm afraid. We've got a big problem down here and we could really use your help."
Joh hesitated for a moment, thrown slightly of balance.
"Er, this is Jon," he said, a little embarrassed.
"Oh," the disappointment in Ben's voice was palpable.
"Can I help?" he offered.

"Er… not really buddy, I kind of need Cam's expertise," he paused for a beat, "no offence."
"None taken."
Jon pressed the mute button and went off to find Cam, "Arsehole," he muttered to himself as he went.
Cam was still in the cockpit going through the landing sequence for the third or fourth time that shift. As usual he was mumbling inaudibly to himself and making notes in one of his impossibly thick journals.
"Hey Cam!"
Cam waved a hand to shush him and continued with his furious note taking without even looking up. Jon shrugged and waited, looking around at the ships display monitors and whistling some nondescript melody, loudly and untunefully.
Cam sighed and made a big show of slamming his notepad on the console top, he turned to face Jon.
"What the fuck is it?" he said.
Jon blinked out of his daydream, "Huh?"
Cam sighed again, "What the fuck do you want? I'm kinda busy here!"
Jon rolled his eyes; he was growing tired of Cam's surliness.
"Jesus Cam no need to bite my head off! I know you're busy but Ben is calling from the colony, they've got some kind of problem apparently."
"A problem? What is it?"
Jon shrugged, "I don't know. It would seem that I'm not deemed important enough to warrant any details."
It was Cam's turn to roll his eyes, Jon's inferiority complex had also been getting more and more pronounced and he was not entirely enamoured with it.
"Oh for fucks sake Jon!"
"What?"

“Stop being such a fucking old woman.”
In a moment of pique Jon threw the communicator at Cam’s head. He ducked just in time and it slammed into the monitor behind him. Jon turned and walked away without watching it land.
“Yeah well fuck you too eh?” he called as he went.
Cam picked up the handset and checked it for damage. He considered shouting after him but thought better of it. Instead he lifted the communicator to his ear and switched it on.
“Hey Ben, what's up?”
“Finally! Jesus Cam what took you?”
Cam shrugged, “Jon’s having one of his fucking moments again. Anyway what the fuck can I do for you? Is everything okay?”
Cam heard Ben take a deep breath before speaking. He felt a cold chill slide down his spine.
“No Cam. Everything is… goddamn far from okay,”
“What?”
“I said everything is pretty goddamn far from okay!”
The communicator crackled; evidently it had been damaged when Jon threw it. Cam listened intently. From the pattern of his voice Cam could tell that Ben was walking as he was talking, and walking quickly.
“We’ve had an accident Cam…a bad one I’m afraid.”
“Shit!” he said, “Is everyone okay?”
Ben paused again, “No I’m afraid not.”
“Ben? What the fuck happened Ben?”
“It’s Felix”
“Felix? Is he okay?” the fear in Cam’s voice was becoming more obvious,
“He’s… stable at the moment but he looks like…”
“What happened?”

"That's what I'm calling for. I think maybe an issue with one of the canaries."
"Really? One of the canaries? That's not good."
Cam slipped into thought. Mentally he was pulling up the blueprints, schematics and operating manual for the canaries.
"Cam?"
"Shush," he said, "I'm fucking thinking,"
"I haven't told you what happened yet what the hell are you thinking..."
Cam ignored him,
"Are you in the bio-pod yet?"
"Er, yeah,"
"Good, I want you to go to one of the canaries and do a hard reset on it."
"A what?"
"A fucking hard reset, seriously Ben? You don't know what that is?"
"Of course. Just not on these."
Cam heard another voice in the background, it sounded like Jim. Jim would know what to do.
"Put Jim on, Ben, would you?"
Reluctantly, Ben passed the communicator over to Jim. A hint of triumph touched Jim's face and Ben inwardly seethed.
"Hi Cam."
"Hey Jim, can you do a hard reset on the canaries?"
"Sure."
Jim moved over to the first of them, flipped down a cover panel and pressed series of buttons. The lights went off then flickered back into life, an alarm immediately began to sound. At the other end of the communicator Cam listened intently to the beeping
"Can you try the other one?"

“Already on it.”
Jim repeated the procedure on the second canary with a similar result.
“What temperature does it say?”
“52 degrees.”
“Shit. Guys you need to get out of there now!” Cam was shouting,
“What? Why?”
“Just do it guys. Now!”
Cam had pulled up a remote display of the canaries readouts. He checked and double checked the settings and kept coming back to the same point.
“Are you out?”
Ben had grabbed the communicator from Jim, ”What’s going on Cam?”
“I’ll explain later. Are you out?”
“Yep…outside!”
“Seal the dome and get away from it. I’ve got to vent the dome before it explodes.”
“What? NO!” Ben screamed into the communicator.
Cam knew what this process would mean to them on the surface but he had no choice. Back on the Nerine Three Cam began to remotely initiate the gas venting sequence. A gas vent was a last resort, everything within the pod could be irreparably damaged which potentially meant all of the food as well. The buildup of hydrogen within the pod not only made the atmosphere toxic but also highly flammable. Unconfined highly flammable substances were never a good thing around electricity.
The door to the pod locked and Cam started to input the final commands
“Cam! Stop!” Ben was shouting

“What’s wrong?”
“Jim is still in there!”
“What? How?” Cam began to press the keyboard frantically. The door remained resolutely locked. The countdown sequence continued
“Open the door!” Ben screamed.
“I can’t!”
The countdown neared its conclusion and the safety vent mechanisms began to buzz into life, preparing to open the dome. Jim stood at the doorway hammering on the glass with his fists, his face twisted in raw panic, screaming in fear.
Cam continued to try to override the sequence but kept coming up against the same error messages. There were only a few seconds left before Jim would be exposed, unprotected to the thin, unbreathable Martian atmosphere, and then only a few more seconds before he died of asphyxiation.
In a final act of desperation Cam bypassed the computer system and went to remotely shut the whole system down. As he did so the vents began to open and the oxygen began to rush out into the Martian sky.

CHAPTER TEN

Jim fell gasping into the hallway, he pushed himself up onto his haunches and started to gag, his eyes were bloodshot red and his face strained. Ben pulled hard on the door and managed to close it against the partial vacuum. Jim coughed and then collapsed onto the floor, unconscious.

For the second time that evening Ben found himself lifting one of his crew mates into his arms and heading for the medical facilities. He grunted as he secured his weight. Jim was heavier than Felix, taller and more solid. Ben's muscles burned in protest at the extra effort and it took an extra few seconds to steady himself. When he was confident he had his balance he headed as quickly as he could along the corridor.

Rebecca blanched as Ben carried Jim into the med-bay.

"Oh my God, Jim!" She cried.

Her hand went instinctively to her face and tears sprung to her eyes. Ben placed him carefully on the examination table next to where Felix already lay.

"What happened?" she asked, her eyes narrowed, "What did you do to him?"

Ben's face was red and slick with sweat, his clothes still clung uncomfortably to his body and he was breathing even more heavily. He looked directly into Rebecca's eyes and met her glare with as much disdain as he could muster.

"I'm trying to save his life," he said dryly between gasps for air, "or would you rather I had just left him where he fell?"

Rebecca's face flushed but she said nothing and immediately started to examine the unconscious Jim.

Ben turned his attention to Sophie, who had left Felix's side and come over to join them. She placed a gentle hand on

Rebecca's shoulder, "You check Felix, Becky, I'll take look after Jim," she said softly.
Rebecca made a groan of protest but swallowed any argument before it started. She made way for her colleague to take over. Sophie looked expectantly at Ben.
"He was trapped inside the bio-pod when it started to vent"
"You vented the bio-pod? Why?"
Ben's eyes widened and he let out an exasperated sigh, "Really?" he asked.
Sophie shook her head, "Sorry, not the point at the moment is it?"
Ben inclined his head, "Not really."
Sophie busied herself, attaching monitors and grabbing an oxygen mask.
"How long was he in there for?" she asked as she secured the mask onto Jim's face.
Ben shrugged, "Not more than a few seconds really. Cam managed to override the door mechanism remotely and I dragged him out straight away."
"Cam?"
"Yeah he was working the vent from the Nerine Three; it was thanks to him that we got Jim out so quickly."
Sophie checked the pulse-oximeter and adjusted the oxygen flow into Jim's mask
"I think he's been lucky. His o2 levels are low but not worryingly so." She inserted a cannula into his arm and began to take some blood, "I'll do some quick blood tests, make sure there's nothing more sinister going on."
"He's gonna be okay?" Ben asked, somewhat surprised.
Sophie nodded, "I want to check his cardiac output before I commit but..."
"Yeah?"

“But I think he probably just fainted.”
Ben grinned, “Fainted? Really?”
Sophie nodded again, “I think so yeah. I want to give him a thorough check over though.”
Jim groaned, opened his eyes and lifted his head tentatively off the pillow; he turned his head so that he was facing Ben.
“Did it work?” he asked quietly.
Ben nodded at him, “Yeah it did.”
Jim closed his eyes, sighed heavily and let his head relax back onto the pillow. Rebecca had moved back over to his side. Her tears had caused her mascara to smudge and run, but her eyes echoed the smile that played across her lips. She reached out and took hold of Jim’s hand, then without saying anything she lowered her face to his and kissed him.
Ben once again began to towel the sweat away from his head and face.
Becky reached out, took hold of Jim's hand and squeezed it, she looked over at Ben and her eyes narrowed suspiciously.
“What was Jim doing in there on his own?"
"He wasn't, I was with him. Cam locked the door before Jim had got out though."
"Why was Cam locking the doors?" Becky asked, suspiciously.
"He wanted to make sure no-one got hurt," Ben said.
"Well, he didn't make great job of it did he?"
Ben held up a hand, "Cam just saved Jim's life, lets not forget that shall we?"
"The point is that Cam locked Jim in there in the first place though," Becky said, "what the Hell was he doing?"
Ben shrugged, "he was venting the gas build up,"
"Why?" she asked,

Ben sighed, "It looks like at least one of the Canaries failed," he looked over at Jim and then back at Becky, "without a gas vent we could have been looking at an explosion down there."
"The canaries failed?“ Becky repeated.
Ben shrugged again, "So it would seem, we'll know more when we get a proper look at them."
Becky stared at Ben clearly chewing something over in her mind.
"Don't even go there Becky," Jim said with a distinct edge in his voice.
"What?" She said, feigning innocence.
Jim shook his head, Ben noticed and his face flushed red.
"It wasn't Cam's fault," he said loudly to no-one in particular, "in fact if it hadn't been for his quick thinking then Jim might not be here at all!"
“Hmmm," Becky said, "it's just..." she paused for a moment
"Just what?" Ben said his voice heavy with threat.
"Well," Becky continued, "who exactly was it that designed the Canaries?" she asked accusingly.
"Oh don't be so ridiculous," Ben shouted, "it was a simple error. Jesus, no machine is faultless."
"Yeah but all of them at the same time?" Becky shook her head, "I'm sorry, I just don't buy that."
"It was an accident Becky," Jim said quietly, his voice fragile and course.
Becky turned back to face Jim and as she did so the fierceness on her face dissolved. “Shh," she said softly, "don't try and talk,"
"Why not?" Ben asked, "Are you worried you might hear the truth?"

"Look, I like Cam, you know I do but the simple facts are that because of his incompetence we almost lost not one but two crew mates today."
Ben shook his head and looked pleadingly at Jim.
"And if we can't trust his design for a simple thing like a canary then what about everything else?"
Ben threw his hands into the air, "Jesus Becky, just listen to yourself!"
"What?" She said defensively.
"Cam's a goddamn genius!"
"Ha!" she said loudly, "so I keep hearing,"
"He is!" Ben countered.
"Well," she said irritably, "if today's events are the work of a genius then I genuinely worry for the human race as a whole," she looked at Sophie who was standing uncomfortably at the edge of the argument, "perhaps we should all pack up and leave now?"
Sophie flushed with embarrassment but said nothing. She did not like this conflict between crew mates and was determined not be drawn into it.
"Without him none of us would be here at all," Jim said.
"Yeah and because of him, two of us very nearly weren't here today!" tears suddenly sprang into her eyes, but she blinked them away.
Jim placed his hand on Becky's arm.
"I'm fine Becks," he said, "the only reason I'm here at all is because of Cam. Pure and simple."
"But..." Becky started but Jim interrupted her
"...But nothing," he soothed, "I trust Cam with my life and so do you on a daily basis. Look around you, none of this would be here if it wasn't for Cam."

Becky visibly deflated, the fire extinguished from her eyes and she suddenly looked exhausted.
Ben also noticeably relaxed and he turned his attention to Felix who was still lying unconscious on the bed next to Jim's.
"How is he Doc?" he said looking over at Sophie who was apparently lost in her own thoughts
"Hmm?" she replied.
"How is he Doc?" Ben repeated and nodded towards Felix.
Sophie looked over at the motionless form of Felix and then back to Ben, "He's stable," she said with a brittle smile, "unconscious but stable."
Ben smiled, "That's good," he said with a nod of his head and then checked himself, "sorry, that is good isn't it?" he added quickly.
Sophie nodded, "It's the best that we can hope for at the moment," she said with a shrug and then returned her attention back to her patient.
"Cam really likes Felix," Ben said to Becky, "there's no way he would hurt him deliberately."
Becky raised an eyebrow at him, "Deliberately?" she repeated.
Ben's face reddened again, but this time in embarrassment, he raised his hands defensively, "No wait, I didn't mean that," he protested, "I was just thinking out loud."
"Hmm," Becky said thoughtfully.
Ben hesitated for a second, bracing himself for a further confrontation that didn't materialise. He smiled nervously at Becky and then glimpsing an opportunity to leave relatively unscathed, he made his excuses.
"I'm going to take a look at those Canaries," he said, "see if I can't work out exactly what happened."
Without waiting for a response he left the medical bay, leaving behind him an increasingly uneasy Becky.

"Why would he say that?" she asked Jim, conversationally
Jim shrugged, "I don't think he meant anything by it," he said.
"Yeah perhaps, but it was an odd choice of words don't you think?"
"I guess," Jim conceded.
"I mean why use the word 'deliberately' at all?" she continued, "It's not as if..." she trailed off, leaving her thought half formed.
Jim looked at her, "What is it?" he croaked.
"They were pretty close back on Earth weren't they?"
"Who? Ben and Cam? Yeah I guess so,"
"You guess so? Jeez, for a while they were joined at the hip, you never saw one without the other,"
"So?" Jim asked.
"I don't know," Becky said wearily, "but...well, what if Ben knows something about him? Something that might perhaps change the way we all look at him?"
Jim shook his head, "No, I'm sure..."
"But what if there is something?" Becky continued, "Why else would he say that?"
"Cam's a good man Becky," Jim protested, “he didn't mean anything by it I’m sure, it was just a poor choice of words, that's all."
Becky looked at Jim, smiled and then bent over to kiss is forehead, “You get some rest," she said, "leave this to me."
Jim twisted on the bed, "Becky?" He said as loudly as he could manage, "what are you going to do?"
She patted his arm distractedly, "Don't worry," she said, "just try and get some rest."
Without saying anything further, she walked from the room leaving Jim wide eyed and as far from restful as he could possibly be.

CHAPTER ELEVEN

Cam was shaken by the apparent failure of the canaries. They were amongst the simpler devices that he had designed, so the fact that they had failed so spectacularly cast a shadow of doubt across the whole project as far as he was concerned. As he understood things, both Felix and Jim were going to be okay but it could have been so much worse. He tried to keep the two of them from his thoughts, but he shuddered each time he allowed the possible consequences to cross his mind. He pored over the designs and specifications of the canaries again and again, desperately trying to spot any weakness or some overlooked fatal flaw. However if there was a fatal flaw, it remained resolutely hidden from him.

He would figure it out, of that he was convinced, but without physically seeing the units himself he could establish no apparent reason for their failure. He needed time but that was a luxury that he could not afford whilst the landing loomed so large ahead.

The careful weeks of preparation for their imminent landing had suddenly been thrown into turmoil, with Cam second guessing himself at every calculation. Convinced that he must have made an error somewhere, he revisited each constituent part of the landing sequence and mechanism in finite detail. Searching for a design flaw or an errant line of code. He hadn't slept in any meaningful way for days and despite the continual badgering from Jon, he was barely eating either.

“You’re going to make yourself ill, Cam,” Jon chided, his face lined with concern.

Cam snorted his reply and continued with his studies. In desperation, Jon grabbed hold of his chair and spun it around so that they were face to face.

“I’m serious," he said, looking directly into his friends eyes, "you have to stop. Now, before you keel over.”
Cam squeezed his eyes closed and rubbed his face with his hand. The rings that circled his eyes had been growing progressively darker and darker almost by the hour. He stretched, shook his head and focussed on Jon’s face.
“I’m not doing this for a fucking laugh you know?”
“I know you’re not," Jon said soothingly, "but it’s not your fault Cam. What happened with the bio-pod? It was an accident."
“You don't fucking know that,” he snapped.
"Yes I do," Jon said
"How can you?"
"Because I know you and you don't make mistakes," Jon said.
"Everyone make mistakes," Cam replied.
"How many errors have you found since you started going through the landing sequence?" Jon asked.
"A couple," Can replied.
"In how many calculations?"
Cam waved him away like an annoying bug.
"That not the fucking point!" He shouted. "What if someone had died?”
Jon reached out and placed a hand on Cam’s shoulder, “But they didn't did they?” he said softly.
Cam’s head dropped slightly and he shook it, “No,” he whispered.
“You don't know what happened, and you won’t know until we get down there. You’ve studied the technical readouts and have said yourself that they're inconclusive,”
“Aye. I suppose,”
“So go and get some rest.”
Cam sighed heavily, “In case you’ve forgotten we’ve got to land this fucking thing in less than 48 hours.”

"No, of course I haven't. Which is exactly why you have got to look after yourself?"
"I'm fine," Cam protested.
"No," Jon said, "you're bloody well not fine Cam. When was the last time you slept? Hmm? When was the last time you sat down and had something substantial to eat?"
Cam shrugged, "I dunno."
"Well, I do! It was almost three days ago!"
"It cannae be!"
Jon nodded. Cam pondered this by counting on his fingers, "Aye, no, fair enough. You're probably right." He nodded.
"So go and get something to eat, and then have a nap, please," Jon said, "before you pass out."
"You're not my fucking mother you know?" Cam said, only half joking.
"No, but I am the poor sod that is relying on you to get me down on that planet's surface in one piece. And preferably not one big flat piece!"
Cam visibly sagged as yet another wave of tiredness washed over him. He ran his fingers through his hair and scratched at his unshaven chin. He sighed deeply.
"I've got to work this out Jon," he said wearily, "I can't make any mistakes," he managed a thin smile.
Jon nodded, "I know. Really I do. But come on..."
Cam nodded, stood up from his chair and stretched elaborately.
"Let me talk to the colony first and then I promise I'll do as I'm told."
Jon rolled his eyes, but nodded, "Okay," he said, "but be quick about it."
Cam headed off to the communications panel where he picked up one of the handsets and switched it on. There was a

crackle of static and then it found its frequency. Jon, meanwhile, headed off to the Galley to prepare some food.
"Mars colony Alpha. This is Captain Harrison on board the Nerine 3. Is there anyone there?"
He waited patiently as the signal was transported to the planet's surface and then bounced around the base, waiting for someone to pick it up. After a few minutes the handset came alive. Cam pressed the 'connect' button and the monitor flicked into life. Simon's broad, serious face filled the screen.
"Hi Simon, how are things down there? How are the patient's doing?"
Simon smiled, "Hello Cam. Yes, we are all okay at the moment here. Jim is out of the medical bay and resting in his quarters. Felix woke up yesterday briefly, but he seems much better."
"That's good. Did he say anything about the accident?" Cam asked, "Can he remember anything?"
Simon shook his head, "He remembers nothing I'm afraid. He is still suffering from the after effects I think. He is still very confused."
Cam sighed, "How about the canaries? Has anyone had a chance to look at them yet?"
Simon shook his head, "No we wanted to re-oxygenate the bio-pod before we extracted them. Ben took them out this morning; he may be running some diagnostics through them now. Would you like to talk to him?"
Cam nodded, "Aye, if he's there?"
"I will transfer you to the workshop," He smiled and the screen went blank as he put the call through. After less than ten-seconds the screen lit up again but this time Ben's face filled it. He smiled when he saw Cam.
"Hey Cam! How are things? Ready for impact?"

Cam flinched at the word “impact” but said nothing; instead he used some of his final reserves of energy to force a smile onto his face.

“Hi Ben. Good to see you. What can you tell me?”

Ben looked down at the bench in front of him where the second of the two canaries lay in pieces. He shrugged.

“Nothing much," he said, "they both seem to be in perfect working order. There are no obvious signs of malfunction and no internal signs of damage.”

Cam rubbed at his stubbled chin again and let out a long breath through his nose.

“I don’t get it Ben. They should be fool proof. Even if one had gone down the other should have been more than capable of looking after the dome on its own. How are the other bio-pods? Any problems there?”

Ben shook his head, “Nope, everything is fine as far as we can tell.”

“Did you save any of the plants from bio-pod Three?”

“It’s not as bad as we figured. We think we can save some of the plants but it’ll be a while before we start getting regular strawberries again I’m afraid.”

Cam sagged. He’d been looking forward to some strawberries for weeks. Weirdly, it was one of the things he had missed the most from Earth.

“Cam?” Ben asked.

Cam shook himself out of his daydream, “Hello? Yes?” he said,

“Are you okay Cam?” he leant in closer to the camera, "Coz you look like shit buddy!”

“Thanks Ben! I can always rely on you to make me feel better!”

Ben winked at him, "That’s what I’m here for.”

Cam laughed, “Okay, well my doctor says I need to get some rest so I suppose I should get off. Let me know if you find anything though won't you?”

“Absolutely, Is Jon there? I’d like to have a quick word if I can?”

Cam nodded. “Sure, I’ll patch you through.”

This time it was the colonies turn to wait for the call to transfer. Ben waited patiently but he chewed on his giant moustache as he waited. The smile had faded from his face and his expression had turned serious, making him look ten years older. The monitor flicked on again and Jon’s handsome features filled the screen.

“You okay Ben?” he asked, his voice touched with concern. It was unlike Ben to ask to speak to him directly, “Is everyone okay down there?”

Ben nodded solemnly, “Yeah, we’re all fine. I’m worried about Cam though, he looks terrible.”

“I know, he’s taken the accident pretty hard. He’s blaming himself.“

“But that’s ridiculous!” Ben was almost shouting at the screen

Jon held his hands up, “Jesus Ben, I know that. He’s not eating or sleeping though. I’m not sure how much more he can take before he snaps,”

“I was afraid of that,”

“He’ll be fine,” Jon shrugged, “at least I think he will. I think we should try not to add any more stress to him though in the next 48 hours.”

Ben nodded, “Agreed,” he paused and looked around, “it’s just…”

Jon waited, “It’s just what? What’s going on?”

Ben chewed at his moustache again, ”It’s just I don't think that anything went wrong with the canaries.”

“I’m not following you I’m afraid.” Jon’s forehead wrinkled in confusion.

“Well, I can’t find anything wrong with either of them,” Ben said, “in fact, I think that they're both working perfectly fine.” He looked at Jon knowingly.

Jon’s face fell as the implication hit him. He shook his head, “No,” he said quietly.

Ben nodded, his expression suddenly darkened.

“I’m only telling you this because I think that you can handle it. You’re the only person that I can fully trust on this.”

“Why me?” Jon said, surprised.

“Because if it’s what I think it is, then it would have to be someone with direct access to the bio-pod. And as you're currently hundreds of miles away on a giant spaceship, I reckon that pretty effectively rules you out!”

Jon said nothing.

“I want you to be clear,” Ben continued, ”that this is only speculation at this point. I have no solid evidence, and I certainly don't want Cam to find out. Like you said, he’s got enough on his plate as it is. Is that understood?”

Jon bristled slightly with annoyance ”Yes of course. I can’t believe it though.”

Jon stared into space for a few seconds, and then another thought came to mind.

“But why? I mean Felix could have died!”

Ben shrugged, “I don’t know. Until we do know though we’re gonna have to keep this between us. It’s only luck that Felix is still alive and that means that there’s someone down here that doesn't care if anyone gets hurt, or how badly.”

Jon agreed and with a conspiratorial nod they ended the call. Jon had duties to perform and he was determined to keep a calm facade. If Cam realised that anything untoward was happening he would lose his focus entirely, and he was perilously close to the edge as it was.

Meanwhile Ben looked at the blank screen and dropped his face into his hands. Despite his initial thoughts, the sharing of this burden had made him feel worse if anything. Ben kept his eyes closed and breathed deeply; his hands shook slightly from the adrenaline that had been coursing through him during the conversation. He didn't like weighing Jon down with this. Especially without any firm evidence. He had to tell someone though and he suspected that he was going to need an ally in the coming weeks and months. He would talk to Cam when they landed and his mind was clearer. Together then they would be able to get to the bottom of this. One way or another Ben remained seated, his chair facing the monitor. From his position he was unable to see Sophie standing motionless at the doorway of the workshop. He was also unaware that she had overheard the entire conversation.

CHAPTER TWELVE

Jim watched the display panels with an uncomfortable mix of emotions. The excitement of the Nerine Three finally landing had been somewhat diluted by the events over the previous few days. There was a tangible feeling of hostility towards Cam from several of the colonists. They blamed him for the failure of the canaries and by association the current precarious physical condition of Felix, who remained in a serious, but stable condition in the med-bay.

Ben had tried to allay everyone's fears but ironically his vociferous protests of Cam's innocence had only served to add further fuel to their fires of suspicion.

He was facing his most delicate and dangerous time as senior officer and the new ship hadn't even landed yet. He ran his fingers through his hair and then moved to get himself a bottle of water from one of the dispensers. He cracked open the seal and took a tentative sip of the ice cold liquid before taking a long slug. It tasted good and he found himself casually marvelling at the technology that allowed him to get an ice cold bottle of water almost thirty-four million miles away from the nearest freshwater tap.

Cam, along with his team, had designed this dispenser along almost everything else he could lay his eyes on. They had worked wonders, redesigning even the most simple of machine in order to maximise their working capacity for the altered living conditions on Mars.

They also understood that it was the tiny details that made all the difference. The tiny details that helped the crew forget how isolated they really were, tiny moments of familiarity in an alien environment, things like a resealable, recycled bottle of water

that satisfyingly cracked open as if for the first time each time it was opened.
Jim allowed himself a small smile and took a long drink. As he did so Becky came round the corner and seeing him standing there, stopped immediately in her tracks.
"Hi handsome!" she said warmly, "You look happy." Jim arched his eyebrows at her, "It's not a crime you know. Looking happy that is," he said defensively.
Becky let out a snort of laughter, and immediately covered her mouth, "I know, she said, it makes a nice change is all. Since the accident you've been...distracted."
"Can you blame me?" he said.
Becky shrugged, "I guess not," she bowed her head slightly, "in fact I think I might be at least partly to blame for that," she said quietly.
Jim shook his head a little too quickly, "No," he said, "not at all."
Becky looked at him and laughed again causing Jim to blush with embarrassment.
"Jesus you're a terrible liar," she said.
"What?"
"I know that what I said about Cam has had you worried,"
Jim tilted his head, "hmm," was all he could manage by way of a response.
"Well, I've come to put your mind at rest," she said happily, "I was worried about you that's all. I was upset."
Jim looked at her but said nothing.
"Anyway," she continued, "I just wanted to come and say that I'm sorry and that I've decided that I know that you're probably right,"
Jim continued to stare, “Probably right?" he repeated.

Becky shifted a little uncomfortably on her toes, "Okay?" she asked.
Jim nodded, "Okay," he said with a faint grin.
Becky noticed this and leapt upon it, "What?" she said feigning annoyance.
"Nothing," Jim said his smile widening.
"Goddamn it Jim, what are you smiling at?"
Jim sighed, "I know you," he said, "and the only way that you would be standing here telling me that you were not going to bother with this anymore, was if you had already done all the digging that you could, and came up with nothing," he paused for a moment, "is that about right?"
It was Becky's turn to flush with embarrassment.
"I told you he's a good guy," Jim said and held his hand out to her which she took instinctively, "speaking of which shall we go and see if he can land this massive goddamn skyscraper on a football field?"
Becky reached up and kissed him.
"Yes, let's," she said and they headed back into the control centre hand in hand.

* * *

The ship buffeted through the thin Martian atmosphere and moved into low orbit above the planet's surface. It was still travelling at more than 15,000 miles per hour but Cam was unconcerned. As long as he maintained a steady altitude he would be able to gradually bring the velocity down until they were able to bring the ship into land. He had practiced this procedure a thousand times and was confident that he could land this ship with his eyes closed if necessary. Jon was sure that he had been joking when he'd said this but had still made him promise that he wouldn't try. Cam smiled, the adrenaline coursing through his body was keeping the accumulative fatigue of the previous days and weeks at bay and he felt sharper and more in control than he had done for almost as long as he could remember. He looked over at Jon who was manfully, trying to look as calm as the circumstances would allow.

Cam felt utterly tranquil though, this was his ship and he was going to land it.

And land it he did.

The massive bulk of the ship settled with an incongruous lightness on the planet's surface. The years of planning, the countless calculations and endless simulations and computer modelling had ultimately paid dividends. The Nerine Three came to a final, unspectacular, sedate halt after more than nine months of space travel.

Cam exhaled heavily and glanced over to Jon, who was grinning widely,

"Nice job sir!" he said, happily.

Cam managed a smile of his own in return, "Thanks," he said a little breathlessly, "are you okay?"

"Never better my friend, never better," John took a deep breath, "how about you? Are you all right?"

Cam shrugged, "Aye," he said and lifted his right hand until it was straight out in front of his face. It was trembling gently but determinedly, "more or less anyway!"

"I never had a single solitary doubt," Jon said.

"Aye, but then again, you had no fucking idea what was going on!"

"I'm a doctor, Cam," he said with a shrug, "I am familiar with effects of the bliss of the ignorant, and I know it's not something to be underestimated."

Jon laughed and slapped Cam heavily on the shoulder. Cam nodded but remained quiet, staring out of the cockpit.
Cam was a scientist and an atheist and the landing had gone as well as he could ever have hoped, however there were still enough moments during the final descent that had made him silently pray to any God that was willing to listen. They had done it though and they were now sitting on the surface of an alien planet. He had brought the ship down within one hundred metres of the landing site, which was frankly astonishing.
The huge red dust cloud that had been thrown up during the final stages of the landing still engulfed the ship. This had no practical impact but in did mean that there was no spectacular Martian vista to greet them to their new home.
“Great view, huh?” Jon said and then began the laborious process of unbuckling his safety harness.
"You want a hand?" he asked.
Cam shooed him away, "I'm fine," he insisted.
"It's not exactly awe-inspiring is it?" Jon said, peering at the glass.
"I'm guessing that you can see your own reflection," Cam said quietly, "that usually inspires your awe."
Cam was also struggling to free himself from his bonds. The artificial gravity on board the Nerine Three was set at approximately ninety percent of Earth's in order to acclimatise the crew members for their time on Mars. It was apparently running a little light though because Cam was suddenly, uncomfortably and acutely aware of his arms and legs in a way that he had forgotten about. His chest felt unpleasantly heavy and his breathing had become laboured and difficult. He looked over at John to see if he was suffering from similar problems and was irritated to notice that his companion was

stretching and flexing his muscles like a gymnast with an oddly serene look on his face.

This irritation passed quickly though as he began to rediscover his own strength. Now free from the safety harnessing, he tentatively tried to stand up. The weight of his body, coupled with the expenditure of his adrenaline reserves, caused the muscles in his legs to strain, he felt himself wobble slightly before quickly regaining his balance, his hand clutching at the back of his seat for support. Jon looked over at him.

"You okay?" he asked.

Cam nodded, before wincing in pain. He swallowed hard,

"Aye, I'm fine," he managed.

Jon took a half step towards him.

"You don't look fine. Sit down," Jon said, worriedly.

"I said I'm fucking fine!" Cam said defensively.

"And I said sit down! Before you fall down," Jon insisted.

Cam glared defiantly at him and stood his ground.

Jon sighed, "Please?"

Cam said nothing.

"Look," Jon said gently, "it's a shock I know."

Cam was exhausted. They had landed safely and all of a sudden, the adrenaline that had kept him alert and focussed throughout the descent was washing away in a tide of lethargy.

His legs were visibly shaking now, but he somehow managed to maintain a resolute grip on the chair back. Sweat began to bead upon his face and forehead and his breathing became increasingly laboured with his every inhalation. He blinked determinedly and shook his head in an attempt to usher away the worsening blurring of his vision.

Jon made another movement towards him but Cam held up his free hand.

“I’m fine,” he said determinedly, "back off!"
Jon shook his head and turned away in mock disgust, he stared at the window and tried again to see something through the impenetrable cloud of red dust.
In a show of defiance Cam released his grip on the chair and took a deliberate step forwards. He paused, wobbled slightly and then found his balance. Jon looked round and tutted. Cam saw him looking and smiled before giving him a triumphant single finger salute. Jon turned away again.
“Told you. I’m fucking fine,” he said before his legs crumpled beneath him and he collapsed onto the floor of the cockpit.
Jon looked back at the noise. Cam was lying on the floor, a pool of blood ballooning around his head like a satanic halo from a long gash on the side of his forehead.

PART 4

Planting Trees on Mars

CHAPTER ONE

MARS COLONY ALPHA, 2023

The colonists took two transports out to the landing site and had watched the descent of the Nerine three with a combination of fear, trepidation and awe. However, the giant dust cloud created by the ship, had engulfed the entire area, rendering the final stages of the spectacle a little underwhelming. It was only when the noise of the retro thrusters finally ceased that they knew for certain that the ship must have landed. As per standard protocol, they had maintained radio silence throughout the landing. However, now that they had safely touched-down, Jim set about hailing the new arrivals.

"Nerine Three, can you hear me?" He called, into the handset. "Guys are you okay in there?"

The colonists all stared at the small electronic device, waiting for a response with collective bated breath. Jim looked uneasily at Becky, before raising the communicator to try again.

"Nerine Three? Can you hear me?" he repeated.

Still, there came no reply.

Ben stepped forward and clapped Simon, heavily on the back.

"Come on big fella," he said and the two of them started walking the three hundred metres or so towards the epicentre of the dust cloud. As they passed Jim, he reached out a hand and grabbed Ben's arm.

"Wait," he said quietly.

"Not on your life," Ben said.

"Ben?" Jim said, tightening his grip.

Ben shook his arm free and without saying another word, continued on his journey into the terracotta darkness ahead. Simon glanced over at Jim, shrugged and then dutifully tagged along behind him.

"Ben!" Jim called, "You don't know what you're heading towards! Wait!"

Ben waved a hand over his head but otherwise, completely ignored Jim's plea.

Jim cursed loudly to himself and then turned to Becky who wore a worried expression on her face.

"Come on," Jim sighed, and moved back towards one of the transporters, "if they're in trouble then we're gonna have to get back quickly."

He looked down at the communicator again, "Nerine Three, are you there?" he said, more in hope than expectation.

He looked up at Becky, "You drive," he said, "I'll keep trying them on this."

"Cam? Jon?" He said, but once more there was only silence in reply.

"Dammit guys, will one of you answer me for God's sake!"

He toyed with flinging the communicator across the cabin, but thought better of it and instead kicked the dashboard.

"Shit," he said, loudly.

Becky steered the transporter forward slowly and carefully. The dust was slowly starting to settle again around the landed ship, but she could see very little and she didn't want to accidentally run into anything, or anyone. When The headlights picked up the outline of Ben and Simon's planet suits through the gloom, she carefully pulled alongside them. She released the airlock on the door and it slid, softly open, with a hydraulic hiss, allowing the two men to climb inside.

The air was still thick with dust as the transporter continued through the mirk. The headlights provided little in the way of visual information, so Becky was using the sonar system as her main means of guidance. Despite the massive bulk of the Nerine Three, it wasn't until they were within ten metres of the hull that they made any kind of visual connection. It looked really quite sinister as it loomed out of the darkness like a giant haunted sandcastle. There was no sign of any landing lights or any movement at all. Becky brought the vehicle to a gradual stop and then beckoned to Jim.

"Look at the size of that thing," she said.

"I knew it was big, but up close..." Jim replied, "it's pretty impressive, eh?"

"Still need convincing that Cam's a genius?" Ben said.

"Huh?" Jim said, "No, not anymore."

Finally, as the dust continued to reluctantly settle around the ship, more of it slowly loomed into view. The size and scale of it were difficult to fully comprehend from the schematics, and it was the first time that any of the colonists had seen it up close.

The vastness was genuinely breathtaking. In an area of previously unblemished landscape there now stood a structure that was roughly the same size and shape as a sizeable Manhattan skyscraper. Becky carefully began to steer around the perimeter of the hull looking for the main entrance hatch.

"Come on," Ben whispered under his breath as they moved past a wall of featureless blackness, "where are you?"

After almost ten minutes of painfully slow progress, the transport finally pulled up opposite the main access hatch for the ship. It was dark and the doors remained steadfastly closed. Jim exchanged an uncomfortable look with Ben.

"They're okay," Jim said, "they'll be here any minute."

"Why aren't they answering then?"
"I'm sure there's a perfectly good explanation," Jim said.
Ben looked at him sideways, "Let’s go," he said and began to reattach his helmet to his planet suit.
Jim nodded, reluctantly. He looked out of the window at the inert ship and rechecked the stubbornly quiet communicator. He eyed it, suspiciously before speaking into it once again.
"Nerine three? This is colony base Alpha, please respond?"
Once more there was no response. Jim sighed and headed towards the transporters air lock with Ben. Simon put his hand out and held his progress.
"I will go," he said simply.
Jim moved to argue but Simon talked over him before he had chance to protest.
"I am stronger than you James," he said matter-of-factly, "if there is a need for carrying them. I am better...equipped to help."
Jim's mouth hung open slightly, he looked over at Ben.
"He's right," Ben added, "no offence, but we don't know what we're heading into."
"I'm hardly incapable of lifting," Jim bristled.
Ben rolled his eyes, "We need you here," is all he said, but it was enough to placate Jim, at least temporarily, and he halted his progress towards the airlock.
"Keep me posted," he said.
Ben nodded and Simon pulled his own helmet over his head. They squeezed into the small transporter airlock and Jim closed the internal door behind them. Once it was locked the outer door immediately began to open.
"Look!" Becky called from the front of the vehicle, "The hatch is opening."

Jim rushed forward and peered through the gloom at the giant vessel's entrance; the lights around the doorway had fully illuminated and the door was slowly starting to open, revealing a single figure, fully dressed in his surface suit. The colonist's suits now carried the physical evidence of over two years of planetary dust and staining. Staining that could never be completely removed no matter how thoroughly they were cleaned. By comparison the suit of the newly landed crew was so pristine and white, that is seemed to be possessed with an iridescent glow.
Pristine, that is, apart from the dark red blood stain that covered most of the right side of it, making him resemble a walking, half completed Rorschach test.
Seemingly oblivious to his alarming appearance Jon raised his hand in welcome. He saw the approaching figures of Ben and Simon and gestured back towards the airlock.
Simon took one look through the hatch before disappearing into the ship and out of view of the cockpit of the transporter. Ben meanwhile grabbed the suited Jon by the shoulders and shook him violently; Jon pushed him away and tapped the side of his helmet, indicating a communicator problem. Ben hesitated momentarily before moving menacingly towards him once more, just as he reached out to grab him again Simon emerged from the airlock with an apparently lifeless figure draped over his right shoulder in a fireman's lift. Ben changed direction in a moment and headed over to help manoeuvre the unconscious Cam into the transporter. The airlock wasn't big enough for all four of them to enter at the same time so after Simon had carefully laid him into it he took a step back. Immediately Ben stepped forward but Jon grabbed his arm to stop him and moved forward in his place. For a second it looked very much as though Ben was going to continue his

assault upon Jon. However, a well-timed, steadying hand placed upon his shoulder by Simon seemed to discharge the moment. He grudgingly stepped back to allow Jon to accompany Cam into the vehicle.

When the inner door opened Becky was already waiting with a field first aid-kit open and prepared

"What happened?" she asked instinctively as Jon fumbled to remove his helmet

Once it was off he took a quick, cursory glance around the transporter and then settled his attention upon Becky.

"He collapsed as soon as we landed," he said calmly, "poor bastard was absolutely exhausted, and I suppose the accumulation finally beat him when the task had been completed."

Becky looked at him, her face set in serious expression.

Jon shook his head, before deciding to elaborate, "You know the task of getting that massive spaceship safely onto the surface?" he said with a nervous smile.

Becky continued to examine the unconscious Cam, and by now both Ben and Simon had reentered the transport, and were removing their helmets with practised speed and ease.

Ben looked furious and Jon recoiled, slightly from his stare.

"What happened?" Becky asked again.

"I told you, he collapsed," Jon repeated.

Becky raised her eyebrows and looked at Jon's blood spattered suit and then at the open wound on Cam's head. It was oozing blood through a makeshift dressing.

"What?" Jon said, genuinely puzzled, “he hit his head on the way down," he said with a shrug, "there's a lot of sharp edges up there and he came down with one Hell of a bang," he slapped his gloved hand hard against the side of his seat.

"Hmmm," Ben said suspiciously.

"What? Wait, you don't think? Oh, come on!" Jon said raising his voice, “Don’t be absurd! Why would I do anything to Cam?" he asked rhetorically, he looked around at the collection of suspicious expressions, and sighed, "tell you what?" he said, the irritation growing in his voice, "why don't we get him into the medical facilities, make sure he's okay, and *then* you can all play your little fantasy game of 'Blame the Brit'"
He shook his head and mumbled something inaudibly beneath his breath.
"What did you say?" Simon asked him.
"Nothing," Jon replied.
"You said something, goddamn it," Ben added with a snarl.
Jon sighed, "I said nice fucking welcome!"
He slid unhappily into the upholstery of his seat and shook his head. He looked over at Cam who was lying perfectly still, blissfully unaware of the tension that his defiant and misguided show of pig-headedness had caused him.
"I hope that leaves a scar," Jon muttered bitterly to himself.
He was surrounded by suspicion, doubt and anger, so he decided to stare out of the window at the Martian landscape.
At his new home.

CHAPTER TWO

Jon stood alone in the main meeting room of the colony. He had been on the planet's surface for less than an hour, but it already felt like a week. He nervously transferred his weight from foot to foot as he considered what was to come next. He looked around at the simple, yet impressive design of the room and marvelled at the engineering and cost that this single room alone represented. It was the jewell within the Martian crown, and as such was the colonies largest and most elaborate accommodation.

The central dome of the colony base rose from the barren Martian landscape like the bloated body of a giant, gilded spider. A series of covered tunnels and walkways sprouted from beneath the belly of the beast, twisting and contorting through the dust like legs hugging the planet's surface.

Each tunnel led to a different part of the colony, some of which hadn't been built yet, but the dome itself acted as physical hub for the colonists. It was the focal point of the colony and provided an area for the colonists to relax and interact with one another, away from immediate pressures of the daily travails. The interior was based on a small town park or courtyard and had several seating areas dotted around a central paved area. There were carefully planted bushes and a handful of youthful fruit trees and bushes that had already flourished within their alien environment.

At the centre of the dome, like a giant water feature, was a huge architectural sculpture, designed to resemble the splash corona of a single drop of water. It utterly dominated the space within which it sat. It was over 10 metres in diameter, more than six metres tall at its highest point and was assembled

from more than a hundred smaller component parts, each of which slotted together seamlessly.
This was the centre of the colony and the location of the main meeting room. In the side of the sculpture, there was a hidden doorway that led into the meeting room itself. In the centre of which stood a large, round wooden table, surrounded by twenty, equally spaced, wooden chairs in homage to the Arthurian table of legend. The room had no ceiling and the diffuse light that filtered down through the dome caught the polished edges of the walls, sending pools of light and shadow spilling across the room's interior.
Jon looked up at the apex and marvelled at the complex, simplicity of the design. He was trying to swallow his both his anger and his apprehension, but he hasn't been terribly successful, so far at either. He paced, restlessly muttering to himself the whole time.
He had been invited here for an official welcome to the colony. However, with Cam lying in the medical bay along with a still unconscious Felix, he felt more like he was waiting inside the headmaster's office with a poorly concealed packet of Marlborough light's in his trouser pocket.
When the others arrived they did so, in a single group. They were led by a stony faced Jim. They filed into the room one after the other and headed straight for the table and chairs; It was immediately evident that they each had a favourite chair and within seconds everyone was seated and every face was turned expectantly towards Jon, who smiled nervously in return.
Becky flashed a smile back at him and was the first to speak.
"First of all Jon," she began, "I would very much like to take a moment to officially welcome you to our home. Your home, in fact!"

Jon laughed.
"Something funny?" Ben asked
Jon shook his head.
Ben opened his mouth to say something else, but Becky cut over him before he had chance.
"On behalf of every single person here tonight, I'd like to say that you are most welcome."
There was a general murmur of vague consent, which was as underwhelming as it was ambivalent.
Jim pushed himself up from his chair. Jon wasn't sure how he had managed it, but he somehow seemed to be at the head of a completely circular table.
"It really is good to see you Jon," he added, "but before we all get too comfortable I think that it would be best if we get some awkward questions out of the way?" His smile didn't falter but his eyes betrayed him. "Don't you?"
"Awkward questions?" Jon asked. "What about?"
Jim's smile didn't falter, "Well...about the landing, about what happened to Cam, about what happened to Felix and I in bio-pod three."
"How is Cam? Is he wake?" Jon asked.
"We'll get to that," Jim said.
"No," Jon shot back, "you'll tell me now, or I will walk out of that door right now!"
He pointed at the opening in the wall.
"Jon, I really don't think..."
"He's fine," Becky interrupted, "his vital's have all levelled out."
"Is he awake?" Jon asked.
Becky looked over at Sophie, who took a half step forward.
"We decided to place him into an induced coma, " Sophie said, "to give him chance to properly recover."
"A coma?" Jon asked.

Sophie nodded, "We wanted to keep him sedated while we did a thorough examination."
Jon nodded, he wasn't convinced but he would accept it.
"Now," Jim said, "can we get back to the matter at hand?"
"What? Your lynch mob, you mean?" Jon said waspishly, "No we wouldn't want to interrupt that now would we?"
"It's not like that Jon," Becks said.
Jon nodded, "If you say so."
"What happened with the landing and in the bio-pod has to be addressed," Jim insisted.
Ben shot a warning look directly at Jim, but either he didn't notice or he didn't care and instead, ignored him.
"Okay then, what do you want me to say?" he asked, through clenched teeth.
"Just tell us about the landing, thats all." Becky soothed.
"Theres not much to tell," he said, "the landing was pretty much textbook. However after we touched down, Cam fainted, probably due to exhaustion and stress and split his head open in the process," he reached out towards the table and helped himself to a glass of water before continuing.
Becky wrote something on her notepad and looked up, "Go on," she said.
Jon shrugged, "And as for what happened in bio-pod three?"
Jim leant forwards expectantly.
"Well, in bio-pod three, it seems to me, that Cam saved both of your lives!"
"And what about Felix?" Jim asked.
"What about Felix?" Jon asked simply.
"In case you hadn't noticed, he is still unconscious in the medical bay!" Andrew stood up from his chair and pointed at Jon.
"Yeah, but he's still alive in there isn't he?" Jon shot back.

"No thanks to your friend," the emotion, cracked at Andrew's voice.
Jon took a half-step backwards and turned to face Andrew, "What happened to Felix wasn't because of anything Cam did or didn't do..."
"Really?" Andrew said angrily, "because from where I'm sitting it would seem that it's entirely because of Cam and his inability to do a simple job properly!" his voice cracked again and Sophie put a comforting arm around him.
"It's okay Andrew," she said soothingly and then stared accusingly at Jon.
Jon threw his hands into the air, "What?" He said laughing with incredulity. "Are you seriously blaming Cam for your collective inability to maintain one of the simplest machines that he has probably ever designed?"
"No-one's accusing any one of anything Jon," Becky soothed.
"Aren't they?" Jon said looking at Andrew, "Are you sure about that?"
"No, they're not," Jim said firmly, "however, the fact remains that Cam had fully automated control over the canaries and when we came to examine them, we could find nothing wrong with them," he turned to look at Ben who shrugged helplessly, "it's true Jon," he said simply, "I checked them all myself and there wasn't a single obvious malfunction present."
Jon sighed, "So that's it, is it? You've all put two and two together and come up with a hundred?" he shook his head.
"We just want to know what happened on board the 'Three' that day," Becky said.
Jon shook his head again, "Cam had been working on the landing procedure and then Ben called through to talk to him."
"How can you be sure that he was working on the landing procedure and not something else?" Andrew asked bitterly.

"Because I said so!" Jon said. "And because, you can check can't you?"
Andrew looked at Jim, "Can we?"
Jon laughed, "How the Hell are you people still alive?" He asked incredulously. "When you don't know how simple computer systems work?"
The room stared at him.
"Everything that any of us do is logged and saved; The time, the place and the action," he looked around from face to face, "you must all know that, surely?"
"Of course," Simon said.
"Then if you don't believe me, download the log details for the time and date of Felix's mishap and double check."
Becky wrote something else in her notebook.
"You don't need to be a rocket scientist," Jon said, looking around the room again, "which some of you actually are, by the way!"
A tiny ripple of embarrassment went through the room.
"I thought he was a genius?" Andrew said, undeterred, "Why the hell would a genius need to spend so much time preparing to land a ship that he himself designed?"
"Oh, I've had enough of this bullshit!" Jon said loudly, and turned to leave.
"Please Jon, we just need your help to understand," Becky said.
Jon looked at Andrew, "I know your upset Andrew," he said sympathetically, "but please, for the love of God think about what you're saying? You sound like..."
"Yes?" Andrew bristled.
"It doesn't matter," Jon sighed, "you're not thinking clearly, that's all."
"What do I sound like Jon? A hysterical queen?"

Jon slumped, "Of course not, " he said, "come on Andrew, you know me better than that?"
Andrew's eyes dropped to the table top
Jon took a deep breath, "Look," he said, finally, "Cam may well have designed the Nerine Three, but in case you have all forgotten it was built in orbit, so had never had to transverse an atmosphere before," he took another drink from his glass, "also, if you care to look outside, you might just notice that the bloody thing is absolutely fucking massive!"
Ben shifted uncomfortably in his seat, “None of us think Cam has done anything deliberately," he said quietly.
"Deliberately?" Jon said looking at Ben.
"Well..."
"Did you say deliberately?" he laughed bitterly "So what you are now suggesting, is that he is so incompetent that he did something potentially fatal by accident?"
"That’s not what I said," Ben protested
"Yes, it fucking is!" Jon yelled
"Jon..."
"Jesus Ben," Jon said, "I'm surprised at you especially. You know Cam probably better than anyone else here. You know that he would never do anything to hurt anyone, don't you?"
Ben shook his head, "Of course," he said softly.
"Then why are you letting these arseholes question his integrity?"
"Excuse me Jon," Jim interjected, "but no one is 'letting' us do anything. We have legitimate questions to ask you, and it would be helpful if you could answer them in a calm manner, without resorting to insults."
"This is a witch-hunt," Jon said, waving away Jim's comments, "you have already come to your conclusions and now you

want me to help you to manufacture a story that fits with them."

"Jon!" Ben said, "Please if you'd just listen to us?"

"No," Jon said angrily, "I've listened to enough of your bullshit for one evening thank-you."

He slammed his water glass back onto the tabletop and several of the colonists flinched in response.

"So if you're finished with all of your conspiracy theory bollocks? I think I'll go and see if the man that you all owe you goddamn lives to, is still alive!"

With that Jon stormed out of the room without a backwards glance. When he reached the edge of the dome he slowed his pace and took a deep calming breath. He looked back at the giant sculpture and swore under his breath.

"Arseholes," he muttered.

He knew that emerging onto the planet surface, covered in blood, with an unconscious pilot would need some explaining. He knew that there was still probably some negativity harboured towards them after Felix's accident. What he wasn't expecting though was that they were going to turn on Cam so quickly, or with such apparent ferocity.

He wished that Cam was awake so that he could talk to him about what was going on. He also wanted a good strong drink, for probably the first time in his life.

* * *

After Jon's explosive exit, the mood within the meeting room was uncomfortable to say the least. Initially no one spoke or made eye contact with one another.

Ben looked around the room and decided to try and break the ice.
"Well, that went well!" he said to the group as a whole, a sarcastic smile spread across his face.
Jim bristled, “There was no need for that reaction, if you ask me," he said looking to Becky for support.
Becky shrugged, "I dunno Jim. I mean the poor guy has only been here for a matter of hours, his crew mate is lying unconscious in the med-bay and..."
"...And he completely overreacted!" Jim cut across her loudly and instead looked to Andrew for support. Andrew, however, was staring at the tabletop, his face set in an unhappy frown.
"He probably wasn't expecting an interrogation though, was he?" Sophie chipped in.
"What?" Jim looked around the table, his voice rising in irritation, "We all agreed that we would have this discussion when they arrived didn't we?"
Jim waited for a reaction but found little in the way of encouragement in response.
"Didn't we?" he repeated but with greater force.
"We did yes," Simon volunteered, "but perhaps the timing could have been a little more...sensitive?"
Jim slapped the palm of his hand on the table top, "Jesus Christ!" he shouted. "So now I have to take sensitivity training from Simon?" He laughed bitterly, "That's fucking rich!"
Simon raised an eyebrow at this remark, but made no other response.
"We've got to live with these guys," Ben said, "and you just accused one of them of dangerous levels of incompetence and royally pissed of the other one."

"Back off Ben!" Jim said angrily, "You were the one that suggested that Cam had something to do with Felix's accident in the first place!"
Ben rose from his seat, "Whoa!" he said, "Hang on a minute there Jimbo, I did nothing of the sort!"
"Don't call me that!" Jim said loudly. "And yes you-fucking-did, remember?" he looked at Becky for support and she nodded faintly at him. Jim pointed at her, "You see?" he said triumphantly, "you did! And now you're trying to make me look like an insensitive prick for acting upon it."
"Hey, it's not my fault that you look like a prick," Ben replied.
Jim now stood from his chair and leant towards Ben, "Just coz you aint got the balls for the difficult stuff!" he growled.
Ben grabbed at his crotch, "You want balls? Well, come and get them sweetheart!" he said with an evil grin.
Jim's face flashed red with anger, "Fuck you!" he shouted.
Becky stood, placed her hand on Jim's shoulder and gently pushed him back towards his chair.
"Now then boys," she said quietly, "do you think that we could all calm down a little here perhaps?"
Jim swallowed his next sentence, but stared sullenly at Ben who returned the look with interest. Becky looked from one to the other and rolled her eyes.
"The fact remains," she said, "is that we have two new colonists. Both of whom are probably wishing that they'd stayed back on Earth, coupled to the fact..."
"It's not my fault that he..." Jim said sulkily.
"Coupled to the fact," Becky continued doggedly, "that we now have a spacecraft the size of a small town to unpack and utilise. Also we are expecting the Nerine Four to join is in...?"
She looked to Simon.
"Four days," he said in immediate reply, "and sixteen hours."

"Four days," Becky parroted, “thank-you."

"So?" Jim said without any real intent.

Becky arched an eyebrow at him, "So," she said, "we have got an awful lot to accomplish in a terribly short amount of time. It will be far easier to get everything done if we can manage to work together as a unit, wont it?"

Jim glared at Ben.

"And, as the two senior officers within this colony," Becky continued, looking pointedly at Jim and then Ben, "it would make sense if you two could stop with the dick wrestling and try just a little harder to get on with one another. What do you say?"

Ben shrugged and Jim nodded.

Becky rolled her eyes, "We'll take that as a yes then, shall we?"

Without waiting for any affirmation, she turned her attention to Andrew. "We will find out what happened to Felix," she said gently, "and we will make sure that he's back on his feet in no time," she smiled reassuringly and Andrew blinked slowly in return.

"Thank you," he said in a hoarse whisper.

Becky turned back to the group as a whole;

"What do we think then ladies and gentlemen? Perhaps one of us should go and invite Jon back into the meeting?"

Jim moved to stand again, “I guess as it was me that apparently upset him..."

Becky once again applied some gentle pressure to Jim's shoulder and made him pause in his movement.

"Perhaps someone else?" she said softly, “someone less...inflammatory."

Jim shot her a dirty look but nevertheless sat back down again.

"I'll go," Andrew said, "it is kind of my fault after all, I shouldn't have lost my temper with him."
Becky smiled at him, “That’s a very kind offer Andrew but perhaps Ben might be the best person to go."
Jim couldn't contain his outrage at this suggestion.
"Ben? That fucking Neanderthal?" he said incredulously, "Really?"
Becky smiled at him, "Play nicely Jim," she warned.
"I will, but is he really the face of conciliation?"
Ben smiled, but said nothing.
"Perhaps not on every occasion," she said diplomatically, "but you heard what Jon said didn't you? He trusts Ben, and more importantly, he knows that Cam trusts him too."
"He seemed every bit as pissed at Ben, as any other of us," Jim said, "probably even more so in fact."
Becky nodded, "True, I know he was pissed at him for a moment, but I still believe that he sees Ben as an ally," she looked at Ben who was still staring at Jim, "what do you think Ben?" she asked directly.
Ben shook his head and looked up into Becky's face; "hmmm?" he said distractedly, "Sure, I'll go. I could do with a walk anyway." He moved his large frame from in front of his chair and headed towards the exit.
Becky watched him leave, but as he got to the exit she stopped him, "Ben!" she called, "Be nice!"
Ben grinned, "Of course." He said, and then disappeared out of the room.
The rest of the colonists were left in silence, ruminating about what had just happened. The tension within the room was palpable and the universal joy and unity of the celebration dinner, now seemed like a lifetime ago.

Becky turned her attention to Sophie, "Maybe you should go with him?" She said thoughtfully. "Dilute some of the testosterone perhaps?"
Sophie smiled and then nodded. She looked down at the computer tablet she had carried with her into the meeting, upon its display were both Cam's and Felix's monitor readouts directly linked from the med-bay.
"One of us should be in med-bay, in case one or other of the boys wakes up anyway," she said as an afterthought and then without another word, she stood up from her seat and then hurried out of the room in a bid to catch up with Ben before he reached Jon.

CHAPTER THREE

Ben walked quickly after Jon, and when he was within earshot he called after him;
"Hey Jon hold on," he shouted, and Jon instinctively stopped and turned around to see who was there.
"Fuck off Ben!" he called back and continued on his way.
Undeterred, Ben tried again.
"Jon!" he called, "Goddamn it, wait up will you?"
He broke into a slightly ungainly jog as he tried to bridge the gap between them. Jon heard him coming and when he was within a few metres he suddenly stopped again and spun around to confront him.
"What do you want Ben?" he said irritably, "I'm not really in the mood for any more of your collective bullshit."
Ben shrugged, "We were just talking to you," he said nonplussed, "it's hardly our fault if you're so easily offended."
Jon raised his eyebrows and laughed harshly, "Yeah right," he said, "just talking to me? You're either joking or a moron, possibly both."
He shook his head and then turned to continue on his way.
"Wait!" Ben said and reached out to place a hand on Jon's shoulder.
Jon looked down at Ben's hand as if it were some form of poisonous fungus; he then raised his eyes and looked at Ben.
"Really?" he said, "You gonna start getting physical now as well?"
Ben removed his hand instinctively.
"No," he said, "but we do need to talk."
"Yeah?" Jon said, "We tried that, It didn't go too well, did it?"
"Jesus Jon, you guys have just arrived. No-one wants this to turn nasty."

"Turn nasty?" Jon said incredulously, "Turn nasty? What the Hell would you call what happened just now?" he pointed down the corridor towards the meeting room. "Was that supposed to be you guys rolling out the red carpet? Because let me tell you, if it was, then you seriously need to work on your social skills. I've had warmer welcomes than that touring Afghanistan in a fucking tank!"

A flash of irritation touched Ben's face and he reddened noticeably. Jon meanwhile turned once again and continued, determinedly along the corridor.

"Where are you going?" Ben called after him.

"I'm going to see Cam," he replied, "see if he can give me a lift back home," he continued under his breath.

Ben watched him go as he weighed up his options. His instinct was to give him some time to calm down, but he also wanted to stop this feeling of bad blood before it fully took hold and became permanently toxic. He waited until Jon was a good twenty metres or so further along the corridor before he set off after him again. He kept at that distance until they reached the medical bay. Jon opened the door and then slipped inside leaving Ben alone in the corridor to consider his next move.

He slowly walked up to the doorway that Jon had just disappeared through and looked through the window to see what was going on.

Jon was looking at Cam's chart and then he checked his IV infusion and his monitor readouts. Apparently satisfied, he dragged a chair across the floor and collapsed heavily into it. Ben saw for the first time what the last twenty-four hours had cost Jon, and felt suddenly guilty about his behaviour. He looked almost broken, his shoulders drooped and his face was suddenly drained of all of the colour that his anger and frustration had afforded him. Jon lifted his hand and then

tenderly rested it on Cam's. He then leant his body forward and touched his forehead against them both before closing his eyes.
Suddenly, Ben felt like a voyeur, intruding on a moment of private intimacy. This was probably not something that Jon would have wanted to share with anyone else and for a split second Ben toyed with the idea of just turning away and leaving, but he didn't. Instead after hesitating by the door for a few moments longer, he finally pressed the release mechanism and it slid open. Jon barely looked up from his position alongside Cam, but as he heard Ben's footsteps enter the room, he sighed heavily.
When he eventually made eye contact, Ben was surprised to see that his eyes were red and swollen.
"Are you okay?" Ben asked gently.
Jon wiped his hand over his eyes and sighed again,
"Honestly?" he said quietly, "I'm not sure that I've ever been further away from okay in my entire life."
"Look..." Ben began, but Jon held up his hand to stop him.
"Please Ben," he whispered, "can we just leave it for tonight? My friend is in a coma and I'd like some time alone with him if that's okay?"
"He's my friend too you know," Ben said, quickly and then kicked himself.
Jon laughed, closed his eyes but said nothing more.
Ben smiled sheepishly, "Sorry," he said, "not really the point I guess?"
Jon nodded and rubbed his eyes with the heels of his hands,
"It's okay," he said after what felt like a lifetime, "it's..."
"What?" Ben pushed,
"It's been a long day that's all."

Ben smiled and took a step closer to where Jon was sitting and then stopped.
"Mind if I join you?" he asked.
Jon shook his head, "I suppose not," he said quietly, "if you must."
Ben pulled over another chair and positioned it next to Jon. Close enough to have a conversation, but not so close as to be mistaken for an aggressive move. He sat down and placed his hands on his lap. Jon stole a sideways glance at him but said nothing; instead he let the silence engulf the room like a newly settled snowfall.
The two men sat, noiselessly, side by side for more than ten minutes, neither of them saying a word, both of them taking the opportunity for a quiet moment of reflection.
Surprisingly, it was Jon that finally broke the silence.
"How's Felix doing?" he said and glanced over to the side room where Felix was lying.
Ben shrugged, "You're asking the wrong guy," he said, "he was awake and talking only two days ago and now..."
"Yeah?" Jon asked
"...And now...well, he doesn't seem to be doing so well anymore. He had another fit yesterday as you guys were landing and according to Sophie, Sorry Doctor Torres, things look bit shaky at the moment."
Jon nodded, "Poor guy," he said solemnly.
Ben nodded, "Yeah,"
"Sorry," Jon said, "about what I said before. It's just that everyone seems so, so fucking angry with us!"
"They're not," Ben said, with a shrug, "not really. But emotions are high and you guys are new," he paused for a moment, "I guess they're just scared and you guys are easy targets."
"Hmmm," Jon grunted.

"How's our friend here?" Ben asked nodding towards Cam.
"He's resting," Jon said simply.
"How about this coma thing? Is that normal?"
"No, not really. Especially not with a head injury, but it looks as though the trauma is relatively stable, but the rest of his system has gone into anaphylaxis."
"Shock?" Ben said surprised
"The fall was a symptom of something else and until we can be certain what it was we want to keep him safe. It's probably just exhaustion but until we can be sure..." he trailed off and looked up at the peaceful face of his friend.
Ben nodded.
"How are you doing?" he said, and placed a hand on Jon's shoulder.
Jon sighed, "I'm tired," he said, "it's been a busy couple of days."
Ben laughed and patted Jon with a heavy hand.
"Look Jon," Ben said, suddenly serious, "I've got something that I think you need to know, something that you're not going to like."
Jon arched his eyebrows at him, “That doesn't sound good," he said.
Ben shook his head, "I'm afraid it's not."
Jon sighed, "Then can it wait?" he asked, "I'm exhausted and I think that I've had enough to deal with over the last couple of days don't you?"
Ben shrugged, "I know," he said, "but I have to tell you...it's important, it’s about Cam,"
"Cam?" Jon said. "What about him?"
Ben sighed.
"Ben?" Jon said, "What about Cam?"

Ben turned his head towards the door as it slid open and then shook his head, "You're right," he said, "it can wait."
Jon opened his mouth to protest, but at that exact moment Sophie walked in through the medical bay door, staring at a tablet screen as she went. She stopped in front of where Cam was lying and then looked up. If she was surprised to see either Jon or Ben it certainly didn't show on her face.
"You two look cozy," she said with a wry smile.
She walked over to Ben and kissed the top of his head, causing Jon to raise his eyebrows and Ben to blush fiercely.
"Do I need to be jealous?" she asked an increasingly uncomfortable looking Ben, who said nothing but flushed an even darker shade of red.
"No fighting then?" she said with a slight giggle.
Ben and Jon looked at each other but neither of them managed to speak.
"That's good," Sophie continued whilst she circled Cam checking his monitors and charts. "Now if you boys could give me some room, I would very much like to check on my patients please."
Jon stood from his chair, "Can I help?" he asked hopefully.
Sophie shook her head, "There is no need," she said, "you are tired I think, and need to get some sleep," she smiled at him.
"I want to though," Jon replied, "he's my friend and I want to..."
"This is exactly the reason you should go and get some sleep," she cut over him, "because it may be that we will need your help in the coming hours and if you are exhausted, you will be unable to assist anyone."
Jon slumped, visibly and then nodded weakly, "Okay then," he said and looked over towards firstly Ben and then the door.
"I'm coming back though," he said defiantly as he moved to leave.

"I should hope that you are," Sophie said seriously.
Ben watched Jon leave and then turned to face Sophie, "I didn't know we were telling people," he said.
Sophie shrugged, "News travels fast in such a small environment as this," she said with an innocent smile, "but, you too can leave now please. I do not want any distractions."
She walked over to the drug cupboard, unlocked it and produced a small glass vial which she studied briefly before heading over to a work bench and filling a small syringe. She glanced back at Ben whose mouth had dropped slightly open in surprise.
"You're dismissing me?" he said aghast.
Sophie nodded, "Yes," she said simply before heading back over to Cam.
"Now if you don't mind?" she gestured to the door, "I have work to do."
Without saying anything else Ben rose and moved towards the door. Before he left he turned back to look at Sophie who was smiling innocently at him.
"Bye," he muttered, then departed from the room and into the corridor beyond.
As he walked, he considered the fact that he now seemed to be in a relationship.
It had been a long time since Ben had even had a girlfriend, never mind taken orders from a girlfriend. He liked to think of himself as an independent spirit, married only to his career. And yet here he was out in the corridor and heading towards his quarters, his tail firmly between his legs, before he even really had had the chance to appreciate what had happened.

CHAPTER FOUR

When Cam awoke, he was alone. His head hurt like molten metal and his throat felt acrid and bitter. Instinctively, he turned his head to better acquaint himself with his immediate surroundings. That was when the first wave of panic crashed over him. He had moved to look to his left but instead of taking in the med bay, his gaze remained resolutely focussed on the ceiling above him. He repeated the motion but this time to the right and had a similar response.

Nothing happened.

He swallowed and then refocussed his efforts. He concentrated all of his strength and effort into his neck muscles and willed them into movement, but again nothing happened. His panic moved up a further notch as the awful realisation of the situation unveiled itself to him. His paralysis seemed to be almost total. He could open and close his eyes, swallow, which was exquisitely painful, but other than that, and the unsettling ability to feel the blood coursing through his vessels, there was nothing. He concentrated and fought down his rising panic to see if he could decipher any sounds or evidence of someone else in the room. There were only the electronic sounds of medical monitors and machines that syncopated, unsettlingly, with the beating of his heart.

He strained until he thought that he could hear voices nearby but such was their distance to him that he was unable to filter the noise into anything recognisable. He vaguely thought that one of the voices might have belonged to Jon, but it was too dislocated and indistinct for him to be certain. He tried to speak, more out of desperate hope than expectation, but all he could manage to emit was a pitifully low moan which was barely audible even to himself.

His heart was racing, his head was pounding, and so he closed his eyes and tried to relax.
"If Jon is here, he will look after me," he thought to himself, "I'm safe and amongst friends."
He repeated this mantra over and over in his head, "I'm safe and amongst friends," he thought until, finally, he slowly started to feel his heart rate gradually slowing.
Just as he was becoming a little calmer a terrible thought struck him; What if Jon's not here? What if he's not looking after me? What if I crashed the ship and all that's left is an expensive collection of twisted metal and body parts? He tried to focus his mind and slowly attempted to recall the events that had brought him to this hospital bed. He remembered the landing; at least he remembered most of it. Had they crashed? There was spike of panic again as he forlornly searched his mind for any memories. However, anything that was there remained in the shadows of his psyche, resolutely hidden. Determined to gather some answers he decided to compile a mental list of things that he knew for sure. Firstly he was alive, and that was a good start. Secondly he was clearly injured; he knew that because he hurt all over. This lead him to his next point. He was clearly, quite seriously injured because not only was he in the medical bay surrounding by all manner of machines and monitors, but he was also apparently paralysed. Something gnawed at him, something remote yet immediate. It remained resolutely hidden though, so he continued with his internal, fact finding mission.
"So what had happened?" he asked himself, "Perhaps they *had* crashed after all?" After a moments consideration he mentally shook that thought out of his head. No, he was sure that they'd touched down safely, he remembered talking to Jon on the bridge, he remembered the childlike look of excitement

on his face and the terracotta coloured dust that had covered all of the windows.
They had landed safely, he concluded with a painful sigh of relief, excellent.
So how did he end up like this?
His head throbbed and his arms ached with what felt like a hundred tiny bruises. What's more, his feet were cold
"Wait a minute," he thought suddenly. "If I'm paralysed then how do I know that my feet are cold?"
This thought dropped from his head as he heard the voices become noticeably louder and Cam recognised now not only Jon's voice but Ben's as well. He strained against the insistence of his uncooperative body to move and make his presence known but all that happened was that the pain in his head intensified with an alarming jolt and he felt the brittle kiss of unconsciousness lay him back into a dreamless sleep.

* * *

Jon and Ben were back in the med bay. Jon stared blankly at Ben's face and licked his, suddenly dry, lips.
"I don't believe you," he said simply.
Ben shrugged, "I don't blame you, it took me a while to come to terms with it as well."
Jon shook his head, "Jacob?" he said, "Jacob killed Cam's wife and daughter?"
Ben nodded, "So it would seem."
Jon laughed, mirthlessly and shook his head again, "No," he said, “that’s not true, it can't possibly be true!"
"It is Jon, I'm sorry," Ben said apologetically, "I only found out a few weeks ago, if that's any consolation?"

"Not really," Jon said, "but how did you find out anyway? Who told you?"
Ben hesitated for a moment, "It doesn't matter," he said finally, “but the fact is I believe them. And so should you."
Jon walked towards the back of the room and sat down in a chair that was immediately behind a large, white Formica desk. It was covered with loose papers, medical journals and stationary. Ben watched him and then went over to join him; he looked disapprovingly at the accumulated clutter and shook his head.
"I thought we were supposed to be operating a paperless system everywhere?" he asked rhetorically.
Jon smiled, "Doctors like paper," he shrugged, "makes us feel official."
Ben forced a smile, picked up a notebook that lay upon the desk and idly thumbed through it without really looking at it. He looked up at Jon and tossed it back onto the desk top.
“I'm not sure what I'm meant to do with this?” Jon asked.
Ben opened his mouth to reply but nothing came out.
“Why tell me at all?”
“He’ll be here in less than seventy-two hours,” Ben said and glanced nervously at the unconscious figure of Cam. He lowered his voice. "The man that killed Cam's family will be living and working side by side with us in three days.”
Jon bowed his head.
“What do you want me to do about it?” Jon looked up into Ben’s bright blue eyes, “It’s a hell of a thing to suddenly land on my shoulders...”
"I did try and tell you before, remember?"
Jon's face wrinkled in thought, before the memory hit him, "That's what you wanted to tell me before?" he said incredulously.

Ben nodded a little sheepishly.
"Jesus Christ! You weren't planning on hanging about were you?"
"There's no time for timidness," he said, “events have almost caught us up."
Jon sighed and picked up an elastic band from the desktop. He twirled it through his fingers and jiggled his leg nervously.
"And you're certain?" Jon asked.
"It was straight from the horse's mouth," Ben nodded.
"Jacob told you himself?" Jon said, surprised.
"Okay," Ben conceded, "The horse's brother, then,"
Jon looked over a Felix, "Oh," he said, "not a good week for the Mbamwa family?"
Ben sniffed, "No, not exactly."
Jon continued to watch Felix for a few more seconds, before turning his attention back to Cam. He was chewing this over and could only come to one conclusion.
"If you're sure..." he said, thoughtfully.
Ben nodded, "Like I say. Theres no doubt."
"Then we have no choice. We've got to tell Cam," Jon said, finally.
Ben shook his head, appalled, “No!" he said
Jon sighed, “We don't have a choice, and he has a right..."
“No!” Ben repeated, but he was suddenly angry.
Jon ignored him, “He has a right to know.”
“No," Ben repeated, "it'll kill him!”
“You don't know that. You said yourself. He’s stronger than he looks.”
“I know, but we can’t take that chance!”
Jon shook his head, "We have no choice.”
“You can't take risks with people’s lives Jon."
"I'm a doctor," Jon said, "thats precisely what I'm paid to do."

"What If it breaks him? What then? How do you cope with that?"
Jon sighed, unhappily.
“I’m right," Ben said, forcing his point, "you know I am. It’s too much. It’ll be like losing them all over again.”
Jon looked at Ben and then at Cam. He nodded slowly.
“Okay,” he said.
“Okay?” Ben repeated, forcefully.
Jon nodded again, “I don't like it, but yeah, okay.”
Ben visibly relaxed, "Good."
"Who else knows?" Jon asked.
Ben stroked his moustache, "No one."
"Why?"
Ben shifted uncomfortably, "It's not the kind of thing you just blurt out to someone."
"You mean, someone other than me?" Jon asked.
Ben blushed, "Yeah, sorry about that."
"No one else though?"
Ben considered telling Jon about Sophie, but he didn't want to field the resultant questions, he wanted to protect her as far as he was able.
"No one," he said simply.
"Hmmm," Jon said. “It still leaves us with the question of what to do about Jacob though? Any thoughts?”
“I don't know yet," Ben said, thoughtfully, “but he’s a dangerous man. Whatever we decide, we'll have to act together. Agreed?”
Jon nodded, “Agreed!” he said.
“We need to careful.” Ben said.
“Hmm.”
Ben stood to leave, Jon watched him, his face expressionless.

Ben looked at him, ”We don't have a choice Jon. You do know that, don't you?”
Jon nodded but said nothing.
“Jon?”
“I’m okay.”
"Trust me, we'll sort something out."
Ben headed to the door. As he went, he paused at Cam’s bed. He placed a hand on his leg, patted it and then squeezed it affectionately. He lingered for a moment and then left without looking back.
If he had looked back, perhaps he would have seen that Cam's eyes were, once again, wide open. He had again woken from his catatonia and had heard the entire conversation between Ben and Jon.

CHAPTER FIVE

Jon was sitting in a chair behind the desk in the Medical bay, he had a book open in front of him. He couldn't concentrate properly and consequently, had reread the same sentence at least four times already. He sighed and in an admission of defeat he closed the book without bothering to mark his page. He stared distractedly over at where Cam lay and tapped his fingertips on the desk top.

It was almost seventy-five hours since he and Cam had landed and Cam was still in his induced coma. Sophie had been keeping a close eye on him and was happy enough with his progress that she was beginning the process of bringing him out of it. The head injury had stabilised and the threat of infection had finally receded after an aggressive bout of antibiotics.

Jon watched him nervously, but as yet he had shown no signs of coming round. He picked up the controlled drugs book and idly flicked through it. He shook his head sadly as he noticed all of the drugs that his friend had been subjected to in such a short period of time.

Cam was awake, it was almost two days since Cam had overheard Jon and Ben talking about Jacob. Two days of almost unbearable torture. The pain and fatigue that had so worried him when he had first awoken had been replaced by a growing sense of impotent rage and frustration. The waking prison that his own body had become had been filled by an old familiar pain, one whose sting he had not felt for almost 10 years. The tears came easily and without thinking, he raised his hand to his face.

He raised his hand...

"Oh my god," he thought to himself I can move. His arm ached, as his muscles protested and then stung as his skin pulled against the connected IV line, but he could move. He winced in pain and heard his own voice again. The accumulative frustration of the previous forty hours broke forth from him in a guttural cry of relief and anguish.

The noise cut through the silence in the room like a 3am car alarm and Jon leapt up from his chair sending the drug book flying across the med bed floor.

“Cam?" he shouted, and rushed over to his bedside.

As he arrived, he immediately he saw the fresh blood that had leaked from his arm, where he had pulled out the cannula. The bright red stain blossomed out over the crisp white hospital sheets and Jon instinctively grabbed a swab and held it against the puncture wound on his arm. Cam raised his hand and looked down at the blood, his eyes flicked to Jon and he opened his mouth to speak.

“It’s okay Cam, it’s just from the needle in your arm. It looks worse than it is. You're okay.”

Cam grunted and turned away from Jon’s stare.

“Hey it's okay,” he said quietly, “you’re going to be fine. You had me worried for a while though.”

Jon laughed quietly, ”I thought I might have to stay here on my own without you!” he shuddered theatrically, “Urgghhh!”

Cam remained still, resolutely staring at the ceiling; he swallowed and coughed a little to clear his throat.

“Cam?” Jon gently rocked his shoulder, “Cam? Can you hear me?”

“I can hear you,” he said tentatively as he tested his voice out again, “there’s nothing wrong with my hearing.”

“Okay, well that’s good!” Jon was smiling, but slightly confused by his friend's apparent coolness.

“Not really,” Cam whispered, wiping away another tear.
“Pardon?" Jon asked, "What’s the matter? Are you in pain?”
Cam shook his head. Jon looked relieved.
“I heard you,” Cam whispered.
“I'm sorry?" John said
"I heard you," cam repeated, a little louder.
"Heard me what?” Jon asked, "I've been sitting here reading."
He looked over at the desk and the discarded book, "Actually I've been sitting here not reading, to be honest, couldn't concentrate."
“I heard you talking," Cam said, "you and Ben, I heard you.”
He turned to face Jon. His face was pained, but resolute.
The colour drained from Jon’s face and his heart started hammering in his chest as the realisation settled over him. He swallowed loudly.
"But that was days ago," he protested, "how could you possibly have...?"
His eyes widened, as the realisation struck him, "Oh god no!" he said desperately.
"How long? I mean when did you wake up?"
He shook his head, "Not two days ago? You can't have been lying here for two days?"
Cam closed his eyes and more tears fell.
"Oh Cam..." Jon said, “I…I’m so sorry," he whispered and took hold of Cam's hand.
He sat down on the edge of his bed and shook his head sadly.
“I don’t know what to say.”
Cam tested his newly recovered control by clenching and unclenching his jaw, “Nothing,” he said bitterly, ”there’s nothing you can say.”
“I’m sorry Cam. I really am.”

“Aye, you said,” he swallowed and flinched with the pain before turning his head to face Jon again, “when did you find out?” he asked

“When you did, I guess. Just when Ben told me the other day.”

Cam nodded, ”Who else knows?”

Jon sighed again, “No one. I promised Ben I wouldn't say anything,” he paused for a moment, “well that’s not strictly true. Felix…”

“Felix?” Cam considered this for a moment, “Aye, that makes sense I suppose. Bastard!”

“Cam, It’s not Felix’s fault and…”

“Aye?”

Jon sighed heavily and allowed his eyes to flick over to the adjacent room where Felix still lay comatose, ”Shit Cam, I didn't expect to be doing this today,”

“What?” Cam asked.

Jon sighed, "It's not looking too good for Felix at the moment," he said reluctantly, "he had another fit as we were coming in to land and..."

Cam arched his eyebrow quizzically, "...and?" he said

"Well, the second fit was a big one, so big in fact that it caused him to have some kind of cerebral event."

"English please," Cam said irritably

"Like I say it's not looking good," Jon said with a shrug, "he's been unconscious ever since the second seizure and whilst he's stable, his prospects are getting worse with every passing hour..." Jon trailed off.

Cam looked at him, some of the fierceness drained from his expression to be replaced by guilt.

"Shit." He said.

He tried to manoeuvre his arms into a position whereby he could sit himself up.

He winced in pain as he tried to push himself up onto his elbows.
“Give me a hand will you?” he said to Jon who instinctively reached out and helped him to sit upright.
“You need to rest,” he said.
Cam glared at him, ”I think I’ve rested enough don't you?” his voice was calm, but threatening.
Jon swallowed, “You’re not well,” he pleaded, “please Cam, lie back down.”
“Can I have a drink please?” Cam said ignoring him, "My throat feels like broken glass!"
Jon sighed and went to the sink where he poured a cup of water. He returned to the bedside and held it out to Cam, who took it a little shakily and tentatively sipped it before gulping it down greedily.
“How long have I been in here?” Cam asked.
“Three days”
“Why?”
“Pardon?” Jon had been prepared for further questions, just not that one.
“Why have I been here for three days? What’s wrong with me?”
Jon shrugged, ”Exhaustion Cam, pure and simple. You’d pushed yourself so hard for so long, there was nothing left to give,” he put a hand on Cam’s shoulder.
Cameron flinched, but didn't try and shrug it off.
“I think when we landed, you relaxed for the first time in weeks and your system just… shut down.”
Cam considered this for a few seconds and seemed to accept it with a small nod.
"Okay, " he said, "what about the paralysis though? Was that part of it?"

"Jesus no!" Jon said appalled. "The idea was to give your whole system a chance to recover. To fight any infection. You weren't meant to be awake for any of it..."
"So what happened?" Cam asked bitterly.
"I don't know," Jon said, unhappily. "There must have been a mistake in the calculations for the anaesthetic...It shouldn't have happened Cam, I'm sorry."
Cam shook his head stiffly, "It's not your fault," he said and then looked at him straight in the eyes, "I need to see Ben."
Without warning, he swung his legs over the bedside and shuffled his bottom forward to the edge of the bed until his feet reached the floor. He wriggled his toes as they touched the cold laminated flooring and looked up at Jon again.
"Any chance of some clothes?" he said.
"What are you going to do Cam?"
Cam looked at him, "I need to talk to Ben," he looked down at his half covered nakedness and tugged at his hospital gown, "I'd rather not do it with my arse hanging out though!"
"It's not his fault Cam; he was trying to protect you," Jon said.
Cam nodded, "I understand," he said calmly, "I still need some clothes though."
"Cam?"
"I need some clothes," he repeated.
"Cam, please," Jon pleaded.
"I said, I need some fucking clothes Jon!" he screamed at the top of his fragile voice.
His hand flew up to his throat and he winced in pain, "Ow," he croaked.
Jon lifted his hands in surrender, "Okay Cam, Jesus!"
Cam stood perfectly still for a moment, staring straight ahead, then he began to sway slightly as his legs struggled to adjust to their task of baring his weight. He kept a hand on the bed

for balance, took a series of slow, deep breaths and blinked slowly and deliberately. Jon obediently headed off to one of the storage lockers and found a pair of jogging bottoms and a white t-shirt, he grabbed a pair of balled up sports socks and then headed back to over to where Cam was standing. He handed the clothes to Cam who took them and immediately started remove the hospital gown. As he undid the ties he paused and turned to address Jon.
"Did you particularly want to see my bollocks?" he asked, matter of factly.
Jon shrugged, "It's nothing that I haven't seen a thousand times before."
"Aye, well fair enough," he said.
Cam stripped off the gown and slowly and carefully, climbed into the jogging bottoms. He groaned as he pulled the t-shirt over his head, he'd forgotten about the head wound. He raised his hand to the bandage that circled his head and touched it tentatively; once again he flinched because of the pain and looked quizzically over to Jon.
"You cracked it against the edge of the console when you collapsed," Jon said, by way of explanation, "you lost a fair bit of blood. Made a bit of a mess of the cockpit as well if I'm honest," he smiled nervously at Cam and was relieved to see a flicker of a smile in return.
This brief show of emotion seemed to break his concentration and Cam faltered on his feet, he took a step backwards and took a firmer grip of the edge of the bed. Jon stepped towards him and put his arm around his waist.
"Hey easy Cam," he said gently, "you've got to sit back down"
Cam rested against the bed and looked at Jon, "I've got to see Ben," he bowed his head and once again, but now the tears flowed freely from his eyes.

When he spoke again, it was in a barely audible whisper, "I've got see Ben."
Jon kept his arm around his waist and pulled him closer, "You've got to rest, that's what you've got to do."
Cam broke away from the hug and stumbled away from Jon, he drew his arm across his face to wipe at the tears and turned back to face Jon, his face twisted in rage and anguish "I've rested enough!" he screamed at him, "Now fucking take me to see Ben or I'll go and find him myself!"
Cam was sobbing freely now, Jon nodded and moved towards him again.
"You sit down; I'll go and get him."
Jon walked past him and headed out of the room, as he left Cam's legs buckled and he moved to the chair that was positioned by the bed. He collapsed into it and buried his face in his hands, sobbing. The accumulative pain of ten years repressed emotion was now crashing over him in wave after wave of raw anguish. He breathed, and caught the smell of Karen's favourite moisturiser in the clinical air around him. He wrapped his arms around himself and could feel the determined pressure of his daughter's tightest hug around his chest. He listened and could hear the sound of her voice, endlessly chatting, asking questions, and telling him stories. He closed his eyes and once more he could see his beloved Martha lying on the mortuary table, her skin porcelain white, her eyes open, staring sightlessly into eternity.
He tried to stifle a primal scream of torture, but it was too big, too powerful and it burst from his lungs like fire, igniting a fresh stab of searing pain in the centre of his chest.
He slumped forward in the chair and slid helplessly onto the floor. He rested his face against the cold linoleum and fought

to breath; he closed his eyes again and slipped once more into blissful unconsciousness.

CHAPTER SIX

Sophie surveyed the room slowly and carefully, taking time to rest her eyes on everybody's face in turn before moving onto the next one.

"Thank you all, for coming here on such short notice," she said unable to hide the tension in her voice.

"This had better be good doc," Jim said irritably, "the Nerine Four is gonna be here in..." he checked his watch which he had set to a timer,"...exactly eight hours and twenty-seven minutes time," he looked up into Sophie's face, "so we are kinda on a tight schedule here, okay?"

Becky placed a calming hand onto Jim's arm, "If Sophie has called us all here, then I'm sure she's got a good reason,“ she said gently.

Sophie blushed and whispered something inaudible before looking, intently at the computer tablet that she was holding. Her hands were quivering slightly and she had to place the tablet onto the desk top in order to be able to read it properly.

"As I said," she whispered, her face burning with embarrassment.

"Goddamn it woman! Speak up for Christ's sake or we'll never get out of here." Jim barked.

"I agree," Simon said loudly and Becky rolled her eyes in frustration, "I have much to do and this will not help with my preparations."

"And I would really like to go and spend some time with Felix," Andrew said, "I've been so busy for the last few days that I've barely seen him."

There was a background murmur that slowly got louder as each member of the colony started to discuss with the others

the list of things that they would rather be doing than sitting in the meeting room.
Ben stood from his chair and slapped his hand down hard on the table top. The general discord in the room stopped suddenly.
"Perhaps if you'd all shut the Hell up then the poor girl would be able to get a goddamn word in edgeways!" he said loudly. He looked around the room, his face fierce and then turned to Sophie, "Go ahead sweetheart," he said with a theatrical wink, "give 'em what you've got."
Sophie smiled gratefully at Ben and then took a fortifying breath before starting again.
"I know that you are all busy," she said, her voice clear and stable, "so I will skip straight to the important bit," she waited for any voices of dissent, when none were forthcoming she continued, her confidence renewed. "As you are all no doubt aware we have had two colonists in a coma over the past few days," her eyes flicked guiltily to Andrew for a second, "thankfully though, Professor Harrison seems to be on the mend and given the fullness of time I am confident that he will go on to make a full and sustained recovery."
There was a rumble of indistinct sentiment that rolled around the room but Sophie did her best to ignore it.
"And we all know that Felix is..." she shot another nervous look over at Andrew but he had momentarily dropped his head, "...is struggling and unfortunately his prognosis is still far from certain."
Jim sighed, "If this is a medical update, then the timing is not the greatest doc," he tapped his watch, "no offence Andrew." He added quickly.
Andrew shook his head numbly and waved his hand, "None taken," he muttered quietly.

"No, it isn't a medical update," Sophie said determinedly, "but what I have to say will greatly effect the newly arriving colonists."
Jim sat up, "The Nerine Four?" He said worriedly, "What has this got to do with them?"
"Everything," Sophie said, "and nothing."
"Could you be a little less cryptic doc? Some of us are only rocket scientists," Jim said bitterly.
Becky shot him a warning look and he settled down almost instantly.
"Sorry," he said meekly, "please continue."
Sophie nodded, "Thank you," she said, "as you know captain, I recently ran some colony wide blood tests to see if there was any link between the sudden seizure that Felix suffered and the low grade illnesses that the general population have been suffering with."
"I didn't know that," Andrew interrupted, "is there something you can do for Felix?" he asked hopefully.
Sophie shook her head, "Not at the moment Andrew, I am sorry."
Andrew's head once again bowed.
"However I have new hope," Sophie continued, "because I have isolated what seems to be a viral pattern that has shown up in everyone's blood work. Everyone's that is except Felix's."
"Really? What is it?" Andrew asked.
"Has this always been there?" Becky asked, "How is that possible?"
Sophie shrugged, "It is a fairly common virus," she said simply, "it's measles."
"Measles?" Simon said loudly, "But Felix is dying. No one dies from measles, do they?"

Andrew winced and Anna moved to put a comforting arm around him.
"What?" Simon said genuinely confused, "It's a perfectly valid question. They don't, do they?"
"Not anymore," Sophie conceded, "but that's not the full story. I do not think that it is the illness itself that has caused the problem, at least not in isolation. I think that perhaps Felix has a rare congenital condition that may have reacted with the virus to trigger his seizures."
"How did he catch it?" Anna asked, "If the tests on the rest of us are all immune?"
"We are not all immune necessarily, but we each carry a version of the virus. If the virus was dormant in someone's system it is perfectly possible that some infection could have reawakened the virus and made it briefly contagious again," she looked around the room hopefully. Becky was nodding in agreement but Jon had his head bowed and determinedly looking at the carpet.
Sophie continued, "Also he may not have been immunised as a child," not everyone was.
"Oh God," Andrew said suddenly, "this is my fault! I had that cold he must have caught it from me!" he sounded distraught and tears had started to redden his eyes.
"It's not your fault," Anna said soothingly, "is it?"
Sophie smiled, "No of course not."
"If it's measles then we can treat it?" Becky said excitedly.
Sophie nodded, "Potentially yes, in the long run," she smiled sympathetically at Andrew before looking back at Jim, "I'm sorry to say this, but the bigger issue at the moment is that the Nerine Four is about to land with twelve new colony members. One of whom happens to be Felix's brother and may therefore have the same congenital predisposition to this reaction."

"So what are you saying doc, we quarantine Jacob when he arrives?" Ben asked
Sophie shook her head again, "Not just Jacob," she said flatly, "the whole ship."
"What?" Jim said suddenly furious. "No way!"
"All I have, is a single hypothesis at the moment," Sophie said, "until I can be sure, I think it is for the best that we don't take any unnecessary chances," she turned to look directly at Jim "Don't you?"
Jim shied away from her stare, but swore to himself as he did so.
"I'm sorry, did you say something?" Sophie asked.
"Fine!" Jim said loudly, before standing up from the table, "Well, if that's all?"
"Where are you going?" Becky asked.
"I'm going to tell those poor bastards that are coming in to land that they can't actually come in when they get here," he said, and stormed off around the table and out of the meeting room.
Sophie blinked as she watched him go and then turned to look at Becky.
"It is the only course of action," she said, confused.
Becky stood, "I know," she said assuringly, "and so does he. He'll be fine when he's calmed down."
Sophie looked worried.
"That was great work by the way," Becky said as she made her way out of the room, "it was a brilliant spot, well done!"
Sophie blushed again and bowed her head; she gathered her notes together and then turned to Ben.
"Are you coming?" she asked.
Ben nodded his head, "I'll be right with you sweetheart," he replied and nodded towards Jon. “Just want to check something with Jon first."

Sophie smiled and then began to make her way out of the room along with the other colonists. Andrew had made a beeline straight for her and Ben had to push down his instinct to step in to protect Sophie from the inevitable grilling she was about to receive. Finally the room was clear and only Ben and Jon remained behind.

Jon walked around the table until he was standing right next to Ben.

"That was convenient" he said.

"What?" Ben asked innocently.

"The discovery of a virus that might potentially affect the only two related members of the colony."

Ben shrugged, "I guess," he said, "I'm not a doctor though, am I?"

"Its bullshit!" Jon said angrily, “And what's more that poor son-of-a-bitch now thinks that his true-love is only a simple injection away from being back to normal," he pointed out of the door after Andrew who was bouncing around Sophie like an excited puppy.

"It's bought us some time," Ben said.

"It's cruel, is what it is!" Jon said loudly, "And now Sophie knows? This just gets better!"

Jon threw his arms into the air in exasperation.

"I didn't want to tell her," Ben said, "but I trust her and time was running out. I had to do something."

"You don't think that this is perhaps a little extreme then?"

Ben laughed, "It's an extreme situation for Christ's sake," he said, "and what's more if you want to know what I think? I think it goddamn-well worked, that’s what I think."

Jon shook his head sadly, "Yeah but at what cost?"

"Don't get all fucking pious with me!" Ben spat, "What it has done is bought us the time that we needed, and not only that it

has provided a way to keep Cam away from Jacob until we can sort something out."
Jon shook his head again, "Cam wouldn't do anything stupid," he said.
"Wouldn't he?" Ben asked, "Are you sure about that?"
"He isn't stupid," Jon said.
"No, he isn't," Ben replied, “and that's what worries me. He is so fucking far from stupid that he might think of something...rash. He's upset and he's also not thinking straight."
Ben moved around the table adjusting the chairs as he went.
"You don't know what he's thinking," Jon said.
Ben stopped walking and looked at Jon his expression one of disbelief, "Oh come on Jon don't be an idiot!" he said with a bitter laugh.
Cam walked into the room, but remained unseen by the others, “Why break the habit of a lifetime?" he said by way of announcing himself.
The other two men both stopped dead and turned to face Cam who looked pale and gaunt, but had the hint of a smile on his face.
"Cam!" Ben said, quickly pushing down his surprise, "Great to see you up and about!"
"Liar," Cam replied, "I'm much more predictable when I'm confined to the sick bay."
Ben arched his eyebrow at him, "Well partially at least," he said smiling.
Jon was not smiling though; Cam's arrival had not done anything to improve his mood.
"You should be resting," he suggested, a little weakly.
Cam did look much better than he had done even a few hours ago but he was still clearly struggling. The walk to the meeting

room looked as though it had taken a considerable physical toll on him.

"You've both avoided me for long enough," he said quietly.

"Now it's time you answered some of my questions," he turned his head and deliberately looked directly at Ben, "especially you!" he said.

CHAPTER SEVEN

Forty-eight hours is how long it had taken Cam to devise a plan. Forty-eight hours of meticulous planning and replanning. He had secreted himself away in his quarters for the duration but no-one had thought anything of it. He had experienced a trauma and deserved some well earned rest and recuperation. It was a little after two-thirty in the morning and the colony was peaceful. Most of the crew were in their quarters resting.
Most, but not all.
Cam lay on his bunk and checked his watch for umpteenth time, his leg jiggled restlessly as he mentally went over his plans yet again, checking and double checking that he had left nothing to chance.
He had to talk to Jacob, he desperately needed answers and as far as he could tell, Jacob was the only man that would be able to provide them. He checked his watch again, before swinging his legs over the side of his bunk and standing up, he walked into the bathroom and glanced into the mirror that hung above the sink.
"It's time," he said quietly to himself, before splashing some cold water on his face and turning to leave.
He paused as he reached the doorway to his quarters and his hand wavered, hesitantly, over the release mechanism for a few seconds. He finally activated it and slipped out of the room into the darkened corridor beyond. However, once out of his room his previous hesitancy evaporated and he moved quickly through the colony with a focus and quiet fluidity that belied the turmoil that churned at his insides.
The quarantine that separated the existing colony members from the newly arrived crew of the Nerine Four was both procedural and physical. The security systems that were in

place to prevent any cross-site contamination were as complex and tamper proof as any within the colony, meaning that the chances of working out how to override them were virtually impossible.
Unless, of course you happened to have been an integral part of the design team that had originated them.
Always leave a backdoor. It was an elementary part of every engineering project. No matter how complex the programme might be, the chief engineer always left a way to quickly bypass the security settings in order to repair the system if anything went wrong.
A record of his movements would still be stored but Cam was more than capable of altering the log afterwards. Even if he couldn't, he was working on the principle that it was easier to ask forgiveness after the fact, than it was to seek permission before hand.
He reached the air-lock that separated the colony from the outside world and looked nervously over his shoulder, as if expecting some unwelcome company.
There was no one around.
The release sequence was heavily encrypted and contained an algorithm that meant that the cypher was constantly changing and evolving. Only those with the necessary security clearance were granted knowledge of the current code and that necessity was established by mission control back on Earth. During a time of quarantine that meant no-one other than the Sophie and Jim had access to the code. The algorithm required to track these changes was complex and only a hard reset would allow access to anyone else. A hard reset had to be performed by two senior colony officers simultaneously and even if performed correctly it would still set off colony wide alarms. Colony wide alarms and stealth

missions were not the easiest of bedfellows and Cam was keen to avoid the attention.

A hard reset was the last resort but Cam did not require any such extreme action because he had his backdoor. He simply punched in a sixteen digit code and presented his eye for retina scanning. The display flashed up a message and the door slid open:

Security override 0001. Welcome Mr. Williams.

"That ought to confuse the Hell out of them," Cam whispered to himself with a half-smile. He stepped through the doorway and into the airlock beyond. Once the initial door had closed behind him he quickly dressed into one of the lightweight planet suits and let himself out into the open expanse of the planet's surface.

* * *

Ben was already awake when the alarm on his watch went off. Someone was breaking quarantine. It had happened a few times before but it had always been Sophie in the past heading over to the Nerine Four to check on their wellbeing. However, she didn't generally make social calls at three o'clock in the morning. Immediately concerned, he swung his legs out of his bed and instinctively headed to the large landscape window that almost filled one entire wall of his quarters.

He rubbed his eyes with the knuckles of his left hand and yawned loudly, before casually picking up a pair of field-binoculars from his bedside table. He put them to his eyes and squinted as he tried to see through the darkness and out into the gloom outside. He could see nothing. The ever-present surface dust was covering everything and made the air thick

and opaque. It was so bad that he could only just make out the giant half silhouette of the Nerine Four that rested less than two hundred metres away.
He checked the readout on his watch and then shook it, roughly.
"Goddamn piece of junk," he cursed.
He looked at it again, but it still told him an impossibility. He looked back at out of the window, and then back at his watch. According to his wrist-wear, the exterior door had just been accessed by Gareth Williams.
He shook it again, It must be a glitch he thought to himself. He would investigate in the morning. He went back over to his bunk and climbed back under the covers. He lay on his back for a moment staring at the ceiling. He felt his eyes grow instantly heavy, but a nagging thought kept flicking his subconscious mind. If there was one lesson that he had learned over the years it was that an assumption of error was quickly checked but long regretted.
This reoccurring niggle, wouldn't allow him to resettle. He sighed and decided to go and examine the airlock anyway. Error or not, it still demanded attention, he pulled on some clothes and went back to the window for one final look. He still couldn't see anything of consequence. Then, just as he went to take the binoculars from his eyes he saw something. A vague electrical glow from a door hatch release, over on the Nerine Four, it shone through the gloom like a beacon, red and unmistakable.
"Hello, someone's out for a late night stroll," he said to himself, "naughty, and naughty!"
He slipped his feet into his boots and headed straight out of his quarters. Whoever it was had a good head start on him but he would catch them soon enough. He smiled to himself, and

when he did there was going to be a hell of a lot of explaining to be done.

* * *

Cam had crossed the distance between the two structures as quickly as the limitations of both his suit and the planetary conditions allowed. As was often the case, the wind whipped over the barren planet, bringing with it a fine rain of dust that clung to his suit and helmet compromising his ability so see where he was going to such an extent that by the time he reached his destination he was staggering across the landscape like a lost man in an arctic blizzard. The storm did bring some advantages with it though, and the wind covered his footprints with a thick layer of dust as he went, obscuring his progress and making him almost invisible from any of the colony's windows.

He pushed the pressure pad on the door release and it slid open quietly. He stumbled gratefully into the airlock and mashed the palm of his hand against the door release so that it slid closed again. When the pressure had normalised he removed his helmet and gasped as he sucked in a big lungful of the Nerine Four's cool artificial air. His adrenaline had made his breathing rapid and uneasy, so he tried one of his counsellors meditation techniques to clear his mind and calm his thoughts. After a few minutes he had regained his composure and then turned his attention to the next threshold that he had to cross. He raised his hand towards the keypad to enter his code and then hesitated. A terrible thought flashed through his mind, what if the security systems on board the Nerine Four had been updated after he had left Earth? What if

the code was obsolete on this ship? What if he woke up the whole bloody colony?
He lowered his hand, leaving the panel untouched and then sat on an upturned storage crate and sighed. His fingers trembled slightly and he closed his eyes again, he took a few more cleansing breathes and looked back at the door panel.
He was too close to abandon now, he had to assume that he would be granted access to the ship as a colony member. It would undoubtedly get him in to more trouble, but that was risk that he had been willing to take ever since he left his quarters.
He stood up from the crate and walked the three or four paces to the doorway. He took a deep galvanising breath and then presented his eye to the retina scanner. The laser moved across the surface of his eye and then the stopped. The door remained resolutely closed and Cam could feel the unmistakable rumble of panic slowly rising through his body. He licked his lips nervously and considered his options. Just as he was deciding to abort and head back to the colony the door slid open.
"Welcome on board Professor Harrison." Said a quiet electronic voice.
Cam looked at the panel with mild suspicion but then moved through the doorway and into the corridors of the Nerine Four.

CHAPTER EIGHT

Jon could have looked at his watch, but he knew, with unshakable certainty what the time was. It was almost three o'clock in the morning and the familiar, unquenchable dread of the graveyard shift had reached its desolate nadir. He sighed but he had no-one to blame but himself. He had volunteered for this particular graveyard shift, but that didn't make it any more palatable.

His arrival into the colony had been less than auspicious and he wanted to prove that he had something to offer. Sophie was exhausted and seemed endlessly distracted. Meanwhile, Becky had enough on her plate, apparently running the colony.

Felix was stable, but he still needed twenty-four hour observation. Jon had therefor, gamely offered to cover the night shift, whilst Sophie got some much needed rest.

In all honesty, he was finding it hard to sleep anyway. Despite being physically drained, the new environment, coupled with the events of the past few days meant that no matter how hard he tried, he couldn't manage to shut his mind off.

At least here, he figured, he would be able to put his insomnia to some good use. The desk in front of him had an open lap-top sitting on it and was surrounded by ream after ream of paper.

The med-bay's record keeping was patchy at best. On his arrival, he had initially taken a cursory glance through the system and had been dismayed at all the apparent gaps and mistakes.

Jon had been impressed with Sophie's handling of the various crises that had arisen. She was clearly a very capable physician but, despite her meticulous attention to detail in other areas, her documentation skills were evidently not her strongest attribute.

The documentation was seemingly all present and correct and Jon could track the record of each pill and vial of medicine that had been prescribed. It was just not ordered correctly or logically and needed reevaluation. There was a large desktop, day to day diary that had notes on each day's attendees and their requirements.

Jon flicked through the pages randomly and rolled his eyes in frustration. It never ceased to amaze him that in a world that had been using computers so effectively for more than sixty years, that there were still those that preferred a pen and a piece of paper.

It all needed recording and transferring onto the computer, which would take time and patience. Jon set about the task with an unexpected enthusiasm, because although it was clerical busy-work, he needed something mundane at the moment, to occupy his restless mind.

One thing quickly became clear as he compared the physical records with the digital ones. Sophie was doing the lion's share of the work within the med-bay. Becky, it seemed, was a fairly infrequent visitor, and even less frequent contributor.The colonists also seemed to favour Sophie for their one-to-one time as well and her call sheet was as extensive as it was illegible.

Jon had always had a low-level suspicion that the inclusion of Becky in the crew had been little more than a cynical publicity stunt. A publicity stunt that had been squarely aimed at the great American public. She was however, a natural born leader and the way she skilfully juggled the various personalities within the colony more than justified her inclusion. This had evidently impacted upon her work in the colony as a medical officer, and poor Sophie had been left to pick up the slack. Given how busy she evidently was, It was strange then that Sophie had been reluctant to delegate some of her duties over to Jon now that he had arrived. Jon suspected that Sophie had become so inured to the workload though, that not only had she become accustomed to it, but she had also perhaps started to enjoy the associated responsibility. He had no doubt it would take time before she would be able to trust him fully with any of her extra duties, but Jon was certain that given the right amount of time she would soften her view and start to allow him to lighten her workload. Tonight's graveyard shift was the beginning of that process. Jon flicked through the diary and then picked up the major incident logbook.

Because this was once again a paper document, Jon let out a loud groan.

However, it was at least, mercifully short. It seemed that before Felix's accident the biggest event was a building site incident that led to Simon breaking his leg. Jon studied the report that Sophie had written and it looked like Simon had only avoided requiring an amputation by the tiniest of margins. Ben had brought him in so quickly that she had been able to get to work straight away. It was lucky that Ben had been so clear headed and acted so speedily, Jon thought to himself. Time in these situations is never your friend so Ben's quick response had almost certainly saved Simon's leg if not his life. Jon turned the pages of the book, examining the other accidents. It had been the same with Felix and then Jim, if Ben had not been there to carry both of them to the med-bay when he had done, then they too almost certainly would have died.

Jon flicked through the pages of the diary looking at all of the attendances for accidents. Ben's quick actions were a recurring theme. It seemed that he was owed a debt of thanks by almost the entire colony.
Almost every single attendance to med-bay had Ben as the supervising officer. Also, almost every incident report mentioned how his bravery or quickness of action had prevented the situation from being far worse than it actually was.
"Lucky he was around," Jon said out-loud to the darkened room,
He continued to flick idly through the logbook.
As he did so, an uncomfortable thought jostled its way into the fore of his mind. It started as an uncomfortable thought but it quickly blossomed into a more sinister suspicion.
A lucky coincidence taken in isolation was one thing, but a whole string them, one after another was a different matter altogether. In fact it was in real danger of crossing the border from happy coincidence to downright suspicious. Jon's brow furrowed.
"No," he said out loud.
He shook his head in an attempt to remove the insidious little thought, but he couldn't dislodge it.
"What," he wondered to himself, "if the reason that Ben has been so quick to respond to each of these incidents is because he somehow orchestrated them?" Jon allowed this thought to settle over him for a few seconds and he could not suppress an instinctive shudder at the possible implications.
He shook his head again, it was too terrible to consider.
The ripples from this would potentially be catastrophic, for not only Ben but the colony as a whole.

There was no-one to talk to about this though, he already wasn't overly popular with the existing colonists and Ben had presented himself as his only ally other than Cam.
Jon pondered on the idea for a few minutes before reaching the decision that he was probably jumping to unwise conclusions. He decided, therefor, to attempt to force the idea from his mind.
He picked up one of the other large hardback drug ledgers that lay in front of him and began to look through the colony's inventory in an unlikely attempt to make some sense of Sophie's somewhat erratic record keeping. However after only a few minutes of rapidly building frustration he threw the ledger onto the desktop with an exasperated cry and stood to go over to physically check the drug cupboard instead. Only the medical staff had access to these supplies and he gained entrance to the locked cupboard via a retinal scan. He opened the door and started flicking through the packages, mentally counting and checking them off as he went. After he had miscounted the morphine vials at least three times though he slammed the cupboard shut and swore loudly into the gloom of the empty room.
"Shit!" he said.
Try as he might the horrible implications of what he suspected wouldn't leave him alone. Despite his best efforts to disregard his suspicions as nothing more than paranoia born out of a tired and emotional mind, he couldn't shake off the feeling that there was something intrinsically wrong about the evidence that he had read.
He needed to talk to someone, he looked at his watch.
"Dammit!" he shouted into the silence.

His first instinct was to go to Cam, but what with one thing or another he quickly put this idea out of his mind. After all Cam wasn't exactly in a fit state to discuss anything at the moment. With Cam discounted, Jon made the only decision that he felt was left available to him. If there was a potential problem within the colony then he had no alternative than to go straight to the top.

He needed to speak to Becky.

Emboldened by finally making a decision, he folded up the notebooks and ledgers and headed out of the door at a determined pace.

He was so concentrated on his newly formed mission that he didn't see Sophie, who was heading towards the med bay carrying a freshly brewed hot cup of coffee. He bowled into her with an unceremonious clatter and sent her hot drink spilling all over her newly laundered scrubs. She squealed first in surprise and then in pain as the boiling liquid soaked through the thin cotton of her top instantly and scalded her unprotected skin underneath.

"Arghhh!" she cried and fell backwards clawing at her top and pulling it over her head as quickly as she was able.

Jon looked at her in astonishment, as though she had somehow materialised straight out of thin air.

"Sophie!" He said shocked, "what are you doing here?"

He looked down at the mess he had created and then back at his half-dressed colleague.

"Oh my God," he said as realisation finally dawned on him, "I'm so sorry. Quick let's get you into the med bay and sort you out!"

He helped her up from where she lay on the floor and then put an arm around her shoulders before ushering her back into the med-bay.

"Let me have a look," he said and bent down to examine the angry red welt that had sprung up on her chest.
"Do you mind?" Sophie said a little flustered.
Instinctively, she grabbed a gown from the linen cupboard and covered herself over
"What?" Jon said defensively and then remembered himself, "Oh yes, of course. Sorry," He blushed slightly.
Sophie glanced down at burn and then back up at Jon.
Jon hurried over to the drug cupboard and began searching for some cream.
"Third shelf down, second from the left," Sophie called after him.
Jon grabbed the tube and then headed back to where Sophie was sitting, unscrewing the cap as he went. He squeezed a little ointment onto his fingers and started to rub it over his palms. Sophie watched him as he approached with an increasing look of horror spreading over her face.
"I think I can apply my own cream, thank-you Jon," she said with an arched eyebrow.
Jon looked at her blankly and then down at his hands guiltily.
"Of course," he said quickly, "I'm sorry...again"
He handed her the tube of ointment and then turned his back as Sophie applied it to her injury.
"Where exactly where you going in such a hurry anyway?" she asked as she rubbed in the cream wincing slightly as she did so.
"Eh?" Jon said distractedly, "Oh yes, I was going to see Becky about something."
"At three in the morning?" Sophie asked surprised.
Jon nodded, "Yes well it's important," he paused a little hesitantly before continuing, "at least it might be important," he said a little weakly.

"Really? Anything I can help you with?"
Jon considered this for a moment before shaking his head, "No," he said simply. "Can I turn around yet?"
Sophie had retrieved a new set of scrubs from her locker and had pulled on the top to cover her modesty.
"Yes," she said, "I'm decent again."
Jon turned back to face her, expecting her to look angry or at least mildly irritated but instead she looked as she always did, he relaxed when he saw her face.
"I really am sorry about that," he said again, "I just didn't see you."
Sophie laughed, "I'm not that small, am I?" she said.
"That's not what I meant," Jon said, once again a little flustered.
She stared at him for a few unblinking seconds before finally releasing him from his awkwardness, "Don't worry about it," she said with a light smile, "are you sure that I can't help with..."
An alarm went off on Sophie's watch which she checked reflexly. Her face darkened with concern.
"Someone's breaking the quarantine," she said, seriously.
"What? Who?" Jon asked.
Sophie shook her head, "I don't know," she said, "but I had better go and check it out."
"Shall I come with you?" Jon offered
She shook her head again, "No, you stay here and get things prepared. If someone has broken quarantine then they might be in more danger than they realise."
Jon rolled his eyes, "Danger?" He said sceptically, "really?"
"The quarantine itself might not be entirely necessary," she said calmly, "but the security systems that are in place to enforce it are very real," her forehead wrinkled with concern,

"So much so that if someone doesn't know what they're doing then they could end up hurting themselves...or someone else."
Jon's face went pale, He knew the level of security that Sophie was talking about and she was right. If, whoever it was, didn't know exactly what they were doing then the ship had some very determined and unambiguous ways of deterring any intruders.
"You had better get after them then," he said, his voice suddenly full of urgency, “I'll cover here."
Sophie looked at him, “What about your visit to Becky?" she asked as she gathered some things together and placed them into her bag.
"It'll wait," Jon said, "now you'd better get going."
Sophie nodded and then headed out into the colony, hoping to intercept the intruder before they did any lasting damage.

CHAPTER NINE

The door to Jacob's quarters slid open quietly and he was standing in the doorway with a friendly smile spread across his face. The colonists all wore basically the same outfit for practicality purposes. However, Cam couldn't fail but notice that the material of Jacob's standard issue white t-shirt was stretched tightly across the muscles of his torso and upper arms.

Jacob stared at Cam for a few seconds, a look of mild bewilderment on his face.

"Cam?" he said finally.

"Hello Jacob," Cam said.

Jacob looked beyond Cam into the hallway, "Are you okay?"

Cam said nothing.

"What are you doing here?" Jacob said, "I thought that we were still in quarantine?"

Cam stared at Jacob, and clenched his jaw. Jacob shifted a little uncomfortably where he stood.

“Cam?" Jacob tried again to engage him, "Don't get me wrong it great to see you, but..."

"Is it?" Cam said, bitterly.

Jacobs face creased with confusion, "Sure it is," he said, "are you sure you should be here, though?"

Cam nodded, "Aye, I'm sure," he said.

Cam stared at Jacob, "We need to talk,"

Jacobs's eyebrows arched in surprise, "We do?"

Cam nodded, "Aye," he said, "we do."

"What about?" Jacob asked.

Cam looked up and down the hallway, "Do you really want to do this here?" he said, "in the corridor?"

Jacob shrugged, uncertainly.

"Come on in," he said after a moments pause.
He stood to one side and ushered Cam in through the door and into his quarters. Despite his size and condition, Jacob looked tired, his face was drawn and careworn and his shoulders were slumped with fatigue.
The news about the immediate quarantine had been a lot to process for the crew when they had landed. Coupled to this, Jacob also had the extra concern of Felix's illness and ongoing coma to deal with.
"Have you seen Felix?" he asked as Cam shuffled past him.
Cam looked at him, momentarily distracted from his anger.
"No," he whispered, "not for a couple of days, I think he's okay though."
Jacob laughed, "We clearly have very different definitions of 'okay'" he said.
"I didn't mean it like that," Cam said, awkwardly.
Jacob waved his hand, "It's okay," he said, "I'm finding it all very frustrating, being stuck here, thats all."
Cam nodded and looked at the floor, trying to recompose himself.
"I just want to see him," Jacob shrugged, "check he's safe, I suppose."
"I'm sorry about Felix, we always got on pretty well," Cam said quietly.
"Thanks," Jacob said, unhappily.
Cam had been knocked off his guard, his anger had, unexpectedly subsided slightly and he found himself suddenly conflicted. He hadn't really considered how Jacob would be feeling about his brother. His pain was too raw, his emotions too unpredictable.
"I was in the bed next to him for a couple of days," he said with a half-smile, "I'm sorry, it's just..."

Jacob nodded sadly, “Its weird," he said with a half laugh, "it was the one thing that got me through the journey,”
"Seeing Felix?"
Jacob smiled, “I had been looking forward to seeing the little bugger for so long that I began to think it would never actually happen,” he stared at the floor before continuing, “and then of course it didn't happen.”
"It will," Cam said, "soon, I'm sure."
"Yeah, hopefully," Jacob said, without looking up, "hopefully."
Cam didn't know what to say, so he erred on the side of caution and remained silent. Jacob lifted his eyes from the floor and then stared, unblinking at the wall behind Cam's head. Instinctively, Cam turned to see what he was looking at and he saw a small framed photograph hanging behind him. It showed Felix and Jacob smiling broadly into the camera, a tiny woman sandwiched between them, looking small but incredibly proud.
The sight of this family portrait, sparked a visceral reaction in Cam.
Family, the word echoed around his head, mocking him, laughing at his pain. He closed his eyes to stop the tears that had suddenly welled there, from falling. He focussed his emotion inwardly and found an ally in the form of his simmering bitterness.
Jacob continued to stare at the photograph for a few seconds longer, before turning his attention back to Cam.
His eyes were red and pained, but he forced himself to smile broadly.
“It’s good to see your face though Cam. How are you feeling now?”
Cam reflexly lifted his hand and touched the scab that was healing slowly upon the side of his head, he flinched.

“Yeah, it’s been crazy. One thing after another,” he looked directly into Jacob’s eyes, and held his gaze for an uncomfortable moment.

He looked away and glanced around Jacobs quarters. His eyes fell towards a large stone grey designer sofa that ran along the length of one sides of Jacobs living quarters.

“Nice,” he said.

"Thanks," Jacob replied.

"Not exactly standard issue though, is it?"

Jacob shrugged, “Yeah, well this was always going to be my permanent quarters when we arrived."

The rest of Jacob's quarters were decorated like a relatively high end hotel room, with designer fixtures and fittings and a surprising amount of living space.

"We were always essentially little more than a flying annex after all," Jacob said, "so I thought I might as well be comfortable."

Cam thought bitterly back to the considerably more Spartan conditions upon the Nerine Three and couldn't help but feel a surge of jealousy towards the ship and all its inhabitants

"No one else on this deck?" Cam asked.

Jacob shook his head, "Nope, just me. In fact you'd be hard pressed to notice anyone else was on board at all unless you purposefully went looking for them," he grinned his big toothy grin again and once again, Cam felt his anger swell.

“Nice to see you have your priorities in order,” he said, "may I?” he asked, inclining his head towards the sofa.

“Of course, be my guest,” Jacob said.

As Cam perched himself on the edge of one of the cushions, Jacob walked over towards the kitchen area of his quarters. He bent down to a counter-level fridge and pulled out a small bottle of water, which he unscrewed and took a long swig of.

“Do you want one of these?” he asked.
Cam shook his head, “No” he said, "thanks."
He swallowed and his throat felt uncomfortably dry.
“Actually, aye chuck us one over,” He said.
Jacob tossed over a bottle and Cam caught it in his left hand. It was cold and slick with condensation. Cam unscrewed the cap and took a long gulp from the bottle. He wiped his hand across his mouth and looked over at Jacob.
“It's hard,” Cam said, sadly.
Jacob looked at him, "What is?" he asked.
"Losing someone close to you," Cam replied.
Jacob nodded, “I haven't lost him yet,” he said defiantly.
"I didn't mean anything by it," Cam said, defensively.
"I know," Jacob said, "although, I am trying to prepare myself....You know just in case.”
He moved around from the kitchen area and sat down on a white folding metal chair. He was now directly opposite where Cam was sitting, he took another sip of his water.
“It’s all bullshit you know?“ Cam said evenly.
“What is?” Jacob asked.
“What everyone tells you, it’s not fucking true.”
Jacob looked at him blankly, “I'm not following you Cam.”
“Everyone tells you that it gets better with time,” Cam said, “but don't listen to them. If the worst happens with Felix, that's what everyone will tell you."
Jacob blinked, and gave a shallow nod.
"It's a lie though, it never gets any better, not really,” he looked at Jacob, "all that happens is you learn to live with it," Cam sighed, "it doesn’t ever go away though,” he said, “you think it has, but then something happens and *Boom! Y*ou're right back in the middle of it all,” he swallowed, “flailing about like a fucking drowning man.”

Jacob nodded, but said nothing.
“When I lost my wife and daughter,” he continued, “I didn't think I’d ever get over it. I remember wondering if it would ever stop hurting…” He drifted off, leaving the thought hanging in mid air.
“Sorry Cam," Jacob said, "I’d forgotten that you've lived through this. Lived through worse."
Cam laughed bitterly.
"I can’t imagine what it must be like, losing a child," he shook his head, "it must have been terrible?”
Cam nodded, “It still is,” he said sourly.
The two of them sat in silence for a few minutes, each apparently lost in their own thoughts. Cam broke the silence with a cough to clear his throat; he looked up again, straight into Jacobs eyes.
“How do you sleep at night?” he asked,
"Hmm?" Jacob said.
"I keep going over things in my head," Cam said, "and that's the question that I always get stuck on."
Jacob shrugged, “It’s not brilliant, to be honest. But I’m sure it’ll settle down in time, you know once I’ve seen him, perhaps even talked to him.”
“That's not what I mean,” Cam blinked and his eyes suddenly filled with tears.
Jacob looked at him, "I'm not sure I'm following you here, Cam," he said.
“I mean having done the things that you've done. How the fuck, do you ever sleep at night?”
Jacob looked confused, "I don't understand,” he said.
Cam breathed deeply, “Oh right sorry," he said bitterly.
"Are you all right?" Jacob asked.
Cam sniffed, "Let me explain then, eh?”

Jacob shrugged, “I think you're going to have to," he said.
Cam wiped his hand across his eyes and nose, sniffing loudly as he did so. He coughed again.
“After you had my wife and daughter murdered," he swallowed hard, "how the fuck did you ever get to sleep, ever again,”
Cam's face was suddenly twisted in bitter anger.
“What?” Jacob said, baffled,
"You fucking heard," Cam spat.
“What the Hell are you talking about?” Jacob said.
“Don’t lie to me, you fucking bastard,” Cam screamed at him, “I know everything. How could you? How could you kill a little girl? My little Martha?”
The tears that he had been trying to keep in check now burst from him in a loud sob and ran freely down his cheeks.
Jacob raised his hands defensively.
“I don’t know what you think you know Cam, but you’re wrong,” he said, his voice cracking.
“Liar!” Cam shouted.
“Cam? How could you think that? That I would do something like that?”
“Don’t fucking deny it. Don't you fucking dare!” Cam was sobbing now.
“It’s not true!”
“Felix told Ben,” Cam shouted.
Jacob’s casual denial was fuelling his anger, feeding his pain.
“Felix told Ben what?”
Cam sniffed loudly, “He told Ben everything,” he wailed, “he told him that you arranged everything,” he stabbed his finger at him, ”that you paid that bastard to drive over them. That you paid him to kill my fucking family!”
Suddenly, Cam leapt at Jacob, his fury no longer containable.
He grabbed at a large kitchen knife from the work surface and

swung it wildly at Jacob's face. Jacob was tired, emotional and stunned, but he was also very well trained. He deftly dodged away from Cam's clumsy attack and then grabbed at the knife. Cam reacted quickly and avoided his grasp. He lost his balance though and tumbled to the floor. He banged his head as he went. Jacob took an instinctive step backwards.

"Cam, stop this!" Jacob said, his eyes wide with shock.

"Fuck you!" He shouted and he pushed himself back up onto his feet.

"You're wrong," he said as calmly as he could manage, "think about it for a second, it doesn't make any sense. Why would I do that?"

Cam was fully standing again, "You wanted me!" he screamed,

"What?"

"Gareth wanted me," he sobbed, "he wanted me and he couldn't have me, so you…"

"I what, Cam?" Jacob said as calmly as he was able, "what do you think happened?"

"You knew that I was having second thoughts, so you took matters into your own hands didn't you? Wanted to clear the way, remove any obstacles" flecks of spittle flew from his mouth as he shouted at Jacob.

A laugh burst out of Jacob, but he tried to swallow it instantly.

"Listen to yourself Cam! It's ridiculous!" he said.

"Don't you fucking laugh at me!" Cam said, incensed, "Don't you fucking dare!"

Cam once again charged at Jacob. This time the slashing blade caught Jacob's forearm. He cried out in pain and clamped his other hand over the wound.

"Stop!" Jacob yelled. "Please!"

"You killed them!" Cam turned again and came slashing back at Jacob. This time Jacob was fast enough. He slammed the base of his hand into Cam's face. Jacob winced as Cam stumbled backwards, holding his nose as he went. After a moments pause, Cam threw a wide, sweeping punch at Jacob, who caught his fist easily and then twisted it hard. Cam screamed and dropped the knife. Then in a single fluid movement, Jacob twisted his body and kneed him fully in the stomach. Cam groaned as the wind was knocked from him, and then fell onto the floor gasping for air.

Jacob stood over him, his hand on his back, "Breathe," he said calmly, "I know it hurts, but you're okay, you're only winded."

Cam gasped in pain, as he tried to force some air back into his protesting lungs.

"Get the fuck away from me you bastard," he wheezed.

Jacob put his hand on Cam's shoulder and sighed, "We can talk about this, but you have to calm down. I don't want to hurt you Cam."

Cam howled with rage and twisted frantically to get himself free, he swung his right fist and connected heavily with Jacob's face. Jacob groaned in a mixture of pain and frustration. He knew that he had to keep him down before someone got more seriously hurt but he also wanted to do it without hurting Cam if he could avoid it. Cam was out of control though, the red mist had fully descended and he twisted again wildly to try and punch Jacob again as hard as he could. He had lost his element of surprise now though and Jacob dodged the punch and kneed the side of Cam's face, his lip split open, sending a spray of blood over the pristine white walls. Jacob winced again as Cam landed with a painful smack onto the floor.

"Cam, come on," he shouted, "stay down!"

"Fuck you!" Cam screamed, spitting blood as he did so.

Undaunted, he began to raise himself, gamely, from the floor. Jacob sighed and punched him again, this time breaking his nose.
“Cam, stay down. I really don't want to hurt you anymore, but you’re not giving me a choice.” He was breathing hard but managed to speak calmly and quietly.
Cam opened his mouth to talk, but it was full of blood. He spat blood from his mouth and for a moment it seemed as though he was going to try to get up again. Instead his strength failed him and he slumped back onto the cold, hard floor. He said nothing though he just lay in a crumpled heap, sobbing and bleeding. The blood from his mouth and nose mixed together, along with streams of tears and snot that ran down his face
“Good,” Jacob said, “good. Now stay down, man.”
He felt the bruising on his face and then looked at the wound on his left arm. It wasn't serious but it was seeping blood heavily. He walked towards the bathroom.
“I don't know where all this nonsense has come from, but it's not true” he said as he went, “stay there, I’ll dress those wounds and then we can talk about this rationally.”
Cam didn't reply.
“Okay?” Jacob called.
Again there was no reply. He opened the first aid kit that he kept by the sink and pulled out a dressing pad and a bandage. He ripped them open with his teeth and then set about covering the wound. As he did so he shouted back into the living quarters.
“Are you okay?” he called. There was no response.
“I’m sorry about that, but you didn't give me much of a choice."
Jacob thought that he heard a grunt from the other room.
"I know what you think of me, but it’s not true.”

He finished off the application of the bandage and then looked at his reflection in the large mirror that hung over the sink. Evidently Cam had caught the side of his face as well with the knife, because a small but angry gash snaked along the side of his left eye. It wasn't deep but was bleeding freely.
“Ah shit!” Jacob muttered to himself.
“You got a couple of good shots in there Cam,” he called, with a shallow laugh.
“Cam?” he shouted, but there was no reply.
“Cam? Are you okay?”
Jacob left the bathroom and went back into his living area. There was blood splattered all over two walls and an unpleasant pool of bodily fluids smeared over his floor. Cam however was gone.
“Cam?” he called again
He searched his quarters but found no sign of him. He touched the cut on the side of his face and winced. He sighed and started to try and straighten up a bit. He picked up the chair that had been flung aside and stood it back in its proper place. He noticed with some dismay that his beautiful sofa now not only sported an unattractive blood red splatter pattern, but also a six inch slash along one of the cushions.
“Oh you fucker,” he said to himself and examined the damage in more detail.
He sighed and made a mental note to punch Cam at least one more time, to pay for the damage.

CHAPTER TEN

Jacob stood in his slightly dishevelled quarters and rubbed his hands over his face with a loud sigh. His arm was throbbing from the knife wound and his face stung. He shook his head as he further surveyed the aftermath of Cam's visit.

"Hello Jacob," came a voice from behind him, "long time, no see."

Jacob physically jumped, "Jesus Christ!" He exclaimed.

He turned around and was surprised to see Ben standing behind him, casually looking at the mess.

"Where the fuck did you come from?" Jacob asked.

Ben shrugged, "I followed Cam," he said.

"Oh," Jacob said, "I seem to be very popular this evening."

"Hurumph," Ben said.

"It's a bit late for a social visit isn't it?" Jacob said, in an attempt to engage him.

Ben shrugged.

"I thought that there was quarantine in place?" Jacob said, "Theres not a lot of point in keeping us isolated if every asshole in the colony can wander over whenever they feel like it!"

He looked at Ben for reaction, but saw none, "No offence," he added as a side thought.

"None taken," Ben said.

"Is it over then?" Jacob asked, "Can I go and see my brother?"

"It's not over, " Ben said, "like I said, I only followed Cam over to make sure he didn't do anything stupid."

"Yeah? Well, you're a bit late for that," Jacob said bitterly.

Ben glanced around the room and his eyes settled on the bloodstained couch.

"So I see," he said.

Jacob looked at the stain and once again vowed to punch Cam at least one more time when he got the chance.
"What did you do to poor old Cam?" Ben asked.
Jacob waved this away with his hand, "Nothing," he said.
Ben arched an eyebrow, "Nothing?" he repeated, "doesn't look like nothing to me."
"Self defence," Jacob said.
Ben snorted, "You, against Cam? Self defence? Don't make me laugh."
"He attacked me," Jacob said.
"So you beat the shit out of him?"
Jacob's expression suddenly darkened.
"Look Ben," he said, "he came looking for a fight and he got one."
"He got more than a fight," Ben said
"He got what he deserved," Jacob insisted. "Where is he anyway?"
"Crawling back to the base with his face in tatters, I imagine," Ben said unpleasantly.
"Yeah, well, I warned him," Jacob said with a shrug.
Ben moved closer to Jacob, very deliberately, "He's my friend," he said quietly.
"Well, that just shows what a bad judge of character he is then, doesn't it?"
"There was no need to hurt him that badly. All you had to do was put him down."
"I tried that, but the stupid bastard kept on getting back up," Jacob said.
Ben shrugged, "He can be quite stubborn," he said, "ah well..."
Without pausing, Ben swung a full arm punch at Jacob's face and connected heavily with his cheek. Jacob was knocked to

one side briefly, but quickly recovered and was soon standing back toe to toe with Ben.

"What the fuck?" he shouted in Bens face.

Ben watched him, wearily, waiting for his retaliation, but none came.

Instead, he carefully touched his face and felt the warm sting of fresh blood against his fingertips. He sighed, looked down at his hands and then back at Ben. Once again Ben braced himself for a response, but instead Jacob laughed.

"You're pathetic," he said through his laughter, "you can't do anything right can you?"

Ben looked confused, and his face reddened in anger,

"What?" he said.

Jacob shook his head and moved closer to Ben.

"I tried to tell Gareth that you were a fucking liability," he said, "but he always stuck up for you, told me of your great experience."

"Shut up," Ben said through gritted teeth.

"International space station," he said, mockingly, "what a bunch of pussies!"

"I said, shut up," Ben said.

Jacob laughed again and moved his face inches from Bens,

"Or what?" He said.

He waited for a moment and then he turned away. He bent over and picked up his towel which he dabbed against his bloodied face. When he turned back to face Ben, he hadn't moved.

"It all makes sense, now," Jacob said, thoughtfully.

"What does?" Ben snarled.

"I couldn't work out why Cam thought what he did, but it's all starting to come into focus."

"I don't know what you're talking about," Ben said.

"It was you that told Cam that I killed his family wasn't it?" Jacob asked.
Ben's expression wavered, he opened his mouth to speak but Jacob raised his hand to stop him before he started.
"Don't bother denying it," he said,
"Okay," Ben said bluntly.
"Jesus Ben! I knew you were a petty little fucker, but trying to get poor little Cameron to do your dirty work?" he shook his head, "That really is some cowardly shit, even for you."
"So what if I did tell Cam?" he said, "What difference does to make how he found out?"
"What?" Jacob looked at Ben, bemused.
"You heard," Ben said.
Jacob snorted with laughter again, "You poor dumb fuck," Jacob said.
It was Ben's turn to look confused.
"It wasn't me," Jacob said with a quiet huff of laughter. "Shit Ben, even if I had done something that heinous, why would you tell Cam? What purpose could it possibly serve? I don't understand."
"Because you're a sadistic fuck Jacob," Ben said calmly, "and you deserve it!"
"What about what Cam deserves?" Jacob asked, "You don't seem to have considered your friend in all this."
"He had a right," ben said, simply.
"A right to what?" Jacob shouted, "Some baseless fabrication?"
"The truth," ben said.
"The truth?" Jacob asked.
Ben nodded, "You can deny it all you like but you're finished here Jacob, finished before you've begun."

Jacob narrowed his eyes and shook his head again, “Well, I guess the truth's going to come out now isn't it?"
Ben stared at him defiantly.
"We've all got our guilty little secrets though, haven't we Ben?"
Ben's face creased in confusion, “What do you mean by that?"
"You think that this will stick? Because it won't," Jacob said smiling.
"We'll see," Ben said.
Jacob nodded, "Yeah we will," he looked at Ben and his grin widened, "we've all got skeletons in our closets Ben, you, me, even the sweet little doctor Torres..."
He let that hang for a few seconds, noting with satisfaction that he seemed to have touched something of a raw nerve with Ben. His fists clenched with tension.
Jacob grinned, "Now, if you wouldn't mind," he said, "I would like to go and see my little brother. So do me a favour will you? And get the fuck out of my quarters!"
Once again he turned his back on Ben and went off to get a fresh t-shirt to put on.
Ben watched him go and he contemplated what he had just heard. He knew that everything that he had worked so hard to build was now under threat, he knew that Sophie was going to get dragged into an argument that she had no part of. Jacob was right though, they all had skeletons, and he was damned if he was going to let this son-of-a-bitch threaten everything that he held dear.
The anger swelled in his chest as he watched Jacob pull a clean shirt out of his wardrobe and slip it over his head. He still had his back to Ben, If he was going to act, he had to do it now.
This time Ben attacked with a ferocity that even Jacob didn't expect or could handle.

He picked up a fire extinguisher that had been sitting next to the kitchen units and before Jacob even had time to look around he smashed it into the side of his head with all of the strength and momentum that he could muster. A spray of bright red blood looped over Jacob's cleanly pressed laundry, Jacob noticed this with some dismay before he fully realised what had actually happened. Belatedly he turned to face his attacker, his hand rising to the new wound on the side of his head.

Something inside Ben had snapped and his rage now had total control of him.

He screamed with fury and lunged forward holding the base of the extinguisher in front of him, which he slammed in to Jacobs's chest like a battering ram. A loud crack resonated around the room, as several of his ribs fractured under the impact. Jacobs eye's widened in shock and pain, he gasped for breath as he stumbled uncoordinatedly backwards. Ben saw his chance and swung the extinguisher once again. It connected heavily, with the side of Jacobs head, causing it to split instantly. Ben took a half step backwards and balanced himself on the balls of his feet, ready to strike again.

Jacob staggered backwards and tried desperately to keep his balance, he was too uncoordinated though and he fell to the floor unceremoniously with a loud crash. Ben threw the extinguisher to one side and leapt at Jacob, his face twisted into a frenzied mask of rage. Jacob had barely even landed on the ground before Ben was on top off him pounding at his face with his fists. Jacob's once handsome face split into a series of fresh cuts and was bruising almost by the second.

He raised his arms in an attempt to cover his face and forced out a guttural scream as Ben rained punches down on him. He squirmed and writhed, and then with a giant effort of will, he

bucked his hips and managed to push Ben off him. He lay on the floor panting for a few seconds, trying to find some protection close at hand. His eyes were swollen though and his sight was poor. Ben had jumped quickly to his feet again though and once more he picked up the discarded fire extinguisher. He walked over to where Jacob lay helplessly on the floor, bleeding and shivering with shock. He grinned, a huge ugly grin at him and then lifted it high over Jacobs head.
"I'll show who's a fucking pussy," he said and steadied himself for what would surely be a killer blow.
Jacob looked at him, "Fuck you," he said through his blood filled mouth, and then braced himself for impact.
"Ben, No!"
A loud piercing cry echoed through the room and Ben paused, he turned to face the door felt his resolve suddenly melt. Distracted at the vital second, Jacob seized the unexpected opportunity and kicked at Ben's standing leg with all of his strength. His right knee buckled beneath him and he cried out in pain, dropping to the floor in an undignified heap. The fire extinguisher landed on his shoulder and he cried out in surprised pain.

Sophie stood in the doorway her eyes wide with fright.
Ben coughed and winced in pain whilst Jacob sagged back onto the floor, exhausted and bleeding.
"What on Earth are you doing?" Sophie asked, her voice quivering as she spoke.
"Go away!" Ben shouted at her. "This is my fight."
"You were going to kill him!" Sophie said appalled.
"Mother-fucker deserves it," Ben said bitterly.
Sophie stepped into the room; she had a brown canvass satchel slung over her left shoulder.

She walked up to Ben and crouched down to where he lay, she put a hand on his shoulder.
"Oh my darling," she said, her eyes wet with tears.
Ben looked suddenly ashamed, "I'm sorry," he said quietly.
Sophie nodded, "I know, its okay," she said.
She kissed his cheek and he pushed himself, unsteadily onto his feet. Once up, he looked back at Jacob and took a half step back towards him. Sophie lifted her hand and placed it gently on his chest.
"No," she said, "enough."
Jacob breathed a sigh of relief, and Ben shot him a dangerous look.
"Just go please," Sophie said, soothingly, "I'll sort this out."
Ben opened his mouth to protest but took one look at the determined expression that was etched onto Sophie's face and decided against it.
"Just go," she repeated.
She smiled at him and he bowed his head. She looked down at the heavily bleeding Jacob and sighed.
“Don't worry, it looks worse than it is," she said, "now go, before anyone notices that you're missing!"
Ben looked over at Jacob and then back at Sophie. He said nothing, but he nodded his head and bent down to kiss Sophie on the forehead. She smiled up at him and then gestured to the door with her eyes. Ben took the final hint and reluctantly started to leave Jacobs quarters.
"Wait!" Sophie called after him, and he stopped dead in his tracks.
She was looking down at Jacob, her hands on her hips.
"On second thoughts there's no way I'm going to be able to help him while he's lying on the floor. Help me move him to his bunk will you?"

Ben groaned, but headed back over to where Jacob lay and took hold of his hand. Too weak to protest, Jacob allowed himself to be pulled onto his feet. He winced in pain and tried desperately not to look directly at Ben. With a little help, Jacob staggered over to his bunk and then collapsed onto the mattress.

He was breathing heavily and his chest gurgled, unpleasantly with his every breath, he looked up at Ben and blinked, painfully.

"Thanks," he said, with a bloody smile.

"Fuck off." Ben said before turning to once again leave the room.

He walked passed Sophie and instinctively reached out a hand towards her, she reciprocated and their fingertips brushed, fleetingly as Ben headed out of the room, closing the door behind his as he went.

Once he had gone Sophie walked over to the bunk and looked down at the bloodied mess that was Jacob.

She shook her head sadly, “Jesus," she said quietly, "look at the state of you. It's lucky I arrived when I did."

Jacob looked at her and nodded gratefully. He coughed and then wiped away some of the blood that had bubbled to his lips.

"Thanks,” he said croakily and Sophie nodded at him with a tight smile.

She placed her bag down and pulled out some dressings and some vials of medicines, which she lined up along the edge of his bedside cabinet. Jacob strained his neck to try and see what she was doing but the effort caused him too much pain and he let his head slump back down onto the pillow.

Sophie, meanwhile, drew up a clear liquid into a syringe. She moved towards him and sat down on the edge of the bed. She gently took hold of Jacob's hand and looked into his eyes.
Jacob glanced nervously at the syringe, "What's that?" he slurred through his broken face.
"Something for the pain," she said.
He nodded his consent and she tied a tourniquet around his arm. After quickly finding a vein, she let the tip of the needle break his skin.
"This will work in just a few seconds," she said, soothingly and then started cleaning away some of the blood from around his face.
Jacob smiled painfully at her, as the morphine rushed into his system.
His smile failed though as he realised that he was also losing the feeling in his legs. He tried to wiggle his toes but they didn't move.
"What's going on?" he asked, panicked
"Shhh," Sophie said with a delicate smile.
"I cant feel my legs," he said. "Why can't If eel my legs?"
"Don't worry," Sophie said calmingly. "That’s just Vecuronium bromide, it's a paralytic drug."
Jacobs eyes widened in panic, "What?" he managed to ask before he slumped back onto his pillow.
"It will help to keep you calm," Sophie said, stroking his head, "but don't worry you'll still know whats going on."
Jacobs eyes widened further.
"Don't panic," Sophie said again as soothingly as she could, "it's going to be a long night though I'm afraid."
She looked over at the lined up vials and drugs that she had unpacked from her bag, Jacobs eyes followed her stare, but his vision was blurry and he couldn't see any details.

"If you panic," Sophie continued, "then I'm afraid that it'll only end up hurting more,"
she smiled sweetly at him, “and you and I have got an awful lot to talk about..."
Jacob swallowed awkwardly and then slipped into a brief, dreamless sleep of blissful unconsciousness.

CHAPTER ELEVEN

When Jacob awoke, he was still unable to move. His eyes darted around as much of the room as he could see but there was no sign of Sophie or anyone else in his quarters. He could just about see a pile of bloodied swabs and bandages on the far right of his peripheral vision. He tried to move his head but to no avail.

"Well, hello again sleepy head!" Sophie said from somewhere off to his left.

He felt her walk closer to him and then her face appeared in front of his, her eyes wide behind her glasses.

"Looks like our Major Sutherland really went to town on you doesn't it?" she asked.

Jacob tried to speak but couldn't make any noise other than a vague grunt.

"Don't try and talk," Sophie said soothingly, "the drugs that I've given you will allow you to breathe and move your eyes, but little else I'm afraid."

Once again, Jacobs eyes widened in panic.

"So I think its best if we come up with a little system to help us along don't you?" She laughed lightly, "But it's not like you have a lot of choice now is it?"

Her face disappeared from view and in its place there came a mirror. Jacob flinched from its proximity, at least he tried to, but when his eyes adjusted they showed him his reflection. His face was bruised and bloodied but the bigger cuts had been expertly stitched together and the smaller ones had all been cleaned and dressed.

"Now," Sophie said, "how about you give me a single blink for 'yes' and a double one for 'no'? How does that sound?"

Jacob looked at his reflection and blinked once.

"Is that a yes?" Sophie asked.
He blinked again.
"Oh good, because you may have just been blinking and then we would have been in all sorts of confusion, wouldn't we," she laughed again and then said quickly, "it's okay you don't have to answer that one."
Jacob swallowed, his throat was dry and sore and his face and arms stung from the cuts. His eyes watered slightly from the pain.
"Ah," Sophie said, as she dabbed away his tears, "you're probably realising about now that although you can't move, you can still feel everything, yes?"
Jacob blinked once and more tears leaked from his eyes.
Sophie sighed, "Yes, well, I'm sorry about that but it's the quickest way to get through this as painlessly as possible."
Jacob blinked.
"Of course it wasn't so quick for poor Cam. He was paralysed for more than two days whilst at the same time being fully conscious," she shook her head unhappily, "I didn't want to do that, but It was the only way I could be sure that he would find out about your murderous ways!" she waggled a disapproving finger at Jacob, playfully.
Jacob blinked twice, very deliberately.
"No?" Sophie said, "No what? No, you're not a murderer? Is that what you're trying to say?"
Jacob blinked, Sophie laughed again.
"Oh come on now Jacob, we both know that's not true don't we?"
Jacob blinked twice again.
"Don't misunderstand me, I know that you didn't kill Cam's family, but you have plenty of corpses hid under plenty of beds don't you?"

Jacob stared at her, his eyes filling with hatred; Sophie looked at him and took half a step backwards.
"Oh dear! If looks could kill, I would be in very deep trouble now I think?" she said a little uncertainly.
Jacob blinked once very deliberately.
"And as for Felix?" she said with a shrug. "Well, who knows what kind of state his poor mind is in by now. I'm afraid that what with all of his problems and the mixture of drugs he's endured he could be in any kind of condition by this point."
Jacob managed to emit a groan of anger and frustration.
Sophie moved over to the cannula and injected another syringe into the port.
"Don't want you breaking free and getting hold of me do I? There's no telling what you would do," she pulled a mock horrified expression and then moved back into position above Jacobs face.
"Now then," she said lightly, "let's get down to business shall we? I'm going to ask you series of questions and then you will answer me either with a yes or a no. Okay?"
Jacob blinked once.
"However," Sophie said, "if at any point I think that you're lying to me or even just not being completely truthful then I'm afraid that I'm going to have to punish you. Okay?"
Jacob blinked again.
"Excellent!" she said. "Now then, firstly I want to know if you had any prior knowledge of me before I enrolled on to this project?"
Jacob blinked twice.
"Okay, then did your brother contact you in any way to tell you anything about me?"
Jacob hesitated for a moment then again, blinked twice.

"Oh dear," Sophie said unhappily, "now you see i'm afraid that I don't believe you there."
A flash of panic flashed across Jacob's eyes and he blinked twice again.
"I know that Felix contacted you about something, so now I'm going to have to punish you," she made a mock frown with her mouth.
Without another word, she removed her face from his field of view, Jacob desperately tried to see what was happening but all he could hear was her moving some equipment around on the kitchen counter.
"I know that you're a big, strong, brave soldier type so I'm not going to bother starting with any of the little things that I would normally do in this situation," she called from across the room, "What you need is convincing that I am, in fact, serious about my threats," she continued as she made her way back over to where he lay.
She showed him his heavy kitchen knife that Cam had wielded so poorly earlier
"This knife for example, still has your blood on it from before by the looks of it?"
Jacob blinked.
"I could use it to...I don't know, cut off one of your fingers perhaps?" she said, lightly.
Jacob stared at her defiantly, and blinked.
Sophie laughed, "Ah!" she said, "You see, that's my point. Big brave soldier," she sighed.
She passed the blade in front of Jacobs face and he traced its path with his eyes. Then, without warning she put it down again, right next to his head. So close that he could smell the copper tang of the blood stained blade.

"I think that threats of physical violence, would be wasted on you," Sophie said, "I do not like this violence anyway. It is too...messy, I think."
Jacob blinked.
"So if I cannot threaten you physically, how shall I be able to persuade you to tell me the truth?"
She paced around his quarters, slipping in and out of his field of view.
"If only there was something, or someone else that you cared about more than yourself?" She continued.
Jacob blinked twice.
"What?" Sophie asked, "No, there isn't someone else?"
Jacob blinked twice. Sophie laughed again.
"I am teasing you," she said.
She produced a computer tablet and held it in front of Jacob's face. The screen was on and it showed a live feed of the colonies Med-bay. Lying in the centre of the shot was an unconscious Felix. He had seemingly, endless infusions and wires running from his inert body. Sophie tilted the screen and looked at it before showing it again to Jacob.
"Can you see that?" she asked.
Jacob blinked.
"Can I assume that you know what you are looking at?"
Jacob blinked.
"Oh, good," she said, "that will make this much easier."
She held the screen in front of Jacob for a few seconds, allowing him to take in the full picture of where his brother lay. Then she removed it and placed it on one of the counter tops.
"I think you know where I am going with this?" Sophie said.
Jacob blinked.

"I have complete control of your baby brothers comfort and wellbeing," she said. "And I am afraid to tell you that he is not very comfortable at the moment."
Jacobs eyes filled with hatred.
"However, the good news is, you have the power to make him more comfortable."
She held up a remote handset and showed it to Jacob.
"This little device gives me complete control of what your brother is feeling."
Jacob blinked.
"I realise that I am expecting you to take a lot of this on trust, so perhaps a demonstration might be in order?"
Jacob blinked twice.
Sophie shook her head, "No, I think a demonstration would help to convince you," she said, thoughtfully.
Once again, she held the screen on front of Jacob's face. She pressed an icon and the camera zoomed into Felix's face. With her other hand she pressed something on the remote. At first, it seemed as though nothing had happened, but then after ten-seconds or so, Felix's face twisted in agony. Jacob grunted and tried fruitlessly to move. Sophie pressed the remote again and after another ten-second pause, Felix relaxed back into an emotionless stupor.
Jacobs eyes had once again filled with tears. He closed them and tried to calm his tortured mind.
Sophie slapped his face and his eyes snapped open, filled with determined ferocity.
"Now, now," she said, "let's keep our mind focused on the here and now shall we?"
Jacob looked into her eyes and vivid fantasies about the form his revenge would take on this bitch when he got free, filled his mind.

"Let's try again, shall we?" she said.
Jacob blinked.
"So, I will ask you again, did your brother contact you about me?" she said.
Jacob blinked.
"When was that? Recently?"
Jacob offered another blink.
"Good," Sophie nodded, "and did you in turn, talk to anyone about what he had said?"
Two blinks.
Sophie looked at his sceptically, "Hmmm," she said thoughtfully, "do I believe that? Or shall I let Felix have another wake up call?"
Jacob blinked twice again, the fear burning in his eyes.
"Sorry," she said, sadly, "but I'm not convinced."
She once again picked up the remote and pressed the same button. She waited for longer this time before pressing it again to turn it off. Jacob tried his hardest to scream in protest.
"Next time I will not turn it off," Sophie said calmly, "now, did you talk to anyone else?"
Jacob once again blinked twice.
"Perhaps you are telling the truth?" she shrugged, "Oh well, not to worry."
"Does your brother have any evidence that incriminates me in any wrong doing?" she asked.
Jacob looked at her, his eyes watering.
"Shall I repeat the question?" Sophie asked, "Do you not understand my accent perhaps?"
Jacob blinked twice.
"Does your brother have any evidence?" she asked again.
Jacob hesitated and then blinked once, his eyes watering.

"What did he do with it?" she asked excitedly, Jacob stared at her,
"Shit," she said loudly as she realised that she had not asked a yes or no question. "Is it in his quarters?"
Jacob blinked twice.
"Is it in your quarters?"
Two more blinks.
Sophie leapt to her feet, "Then where is it?" she screamed and then held the remote directly in front of Jacobs face, "I can let it kill him, if you like?" she said her face wild with emotion.
Jacob stared at her; her expression had lost its calm composure and had been replaced by a haunted look of genuine fear. He blinked away his tears and tried to convey all of the triumphalism that he could manage. Sophie picked up on this and her face twisted into a bitter sneer.
"You have served your purpose," she said with a dismissive wave of her hand.
She moved back over to her medical supplies and picked up a vial of medicine from the bedside cabinet. She lifted it and examined the label before filling another syringe.
"In case you were wondering," she said conversationally, as she worked, "this is a potassium and adrenaline cocktail of my own creation."
She walked back over to Jacob and bent over until her lips touched the delicate hairs on his ear.
"It will make it look as though you have suffered a massive heart attack," she whispered gently, "brought on by the stress of your fight with Cam, coupled with your concern about your brother."
She stood up and smiled, "Cam will no doubt be expelled from the colony for this, and once I have found the evidence from your beloved brother, then I will kill him too."

"Bitch," Jacob croaked.
"My goodness," Sophie said, surprised, "you are stronger than I thought. That last dose should have kept you down for another hour at least."
Her eyes flicked nervously to Jacobs fingers, which had suddenly started to twitch.
Jacob groaned, and with a gigantic force of will, he tried to raise his reluctant body from the bed. Sophie watched in horror as he moved, slightly.
She grabbed the first syringe and darted over to his cannulated left arm. Jacob saw her coming and pushed all of his effort into swinging his arm at her body. He connected with a satisfying thump and Sophie crumpled to the floor, crying out in pain as she went.
"You bastard!" she screamed and rolled away from his reach.
Jacob tried again to push himself from the bed but a combination of fatigue and his own body weight meant that he did not yet have the strength to combat the effects of the drugs.
He sagged back onto the bed with a groan of frustration.
Sophie grasped her opportunity and in this moment of recovery, she jammed the needle into the meat of his thigh.
She then darted away to the other side of the room before Jacob had any time to react. The effects would be lessened because of this delivery method, but they would suffice for what she still had to do.
Jacob cried out in frustration and pain, as he realised that finally, he had been beaten.
Sophie watched him intently, from across the room, and when she was certain that the injection had had time to work she gingerly approached him again.

"That was exciting," she said as she approached, Jacob stared at her, once again immobilised, "if you had been a few inches either side, who knows what would be happening now?"

Jacob struggled against the confines of his own body, but once again was helpless.

Satisfied that he was completely inert, Sophie moved her face directly in front of Jacobs and then, quite suddenly, she licked his lips slowly before kissing him wetly on the mouth. Jacobs eyes filled with revulsion. Sophie looked genuinely offended for a second and Jacob took a crumb of satisfaction from that.

"I believe that this will be excruciatingly painful," she said, recomposing herself.

Jacob blinked.

"I can’t be sure though, because no-one who has ever received it, has ever lived to tell me about it afterwards."

With that she emptied the syringe into the cannula and then stood back to watch him die.

CHAPTER TWELVE

When Jim and Jon arrived at Cam's quarters they weren't exactly sure what to expect. They didn't know if he was going to fight them as well or if his quarrel with Jacob had cleaned out his aggression.

Jon knocked loudly on the door, but there was no answer.

"Cam?" he called, "Cam? Are you in there, mate?"

There was only silence.

Jim stepped forward, "Cam? Are you in there? We need to talk to you."

They looked at each other, "We know that you're upset, but we have to talk about what happened tonight."

The door slid open and Cam stood in front of them. He looked at them each in turn and then walked back into his quarters.

"Jesus Cam, you look like shit!"

"What did you do Cam?" Jim asked, his face etched with concern.

Cam sighed, "I went to see Jacob," he said, "I wanted to talk to him. I wanted to understand I suppose...I don't know, all I ended up doing was losing my temper and getting my arse kicked," he smiled reflexly and then immediately winced in pain.

He slumped down into a chair. There was a laptop open on the table and also a blood stained flannel that he had evidently been using on his bloodied nose and lip.

"Looks like that talk went well?" said Jon as he went to join Cam at the table,

Cam smiled again and then immediately wished that he hadn't.

Jim shook his head sadly, "Why'd you do it Cam?"

He shrugged, “I wanted to talk to him. That’s all just talk.”
“Well, it looks like you did a whole Hell of a lot more than talk.”
“I lost my temper,” Cam shrugged again, “the bastard kept denying everything. I just snapped,” he touched his lip tentatively, “look where it got me though,” he said sadly.
“Jesus Cam! What were you thinking?” Jon said, his face was drawn and pale and filled with concern.
“I guess I’m not much of a fighter eh?”
Ben and Jim exchanged knowing glances.
“What?" Cam said wearily, "Don't tell me that bastard complained about me?"
He shook his head and pointed to his broken face.
"Jesus-fucking-Christ! It was me that took the fucking beating, not him!”
“Cam, do you even know what you did?” Jon said, gently.
“What?” cam said,
"Do you remember what happened?" Jim asked.
"Of course I do."
“You stabbed him.” Jon said.
The memory of the fight washed over Cam, “Well, aye. I suppose so,” he shrugged, ”but it wasn't bad."
"It wasn't bad?" Jim said.
"No. The sanctimonious prick was even cleaning himself up while he mocked me from the bathroom," he shook his head at the memory and immediately winced again.
"I wasn't having any of that though," Cam continued, "I got the fuck out of Dodge before he came back to spout any more of his patronising bullshit.”
“He was cleaning himself up?” Jim said incredulously, “While you were still there?”
“Aye, why what’s he saying?” Cam rolled his eyes.
Jon sat down next to his friend, with a big sigh.

“Well, not much actually,” Jon said.
Cam shrugged, “So?”
“He’s not saying much Cam, because he can't," Jim said.
Cam’s forehead wrinkled in confusion, "I don't understand."
“He’s not saying much Cam, because he’s dead.”
“What?” Cam said, "When? How?"
“He’s dead Cam. He had a massive heart attack.”
Cam shook his head, "I don't believe it, a heart attack?"
"Well, the injuries that he sustained were life threatening anyway,"
"I...I barely touched him," Cam stuttered.
"He had multiple fractures to his mandible, skull, ribs and sternum," Jon said.
"You beat him within an inch of his life," Jim said.
“No, I didn't," Cam protested, "don’t be ridiculous. I barely touched him. He beat the shit out of me!”
Cam gestured to his bruised and battered face again.
“Yeah we can see that Cam,” Jon said.
“Then how?”
“We found the knife," Jim said.
“But...” Cam was in shock, “but, he was fine when I left!”
“No, he wasn't," Jim said, "he was dying when you left. Jesus man, can’t you remember?”
Cam shook his head. This was too much for him to process.
“I don't remember,” he said, uncertainly.
"Sophie found him," Jon said, "she tried to help, but it was already too late."
"Sophie?" Cam said confused.
"When you broke the quarantine, she was alerted," Jim said, "as she is the chief medical officer."
Cam nodded.
"There was nothing that she could do," Jon said.

"No," Cam said again.
"The damage to his sternum must have put pressure on his heart," Jon said, "it was only a matter of time, probably."
Cam sank his head into his hands.
“Come on Cam,” said Jim quietly, “you’re going to have to come with us I’m afraid.”
“Go with you?" he said, shocked, "Why? Where?” Cam stood and instinctively backed away from the two men.
“This is bullshit guys. I barely touched him,” he said and looked at Jon for support.
“Cam, you might not have meant to. However, because of your actions a man is dead,” Jim said with a helpless shrug. “We can’t leave you here.”
"Where are you going to take me?" Cam asked
“We’re going to have to put you somewhere safe,” said Jim, “somewhere away from everyone else.”
“Safe? Safe? Safe for whom?” Cam looked helplessly from one to the other, “Jon?” he said desperately.
“Safe for everyone, you included I'm afraid. Everyone’s going to be scared.”
"Scared of what?" Cam asked.
Jim looked at him.
"Scared of me?" Cam said, incredulously, "For fucks sake, this is crazy."
"We're just going to take you to the med bay for now. I want to have a look at your injuries and we can talk, " Jon smiled.
"Just you and me?" Cam asked hopefully.
Jon looked at Jim.
"We need to talk to you properly," Jim said.
Cam grabbed hold of Jon's wrist, he stared into his face his eyes wide with fear, "I didn't do this Jon," he said, desperately.

Jon shook his head and then turned to Jim, “I’ll bring him," he said.
Jim shook his head.
"I’m afraid not Jon, we do this together," he turned and open the door, "come on, before the rest of the colony wakes up and finds out what’s happened."
Jim led Cam out the door and they headed along the corridor as a threesome. When they arrived at the med bay Sophie, Ben and Becky were waiting for them.
Cam looked at each of their faces in turn, desperately trying to find some sign of an ally but each figure was resolutely refraining from making eye contact with him, as he looked at Ben he noticed that he was wearing his old military issue side arm. He desperately hoped that that was not the sign of what was to come.
"Please, sit down Cam," Jim said and gestured over to a chair by the side of one of the treatment tables.
"I'm fine thanks, I'll stand."
Jim shrugged, "Suit yourself," he said and then turned to face his colleagues, "shall we begin?"
Each of the other assembled colonists replied with a faint nod of the head.
Jim spoke loudly to the room, "Please let it be noted that we are here to investigate the death of Captain Jacob Mwamba. A crew member of the Nerine Four space craft."
He paused, cleared his throat and looked around the room, "Present for these proceedings are: Captain James McLaughlin, Captain Benjamin Sutherland, Rebecca Blank, MD; Captain Jon Daniels, MD; Sophie Torres, MD; and the accused Captain Cameron Harrison. Are we all in agreement?"

There was a vague murmur of agreement around the room. Jim turned back to Cam.
"Captain Harrison? Can you describe your movements this evening please?" Jim asked.
"I don't understand," Cam said, weakly.
"What don't you understand?" Ben said.
"Captain Sutherland, kindly address the accused in the appropriate manner," Jim said.
"The accused?" Jon said loudly, "Is this supposed to be some kind of trial then?"
Jim nodded, "We are investigating a murder, what would you have me call it" he said.
"I thought we were going to hear his side first?" Jon said, angrily.
"We will," Jim said, "we are doing things by the book, thats all."
"By the book?" Jon yelled.
"Yes, Captain Daniels, now if you would kindly calm down, we can proceed."
"This is bullshit," Jon said flatly.
"I beg your pardon?" Jim said angrily.
"You heard me Jim-Sorry *Captain Mclaughlin*," Jon said with a sarcastic smile.
"This is inappropriate," Jim shouted.
"No," Jon spat, "this whole thing is inappropriate."
"What would you suggest Jon?" Becky asked.
"How about employing even the tiniest bit of common sense, for a start!"
"We are trying..." Jim began.
"No, you're not!" Jon shouted, "For Christ's sake look at the man?"

All eyes in the room turned to take in the bruised and bloodied visage of Cam.
"Yes? So?" Jim said,
"The man can barely walk," Jon said, "he has just recovered from a blow to the head and then endured what I can only describe as 'having the shit kicked out of him'"
"So?" Jim repeated.
"Have you ever met Jacob?" He said incredulously, "Do you remember what he looks like?"
Jim coughed, "of course, but I really don't..."
"Do you honestly think that you could take Jacob in it fight?" Jon continued.
"Possibly," Jim said, blushing slightly.
"Bullshit!" Jon roared, "And you are fit, well and fully acclimatised to life on this planet."
Jim shifted uncomfortably from one foot to the other.
"Whereas Cam here couldn't even walk two days ago,"
Jon looked around for support, everyone was looking at him.
"And yet here you are, spouting the infernal nonsense that not only did he get the shit kicked out off him tonight, but at some intervening moment, he managed to beat Jacob essentially to death?"
Jim looked around the room for support, but found none forthcoming. Every set of eyes was trained on him waiting to hear his response.
Every set of eyes that is except Sophie, who instead was staring at the floor.
"He has a point Jim," Becky said gently, "it doesn't really add up"
"Then who?" Jim asked.
Becky shrugged.
Jon was looking at Sophie.

“Are you okay Sophie?" he asked her tenderly.
She looked up and her eyes were red raw, and tears were streaming down her face, she looked over at Jon and then shook her head.
"No," she sniffed, and then she glanced over at Ben.
"I'm sorry," she wept, "but I have to tell them the truth."
Ben's eyes widened in shock, he took half a step forward.
"Sophie," he said. "No!"
Sophie swallowed, "I'm sorry, my darling," she said and shook her head miserably.
Jon had moved over to Sophie and placed a comforting hand on her shoulder. From across the room Ben flinched as though he had been slapped.
Jim looked from Sophie, to Ben. His face wore an expression of angry confusion.
"What's going on?" He said. "Sophie what are you talking about?"
"Please Sophie?" Ben implored.
"We can’t let Cam take the blame," Sophie said, through her tears, "not for something that you did."
The few members of the colony gasped in unison. Ben's face fell and then he nodded briefly.
"Ben?" Becky said. "What does she mean?"
Ben looked over at Sophie, he desperately wanted to go and comfort her. To put his arms around her and tell her everything was all right. But he couldn't move, his feet were rooted to the spot.
Meanwhile, with the focus shifted, Cam had slumped into a chair, his bravado now faded, his stubbornness replaced by exhaustion.
Sophie looked at Ben, "I'm so sorry,“ she said again and then dissolved once more into tears.

"It's okay sweetheart," Ben said with a small smile, "I know that you were trying to protect me, but you're right."
The room slipped into stunned silence for a moment and everyone looked at one another, seemingly unable to speak.
"Ben?" Cam said finally, breaking the silence.
"My goddamn temper," Ben said almost to himself, "I knew that it would get me into serious trouble one day."
"Why?" Cam asked.
Ben shrugged, "Red mist, I guess," he said and waved his hand in front of his own face.
Jim looked at Becky, who nodded at him
"I'm going to have to ask you to submit yourself to house arrest," Jim said.
Ben stared blankly ahead.
"How could you?" Jon shouted furiously, "He's meant to be your friend and you were just going to hang him out to dry?"
Ben looked at him and smiled sadly, "Sorry Cam," he said, “nothing personal eh?"
Cam couldn't make eye contact with him but nevertheless he nodded, "It's okay," he whispered.
"Okay?" Jon yelled incredulously.
Cam nodded, "Aye."
"It's not okay Cam," Jon continued, "you could have been expelled or Christ knows what?"
He looked around at the others in the room, waiting for someone to move. Eventually Jim stepped forward.
"I'm going to have to ask for your gun, Ben," he said and held out his hand.
Ben nodded and unfastened his holster. He pulled his pistol out and looked at it lovingly. It was heavy, polished chrome, high caliber weapon.

"I'll look after it," Jim said with a half-smile and Ben nodded his appreciation at him in reply.
He turned to look back at Sophie and smiled, "I'm so sorry sweetheart," he said.
Then without a moments further hesitation, in a single fluid motion, he placed the barrel of the pistol into his mouth and pulled the trigger.

CHAPTER THIRTEEN

Jim was pacing up and down the floor of the meeting room on his own. As the commander of the colony it was his unpleasant duty to tell those that didn't already know about the previous night's tragic events.

He looked down at his hands and noticed that they were noticeably shaking. He clenched and unclenched his fists and then stretched out his fingers, but it made no difference. He sighed, shoved his hands into his pockets and then continued once again with his pacing.

"Jim?" Becky said quietly, whilst at the same time knocking on the door frame.

Without waiting for a response she took a few tentative steps forwards before pausing again. Jim looked over at her and smiled.

"Hey," he said quietly, "come on in. I could do with the company to be honest."

"Rough night," she said.

Jim laughed, mirthlessly, "Yeah, you could say that."

She walked over to him and slid her arms around his waist. His body relaxed at her touch but his face still carried the visible signs of the enormous strain that he had suddenly found himself under.

"I thought you might want some time alone," she said, "you know, before..." she trailed away and squeezed him tightly.

"How did this happen?" he asked rhetorically

Becky shrugged, "I don't know," she said, "I still can't believe it."

Jim looked at her and smiled, "How are you, anyway?" he said.

"I'm okay, I guess, all things considered."

Jim nodded, "What about Sophie?"
Becky wrinkled her nose and shook her head, "Not great."
"Yeah I can only imagine."
"We've given her something to help her sleep. She had a sedative already mixed in the med-bay so we gave her a dose of that. She went out like a light."
"Thats something I suppose."
"God alone knows what the long term impact of this is going to be on her," Becky said miserably.
"Did she say anything to you?"
Becky shook her head, "No, but what can we expect? After all she's just watched a man that she cared about blow his brains out all over the med-bay."
"I know," Jim said, "and because of her as well."
Jim looked at Becky, noticed her expression and instantly regretted speaking.
Becky pushed away from him angrily, "Is that what you think?" she asked, accusatorially, "do you think that this is somehow Sophie's fault?"
Jim stared at her, but could find nothing to say.
"That it's because of her that Ben killed himself?" Becky's face was flushed with the heat of her anger.
Jim's face had also reddened, but in shame, "No...of course not," he stammered," I just meant..."
"You should know better, in fact you *have* to know better!" Becky said. "You are the commander of this colony. Your words have weight."
"You're right," Jim said, "I'm sorry."
Becky's expression softened, but her tone remained hard.
"You need to be careful," Becky said, "the difference between what you mean and what you say could have far reaching

consequences. It could be the difference between life and death, especially at the moment."
"I know," Jim said meekly, "she does know though doesn't she?"
"Know what?"
"She knows that we don't blame her for any of this?"
Becky nodded, "I think so," she said.
Jim relaxed a little, "Thats good," he said.
"She made a difficult decision today," Becky continued, "an incredibly brave and courageous decision, one that must have carved her up inside," Becky sighed,
"It's so sad," she said.
"I know" Jim said, taking her hand.
"To make that decision, and then..." Becky faltered
Jim nodded, "It's okay," he said.
"She's strong, but we've got to be there for her," Becky said, "all of us."
"I know," Jim said again, "really I do. I just wasn't thinking that's all."
Becky fixed him with a stare, "Well, that's one particular luxury that you can no longer afford I'm afraid," she said and placed her hand on his arm.
Jim nodded, "I know," he said.
"We have seven new colonists on the Nerine-Four that have arrived into the middle of a war zone."
"At least we can break the quarantine now, get them all on board."
"There's Cam and Jon as well," Becky said pointedly, "we haven't exactly rolled out the red carpet for them have we?"
"It's been difficult," Jim started to explain, but Becky interrupted,

"No excuses," she said, "we need leadership right now, we need you!"
Jim looked at her and sighed again, "I'll do better," he said, determinedly
"I know you will," Becky said and squeezed his arm gently.
Jim stared into space for a moment before looking back at Becky.
"Is everyone up?" he asked.
Becky looked at her tablet and nodded, "Yeah, I sent a message to everyones com-pad and there's a notice on the dining hall door telling everyone to head straight here. In fact..."
Jim looked towards the door, "Oh God, everyone's already here aren't they?" he said, his voice suddenly thin.
Becky smiled at him and nodded, "I'm sorry," she said.
Jim gathered himself mentally and then pulled himself up to his full height.
"Better get my game face on," he said.
Becky smiled again, "You've got this," she said.
He looked at Becky, gratefully and nodded, "Okay," he said, "let's get this over with."

The meeting room filled up quickly and the conversation between the colonists ranged from the mundane to the wildly speculative as they arrived. Once everyone was seated Jim surveyed the room slowly, the background chatter continued, but there seemed to be no inclination of what he was about to say. He was grateful for that at least. He cleared his throat and waited for a few seconds for everyone to calm down.
"Good morning everyone," his voice displayed no evidence of the turmoil he felt inside.
The room fell instantly silent.

"I know that this it's a bit unusual to call you all in before the start of the day," he said.
"This had better be good, I'm starving!" Came a voice from the back of the room.
There was general murmur of agreement. Jim raised his hand.
"I know, but this is important," he said.
The murmur subsided and when the room was silent again, Jim continued,
"The fact is, what I have to tell you is not something that could, or indeed should wait any longer than necessary."
This set off a fresh, new round of discussion. Once again, Jim raised his right hand in an attempt to catch everyones attention.
"Thank you," he said loudly, and the noise, once again, quickly abated.
He looked over at Becky.
"There is no way of sugar coating this so I won't try," he swallowed hard. "It is with a heavy heart and no small amount of personal sadness that I stand here this morning, charged, as I am, with the unenviable job of imparting some terrible news to you all."
The chatter re-started as Jim knew that it would but this time he allowed them few moments of conjecture before he started to speak again.
"In the early hours of this morning, Captain Jacob Mbamwa, who was an officer on board the Nerine-Four for those that didn't know. Suffered from a major cardiac event and unfortunately died as a result."
A rumble of surprise and shock reverberated through the room; Jim raised his voice and did his best to talk over the top of it.

“This is despite the very best efforts and remarkable quick response of our dedicated medical team," He looked over at Jon and nodded, but he offered no response. Jim waited patiently for a few moments to allow the buzz to die down a little and then cleared his throat again.
"Please," he said, "I'm afraid that there is more to come."
"More?" Simon said arching his eyebrows quizzically, "What could be more?"
Jim nodded solemnly, "In a separate and completely unrelated incident, I am very sad to report that Major Benjamin Sutherland was involved in a terrible accident, the result of which cost him his life."
This time the room erupted into a sudden cacophony. Jim bowed his head, he had expected this, but the sudden, physical outpouring of emotion had brought an uncomfortable and unexpected lump to his throat which made it difficult for him to continue. He coughed and then took a sip of water.
"Please!" he said, in an unsuccessful attempt to make himself heard again.
"Everyone please calm down!" he yelled whilst slamming his fist against the table. Slowly the wave of sound began to thin.
Anna stood from the crowd, "What happened?" she said, her voice full of concern.
Jim sighed and looked over to Becky for support but all she could offer in response was an determined nod. But this had a galvanising effect on him.
"We don't know for certain yet,” Jim lied, "but we are not looking at any suspicious circumstances surrounding his death."
Anna raised her hand and Jim nodded at her, "Yes, Anna?" he said.

"What kind of accident?" she asked, "Is there something the rest of us need to be careful of?"
Jim shifted uncomfortably, "It was a...weapon malfunction," he said almost apologetically.
"A weapon malfunction?" Anna parroted, "What kind of..." she stopped her question when she caught the expression on Jim's face and fell instantly silent.
As the implications of this struck her, she found herself unable to say anything further so instead she let her eyes drop to the floor. Andrew jabbed her in the ribs and whispered a question to her but she ignored him and simply shook her head unhappily.
Jim continued, "Once again the medical team were on the scene incredibly quickly and worked as hard as they could to save him. Unfortunately, their attempts proved to be ultimately futile, and he died only a few hours ago surrounded by friends."
There was a further rumble of disquiet throughout the colonists as they discussed this new information and Jim said nothing to dissuade them.
Finally as the conversation quietened, he went on. "I only wish that there was some grain of comfort that I could offer you all, something that I could say or do to make all of this better."
He looked down at his hands, they had stopped shaking.
"This is a lot to take in, so I'm not going to say anymore at the moment out of respect for both Ben and Jacob. I understand that there will be many questions amongst you guys and I promise that I will do my best to address each and every one of them in time."
He looked at Anna, but she was still looking at the floor.
"In the meantime however, I would be eternally grateful if you could all exercise your restraint, especially around Sophie.

She has gone through enough without any of us adding to her woes. Is that understood?"
There was a general mumble of consent.
"One more thing," he said over the top of the increasing din, “in light of last night's tragic events, I have decided to abandon all works and duties for the next two days as a mark of respect. However, if anyone wants something to do by way of a distraction then please come and see me afterwards and I will arrange something with you individually. Okay?"
Once more the collective produced a muttering of agreement.
"Then you are free to go about your business."
He watched as the colonists filed slowly from the room exchanging theories and suspicions as they went.
He sighed and then collapsed heavily into his chair, closing his eyes. When they reopened Simon was standing in front of him.
Jim flinched slightly, "Simon? Hi,"
Simon smiled politely and nodded, "I am sorry for the death of Ben and Jacob," he said solemnly.
Jim nodded, "Yeah, it's a shock to us all."
Simon nodded in return, "Ben was a difficult man to get along with," he said pensively, "for me at least. But I liked him and I will miss him."
Jim looked at him but said nothing. Simon took that as a cue to continue, "I would like to work today please," he said.
Jim's eyes widened in surprise, "Really? You sure about that?"
"I am," he said, "I would rather be doing something productive that sitting doing nothing."
"Fair enough," Jim said, "there's plenty to do I guess. Please feel free."
Simon smiled, "Thank-you," he said simply, and then turned to leave.

Jim watched him go and shook his head slowly, "That is one weird son-of-a-bitch," he said to himself.
Becky walked up behind him and placed what she hoped would be a comforting hand, gently, on his shoulder.
"You did a good thing," she whispered into his ear and kissed his cheek lightly.
Jim turned his head to look at her, "Do you think so?" he asked.
Becky nodded. "The truth will no doubt filter out over the weeks, but right now people need to cling to something positive," she smiled at him, “at least for the moment."
"Thanks," he said, "I needed to hear that."
He pulled her closer and slipped his hand under her shirt, letting his fingers caress the skin of her stomach. Becky smiled and made no effort to stop him.
"Perhaps now is a good time?" she said, looking at him expectantly.
Jim caught her expression and his face twisted in to a look of doubt,
“We’re going to have to tell them at some point anyway,” she said quietly.
Jim sighed, “It’s no one’s god-damn business but ours.”
Becky smiled at him, “I know honey, but they'll find out soon enough anyway. Besides it might help to lighten the mood? You know some good news for a change?”
Her hand moved down to where Jim's rested and she patted it through the material of her shirt
“It’s not like I’m going to be able to keep it a secret for much longer is it?”

THE END

Planting Trees on Mars

Printed in Great Britain
by Amazon

58041671R00293